WASHINGTON, AUG. 9, 1940— WILLKIE LEADS ROOSEVELT IN GALLUP POLL!

MAXWELL MUNRO: Captain of Military Intelligence at the U.S. Embassy in London, he was thought to be a spy for his father, a powerful isolationist senator. But when he uncovered the war's most explosive secret, he made his own hard choices. Now no one would stop his daring, deadly plan!

FRANKLIN DELANO ROOSEVELT: The public did not know how crippled he'd become—or of his secret pledge to Churchill. Fighting for re-election, he was playing a dangerous game—and preparing to lead his nation into war. . . .

BERLIN, AUG. 11— ROOSEVELT ENCOURAGES BRITISH TO CONTINUE WAR; REICH MINISTER WARNS U.S. PRESIDENT

BETTY DONALDSON: FDR chose her for a secret mission to London, while his fiercest political rival wanted her for his bed. Caught between America's most powerful politicians, she went after the story her own way—and walked into the eye of the storm. . . .

(more . . .)

LONDON, AUG. 14—
500 NAZI PLANES RAID BRITAIN;
COASTAL AREAS, AIRFIELDS HIT

SEAN DALY: An IRA man with only one cause: to destroy the English. Recruited as a German spy, he was a vital source of intelligence in London—and planned for a Nazi invasion. . . .

MARIE PRICE: A French beauty, she came to Sean Daly with no loyalties—but with a lifetime of pent-up passion. He saw her gifts—and had a job for her to do. . . .

BERLIN, AUG. 29—
REICH ADMITS "SLIGHT" DAMAGE
TO BERLIN;
NAZIS SAY WAR ENTERS NEW,
DANGEROUS PHASE!

WINSTON HAMILTON: He lived a quiet life with his mother—and translated the most important information of the war: decoded messages from the German High Command. When a beautiful woman suddenly walked into his life, he would give her whatever she asked. . . .

LONDON, SEPT. 17—
LONDON IN FLAMES AS NAZI BOMBERS POUND CITY;
10TH CONSECUTIVE NIGHT OF HEAVY BOMBING RAIDS

GOERING: A braggart and a man of extravagance, his Führer had given him a second chance to crush Britain. But the RAF was battering the Luftwaffe— and Goering knew he was being betrayed. . . .

JOSEPH KENNEDY: FDR's Ambassador to England, he had his own agenda: to put himself in the White House, and keep the U.S. out of the war. Beneath his charm and wit was an iron cunning—and a secret plan to drive Roosevelt from office. . . .

BERLIN, SEPT. 28—
NAZIS IN FOURTH WEEK OF LONDON BLITZ;
FLAMES GUIDE RAIDERS TO NIGHT TARGETS;
GOERING CLAIMS BRITISH MORTALLY WOUNDED!

THE ENIGMA MACHINE: Breaking Germany's complex code, American and British Intelligence saw into the heart of the Reich—and intercepted Germany's flow of secret information. But their advantage is about to collapse, and Hitler is prepared to issue—

DIRECTIVE 16!

Charles Robertson

DIRECTIVE 16

POCKET BOOKS

New York   London   Toronto   Sydney   Tokyo

This book is a work of fiction. Names, characters, places and incidents are either the product of the author's imagination or are used fictitiously. Any resemblance to actual events or locales or persons, living or dead, is entirely coincidental.

Another *Original* publication of POCKET BOOKS

POCKET BOOKS, a division of Simon & Schuster, Inc
1230 Avenue of the Americas, New York, N.Y. 10020

ISBN: 0-671-61153-4

First Pocket Books printing May 1988

10 9 8 7 6 5 4 3 2 1

POCKET and colophon are trademarks of
Simon & Schuster, Inc.

Printed in the U.S.A.

For my mother,
Anne Reilly Robertson

DIRECTIVE 16
Preparations for a Landing Operation
Against England

As England, in spite of her hopeless military situation, still shows no sign of willingness to come to terms, I have decided to prepare, and if necessary to carry out, a landing operation against her. The aim of this operation is to eliminate the English mother country as a base from which the war against Germany can be continued and, if it should be necessary, to occupy it completely.

—Adolf Hitler
July 16, 1940

FOREWORD

It is easy now to believe that victory against Germany in World War II was inevitable—easy to believe that such a monstrous aberration as Naziism could not possibly prevail over the democracies. But there was a time when the difference between defeat and survival was razor thin. This book is about that time.

It is also easy to believe that victory in the election of 1940 was a foregone conclusion for a President as popular as Franklin Delano Roosevelt. But there was a time when all the indications said that Roosevelt would not prevail. This book is about that time, and how these facts converged at one incredibly dangerous moment in history.

The principal characters in this work are fictitious; they operate against a background of real people and real events. No historical figure is made to say or do anything that is contrary to his known convictions. Wherever possible these historical figures speak in their own words.

◆ *PROLOGUE* ◆

BERLIN, May 9, 1945—At twilight the city lay in ruins. Row upon row of gutted buildings lined streets that were pocked with craters and strewn with rubble. The empty masonry shells, like skeletal remains in some gigantic elephant graveyard, stood in mute testament to the awesome destructive power of the victorious allied forces. Two years of bombing attacks by British and American air forces, and months of ferocious artillery bombardment from advancing Soviet troops, had left the city a shambles.

The war was finally over. On May seventh at Reims and again on May eighth in Berlin, the Germans had signed the unconditional surrender. Within the space of nineteen days, three of the five war leaders—Roosevelt, Mussolini, and Hitler—had died, and one week later the war in Europe was at an end.

The small convoy, two staff cars and a truck carrying the soldiers of the Red Army escort, weaved its way through the wreckage of what had been one of Europe's finest cities. Several times the convoy had to stop and retrace its path because the street ahead was blocked with the debris of collapsed buildings. Each time their path was obstructed, the young Russian officer, Orlenko, an artillery major, looked with concern at the American brigadier general and to the grim-faced Russian officer of the Chief Intelligence Directorate of the General Staff.

The American general was in his early thirties, a man whose war had begun even before his country's entry into it. He was tall, dark-haired, and confident in the manner that reassured friends and infuriated others. His handsome, almost boyish face, seemed untouched by more than five years of war, but his eyes were cold and hard.

Both Russians had been on hand to greet Brigadier General Maxwell Munro and his two aides—Captain Hunter and

1

Lieutenant Miller—at Staaken Airfield on the outskirts of the Spandau suburb when the American transport plane had arrived from 12th Army Group tactical headquarters in Weisbaden. Major Orlenko, in his early twenties, was excited by the arrival of the Americans. He was openly friendly and eager to try his few words of English. The GRU officer, Yaskov, had been cold and suspicious from the beginning. When the major attempted a greeting in English, the intelligence officer gave him a sharp look. Thereafter Orlenko left the conversation to the others and satisfied himself with an occasional friendly smile and nod.

The American lit a thin cigar and offered one to each of the Russians. Orlenko, with a look at Yaskov, eagerly accepted. Yaskov refused. He spent the remainder of the trip looking out the window so that he would not have to see the American.

The Americans were in Berlin as part of the agreement that had halted the American 12th Army Group's advance across the Elbe and allowed the Russians to enter Berlin first. The British and Americans, though, would be allowed access to any archival documents important to their postwar interests. When the Americans had heard that the Russians were removing documents by the truckload, they immediately demanded the right to send in a team to inspect the material before shipment to Moscow. The Russians denied that anything had been removed, but, in the interests of international cooperation, did not refuse American access to what remained.

A soft drizzle coated the windows of the staff car, distorting the image of the city. To General Munro, the city that slid past his window was an Impressionist portrait, a gray on gray relieved only by an occasional splash of crimson where the flags of the victorious Red Army hung limply in a misty sky.

The convoy made its way through the city, across Berliner Strasse, through the crater-pocked Tiergarten Park, around the rubble of Chaussee Strasse to the Brandenburg Gate. The city was a wasteland of smoldering ruins. Even the drizzle could not extinguish the flames that lurked in the bowels of the shattered buildings, and thin, wispy ribbons of smoke spiraled skyward into the overcast sky. The few standing buildings were pockmarked with artillery and machine-gun fire and it seemed that every window in the city was broken.

The columns of the Brandenburg Gate were festooned with Soviet flags. Above the gate the Chariot of Victory, with three of the four horses toppled, was a twisted wreck. The square itself was strewn with abandoned German equipment —demolished vehicles, spent artillery casings, fire-blackened tanks.

There were civilians on the streets—smaller than life, shabbily dressed, and bent over as if under a great burden. Most pulled small hand wagons that held the remnants of their belongings. They trudged on, heads bowed, oblivious to the soft drizzle that washed the city.

The convoy crossed the Unter den Linden and turned south onto Wilhelm Strasse. The Wilhelm Plaz was piled high with rubble and dotted with bomb craters. On the right the Reich Chancellery was a twisted, charred ruin. Red flags flew from jagged fragments of walls and on the one standing wall hung a huge black and white portrait of Stalin. Uncle Joe looked out across the Chancellery Garden to the demolished entrance of the Führer Bunker, where, it was said, Adolf Hitler had committed suicide and his body had been cremated in the garden.

At the intersection of Wilhelm and Prinz Albrecht Strasse, the convoy turned right and pulled to a stop in front of the huge, block-long, gray granite edifice that had once been the offices of what was called the Reich Main Security Department. The building was extensively damaged, but some portions were surprisingly intact.

Munro stepped out of the car as the Russian guards on duty at the entrance snapped to attention. The American general raised the collar of his raincoat and looked up at the building which was draped in the omnipresent red flags. There, he knew, was where the vast German security apparatus—the Gestapo, the Criminal Police, the SS Security Service—had headquartered. He had come here to find something that must not be allowed to fall into foreign hands.

The Russians stepped out of the car and stood at his side. For a moment there was a respectful silence, as if this place were too terrible for comment, then Major Orlenko slapped Munro on the back and said in halting English, "Follow me, General."

The doors of the second car opened and the others stepped out. Captain Hunter looked at the building, Lieutenant

Miller kept his eyes down. The Lieutenant had been here before.

His identification papers listed him as Lieutenant Robert Miller of the US 12th Army, assigned to the interrogation unit at Magdeburg. His real name was Karl Dietrich and he was a former SS officer who had worked in this building for more than five years. Three weeks earlier Dietrich had escaped from Berlin, crossed the Elbe, and surrendered to the American forces outside Schönebeck. He had been taken to Magdeburg for interrogation, and in order to secure what he hoped would be preferential treatment, Dietrich had told his captors of certain documents that were in the files of the Reich Security Offices in Berlin. Less than forty-eight hours later, Dietrich found himself the subject of intense interrogation by several American officers, one of whom was Lieutenant Robert Miller.

Fearful of immediate execution, Dietrich did not tell his interrogators that he had been an adjutant to both Reinhard Heydrich and Ernst Kaltenbrunner who had both been head of the Reich Security Administration. The Americans, as it turned out, were not terribly interested in the fact that he had been with the SS. They were more interested in the whereabouts of the documents and promised him safe conduct if he would aid in their location. Now, much to his chagrin, Dietrich found himself back in Berlin, surrounded by the very Russians he had been so desperate to evade.

General Munro motioned to his aides and both joined him as they entered the building.

Instinctively Dietrich reached for the metal ID plate used to gain entry to the building, but was able to stop himself before his hand reached his pocket.

Yaskov eyed Dietrich suspiciously. There was something about this one that he did not like.

"Which way?" Munro asked Dietrich quietly.

"Third floor." He looked at the gaping hole where the elevators had been. "Up these stairs."

Munro turned to Captain Hunter. "Tell our Russian friends that we wish to go to the third-floor offices."

Hunter translated. Yaskov, who spoke German and English passably well, waited until the translation was complete before nodding.

The corridors were littered with debris, and everything of

4

any value—desks, carpets, chairs—had been removed from the building. They passed row after row of empty offices, their footsteps echoing across the bare floors of the corridor.

"Here," said Dietrich softly to General Munro, and the group stopped in front of a large set of offices at the end of the corridor.

"Tell our Russian friends we wish to inspect these offices," Munro said.

Yaskov wondered how these Americans, particularly the one called Miller, were so familiar with the offices of the Reich Security Administration.

The three Americans, followed by the Russians, entered the first office. It was empty—stripped to the walls—and Munro had a sinking feeling that what he had come for might already be gone.

Dietrich led them through to the inner office, and there, lined against the wall, stood a row of file cabinets. There was even a table, one leg missing, propped against the same wall.

Dietrich nodded and Munro sighed in relief.

The Russians stood back as the Americans began to pull out drawers and leaf through the stacks of documents. Yaskov watched the one called Miller. Only he seemed to know what he was looking for. Sure enough, Miller soon gave a soft cry of triumph and pulled an entire file from the cabinet. With a slight smile he handed the file to the General.

Munro leafed quickly through the documents, his eyes glowing, his lips curling into a small smile. These were the documents. He had seen the originals almost five years ago in London. He had come to Berlin to retrieve them so that the reputation of a dead President would not be sullied by those who had not understood then and would not understand now. "You're sure," he said to Dietrich, "that there are no other copies?"

"If they had been photographed, they would be stamped by the Reich Photography Service. This is it. There are no more."

The General looked at Captain Hunter, a glint of triumph in his eyes. "This is what we came for."

Yaskov stepped forward. "My orders are that none of these documents are to leave the building. You may inspect them, as was the agreement, but the documents remain the property of the people of the Soviet Union."

General Munro quickly recovered from the shock of Yaskov's facility with English. "The agreement was to inspect and, at our option, remove any and all documents."

"Those are not my orders."

"These documents go with me," Munro said forcefully. "I have the full authority of the Supreme Commander of Allied Forces in Europe."

Yaskov smiled. "I'm afraid your supreme commander does not reign east of the Elbe, General. I have the full authority of the Supreme Soviet Command, and, I might add, a contingent of Soviet troops at my immediate disposal."

General Munro placed the documents on the table and removed his bulky raincoat. Yaskov noted for the first time that the General wore a sidearm. Munro withdrew his Colt .45 from the side holster, moved the safety, and then placed the weapon on the table next to the documents.

Captain Hunter opened his raincoat. He, too, was armed. Dietrich's eyes bulged. This was much more than he had bargained for. The Americans were as crazy as everyone had said.

Major Orlenko had no idea what was happening. Instinctively his hand moved toward the pistol at his belt. Without touching his own pistol, General Munro stared at Orlenko. "Don't do that, son," he said. Orlenko's hand dropped to his side. Something in the American's voice was enough to make him wait.

Munro spoke again. "In the interests of international harmony, Mr. Yaskov, whoever the hell you are, we are going to comply with your request that no documents leave the building."

Yaskov's frozen face broke into a smile and he stepped toward the table as if to gather the file.

"Not just yet," said Munro. "We haven't fully inspected them."

Yaskov stopped. "Of course. That is your privilege."

"Thank you," Munro said. He lit another cigar and opened the file folder. He removed the first page, held it up, inspected it, then crumpled it into a ball and set it afire with his lighter. As the flame grew, he dropped the burning page to the floor.

Yaskov's face contorted in fury. He muttered something to

Major Orlenko, who looked uncertainly toward Munro as if awaiting orders.

"Tell the Major not to try anything," Munro said to Hunter, as he set another page ablaze. "They don't even know what we're burning here. Tell him it's not worth dying for."

Hunter relayed the general's words to Orlenko, who seemed to find the American's reasoning impeccable. He stood back away from Yaskov and shrugged.

Munro, puffing on his cigar, incinerated page after page from the file. When he was finished and there was a pile of blackened ashes littering the floor, he returned his pistol to his holster, put on his raincoat, and turned to Yaskov. "Maybe you'd be good enough to give us a ride back to the airfield."

They rode in silence. Munro knew that he had destroyed important historical documents, but was sure that, under the circumstances, he had done the proper thing. He had performed one last service for the President. Franklin Roosevelt had been dead for almost a month now, but Munro would always think of Roosevelt as "the President." The original documents—those he had first seen in 1940—had been destroyed soon after America's entry into the war. As far as he knew, there were no other copies. If there were other copies, that would have to be a problem for someone else. He had done his part. He had come full circle. Perhaps he could put it all behind him now.

WILLKIE LEADS ROOSEVELT IN GALLUP SUR-
VEY OF ELECTORAL VOTE; REPUBLICAN HAS
304–227 EDGE, 38 MORE VOTES THAN NEEDED
TO WIN

WASHINGTON, AUG. 9

♦ *CHAPTER 1* ♦

WASHINGTON, D.C., August 9, 1940—Betty Donaldson was shown into the White House press room at a little after 9 P.M. on Friday evening. She was a correspondent for *Time* magazine and had been summoned to the White House only a few hours ago. Although she had been busily packing for a trip to London when the invitation arrived, it was a request she could not ignore. Betty was in her middle twenties, but with her short hair, confident posture, and serious expression she seemed somehow older. Hers was a face that had been called beautiful and she was well aware of the advantages of such looks.

She wore her best wool suit—it had been lying on her bed, ready to go into her suitcase—and was quite uncomfortable. The weather in Washington was an un-Londonlike eighty-five degrees.

She was greeted by the President's assistant press secretary, Peter Anderson, who directed her to a seating area in one corner of the room, where they were served coffee by a silent black man in a white jacket.

Betty wasted no time. "So," she said matter-of-factly, "what's this all about?"

Anderson raised an eyebrow.

Betty Donaldson was very busy and didn't have time for the political games played by the people who worked for Franklin Roosevelt. "C'mon, Peter," she said, "Reporters

9

don't get ordered to the White House to have a cup of coffee and a pleasant chat with the press secretary or"—she added maliciously—"his assistant."

If Anderson was offended by the slight, it didn't show. He put his cup on the low table that separated them. "Press Secretary Early apologizes for not being here himself. Unfortunately, he had pressing business elsewhere this evening."

Betty Donaldson shrugged.

"Because of our . . ."—Anderson paused, searching for the right phrase, and then said with a quick smile—"personal relationship . . . it was felt that I would be the proper person to discuss this matter with you."

As far as Betty was concerned, their relationship was strictly professional. She was aware that Anderson felt otherwise, but that only made it easier for her to get information inside the White House. She had been one of the first reporters to break the news that Franklin Roosevelt would indeed accept the nomination of his party for a third term if it were offered. That story had been a coup for her and one that she owed to Anderson. Soon after, over dinner and drinks, he intimated that he felt some sort of payment was due. Anderson was young and not unattractive, but Betty Donaldson was not about to start paying for information with sex. She would repay her sources the way her male colleagues did—with an exchange of information, or a flattering reference in a subsequent article.

When rebuffed, Anderson had feigned wounded innocence. Anything that he gave her was from friendship, he had whined, and not in expectation of repayment. She, of course, had apologized for misunderstanding his intentions. After that, though, there had been fewer bits of inside information.

"You leave for London tomorrow," Anderson said.

"Yes," said Betty, her eyes narrowing.

"You will be one of the very few women assigned to what is likely to be a war zone."

"I think it is already considered a war zone, Peter."

"You know what I mean. If the Germans invade, it's going to get pretty risky over there."

"I've been through it before."

He forced a smile. Her arrogance was her most annoying quality. But it also made her tremendously exciting. He had never met any woman quite like her. "Yes," he said. "The

President was—we all were—very impressed with your despatches from Warsaw last year."

"Unfortunately, I had to get out before the really heavy stuff hit . . ."

Anderson interrupted. "Yes," he said, "absolutely right. And now, apparently, you are being sent to England to cover the same chaos."

"If the invasion comes, I want to be there. It'll probably be the biggest story of the century."

Anderson nodded. "No doubt—end of the British Empire and British civilization as we know it sort of thing."

Betty sensed that Anderson was trying to lead her somewhere. "Something like that," she said.

"How do you feel about it?"

"About what?"

"Invasion, end of the empire, end of British civilization."

"I've seen too much of the British Empire to care much about its survival," Betty Donaldson said. "But . . ."

"But what?"

"I think it would be an immense tragedy if Hitler occupied England."

"We agree," said Anderson.

"We?"

"The President, the administration."

"So do something about it, before it's too late."

"Like what?"

Betty shook her head. "That's your department. I just write stories."

Anderson smiled. "But you can help."

"Me?"

"Can we talk off the record?"

She nodded.

"When you get to London, the President would like you to report back to him with your impressions about how the British people are reacting to the situation."

"You've got people to do that sort of thing."

"Yes, we do," Anderson agreed. "We get reports almost on a daily basis. Unfortunately, they invariably conflict."

"What about the Ambassador? Has he changed his mind?"

"Ambassador Kennedy still sings the same song. The British have had it. The war will be over in a month and the British should sue for peace and get the best deal they can."

Betty Donaldson smiled. She had heard the rumors, prevalent in Washington, that Kennedy was more worried about his liquor contracts that he was about the British getting acceptable peace terms. More than one politician had told her that Kennedy was afraid a German occupational government would not honor any previously written export-import contracts. "I suppose," she ventured, "that a negotiated settlement would preserve his liquor franchises."

Anderson made a face. She had broached a subject that he was loath to discuss. "We can't be certain that his motivations are anything less than honorable."

Betty almost laughed. "Why not? Everyone who knows him seems certain of his motivation."

Peter Anderson looked at the carpet. This was not the conversation he wished to pursue. "There are many who agree with him. Charles Lindbergh is going around the country telling everyone how wonderful—and invincible —the Germans are. Certain elements in the Senate are unalterably opposed to any sort of aid to the British."

"Certain elements in the President's own party are unalterably opposed to any assistance."

Anderson nodded sadly. "There are also publications —with close ties to the opposition party—that are against aid to Britain."

Betty knew that he was alluding to her employer, *Time* magazine.

"Henry Luce has never tried to influence anything I've ever written," she said, knowing it wasn't quite true. Two years ago she had been commissioned to write a puff piece on Ambassador Kennedy. At the time the Ambassador had been Henry Luce's favorite candidate for the presidency. Her piece had not been puffy enough, apparently, because there had been a few deletions and some facts that she had not written were included in the article. When she had questioned her editor about the changes, he had merely pointed to the ceiling to convey the idea that the changes had come from "upstairs."

The look on Anderson's face showed his disbelief. "I'm sure that Luce liked your stories from Poland describing the awesome power of the German military. It fits right in with what he wants the American public to believe."

"Everything in those stories was the absolute truth. If it happens to please some and not others, I can't help that. I only report what I see. Nothing more, nothing less."

Anderson smiled. "That's what the President is counting on. He'd like a personal report from England. What you see—what you hear. Nothing more, nothing less."

"Why doesn't he just read my articles?"

"He wants more than that."

"Like what?"

"An objective appraisal—your appraisal—as to whether or not the British can hang on. If we give them the planes, the tanks, the artillery, the rifles they need, can they hold off the Germans? Do they have the guts for it?"

"Why not just give it to them and find out?"

Anderson shook his head. "It's not that easy. If we give the British everything they need and they still go belly-up—what then? We have lost all of that material which we then may need desperately for our own defense. If that happened, there are people here in Washington who would crucify the President."

"And not without justification."

Anderson ignored her comment. "The President is convinced that if Hitler conquers Britain, it won't be long before he starts looking in our direction."

"He's probably right."

Anderson was silent for a moment. Finally he said, "Will you help us?"

Betty Donaldson lit a cigarette. She chose her words carefully. "I work for *Time*," she said, blowing a cloud of smoke in Anderson's direction. "If I can help you without compromising my position with the magazine, I'll do it. I won't sugar-coat anything that I see over there; I'll report exactly what I feel."

Anderson smiled. "That's exactly what the President wants." He stood up and Betty, assuming that the meeting was over, began to get up, but Anderson motioned for her to remain in her seat. "I'll be back in just a few minutes," he said. "Would you mind waiting here?"

"All right," she said and watched him go. She wondered what she was getting herself into. Her father, who had been a foreign correspondent for the *Washington Globe*, had told her never to trust anyone in government. He was also a dyed-in-the-wool Republican with a deep distrust of Roosevelt and his New Deal administration. Now, apparently, she had agreed to work for the politician her father despised more than any other. She sighed. What her father didn't know wouldn't hurt him.

After the death of her mother, Betty had often traveled with her father. His job took him all over Europe, and the teenage Betty Donaldson had wanted nothing more than to be a reporter like him. She had lived, for varying lengths of time, in Paris, London, Madrid, Berlin, Warsaw, and Vienna and had visited most of the other countries in Europe. She had, at her father's insistence, returned to the United States to attend college, and after four years at Radcliffe she had set out to become a reporter. With her father's connections it was easy to get a job, but she discovered that she was expected to cover the ladies' garden clubs or the latest news from the debutante front. She was a woman reporter and expected to cover women's stories.

In 1937, after a year of trying to find a newspaper that would allow her to do real reporting, she had quit in frustration. She returned to Europe and went to Spain, where her father was covering the Spanish Civil War. From Madrid, using the byline B. Donaldson, she wrote a series of freelance articles about the war that were picked up by some midwestern newspapers.

Someone in New York noticed her work, and she was given an assignment by *Life* magazine. Reporting from a war zone was considered "man's work," and the news that B. Donaldson was a woman caused quite a stir back in the States, and Betty became a minor celebrity for a brief time. By then she had established herself as a competent reporter and Henry Luce hired her to work for *Time*.

Her father, Walter Donaldson, was a staunch believer in isolationism. "Let the rest of the world go to hell," he said often. "Just so long as they don't get us involved." His bitterness stemmed from the fact that his youngest brother had been killed in what had been called "the war to end all wars." "And for what?" Donaldson said. "To save the goddamned British and the French from the Germans? And now they're at it again."

She wondered what her father would think of the Roosevelt request. Probably, she thought, want me to tell him to go to hell.

Anderson was back, interrupting her reverie. "Come with me, Betty," he said from the doorway.

She followed him down a long, carpeted hall to an elevator. Wordlessly he led her on board and pushed a button for the second floor, which she knew was the presidential living quarters. She was suddenly glad she had worn her best wool suit.

As the elevator door opened onto the second floor, Anderson nodded to the Marine guard on duty in the hallway and walked, with Betty following closely, to a double door to the left of the elevator. He knocked and a familiar voice called out for them to enter.

Franklin Delano Roosevelt was behind his desk, working on a small stack of papers, when Betty Donaldson took a deep breath and followed Peter Anderson into the President's study. As she entered, the President looked up as if her arrival had been a totally unexpected but pleasant interruption.

Franklin Roosevelt put down his pen and extended his hand across the desk. "Miss Donaldson," he said, a broad smile splitting his tanned face, "it's so nice of you to stop by."

She took the President's hand. He was strong and robust, the strength of his upper body belying the debilitation of his legs.

"Please, sit down," Roosevelt said. "I've been so looking forward to talking with you."

"Thank you, Mr. President," she said. It was difficult to imagine that this robust, healthy figure who sat before her with a heavily tanned face and a jaunty smile was unable to walk without assistance. Living in Washington, and covering the official events as she often did, Betty Donaldson had seen the Franklin Roosevelt that the public had never been allowed to see. She had seen James Roosevelt, the President's son, support his father as the President laboriously made his way toward the podium at numerous speaking engagements. She had often seen one of the two burly aides who accompanied the President wherever he went scoop him out of his wheelchair and carry him into or out of his car. It was always disconcerting to see the President of the United States, one of the most powerful men in the world, picked up and carried like a helpless child. No photographer would ever think of taking the President's picture at these times. As far as she knew, no one had ever taken a photograph of the President in his wheelchair. If they did, no newspaper or magazine would publish the photographs. The American public had only some vague conception that their president was indeed hopelessly crippled. What they saw in photographs was a vigorous, energetic man behind the wheel of his car or standing at a podium or sitting casually, usually with legs crossed, in an easy chair. His voice, which millions listened to over the radio, projected strength, vitality, and stability.

Now the voice was soft and almost wistful. "Well, Miss Donaldson, I must say that I envy you."

"Envy me, Mr. President?"

Roosevelt smiled. "Yes. Going off to London at the height of all this excitement. I must say that I wish I were a younger man." Betty could not help but think of a younger Roosevelt, walking briskly toward some uncertain future. "You are about to become a witness to history," Roosevelt said. "I wish I were going."

"We need you right here, Mr. President," Peter Anderson said quickly.

The President winked at Betty. "Thank you, Peter," he said. "What would a president be without trusted aides to boost his already inflated ego."

Anderson shuffled his feet embarrassedly in front of his boss.

"Why don't you wait outside, Peter, and let Miss Donaldson and me have our little chat?"

Betty actually felt sorry for Anderson as he backed out of the room, looking at the floor, as if by some royal decree he could not look upon the visage of the reigning monarch.

FDR saw her expression. "Don't worry about Peter," he said. "He does a very fine job here, and I appreciate everything that he does for me."

Betty nodded and the President watched her carefully before going on. "The reason that I asked Peter to bring you here this evening, Miss Donaldson, is that I am besieged on all sides with conflicting information about the war in Europe. If we—as Americans—are going to make intelligent responses to this crisis, we must have accurate information."

Betty, mesmerized by the man, could only nod. "How can I help, Mr. President?"

Roosevelt beamed. "Just be yourself. Just report what you see and hear and feel."

"But I'd do that anyway, Mr. President."

"I know you would, Betty—may I call you Betty?" He went on before she could answer. "And that's why I'm asking for your help. People tell me that the British can't possibly hold on against Hitler. Charles Lindbergh keeps telling me and the American people that this is not our fight and that the Germans are invincible. People in my own party—like Senators Clark and Wheeler—warn me to stay out of this fight or there will be a revolt in my own party. The Republicans are calling themselves the 'Peace Party' and their nominee calls for nonintervention. Can I tell you something that won't find its way into the pages of *Time* magazine?"

"Of course, Mr. President."

"Have you ever heard of the Strong Memorandum?"

"I don't believe I have."

"The Strong Memorandum was drafted by the Army's War Plans Division under the direction of Brigadier General George Strong and was presented to me in June of this year. The memorandum cataloged the limited military capacity of the U.S. armed forces, and the inability of those forces to contest any aggression by Nazi Germany."

Betty Donaldson nodded knowingly. "Our military weakness is a well documented fact, Mr. President."

"The memorandum predicted the early defeat of both the British and French forces by the Germans. Part of that prediction has, of course, already come true. The recommendation of General Strong and his committee is that the United States mobilize as rapidly as possible in preparation for action against hostile forces. What is important, as far as we're concerned, is the final recommendation of the Strong Memorandum. It suggests that, in order to preserve the nation's limited military capacity, all military aid to the Allies be terminated as soon as possible."

"That," said Betty Donaldson, "would ensure the rest of the prediction."

The President nodded. "I have not talked with anyone who believes that the British can hang on without our help."

"But can they hang on, even with our help?"

"Bill Donovan has just returned from London on a personal mission representing me. He thinks the British can hang on."

"Wild Bill Donovan?" Betty said, her surprise evident. Donovan was a prominent Republican, a former candidate for governor of New York, and a war hero of the Great War.

Roosevelt nodded.

"Seems that you're surrounding yourself with Republicans these days, Mr. President." In the last month Roosevelt had added two Republicans, Frank Knox and Henry Stimson, to his cabinet.

Roosevelt grinned. "Any port in a storm."

"These particular Republicans just happen to be advocates of interventionism, which doesn't exactly endear them to some elements in your party."

"You see my dilemma," said Roosevelt, smiling.

"A dilemma compounded by the fact that you are running for a third term."

The President's eyes narrowed.

Betty took a deep breath and plunged on. "You want to do what you think is right, but you'd like to do it without jeopardizing your chances for re-election. And right now," she said, "the polls show Willkie with an early lead."

Betty expected, at the very least, an angry lecture. Instead, Roosevelt put his head back and roared with laughter. "Peter was right about you," he said finally. "You don't miss much of anything, do you?"

Betty, relieved at the President's good humor said, "All part of the job, Mr. President."

"Which brings us back to the topic of our original discussion." The President drummed his fingers on his desk. "As everyone is well aware, even my ambassador to Britain thinks that the war will be over very soon, that the British have had it."

Betty knew that the President was referring to a speech that Ambassodor Kennedy had made in Boston during a recent visit. He had told a cheering crowd that the war was not "our fight" and that the British were as good as finished. The speech had, of course, caused a sensation on both sides of the Atlantic. The British were furious that the Ambassador

18

would voice such opinions and deeply disappointed that he believed such things to be true.

"And if he's right?" asked Betty.

"Then we can't afford to give them what they want."

"When the British knew the French were finished, they got out everything they could," Betty said.

"Yes, but they knew it was over. We don't know and that's where you come in."

"How can I help?"

"I'd like you to send me, via the diplomatic pouch, your estimates of the staying power of the average citizen."

"I'm quite flattered, Mr. President, that you would place such trust in me, but I am sure that others are more capable."

Roosevelt's jaw hardened. "Betty," he said, "I send generals and admirals and politicians to England every day, it seems. They speak to other generals, admirals, and politicians. I want to know about the people—the ordinary people—the shopkeepers, laborers, factory workers, housewives, and common soldiers. If they are willing to fight, maybe we can help them pull their irons out of the fire."

They were silent for a moment, then Roosevelt said, "I read your dispatches from Poland, Betty. Your descriptions of civilians caught in that terrible event moved me very much. That's part of the reason I think you are the right person for this assignment." He smiled, breaking the seriousness of the moment. "But don't think that you are alone in this. I have many, many people reporting back to me on the European situation. Your report will be, however, very important."

The President offered his hand. "I'll expect to hear from you, then?"

Betty could only take his hand and say, "Yes, of course."

Roosevelt flashed the famous smile. His eyes sparkled. "I look forward to reading your reports," he said. Suddenly he seemed very fatigued.

Peter Anderson entered the room, summoned by some silent signal.

"You were absolutely right about Miss Donaldson, Peter. She's perfect for our little assignment."

Anderson gave Betty a wicked smile. "I knew you'd think so, Mr. President."

"Well, goodbye, Miss Donaldson, and good luck over

there," said the President, but it was obvious that his mind was already elsewhere. He picked up the stack of papers on his desk and began leafing through them.

Anderson led Betty Donaldson out of the room and into the hallway. They rode the elevator in silence. At the first floor Anderson walked her to the East Wing exit. "Have you had dinner yet?"

"Yes."

"This could be quite a feather in your cap," he said. "Special assignment for the President of the United States."

"And all thanks to you," she said sarcastically.

"How about a drink? I'm finished for the evening."

"Unfortunately, I'm not. I've got a million things to do before I leave tomorrow."

"Just one drink?"

Betty sighed. "I don't think so, Peter. We've been down this road before and it seems to be a dead end."

Anderson nodded, "I guess your right," he said.

Betty touched him lightly on the shoulder. He was an important source and there was no sense in turning him off completely. "Perhaps I'll see you when I get back."

He immediately brightened and she marveled at his eternal optimism. He watched her walk down the steps to the waiting White House car and watched her slide into the back seat. He gave a soft, low whistle as her skirt rode up a little.

She never once looked back in his direction.

♦ CHAPTER 2 ♦

BALTIMORE, MD., August 10, 1940—The early morning sun sent dazzling slivers of light bouncing across the wavetops of Chesapeake Bay as the *Lisbon Clipper* taxied out from the Baltimore waterfront terminal into the choppy waters of the Patapsco River. The pilot swung the nose of the Boeing 314 flying boat into the wind and slowly revved the four great engines to full throttle. Gradually the *Clipper* picked up speed, and the boatlike hull began to rise above the waves.

At full power the noise was deafening and Betty Donaldson put her fingers in her ears to block out the sound.

The *Clipper* raced toward the bay, great plumes of spray flashing behind her. As it reached take-off speed, the flying boat lifted ever so slightly, and, like a flat stone hurled across a lake, skipped several times before rising completely above the wavetops. For a short time the *Clipper* was no more than five feet above the water, and to a first-time observer the aircraft might have looked as if it would never go higher, but finally, the angle of flight increasing sharply, it rose into the air, banked left, and began a long circle around the Pan Am terminal on the banks of the river.

The captain's voice crackled from the intercom. "Airborne, ladies and gentlemen. We will be making a stop in Hamilton, Bermuda, for fuel and a mail pickup. Then on to Horta in the Azores and then, to our final destination, Lisbon, Portugal, in approximately seventeen hours and thirty-five minutes from now."

There was a small collective sigh of relief from the fourteen passengers on board, as if the pilot's voice had somehow soothed their fears about a four-thousand-mile ocean flight. Although some of the passengers were bound for destinations in Europe, most were destined for England and would have to make connections with British Imperial Airways in Lisbon for the flight to Poole, near Bournemouth, on the Channel coast of England. The Boeing 314 flying boat, because of its great size and cargo capacity, was considered a merchant vessel and as such was not allowed to "sail" into the ports of belligerent nations without fear of attack.

The pilot droned on about altitude and weather and flight procedures, and Betty tuned him out. She settled back into her seat, relaxing somewhat the grip she had on the arm rests. Flying was nothing new to her, and usually she felt no trepidation, but the bouncy take-off and the knowledge that she was heading toward a war zone had left her vaguely uneasy.

She was also troubled by her committment to President Roosevelt. Despite her claims to journalistic impartiality, Betty wondered how objective she could be. Because of her father, she had never been particularly fond of the British. According to him, it had been the British who had encouraged Hitler to gobble up Austria and Czechoslovakia, and then her own experience in Poland, where the Poles had valiantly fought the Germans in the vain hope that the British and French would honor their treaty obligations, had helped cement those negative feelings. The British had declared war on Germany because of the attack on Poland, but it had been an empty gesture. While the Poles fought, the British and the French had twiddled their collective thumbs.

Now she was being asked to evaluate whether or not the British, who had already abandoned the French in that country's most desperate moment, were worthy of American aid.

She sighed. Objectivity might not be easy.

Betty looked at her watch and then at the blue Atlantic below. Hamilton, Bermuda, in a little less than three hours. She settled back in her seat. It was only the beginning of a long, hard journey.

CHARLES LINDBERGH CALLS FOR COOPERATION
WITH GERMANY AFTER NAZI VICTORY; LONE
EAGLE WANTS U.S. NEUTRAL; "AMERICA MUST
STAY OUT OF EUROPEAN WARS," HE TELLS
RALLY

CHICAGO, AUG. 10

◆ *CHAPTER 3* ◆

LONDON, August 10, 1940—Ambassador Joseph P. Kennedy was furious. "That son of a bitch Donovan was here for over two weeks. Sent by Roosevelt to snoop around. And me, the goddamned ambassador. I don't even know he's here until the day before he leaves." He pounded the desk. "Now what kinda shit is that?"

The Ambassador was in his shirtsleeves, his red suspenders dangling by his side. He was fifty-two years old, but his broad shoulders, freckled face, and wire-rimmed glasses gave him a more youthful look. The eyes behind the spectacles were icy blue and capable of freezing a man in his tracks.

One by one he eyeballed the men in his office, daring them to answer. No one did.

"I'm probably the only one in this goddamned room who didn't know that this prick Donovan was here." He eyed them again with a look that was full of malice. "I want to thank you all for telling me that this Donovan, this"—he groped for the words—"this goddamned Republican was here doing what I consider to be my job."

There were seven of them sitting in a semicircle in front of the Ambassador's desk. They had been served coffee and pastries by a servant who had discreetly disappeared before the Ambassador began his harangue. No one had dared touch the pastries, and the coffee had grown cold.

23

The seven were: David Carson, the charge d' affaires, who, officially, was second in command to the Ambassador; Terrence Wymore, the Ambassador's assistant, who in practice if not in title was actually the number two man at the embassy; Colonel Robert E. Jackson, the military attaché, and his recently arrived assistant, Captain Maxwell Munro; Captain Jonathan Studwell, the naval attaché, and his assistant, Lieutenant Commander Ian Forbes; and the air attaché, Colonel Tobias Graham.

"Naturally, I called Mr. Donovan," Kennedy went on in a mock pleasant tone, "just to let him know that I knew he was here. He was staying at the Claridge—practically under my goddamned nose. I met with him—at my insistence—and do you know what the son of a bitch had to say?"

No one ventured a guess.

"Mr. Donovan told me that I should stop bad-mouthing the British. Told me that it was U.S. policy to help these people in any way we can, and that I should stop saying they haven't got a chance." The Ambassador grinned. "I asked him if that 'policy' he referred to was official U.S. policy, and if it was, why hadn't I read anything about it in any of the goddamned newspapers." The grin widened. "He didn't have an answer for that one. I asked him what the 'official' U.S. policy would be after the November election. He didn't have an answer for that one, either. I reminded him that the latest Gallup poll placed Willkie within a few points of Roosevelt in the popular vote and ahead in the electoral vote. Half the Democrats are against a third term. If Wheeler runs, as he threatens to do, he'll take millions of votes from Roosevelt and hand the election to the Republicans."

Kennedy drummed his fingers on his desk. "Roosevelt is finished," he said.

Ambassador Joseph P. Kennedy was being his usual irascible self, thought Colonel Robert E. Jackson. Even though the events he described had taken place one week ago, Kennedy was still angry about what he considered a slight from the White House. The Ambassador's comment about Roosevelt had sparked a memory of the last time the Ambassador had called one of these staff meetings. It had been more than a month ago, and Churchill had just spurned the latest peace offer from Hitler. At that time Kennedy had seemed more casual, more in control of himself. He had had his feet up on his desk, hands behind his neck, as he predicted the future course of the war.

"Three or four weeks," Kennedy had said. "That's it. If the British haven't got the good sense to give in by then, Hitler will invade and cram surrender down their throats." He smiled as if enjoying the prospect. "If that happens, the British deserve everything they get."

There had been a clearing of throats and a slight murmur of disapproval in the room, but no one had said anything.

"It's just sheer stupidity," Kennedy had gone on, "for them to hang on in a fight that everyone knows they can't win. The bastards are hoping we'll rescue them from their own mistakes—just like we did in the last war. But this war has nothing to do with us."

Colonel Jackson was wrenched back into the present by the loud thump of Kennedy's fist on the desk. "I have received no 'official' notification of any change in policy," the Ambassador said, "and until I do, the policy of this embassy will be to offer no encouragement, in any form, to the British. Their best hope of survival is a negotiated settlement."

Colonel Jackson announced his intention to speak by clearing his throat. The Colonel was a tall, slender man in his mid-fifties. He was soft-spoken, but there was an air of authority about him. The Ambassador looked at him in surprise. "The Royal Air Force seems to be doing rather well in the air engagements with the Luftwaffe," Jackson said. "They're reporting combat figures of two or three to one in their favor."

Ambassador Kennedy shook his head sadly. "Even if those reports are accurate—which I doubt—it won't do them any good. Last year Charles Lindbergh told me"—he stabbed a finger at his desk—"right here in this office, that the Germans have such overwhelming superiority in aircraft that they could afford to lose by five or ten to one and still have enough to overwhelm the British. The Germans haven't used half of the forces that are available to them. They keep hoping that Churchill will see the light and avoid a bloodbath."

"I don't know of any military force, Mr. Ambassador, that could accept those kinds of losses."

"That's not what's important here," said Kennedy. "What is important is that we keep out of it."

Now that Jackson had broken ground, others felt free to

speak. Captain Jonathan Studwell, naval attaché, was first. "Mr. Ambassador," he said, "if the Royal Navy falls into Hitler's hands, it could be disastrous for us. Just as the British were concerned with the fate of the French fleet, we must be concerned with what would happen if the Germans gained control of both the French and British navies. These combined forces would—"

"Mr. Hitler has no designs on the United States," the Ambassador interrupted. He eyed Studwell coldly. Kennedy had little use for military men. They had no conception of the economic forces that shaped the modern world. Theirs was a world of tin soldiers and toy guns. "What Hitler has wanted all along is to be secure within his own territorial borders. If the British and French had let him do that, they wouldn't be in the position they are in now—one finished, the other in the middle of its death throes." He shook his head sadly. "I've said it before and I'll say it again—why would anyone want to go to war over Poland?" Kennedy let his gaze fall on Captain Munro. "What do you think, Captain?"

Munro squirmed and sneaked a quick look at his boss, Colonel Jackson, for direction. None was forthcoming. "Mr. Ambassador, we've got to stay out of this war."

Kennedy smiled warmly. "I'm sure your father feels that way."

"Yes, sir," said Munro. "I'm sure he does."

Munro was the youngest man in the room and the son of Malcolm Munro, the senator from Minnesota. Senator Munro was a Democrat and an arch isolationist who opposed Franklin Roosevelt's attempts to aid the Allies because doing so would weaken American defenses. Senator Munro was also opposed to a third term for the President. Only a month earlier, just before the Democratic Convention, he had declared that he would bolt his party if FDR was renominated, or if the Democratic Party became what he called, "the war party." The Senator was a man of considerable influence in Washington and was also a friend of Ambassador Kennedy's. There were those who suggested that he had used his influence and friendship to get the Army to post his son to the London embassy. Some even suggested that his son was in London to keep him informed about what Roosevelt and Churchill were up to.

Captain Studwell sighed inaudibly and looked at Colonel

Graham, who barely shook his head. Both looked at Colonel Jackson, but he, expressionless as usual, gave no indication that he might be insulted that the Ambassador had asked for the opinion of his assistant rather than his.

Terrence Wymore's eyes narrowed as he detected some sort of signaling among the military men. Terrence Wymore was forty-four years old, his hair already gray, and his midriff bulge assuming gigantic proportions. As usual, he thought, the military men show their disrespect for the Ambassador, but don't have the courage to speak out. It was an open secret that the three attachés held the Ambassador in contempt. They thought he wasn't good enough for them. It was like Boston all over again, thought Wymore. No matter how much wealth a man accumulated, there were always those who felt that he wasn't good enough to shine their shoes. That's how it was with this crowd. He grinned as he watched them squirm in their chairs, afraid to contradict the Ambassador. He enjoyed watching Joe Kennedy make them uncomfortable.

Once again Kennedy addressed the group. "Well, the British have stirred up a hornet's nest and they're going to pay for it." He smiled. "This time, for a change, they've picked on a country they can't push around."

The Ambassador removed his wire-rimmed glasses and began to polish the lenses with a linen handkerchief. Colonel Jackson stifled a sigh. He knew the "I told them so" speech was coming.

"If they had only listened to . . ." the Ambassador began, and they all thought that he would say, "me," but instead he paused and finally said, ". . . Chamberlain." He went on quickly. "None of this would have happened. The man was a peacemaker, a statesman, a judge of character." He shook his head sadly. "He and I discussed this many times, and we both agreed that Hitler should not be forced into drastic action."

Colonel Jackson coughed into his clenched fist. It was his opinion that the former British Prime Minister was a thoroughly decent man but basically naive and misguided. Chamberlain had truly believed that he could negotiate with Adolf Hitler. Unlike the others, however, Jackson was never openly contemptuous of the Ambassador. He respected the position but not the man who currently held it.

"Now," said Kennedy, "we've got this Churchill to contend with." It was no secret that Kennedy and Churchill despised each other. "I don't think that I've ever heard a more belligerent man in all my life. He talks as if he really believes that Britain will be able to hold off the Germans." He chuckled. "His only chance is to start negotiating a reasonable armistice, and hope that Hitler is still willing to offer very attractive terms."

He's enjoying this, Jackson thought. The opportunity to see the English battered by an old adversary, and the double pleasure of being able to say, "I told you so." From their first meeting in 1938, when Kennedy had taken over as Ambassador, Jackson had been repelled but at the same time fascinated by this self-made millionaire who had taken London by storm. The man was an anomaly. He could be charming one moment, obnoxious the next. Often profane and irreverent, at times he seemed awed by what he had achieved in his life. After spending a weekend with the King and Queen at Windsor Castle, Kennedy had talked of nothing else. He spoke in hushed tones of the splendor of the castle and heaped praise upon the Royal Family as if in some way they had bestowed on him the acceptance that he had never found in his native Boston.

During the early months of his tenure at the embassy, Joe Kennedy had been surprisingly popular with the British public, who seemed to see in him the embodiment of all their dreams and aspirations. He had brought with him his full entourage of handsome children, and the British had been enthralled with this feisty Irish-American clan that had scrambled to the upper echelons of American society. Soon Kennedy was on intimate terms with Prime Minister Neville Chamberlain and supported him in his futile attempts to appease Chancellor Hitler. In that endeavor Kennedy was in accord with the vast majority of the British public, who wanted only to be left in peace. Feed the dog a bone, they seemed to say, and perhaps he will be satisfied. And so, at Munich, they fed him much of Czechoslovakia and assumed that his hunger would be sated. They had not considered the beast's enormous appetite.

But even after that policy had been discredited and its major proponents removed from office, Ambassador Kennedy continued to insist that Hitler was a man who could be reasoned with. When he spoke of Hitler, he often closed by saying, "We can do business with him."

That was a typical Kennedy response, Jackson thought. The world could always be equated with American business practices—buy, sell, negotiate, compromise, outmaneuver. Profit was everything. War was to be avoided, not necessarily because of the human suffering involved, but because it destroyed goods and capital. War was like a fire in a well-stocked warehouse. To Kennedy, the heads of the various states were like the presidents of American businesses. They could be reasoned with because no businessman wants to see his product and profit destroyed. Just as he had negotiated mergers in the banking and motion-picture businesses, Kennedy felt that he could sit down and strike up a deal with any business leader. Hitler's problem, he felt, was that no one had offered him the right deal.

"For the moment," Kennedy said, "our first concern must be to get American citizens out of the war zone. I've been informed by the State Department that the liner *Roosevelt*"—here he grinned mischievously as if at some private joke—"will be arriving soon to repatriate any Americans who want to get out before the Germans arrive. We don't know what Hitler will do when he gets here."

"I'm sure," said Colonel Jackson, his face and voice without expression, "that we'll be able to negotiate some suitable arrangement with him when he does arrive."

Kennedy eyed the Colonel carefully. He could never tell if Jackson was being sarcastic. The soldier had always treated him with the greatest of respect, but the Ambassador knew that there was an air of condescension lurking in the background. It was always the same with these upper-class snobs. He had dealt with bastards like this all his life.

Kennedy looked at the wall clock. "I have an appointment in fifteen minutes," he said, rising from his seat. The others rose also. "I just wanted to make sure," Kennedy continued, "that we all understand the official policy of this embassy. We must prepare for the collapse of first the economy, then the military, and ultimately the government of Great Britain. I don't care what that damn fool Bill Donovan is telling Roosevelt, I intend to inform the State Department and the President that collapse is imminent and I expect that you military people will make similar reports to your superiors in

Washington. Don't hold out false hope. Now I suspect that we all have a million things to do, so I suggest we get to it."

Everyone began to move toward the door. Kennedy called out to Terrence Wymore. "You can stay, Terry. We'll probably be inundated with requests for passage on the *Roosevelt*, and you'd better set up a staff to deal with the crowds."

David Carson turned to face the Ambassador. "The staff is already in place and anticipating the rush."

Kennedy's expression darkened. "This is going to be greater than you expect," he said gruffly. "Put more people on it."

Carson nodded. "As you wish, Mr. Ambassador."

"That's it, then," said Kennedy. "Let's get busy."

As soon as the others had departed, Kennedy turned to Wymore, "Close the door, Terry. We've got to talk."

Wymore did as instructed and returned to his seat in front of Kennedy's desk. He sat and waited for his boss to begin.

Wymore was a lawyer who had never practiced law. He had spent the last twenty years working for Joe Kennedy in one capacity or another. When Kennedy had decided to get into the motion-picture business in 1929, it was Wymore who was his advance man in Hollywood. He had quickly established a reputation as a no-nonsense, hard-nosed negotiator who was totally dedicated to his boss. In 1933, with repeal only a short time away, it had been Wymore who went to England to set up the meetings that eventually made Joe Kennedy the sole distributor of Gordon's Gin, Haig and Haig, and Dewar's Scotch. There were also rumors that during Prohibition Terrence Wymore had brought Joe Kennedy and underworld figure Frank Costello together as partners in the liquor business.

Now he was known as the Ambassador's assistant, personal secretary, advance man, confidant, or, simply, jack-of-all-trades. There was a bond between them that surpassed all understanding. Although there were only eight years between them, they were like father and son. Kennedy had only to speak and Wymore was ready to do his bidding. Sometimes, even before Kennedy could make his wishes known, Wymore had anticipated his thought and accomplished the task. His dedication bordered on idolatry. He believed that Joe Kennedy was one of the great men of his era, and through Joe

Kennedy he had rubbed elbows with movie stars, presidents, prime ministers, and kings.

Wymore's greatest desire was that Joe Kennedy would become President of the United States. Only a year ago it had seemed very possible that Kennedy would be the choice of the Democratic Party. He held the most prestigious diplomatic post available, was touted for the job by many business leaders, was popular in the press, and with his large, handsome family, was popular with the public, who saw him as the epitome of the American Dream, a man who had built his fortune from nothing. Even Roosevelt had intimated that Kennedy would have his backing—although Wymore was aware that Roosevelt had given his blessing to at least a dozen other potential candidates.

But then came the war. Goddamned war! Everything had changed. Roosevelt had changed his mind about a third term and shrewd politician that he was, had kept Kennedy isolated from the campaign by forcing him to stay in England. While Roosevelt played the reluctant virgin, pretending that only his party's insistence and the will of the people had persuaded him to run for a third term, his opponents squabbled amongst themselves, and Joe Kennedy, the only legitimate contender, was unable to extricate himself from the ambassadorship.

Roosevelt, Wymore thought, had played it perfectly. The one job that Joe Kennedy had wanted above all others was Ambassador to the Court of Saint James. It was the perfect post for the man who wanted to prove something to the Boston Brahmins—the Lowells and the Lodges—who had forced him and his family to flee to New York to find the social acceptance that his wealth and stature deserved. The Brahmins must have died when they saw the pictures in all the Boston papers of Joe and Rose hobnobbing with the King and Queen while young Bobby made conversation with Princess Elizabeth. The London Embassy was also the perfect post for a man who wanted to remind the English that his grandparents, who had fled Ireland in steerage, had been refugees, abused by the world's most powerful country. Now he had returned in first class, as the representative of the nation that had replaced England as the leader of the Western World. It was a Cinderella story of the first magnitude, and the world loved it.

But it was a Cinderella story that had turned to ashes. When Franklin Roosevelt had announced the appointment of Kennedy as the United States Ambassador to the Court of Saint James his advisers had been amazed and distressed. Insiders at the White House had leaked the word to Kennedy, through Wymore, that Roosevelt's closest adviser, Harry Hopkins, had been dismayed by the appointment and had said, "Kennedy will bear watching." Harold Ickes, Interior Secretary and another close Roosevelt confidant, had been even more distressed.

Roosevelt himself had been unperturbed. He had called the appointment ". . . a joke. The biggest joke in the world." It was now clear that Roosevelt's joke was on Joe Kennedy. The post that was to become the stepping stone to the presidency had become a prison. With Europe at war, Kennedy could not return to the U.S. without appearing to abandon a vitally important position. It was with an almost perfect vision of the future that Franklin Roosevelt had removed his prime challenger from the field of contention and made it impossible for him to re-enter the fray.

Terrence Wymore had to admit that Franklin Roosevelt was still the master politician. He had the uncanny ability to get people to work for him without committing himself to any one person or idea. Talk to ten different politicians and you would get ten different impressions of the President and what he really believed. One thing was certain, though; Joe Kennedy believed the President had deceived him. He had promised Kennedy his support for the 1940 campaign and then he had decided that he wanted to keep the job for himself. Sweet Jesus! Wasn't eight years enough for any man? Kennedy was sure that it was the "liberal bunch—the commies and the others," who surrounded the President, who had convinced him to run again. They knew that with Kennedy in the White House they'd be out looking for work. "Bunch of goddamned social workers," he often called them.

As with most things, Terrence Wymore's views mirrored Joe Kennedy's.

Kennedy sat down and put his feet up on the desk. He lit a cigar. "Terry, how good are your contacts at the Hungarian Embassy?"

Wymore smiled. "First class, Joe."

Kennedy nodded. "Good. Do you think they can find out

what the Germans intend to do with the export-import contracts already in place, if they occupy England?"

Wymore nodded.

"Will they honor them, or will they take over everything for themselves?" Kennedy flicked his cigar ash into the ashtray next to him. "Those goddamned liquor contracts are worth over two million a year to us. After occupation they might be worthless. I don't mind telling you, Terry, these German bastards have got me worried. They're tough pricks, and I don't look forward to having to deal with them about continuing the liquor contracts."

"I'll see what I can find out."

"If von Dirksen comes back as German Ambassador, I don't think we'd have any problem. Herbert and I hit it off pretty good when he was here. I'm sure he'd put in a good word for us with Hitler or whoever is going to be in charge when the time comes."

"I'll do what I can, Joe, but don't be disappointed if it isn't much. It's chaos out there. Nobody knows what the hell is going to happen next."

"One thing, Terry. I can't touch any part of this. And none of it can touch me. Clear?"

"As always, Joe. I'm acting on my own."

"I don't know where I'd be without you, Terry." He laughed. "Probably running a bar in the North End."

Terrence Wymore beamed. He lived for this kind of praise from his boss.

◆ CHAPTER 4 ◆

When they left the Ambassador's office, Captain Studwell
whispered something to Colonel Graham and then turned to
Colonel Jackson, who was engaged in discussion with Maxwell Munro. "Bob," he said, "if you have a minute, I'd like to
talk to you."

Jackson smiled pleasantly. "Now would be fine." He
moved toward Studwell with Munro obediently falling in step
behind.

Studwell gave Munro a steely look and said, "In my office,
Bob. Alone, if you don't mind."

Jackson frowned, looked at Munro with puzzlement, and
shrugged. "Of course," he said to Studwell and then turned
to Munro. "I'll talk to you later, Max. Perhaps you can come
to my office?"

"Whatever you say, Colonel," said Munro. "I'll be in my
office whenever you need me."

The senior attaché's offices were on the second floor of the
embassy while the assistant's were on the lower level. As
Munro made his way to the stairwell he noted that Ian
Forbes, the assistant naval attaché, remained with the others
as they headed for Studwell's office. It was apparent that
Munro had been singled out for exclusion from whatever
discussion was about to take place.

Exclusion was not an experience that was new to Maxwell
Munro. For most of his life he had been an outsider. Wealth,

which should have given him easy acceptance, had in some strange way made him uncomfortable. Because of his family's great celebrity, he had never felt that he was accepted for himself, but because he was a Munro.

The Munro name was the most powerful in Minnesota politics, and had been for a long time. Senator Munro's father had been a Democratic congressman from St. Paul and his grandfather one of the state's first governors. The family fortune had been made in mining and the Munro Iron and Steel Works in Duluth was still the largest single employer in the state. Senator Munro was now serving his third term in the Senate after two terms in the House and, as the co-chairman of the Foreign Relations Committee, was widely regarded as one of the most influential politicians in Washington.

His father's increasing prominence had made it even more difficult for Max Munro to find his own niche in life. At Duluth College he had always been "the Senator's son," and even his professors had treated him with the deference usually reserved for visiting royalty. That deference was probably inevitable on a campus where several buildings had been donated by and named for Max's relatives. It had been a mistake to attend college so close to home. He had known that even before his first year was up, but his father would not listen to his protests. He would do what was expected, spend his four years at Duluth, and join the family business.

Instead, Max had joined the Army, partly to escape those expectations, and partly to find a place where he could be his own man. It had not, however, worked out as he had anticipated. Senator Munro's influence was everywhere. Commanding officers were always inviting the Senator's son to dinner. Dinners at which he noticed there were no other junior officers. In a peacetime army, where most officers put in long, hard years between promotions, Munro was promoted regularly and often. His performance ratings were always exemplary, better even than those officers who worked harder and showed greater dedication. It was not difficult to detect the power of the Senator behind the progress of the son. It was even less difficult to understand the resentment felt by many of his less successful fellow officers.

In 1940, after four years, Maxwell Munro had attained the rank of captain at least two years earlier than what was considered normal progress through the ranks. Although, in his own estimation, he had not been a top candidate, the promotion had come through as regularly as had the others. When his commanding officer had given him his captain's bars and told him, "Your daddy would be proud of you," Max had decided to leave the Army. What stopped him was that along with his new rank he was given a new assignment. He was being transferred to the staff of the American Embassy in London as an assistant to the military attaché. It was apparent, once again, that his father's influence was behind this move, but for once he did not protest. London was where civilization stood at the crossroads. He could not miss the opportunity to be a witness.

With a final glance over his shoulder at his departing colleagues, Munro walked down the stairs, aware that once again he was on the outside looking in. The Army should have been different, he thought. A soldier should be treated according to his abilities and not his contacts. An officer should be promoted for his leadership, not because of the influence of his friends. But, to his disappointment, the Army had turned out to be much like the real world. Those with influence and power moved forward, those who did not did most of the work and stayed where they were.

Captain Studwell closed the door to his office and motioned the others into the chairs around his desk. He was a small man, with a ruddy complexion and a pugnacious nature. He stood by the window for a moment, looking over Grosvenor Square before turning back to the group he had assembled.

"What do we do with this guy?" he said, looking directly at Colonel Jackson.

"Which 'guy' are we talking about?"

"C'mon, Bob. This new assistant of yours—Senator Munro's son. Don't you think that it's a little too coincidental that on the day Munro arrived, Kennedy found out about Donovan being here in London?"

Jackson shook his head. "The Ambassador could have found out about Donovan from any of a hundred sources. It's a miracle that word of Donovan's tour didn't get to him earlier."

"No one—from the President on down—wanted Kennedy to know that Donovan was here," Studwell said.

36

"You seem to forget, Jon," chimed in Toby Graham, "that the Ambassador still has some very influential friends in England."

"Yes," said Studwell with a derisive chuckle, "the Ambassador has friends in all the wrong places."

They all knew that Ambassador Kennedy's friends in England were now mostly out of power. Kennedy had been an intimate of the group of English politicians—former Prime Minister Neville Chamberlain, Foreign Secretary Lord Halifax, Chancellor of the Exchequer Sir John Simon and others—who had been responsible for the policy of appeasement. They had been replaced by men—Churchill, Anthony Eden, and Duff Cooper—who had opposed that policy and now had no use for those who had maintained it, or for the American Ambassador who had supported them.

Studwell looked at Jackson. "Bob, this Munro isn't one of us. At every turn he's used his father's influence with the War Department to move up the ladder. How many twenty-eight-year-old captains do you know in the Army?"

Jackson knew that in the peacetime U.S. Army there were very few captains with as little service time as Max Munro.

"I'll tell you something else," Studwell said. "I think that Munro has been appointed to the embassy staff to keep his eyes open and report back to his old man."

When Jackson said nothing, Colonel Graham turned to him and said, "It is possible, Bob."

"I really don't like this sort of thing," Jackson said. "Look at us. Meeting in secret, excluding one of our own, denigrating our immediate superior."

"I answer to the War Department," Studwell said. "I don't consider Kennedy my immediate superior."

Jackson said quietly, "Then perhaps you should reread the orders that appointed you to this embassy, Jon. Although we are all responsible to our superiors in Washington, as members of the embassy staff we report directly to, and are under the direct command of, the Ambassador—whomever he may be. I don't say that we have to agree with everything that the Ambassador says or does. But this constant carping behind his back does none of us any good. He wants to keep us out of this war and we all want Hitler stopped before the U.S. gets involved. We want the British to beat him in the field, and we

37

hope to give them the supplies to do so. The Ambassador wants a negotiated settlement. Either way the result is the same. The war is stopped and we stay out of it."

"But," said Graham, "our way eliminates the possibility that next year, or the year after, or five years from now, this will start all over again."

"Five years from now we, and the British, will be considerably stronger—and wiser. I doubt that we would let this happen again. Hitler preyed on our weakness. No one was strong enough to oppose him. Next time that won't be the case. Our best bet right now is to help the British survive and to hope that eventually they can get the job done."

"If the British fall," Studwell said, "the entire continent will come under German domination, and we will stand alone against Hitler."

"Hitler still has to deal with the Russians," said Jackson.

"The Russians!" Studwell exploded. "Those bastards are as much responsible for this war as is Hitler. The Molotov-Ribbentrop Pact gave Hitler the green light to attack Poland. Without their O.K. he couldn't have done it."

"Then," said Graham, "they helped him carve up Poland."

Jackson said nothing until his colleagues were finished. "And," he said quietly, "when they've finished carving up Europe, they'll have only each other to deal with."

"If Hitler conquers this island," Studwell said, "nothing can stand in his way. Right now he has the most powerful army and air force in the world. If the Royal Navy falls into his hands he will have three"—he held up three fingers of his left hand—"of the world's six most powerful navies at his disposal. The British, the French, and his own. Throw in the Italian fleet and it's four of six. If, as expected, the Japanese form an alliance with Hitler and Mussolini, together they will control five of the six most powerful navies in the world. They will also have access to the British bases in the Western Hemisphere. How would you like the German fleet stationed at Bermuda, or the Bahamas, or Jamaica?" He answered his own question. "It would be disastrous."

"I understand all of that, Jon," said Jackson.

"The Ambassador thinks that Mr. Hitler is satisfied with what he has. I think he intends to dominate the world."

Jackson smiled. "Let's hope that the Ambassador is right."

Graham said, "I had lunch with some people from the

Foreign Office yesterday, Bob. Their feeling is that the Ambassador knows nothing of history, politics, warfare, human nature, or diplomacy. They think he's a double-crosser and a defeatist. They're convinced that the Ambassador's major concern is with his own fortune. This is coming from people like Sir Robert Vansittart and Sir John Balfour at the American desk. Their feeling is that the Ambassador's only talent is making money, and that he cares little for how he makes it."

Studwell said, "Jan Masaryk, the Czech foreign minister, told me personally that the Ambassador had used advance knowledge of the German invasion of Czechoslovakia to sell Czech securities short, making himself a small fortune in the process."

"Then there's the Irish question," said Graham. "The British feel that the Ambassador's Irishness has made him anti-British. That he would welcome a British defeat because that would more than likely bring about a united Ireland."

"That's nonsense," said Colonel Jackson. "We're talking about the American Ambassador here."

"Who happens to surround himself," said Studwell, "with Irish cronies wherever he goes. Look at his personal staff —they're all Boston-Irish. I can't imagine that one of them would give a damn if England went down the drain."

"And look at us," said Jackson. "All from good English and Scottish stock. Perhaps our motives are suspect, too."

Studwell's face darkened. "My only concern is the security of the United States."

"I know that, Jon," Jackson said. "But what I am trying to suggest is that the security of the United States may be the Ambassador's only concern, also. What we see as defeatist, and what the British see as double-crossing and anti-British, may only be his way of protecting the interests of the United States. He's not alone in wanting to deny aid to the British. A lot of good, loyal Americans are afraid that we may strip our own defenses in a lost cause."

"That's true," said Studwell derisively. "The Senate is full of them. People like Wheeler, Clark, Walsh, and"—his eyes widened in mock surprise—"Senator Munro. Then we've got others—like Kennedy and Lindbergh—who wouldn't fight the Germans if Hitler walked up and punched them in the nose."

"We don't know that."

"We do know that the British would like to put Kennedy on the first boat back to Boston."

"Then why don't they speak to the President or the State Department?"

"They can't afford to antagonize the American public. If they didn't need us so desperately, they'd boot his ass right out of here."

Graham interrupted again. "We're getting away from the essential argument here. If the United States turns her back on the British, they're finished."

"Right now," said Jackson, "the German Army is the most formidable fighting force in the world." His eyes caught Studwell in a stare. "I've seen the British Army. It is ill-equipped and undermanned. The Wehrmacht would push it aside as if it were made of papier-mâché."

"If they could get at it."

"I've also inspected the British shore defenses. If the Germans knew how inadequate they were, they'd be here tomorrow. If the Germans could land fifty-thousand troops in England, it would be over in a week—just as the Ambassador says."

"Then why doesn't he come?" Studwell asked. "Hitler knows that the British Army hasn't regrouped from Dunkirk. He knows how much equipment they left behind in France. Why doesn't he come?"

"You're both missing the point," Graham said. "In order to do any of the things you've talked about, Hitler must first eliminate the RAF. Hitler and Goering know—and so do Churchill and Dowding—that without the RAF as an obstacle, the Germans can do what they please on this island. Without the protection of the RAF, it would be suicidal for the Royal Navy to attempt to stop an invasion. Without the elimination of the RAF, it would be suicidal for Hitler to attempt it."

"Go on Toby," Jackson said, "I think you're absolutely right. What happens next?"

"If the Germans fail to entice the British into aerial combat—and I doubt that they will—sooner or later Hitler will attack a target that the RAF will have to defend."

"London," said Jackson.

"Exactly."

Jackson's eyes went to the window behind Studwell. He remembered Charles Lindbergh's warnings about the destructive capacity of the Luftwaffe. He could almost imagine the city in ruins.

Studwell looked at the others. "Do we agree that the defense of this island is essential to our own national security?"

"Yes," said Graham.

They both turned to look at Jackson.

"What we tell the President and the War Department is of tremendous importance," Jackson said. "It is entirely possible that only the military intervention of the United States can save the day. Ultimately, our advice could be responsible for bringing the United States into this war."

The others nodded.

"It is also possible," Jackson went on, "that our country could suffer a crushing defeat. General Tatsumi, the Japanese military attaché, has intimated to me—and I have so advised Washington—that his country is on the verge of a military alliance with Germany and Italy. If that happens we would be faced with war on two fronts."

"The way I see it," Studwell said, "we have no choice in the matter. Sooner or later, the Germans and the Japanese are going to challenge us. If we can save the British, we'll have an ally. If we wait until they are defeated, we'll be all alone. We must convince Washington that the only course is to support the British against Hitler. To do otherwise is suicidal."

Jackson was silent. "I can see no other way," he said softly.

"Then we are agreed," Studwell said. "Now that that's decided, what do we do about your man Munro?"

"What do you suggest?" Jackson asked.

"Keep him in the dark about all of this. We don't want word to get back to his father's cronies in the Senate—or to the Ambassador."

"I don't like it," said Jackson.

"I don't, either, Bob," said Graham, "but it may be the only way."

"Keep him busy," said Studwell. "Send him off around the countryside reporting on anything that will keep him out of our hair."

Colonel Jackson stood up. "Agreed." He sighed. "I'm not

sure it's the right course of action, but I'll find something to keep him busy."

"Perfect," Studwell said. "And now, as the Ambassador would say, let's get busy."

They trooped into the hall, Graham and Studwell and their assistants in animated conversation, Jackson quiet and deep in thought. Although certain that what they had decided was the only safe course for them to take, the actual decision —acknowledging what each had known for weeks—filled him with a dark sense of foreboding. Jackson had served with Pershing in the Great War, and visions of those battlefields still filled his nightmares. He would suffer almost anything before he would let those nightmares become reality again.

ROOSEVELT ENCOURAGES BRITISH TO CONTINUE WAR, GERMANS SAY; REICH MINISTER WARNS PRESIDENT

BERLIN, AUG. 11

◆ CHAPTER 5 ◆

BERLIN—ABWEHR HQ, Sunday, August 11—The headquarters of the secret intelligence service of the German High Command—known as the Abwehr—resided in a row of five-story townhouses on Tirpitz Ufer, around the corner from the headquarters of the High Command of the Army and the Navy and of the main Defense Ministry on Bendler Strasse. These gray, imposing structures were known as the Bendler Block.

The Bendler Block was alive with activity. Throughout June and into early July, Adolf Hitler had continued to hope for some positive British response to the numerous peace proposals he had offered. Finally Hitler decided that invasion was his only alternative. On July 16 he issued Führer Direc-

42

tive 16, which called for his generals to prepare for an invasion of Great Britain. On July 19 he made his final effort to persuade the British to come to terms. When the offer was rejected without comment on July 22, the generals were told that they should be prepared to invade by September 15.

Since that time, the German High Command had worked at fever pitch to prepare what most felt would be the most enormous undertaking of their military careers. The Army High Command designated thirteen divisions from three different army groups to make the initial landings which would be followed by twenty-eight additional divisions within two days. The Naval High Command began the enormous task of preparing the embarkation ports, providing mine sweeping and escort vessels, and gathering, from all over Europe, the barges which would be used to transport the invasion forces. What was apparent to all was that without air superiority over southern England the invasion could not possibly succeed. Both army and naval commanders cautioned the Führer that their plans could only work if the Luftwaffe first neutralized the RAF and then prevented the Royal Navy from disrupting the landings.

This enormous task fell to the Commander in Chief of the Luftwaffe, Reichsmarschall Hermann Goering. Others might have equivocated in the face of such responsibilities, but Goering was not one to underestimate the abilities of his forces. The Luftwaffe, after all, outnumbered the Royal Air Force by almost two to one and had already routed both the British and the French in the skies over France. Goering promised Hitler that his forces would eliminate the RAF in just four days and that, under the protective umbrella of the Luftwaffe, the invasion could then proceed at a leisurely pace.

On this, the eleventh day of August, 1940, the war plans were proceeding at full tilt. Earlier in the day Admiral Wilhelm Canaris, head of the Abwehr, had been summoned to Bendler Strasse to the offices of General Alfred Jodl, chief of the operations section of the German High Command and personal chief of staff to Adolf Hitler. Jodl wanted to know what preparations Canaris had made for the invasion and how many Abwehr agents were in place in England to foment confusion, disrupt enemy lines of communication, and commit acts of sabotage. Jodl would have been sorely disappointed if Canaris had told him the truth. The Abwehr had very few agents in Britain when the war began, and most of those who had been landed since the outbreak of hostilities had been captured within days of their arrival on enemy soil. True to his profession, Canaris wove a tissue of lies, exaggerations and misstatements, that gave the impression that the Abwehr was in control of a substantial network of spies. By including the names of the few German sympathizers left in Britain, the leadership of the Irish Republican Army, the Welsh nationalists, any foreigners in Britain who might conceivably have some grudge against their adopted homeland, and those agents who had been captured but not yet confirmed as such, Canaris made his few agents sound like hundreds.

When Canaris left Jodl's office he was reasonably sure that the General would give a favorable report on the Abwehr's activities to the Führer. His only concern now was to try, in some way, to make the reality of his situation somehow match the fantasy that he had created. To that end, as soon as he was back in his office at Tirpitz Ufer, he called for Colonel Erwin von Lahousen, head of Abwehr II and a former officer with the Austrian secret police who, in that capacity, had helped the Germans take over his country. Lahousen was in charge of saboteurs and particularly those who were members of the Irish Republican Army. Lahousen's answers to his chief's questions did nothing to assuage Canaris's fear that the Abwehr was ill-prepared to play a major role in the coming invasion.

"I don't think we can count on the IRA," said Lahousen. "They are undisciplined and without scruples. They will take whatever we offer them, but cannot be relied upon to give anything in return."

"Who else, then?" asked Canaris.

"It must be remembered, Herr Admiral," Lahousen said, somewhat defensively, "that until recently, the Führer himself had banned any placement of agents on British soil."

Canaris knew that this was true. From 1935 to 1938, Hitler, hoping to form some sort of alliance with Great Britain, had forbidden the Abwehr to meddle in British affairs. The Admiral gave Lahousen a baleful stare. "Would you like to accompany me when I tell the Führer that our problems in England are his fault?"

Lahousen swallowed hard, but did not answer.

"You are well aware, I am sure, Colonel," said Canaris, "that this agency is under the constant threat of dismemberment by the hyenas of the Reich Main Security Office. Our friends in the SS would like nothing better than for us to admit that we have nothing to offer in the war against England."

"Our resources are limited," said Lahousen, "but I wouldn't say we have nothing to offer."

"What, then?"

"Captain Bernhard Ritter has a small but effective stable of agents active in England. He . . ."

Canaris interrupted. "Send him to my office, at once." He looked at his watch. "Better still, tell him to meet me in the courtyard. The young captain can tell me about his stable over lunch."

Lahousen jumped to his feet. "At once, Herr Admiral."

Captain Bernhard Ritter stood next to the Admiral's idling Daimler in the courtyard behind Tirpitz Ufer, nervously shifting from one foot to the other. Like many in the Abwehr, Ritter was a former naval officer. He had served the Abwehr as the Naval Attaché in both the Dublin and London embassies. Ritter was thirty-five and short, with jet black hair and dark eyes. He was well aware that his stature and coloring were not the models of the perfect German. Friends and colleagues often joked about his non-Aryan features. To Ritter, it was no joke.

When Canaris appeared, he brushed past Ritter without a word, slid into the back seat of his limousine, then bent forward to look at Ritter. "Get in," he said.

The ride to the Tiergarten Plaza was brief. The Plaza, a large solarium at the edge of Berlin's Tiergarten Park, was close by and Canaris lunched there at least three times a week.

"Have you eaten at the Plaza?" Canaris asked.

"No, Herr Admiral," Ritter admitted. What he did not admit was that he had already eaten lunch—a sandwich—at his desk back at Tirpitz Ufer.

"Try the Wiener schnitzel," said Canaris.

Ritter nodded.

When they were seated at the Admiral's favorite table,

Canaris waited for the waiter to take their order and depart before broaching the subject of the meeting. "The battle in the skies over England will soon reach a critical phase," he said. "It is my considered opinion that Field Marshal Goering's plan is doomed to failure." He paused.

Ritter said nothing.

Canaris, his face expressionless, went on. "No matter how many aircraft Goering is able to commit to the battle, the advantage belongs to the British." Then Canaris, whom his men called the old man, gave his subordinate a sardonic smile. "Although the military part of this battle will be indecisive, it is my belief that the proper application of intelligence information can turn the tide in Germany's favor."

Ritter, at that moment, knew why he had been given the singular honor of luncheon with the head of the Abwehr. The old man hoped to make a significant contribution to the coming invasion and thereby save his beleaguered agency.

The waiter returned with their order and Ritter used the break in the conversation to take a good look at his superior. The Admiral seemed too small for his uniform. Perhaps it was the tribulations of his job, perhaps it was the constant pressure from the SS. In any event he seemed to have diminished in size over the past year. Canaris was fifty-two. He had a long, narrow face and an expression of perpetual sorrow, and his eyes, heavy-lidded and dark, gave no indication of the fires that burned within.

It was common knowledge that Canaris was involved in a bitter struggle with Reinhard Heydrich of the Reich Main Security Office, which incorporated the Gestapo, the secret state police; the Kripo, the criminal police; and the Sicherheitsdienst, known as the SD, which was the intelligence and counterespionage arm of the SS. Heydrich believed that all intelligence functions should be consolidated under one main office with, of course, himself as head. Canaris was equally determined to protect the independence of his department and, of course, to protect his own position. In this struggle the ruthlessly ambitious Heydrich had several advantages over his older rival. He was a favorite of the Führer himself, and of the Reichsführer of the SS, Heinrich Himmler, who had "discovered" Heydrich and carefully orchestrated his young protégé's meteoric rise through the ranks of the Nazi Party.

Most of Heydrich's rivals had fallen by the wayside or quite simply surrendered to his insatiable lust for power by accepting his hegemony over their function. Not Canaris. For two years the Admiral had been able to resist Heydrich's constant maneuvering for control of his agency. Canaris had held on in the face of what for others would have been insurmountable odds. Canaris had none of Heydrich's style or talents. He was dour and plodding, and he found no favor in the upper echelons of Nazidom. His survival was something of a miracle. His one asset, which he cloaked beneath a mask of polite civility, was that he was as ruthless as his young rival. Captured during the first war, Canaris had escaped from an Italian prison by murdering the priest who came to give him absolution. He then had used the murdered priest's robes to walk out of prison and eventually make his way back to Germany.

There were rumors, of course—in Nazi Germany there were always rumors—that Canaris owed his survival to the fact that he also collected dossiers, and that locked in his personal safe at Abwehr headquarters was the dossier that the Admiral had gathered on Reinhard Heydrich. That dossier, so the rumors said, provided definitive proof that Heydrich—the "Blond Beast," the "Scourge of Poland" —had Jewish blood coursing through his perfect Aryan veins.

That rumor, if true, and the threat of its revelation, would have been enough to protect the Admiral from Heydrich's rapacious appetite.

The law of National Socialist Germany was the law of the jungle. The strong preyed upon the weak, the weak upon the weaker. In order to survive, the weakest developed defenses to enable them to camouflage those weaknesses and protect themselves from the predators. The survivors struggled over every scrap of meat and over every particle of territory.

Ritter looked across the table at the Admiral, who chewed contentedly on his Wiener schnitzel. The long, expressionless face revealed nothing of the mind behind the mask.

Canaris put down his fork. "As I recall," he said, "you still have several active agents in England."

Ritter nodded. He was in fact one of the few Abwehr

officers with reliable sources in England. The Abwehr's attempts to put agents in place had been nothing short of disastrous. Most of those placed before the war had been rounded up within weeks of the commencement of hostilities, and those emplaced since the war had begun were a sorry lot whose training was insufficient to enable them to elude capture for more than a week or two.

"Tell me a little about them," said Canaris.

"There are five under my jurisdiction, but I consider two of them to be unreliable."

Canaris's long face did not change expression, but his left eyebrow raised a fraction. "Why?"

"One, Helmut Stark, I'm sure has been captured. His last three radio communications have neglected to include his secondary security check."

"And the other?"

"The Dutch businessman—Van Ness."

"Yes, I remember him," said Canaris. "What's the problem?"

Ritter shrugged. "Everything seems in order with him, but I have no faith in his ability. I think he was pressured into this assignment and was too afraid to say no. It is probable that on his arrival in England he surrendered himself to the first constable he found." He shook his head. "His transmissions are perfect—security checks properly in place—but they tell us very little that is not available in the American newspapers."

"You do well not to trust either of them," said Canaris. "Tell me about the other three."

"Daly, Benke, and Price. The first, and, in my estimation, the most important, is the Irishman, Sean Daly. You have seen my reports on his background and activities. He has been providing me with information since before the war. In the spring of 1938 I brought him to Germany for two weeks of training at the saboteur's camp in Quenzee. He performed admirably in all phases of his training. He is resourceful and, I believe, dedicated. Since the war began, he has been able to give us technical information, very detailed drawings, and occasional photographs of the British coastal defenses. When the invasion comes, this information could be of incalculable value."

"Colonel Lahousen does not share your enthusiasm for the Irish," said Canaris. "He finds them untrustworthy."

"I agree completely," said Ritter. "The Irish Republican Army comprises mostly simple hooligans who are of little value to us. We must use their limited talents very carefully. Those in the IRA who are legitimate revolutionaries are dominated by Communists. Their goals and ours are incompatible."

"But not Daly's?"

Ritter shook his head.

"His motivation?" the Admiral asked.

"He wants a free, unified Ireland."

Canaris sighed. "Let's hope that someday he gets his wish."

Ritter and Canaris were well aware that in Hitler's grand design for Europe, there were very few free and independent nations.

"What about the others?" Canaris said.

"One, of course, you know quite well. Josef Benke, the second secretary at the Hungarian Embassy in London. He is more your agent than mine. He replaced me as a liaison between agents when we were forced to close our London embassy."

"Do Stark and Van Ness know anything about Benke?"

"Nothing. Benke has no contact with them. His only functions are to gather information in embassy circles and to relay messages from Daly to Abwehr headquarters in Portugal."

"How do you read him?"

"Opportunist," Ritter said. "Benke understands that it is to his advantage to serve Germany. I don't think that he is ideologically drawn to National Socialism. As long as he believes that Germany is going to win, he will be on our side."

"Sometimes that type is more reliable than those who serve from admiration. They are less likely to become disenchanted with one's philosophy, and you always know where they stand."

"I agree, Herr Admiral."

"I take it then that you are satisfied with the reliability of both of these men?"

"Extremely so. With Benke's assistance, Daly and Price have been able to infiltrate the American Embassy. They have passed along to us a great volume of military information that passes between London and Washington. They are about to attempt a similar infiltration of the British Secret Service."

Canaris seemed pleased, but it was hard to tell.

Ritter continued. "Benke's contacts at the American Embassy are still impeccable. He continues to provide information about Roosevelt's deepening involvement with the British. I think that information, if revealed, would cost Roosevelt the election."

Canaris nodded. "I agree with you. The American public would repudiate Roosevelt if they thought for a minute that he was dragging them into a war with Germany."

Ritter's raised eyebrow asked the question that he dared not voice.

Canaris cast a baleful eye on his subordinate. "The reason this information has not yet been released, my curious friend, is that I have determined that the time is not yet right. If we reveal what we know now—three months before the American elections—we only give Roosevelt and his cronies time to concoct an alibi."

And, Ritter thought, give Heydrich and others the opportunity to grab some of the credit for the Abwehr's work. He wondered how much credit the Admiral would be willing to share with him. After all, he thought, I was the one who first brought him the news of the secret correspondence between Churchill and Roosevelt.

To his dismay, the Admiral once again read his mind. He gave an approximation of a smile. "Don't worry Ritter, there will be enough glory in this endeavor for all of us." The smile vanished as suddenly as it had appeared. "Provided, of course, that the glory stays within this agency."

"Of course, Herr Admiral."

"Now," Canaris said, "tell me about your fifth agent."

"She is a very attractive woman. Her married name is Marie Price and she is a Swiss national, born in Basel. In 1926, when she was sixteen, she married a minor Nazi party functionary in Freiburg. His name was Helmut Steinhoff. This Steinhoff was a friend of her father's, and almost as old. The father was a Nazi-sympathizer. He was attracted to uniforms, flags, and marching bands. Steinhoff was attracted to children—of either sex."

Canaris wrinkled his nose in disgust. "Where is Steinhoff now?"

"He was murdered in 1928. Someone slit his throat while he was sleeping."

"The girl?"

"She was a suspect—there had been a history of vile treatment. A police report from 1927, for instance . . ."

Canaris held up his hand. "Spare me the sordid details," he said.

"Anyway, there was no proof that she killed him. She was able to provide an alibi. Steinhoff was little more than a perverted thug. No one was particularly interested in prosecuting whoever had done him in."

Canaris sipped his coffee. He looked at his watch and Ritter knew his time was short.

"After her husband's death she moved back to Switzerland, but apparently it was not exciting enough for her. She moved to Berlin in 1929. Did some modeling. Worked in one of the cabarets."

"Prostitution?" Canaris asked.

"Perhaps," Ritter said reluctantly. "At that time most of the girls in such establishments were. In any event, she lived a somewhat sordid life for almost two years, then she moved back to Basel around 1930. Soon after, she met Reginald Price, the youngest son of an English merchant. He was an officer with the Royal Flying Corps who was on vacation. He fell in love with her, took her back to England, and married her. No one, of course, knew anything about the marriage to Steinhoff, or about his untimely demise."

"A happy union?" Canaris said with barely concealed sarcasm.

"No. She has a habit of attracting men who mistreat her."

"Where do you come into all this?" Canaris asked.

"1938. I was serving at the London Embassy, when someone from the embassy staff recognized her in a restaurant. Someone who had seen her many times in Berlin when she . . . uh . . . worked in the cabaret."

Canaris had a good idea who this someone was, but if Ritter preferred anonymity in this matter, he would not protest.

51

"I had her followed and then paid her a visit. I reminded her of her time in Germany and told her that she might do well to serve the cause of National Socialism."

"Blackmail is so unlike you, Ritter."

"Anyway, she laughed in my face. Said she didn't care what I told her husband."

"And?"

"A few days later she contacted me. Said that she wanted to work for me . . . uh . . . for Germany."

"A true believer," Canaris said sarcastically.

"I think it is the excitement. She craves"—he searched for the right word—"stimulation."

"I had no idea, my dear Ritter, that you could be so"—his pause emulated Ritter's—"stimulating."

Ritter searched his boss's face, hoping not to find condemnation. He was well aware that the Admiral, a man who had committed murder, did not approve of sexual misconduct. As usual the Admiral's face was impossible to read, and Ritter quickly went on. "When I left the Embassy in '39, I turned her over to Benke and Daly, knowing that some of her talents could always prove useful."

"What has she accomplished for us?"

"In addition to her work at the American Embassy, last month she passed along some interesting information about Fighter Command headquarters."

Canaris nodded.

"Her husband was killed in France, in May, and her status as a war widow accords her certain privileges in English society."

"Such as?"

"Because she speaks French, she has been able to get herself a minor position at de Gaulle's Free French Headquarters in London." Ritter smiled. "She has already passed along some interesting information about what is going on there." He smirked. "Mostly internal squabbles, and policy disagreements."

Canaris sighed and shook his head. "The French," he said, almost sadly. "Nothing they do surprises me."

"And you are certain," Canaris said between mouthfuls of strudel, "that these three—the woman, the Irishman, and Benke—have not been turned by the British?"

"Positive," Ritter replied. "There is nothing to give them

away. The method of communication, unlike radio transmission, is absolutely safe. The reports are hand-delivered through the Hungarian diplomatic pouch to our office in Lisbon."

"The method is safe, but very slow. By the time you get the information it may be of no value."

"Five hours to Lisbon from England," Ritter said. "If the information is perishable it can be relayed to Berlin with the Enigma coding device. I prefer hand delivery in all but the most extreme cases."

"You are probably correct," Canaris said. "I don't want anything to disclose these agents to the British. Right now the most important piece of information we have is the disclosure of the Roosevelt-Churchill alliance. If we can use that to prevent the re-election of Roosevelt, I'm sure the Führer would be most pleased." His eyes narrowed. "But what is required to defeat Roosevelt is more definitive proof."

"I'll see what can be done."

"Look," Canaris said, "everyone believes—and the communications we have acquired show—that Roosevelt and Churchill have come to some sort of agreement about the course of the war. Even Roosevelt's opponent, Mr. Willkie, charges that. What is not known is exactly what this agreement is. Is it a promise that the United States will continue to send war material to the British in violation of their own neutrality laws? Is it a promise to strip American defenses by giving American naval vessels to the Royal Navy? Or is it a promise to send troops in case of a German invasion?

"Any of these would force him out of office."

"Perhaps," said Canaris. "But only if we have proof. German claims of this duplicity would be dismissed as mere propaganda."

"According to Benke, the American Ambassador strongly disagrees with Roosevelt's close ties with Churchill and is very close to denouncing Roosevelt's policy.

Canaris's eyes lit up. "That," he said, "would be most advantageous to Germany. If his own ambassador to Britain condemns his policies, the American people would be more likely to reject Roosevelt."

"Without a doubt. Kennedy has tremendous influence with the voters in America—particularly Catholics. If he abandons Roosevelt, the election is as good as over."

"And," said Canaris, "with Roosevelt out of the picture, the British would have to negotiate a settlement. Is there any way we can encourage Kennedy?"

"According to Benke, he is concerned that his liquor contracts will be abrogated after the German occupation. He is hoping to maintain friendly relations with the occupational government."

Canaris chuckled, his smile broader than Ritter had ever seen. He sipped his coffee, placed his cup on the table and dabbed at his mouth with a linen napkin. "Wouldn't it be quite an accomplishment, my dear Ritter, to win a war over lunch?"

Ritter's smile was as broad as the Admiral's. His thoughts were of the honors that would be reaped.

"And all," said Canaris, "for the price of a few cases of whiskey."

Less than two hours later, at his office on the third floor of Gestapo Headquarters, on Prinz Albrecht Strasse, Reinhard Heydrich was reading a transcript of the conversation between Admiral Canaris and Bernhard Ritter at the Tiergarten. For more than a month he had had a listening device placed at Admiral Canaris's favorite table at the Tiergarten Plaza.

Heydrich jumped up from his seat, smashing his fist on his desk. His adjutant, Colonel Karl Dietrich, who had delivered the report and had stood quietly waiting while his boss read it, took a half-step back as if afraid that Heydrich might strike him.

"That old bastard," said Heydrich. "He's got someone inside the American Embassy." He handed the transcript to Dietrich. "Read this," he said. He paced the room, his hands behind his back, while he waited for Dietrich to finish.

Heydrich was a former naval officer who had served for a time under then Captain Wilhelm Canaris. In 1931, Heydrich had joined the SS, after he had been forced to resign from the navy for "conduct unbecoming an officer and a gentleman." That conduct was more than acceptable to his bosses in the SS. In three short years Heydrich had attained the rank of SS-Obergruppenführer, which was equivalent to the rank of general in the regular army, and in 1939 he became the head of the Reich Security Administration. He was now one of the most powerful men in Nazi Germany.

In 1940 Heydrich was thirty-six years old and the golden boy of Naziism. He was tall, blond, and handsome—the perfect Nordic-Aryan type that Himmler admired so much. He was athletic—a skilled fencer, an accomplished skiier, an excellent horseman, and an experienced pilot who on occasion flew combat missions with the Luftwaffe. Heydrich was a concert-quality violinist whose sensitive playing often brought tears to the eyes of his listeners. He was a captivating speaker, his high-pitched staccato voice demanding attention, and, by the somewhat skewed standards of the Nazis, he was considered an intellectual. These qualities might have brought Heydrich prominence in any of a hundred governments, but in the world of Nazi Germany there were other, darker characteristics required for success. These Heydrich also possessed in abundance. He was cold and calculating, the kind of man who carried an icy chill with him wherever he went. His ruthless ambition knew no bounds, and his disregard for common decency made him a man feared even by his Nazi cohorts. Already he had signed the death warrants of hundreds of thousands of Poles and Jews and in his mind brewed the plans for the extermination of millions. Not surprisingly, Heydrich saw treachery and hostility everywhere. No one was safe from his suspicions. He had compiled dossiers on friend and foe alike, using the information to destroy and intimidate rivals, colleagues, and enemies of the state. In less than ten years, Heydrich had used his merciless methods to scramble to the very top of the Nazi hierarchy. In the minds of his superiors Heydrich epitomized what National Socialism was all about.

Finally Dietrich finished reading the transcription. "You are probably correct, Herr General," he said.

"What about us?" barked Heydrich. "Why don't we have a man in there to give us this kind of information?"

"Well, Herr General, we have a very good contact with someone on the inside, but, as of yet, he has not been able to get us this kind of information."

"I want something done about this, do you understand? Now." Heydrich's face was red and his high-pitched voice was almost a whine. "I will not allow that old bastard to put one over on me. I want a man in position at that embassy who can give us this kind of intelligence. Get me the dossier on Ritter. Let's see if he would rather throw in his lot with the Gestapo."

"I know of him," said Dietrich. "He's one of Canaris's best men."

Heydrich's face split in a joyful leer. "I'd like nothing better than to take the old bastard's best man away from him."

As Dietrich nodded and turned to leave, Heydrich said, "Get Obersturmbannführer Kaufmann. I want him to take care of this."

Dietrich winced. Otto Kaufmann was a protégé of Heydrich's, and, as Muller and others were aware, the dog was as vicious as his master. "Yes, Herr General," Dietrich said.

"Check my schedule this evening. I may want to work late."

"This evening, Herr General," said Dietrich, "you and Madame Heydrich are dining with Admiral and Mrs. Canaris at their home. Foreign Minister Ribbentrop will also be there."

For a moment Heydrich said nothing and Dietrich feared his boss was about to explode. Instead, the General said, "Isn't that wonderful? I get to spend the evening in conversational minefields with the craftiest old bastard in Berlin." He laughed, a high-pitched cackle that made Dietrich wince. "I do enjoy these evenings."

As his general's mirth continued, Dietrich slipped through the door into his own office. Once inside, he gratefully closed the door behind him.

◆ *CHAPTER 6* ◆

Monday, August 12—London was strangely gay that morning. The air was clear, the sky blue, and the faces of the
Londoners seemed somehow bright and cheerful as if expecting some wonderful holiday. Many of them in fact were on
holiday. Bank holidays that summer were joyous events that
sent hordes of Londoners scrambling south in search of
beaches to enjoy the exceptionally warm weather that graced
them during June, July, and August of 1940.

Betty Donaldson was on her way from the Savoy Hotel to
the American Embassy and noticed the expectancy on the
faces of those on the street.

"They look like they're on their way to a party," she said to
the embassy driver who had arrived promptly at 8 A.M. to take
her to her appointment with the Ambassador.

"Some party," said the driver without emotion.

"Yes," whispered Betty almost to herself. She had been to
Hitler's other parties in Spain, Poland, and France. Perhaps,
she thought, if these people knew what they were in for they
would not be quite so cheerful.

At the embassy the car was waved through the gate with
barely a glance by the guard on duty. Inside the compound
the car circled the drive and stopped at the side entrance.
Immediately the side door opened and a short, red-faced man
came down the steps toward the car. Betty opened the car
door and stepped out before the man reached her. He seemed

flustered by what was to him either her impatience or ignorance. Betty stuck out her hand. "Good morning. Betty Donaldson, *Time* magazine."

She was given a weak handshake in return. "Yes," said the man. "Terrence Wymore, aide to the Ambassador." He added a cursory, "Pleasure to meet you."

Wymore led Betty Donaldson into the embassy and up to the second floor to Ambassador Kennedy's outer office. "The Ambassador has not yet arrived," he said. "Please be seated. He should be here shortly." With that, Wymore turned and left.

Almost an hour later Ambassador Kennedy burst into the room. "Good morning, Betty," he said, grasping her hand firmly. "It is so nice to see you again."

"Good morning, Mr. Ambassador," she replied, realizing immediately that no apology would be forthcoming.

Still holding her hand, Kennedy pulled her out of her chair. He gave her a quick head to foot once-over and then pulled her closer. She could smell the cigar on his breath and her stomach flopped. He grinned. His voice was a low growl. "You're still the best-looking reporter I've ever seen, Betty."

She pretended to be flattered while trying to extricate her hand from his. "Why, thank you, Mr. Ambassador."

He let her go. "What's all this 'Mr. Ambassador' crap?" he said, leading her into his inner office. "Out in Hyannis, it was Joe and Betty. Nothing's changed."

Betty Donaldson laughed, a low throaty growl. She looked around the room. "Not much."

The Ambassador's office was spacious, with high windows overlooking Grosvenor Square. The furniture was delicate and graceful, curved lines and satin cushions, and Betty Donaldson knew immediately that the Ambassador's wife had selected the furnishings. Joe Kennedy's taste ran more to early American, solid and functional, than to the decorative elegance of his office.

He read her thoughts. "Rose," he said with a shrug that was part apology and part derisive. The Ambassador sat behind his ornate desk, his back to the windows and the view beyond.

"I like it," Betty said. "It's really you." She managed to keep the sarcasm from her voice.

Joe Kennedy's eyes narrowed for just a moment as he pondered her meaning, but her face seemed so open and innocent that he quickly dismissed his suspicions.

Betty realized that she was treading on dangerous ground and flashed the Ambassador her best flirtatious smile. Kennedy, she knew, could be easily disarmed with flirtation. That also was dangerous ground. Kennedy was a legendary skirt-chaser and she had no desire to make herself a target of his amorous advances. Betty saw his eyes settle on her legs. "How is your family?" she asked. She smoothed her skirt, tugging it further down to cover her exposed knees.

"What's that?"

She repeated the question.

"Safe and sound," he said. "That's what counts." Kennedy shook his head sadly. "I miss them all," he said.

For a moment Betty felt sorry for him. She had been with Joe Kennedy and his family at the family estate in Hyannis and knew that his devotion to his family was genuine. Whatever else he was, she thought, in his own way he was a family man.

She had first met Joe Kennedy and his family in June 1938 when the recently appointed Ambassador had returned to the United States for Joe Jr.'s Harvard graduation. After the graduation the family had gathered for a brief vacation at Hyannis before returning to England. At that time there had been intense speculation that Joe Kennedy might make a run for the presidency in 1940. Public opinion polls listed Kennedy as one of several potential candidates. His close friend Arthur Krock of *The New York Times* devoted considerable space in his newspaper to touting Kennedy for the job. Betty Donaldson's boss, Henry Luce, the owner-publisher of *Time* magazine, was equally enthusiastic about Kennedy as a presidential aspirant. He had sent Betty to Hyannis that summer to do a piece on "Kennedy—the family man." It was a piece obviously intended to elevate Kennedy's stature with the American public, and Betty knew that she had been sent to get what was known as the "woman's angle."

"I want the public to see Joe with his family," Luce had told her. "Let them see what a devoted husband and father he really is. Talk to Mrs. Kennedy, talk to the kids."

Betty had arrived at Hyannis and was warmly greeted by the Kennedy family. She was given a room in the main house down the hall from the children's quarters and told to make herself at home. She ate with the family, went sailing with Jack, who was shy and serious, and even flirted a little with Joe Jr., whose loud laugh and boisterous behavior she found exciting. Joe Jr. responded to her flirtation with a slow smile, and quite often she felt his eyes on her when he was sure no one was watching. On her first night at dinner with the family, Joe Jr. was rather obvious. He sat next to Betty in the seat usually reserved for his eighteen-year-old sister Katherine.

"Hey," said Katherine, whom the family called Kick, "that's my place."

Joe Jr. gave her a look and Katherine raised her eyebrows. "Pardon me," she said, suppressing a giggle. "How foolish of me."

The other children made funny faces and dug at each other with elbows. Betty could feel her face grow red but neither Joe nor Rose seemed to take any notice of what was going on. Joe Jr. stared fiercely at his siblings and the giggling stopped. It was obvious that no one was prepared to challenge or make fun of him.

From then on it was assumed that Betty was with Joe Jr.

There was a dynamic quality about the family that ran from top to bottom, a sense of spirited competition coupled with the promise of achievement. There was no doubt that Joe Kennedy expected his children to succeed. At the dinner table he questioned them about their daily activities, plans for the coming weeks, and ambitions for the future.

These question-and-answer sessions impressed Betty. Joe would cross-examine each of his children in turn and expect each to respond seriously to his questions. Even six-year-old Teddy was quizzed on his activities, and his answers were regarded as seriously as those of his older siblings.

On the second day of her stay Betty was surprised when Joe included her in his dinnertime interrogation. "And what about you, young lady," he said. "After you've finished writing about this wonderful family of mine, what are your plans?"

"I'm not sure, Mr. Kennedy," she said. "But I think I'd like to go back to Spain and continue writing about the war."

There was a sudden silence and Betty sensed that the family was seeing her for the first time.

Rose spoke first. "You mean," she said incredulously, "that you've been to Spain and written about the war?"

"Yes," Betty said simply.

"When?" asked Jack, suddenly impressed, his interest obvious.

"Earlier this year," she said as casually as she could, as if one did that sort of thing all the time. "I was there from November of last year until January." She sneaked a quick look at Joe Jr. to see if he was as impressed as his younger brother. He was looking at her with what she was sure was increased interest.

"I was in Europe last summer," Jack said. "I tried to cross into Spain from France, but we were turned back at the border."

"For which we are all very thankful," said Rose.

"I'm afraid you'd need special credentials to enter the country," Betty said.

"Did you get shot at?" asked thirteen-year-old Bobby, his eyes wide as saucers.

Betty smiled. "No. I'm afraid not."

Bobby seemed disappointed.

"Who do you think is going to win?" asked Jack.

Betty shrugged. "It's obvious who's going to win. As long as England and France and the United States refuse to send war materials to the Spanish government, and the Germans and Italians continue sending as much as Franco can use, the result is inevitable. The war will be over by the end of this year."

"Do you think—" Jack began, but was interrupted by his father, who thumped his fist on the dining table. "It's not our fight," he said. "The Communists are helping the Spanish government. God help the Spanish people if that crowd wins." He had spoken with such an air of finality that the table lapsed into silence.

"I don't think you have to worry about 'that crowd' winning," Betty ventured. "They haven't a chance."

Joe Kennedy smiled, almost sweetly, she thought, and turned his attention elsewhere. "So tell me, Joe," he said, "how was the sailing today?"

61

Before answering, Joe Jr. gave Betty a brief smile of sympathy. At least, she thought, I'm making some headway with young Joe.

After dinner she went out to the porch and stood looking across the rolling lawn to the Nantucket Sound. She felt a presence and smiled knowing it would be him. Sure enough Joe Jr. was by her side.

"I thought we might do a little sailing tomorrow," he said. "Like to come along?"

She was coy. "Maybe. Who's going?"

He gave her a smile that was full of confidence. "Just you and me."

"I'm leaving tomorrow afternoon," she said.

"We'll leave early. Be back in time for lunch."

"Sounds like fun," she said.

Joe Jr. moved closer and Betty held her ground. Their shoulders touched but just as Betty was about to turn and face him, the front door opened and Jack stepped out on the porch.

"So there you are," he said to Betty, ignoring his brother. "I wanted to ask you about the war in Spain." He looked at his brother. "If that's all right with you, Joe?"

Jack grinned impishly and Betty was aware for the first time of the intense rivalry between these two elders of the Kennedy clan. She was also aware that she had become an object of that rivalry. For a moment she thought that Joe Jr. might tell Jack that it "wasn't all right," but he did not. After a brief pause he shrugged and, mumbling something about turning in early, went inside.

Betty called after him, "Joe?" and he turned at the door. "Will I see you later?" she said.

He smiled. "Maybe."

She watched him go, then turned to Jack, who was watching her intently.

"You should be careful with my brother," he said.

"Why's that?" she asked.

"He's too old for you."

"I don't think so," Betty said before she caught Jack's drift. "Oh," she said, laughing, "and I suppose you're not?"

Jack laughed. "I think I'd be just about right."

"I thought you were interested in the war in Spain?"

"I'm interested in all sorts of things," said Jack. "I thought that you might like to come sailing tomorrow. You can tell me all about your Spanish adventures."

"You're a little late. Joe just invited me to go sailing with him tomorrow."

Jack's expression clouded, but almost immediately the old ebullience returned. "The early Kennedy gets the worm," he said.

"If that's what you call flattery, it'll get you nowhere."

"Just a figure of speech," he said. "I would never think of you in those terms."

"Apology accepted," she said.

He smiled, but he seemed slightly deflated and Betty could see in him the pain of the younger brother forced to compete with an older brother who was more than he could ever hope to be. After a brief silence Jack said, "So, tell me about Spain."

Later that night, after midnight, the three-quarter moon was obscured behind low-lying clouds, leaving the Kennedy house in a gray darkness. Betty lay awake thinking about her magazine article. Henry Luce was correct. The Kennedys were a remarkable family. In her mind she had constructed the lead to her story and was cataloging the details when she realized with a smile that too many of the details were about Joe Jr. She let herself imagine what life might be like as the wife of a Kennedy. Young Joe Kennedy was probably the catch of the century and if there was any chance for her she knew that she would take it.

There was a noise at her door. At first she was startled, but then as the door began to open she knew with sudden certainty that it was Joe Jr. With amazing calmness she understood that what she said and did now might make all the difference to her future.

She sat up in bed. The door was completely open now but she could see nothing but the inky darkness of the hallway. "Joe," she whispered, "is that you?"

"Yes," came the whispered reply.

Her heart was pounding; her throat was dry. Was this the moment to feign virginal timidity? Or was it time to throw back the sheets and welcome him to her side?

The moon peeked from behind the clouds and a shaft of light reflected briefly off the eyeglasses of the figure in the doorway. Betty almost gasped as she realized that her visitor was not Joe Jr. but Joe Kennedy Sr. himself.

Kennedy closed the door softly behind him. He sat on the bed next to her, placing a hand on her shoulder. "You've known all along, haven't you?" he said.

Betty was speechless.

Kennedy went on. "I haven't been able to take my eyes off you since you got here."

Betty struggled to regain her composure. "Mr. Kennedy," she began but he interrupted her.

"Mr. Kennedy?" he said. "What happened to 'Joe'?"

He was unaware that she had called out to his son. "Joe," she began again, stammering slightly, "I don't think that this is the right time or place."

"Don't be silly," he said. His voice was calm, almost hypnotic. "There's nothing to worry about. Everyone is asleep."

She jumped out of bed on the side away from him. "I couldn't," she said. "I just couldn't." She struggled for an excuse that would satisfy him. "Your wife. She's right here in the house."

"Don't worry about that. She sleeps like a log."

"Your children?"

He chuckled quietly and stood up. "Don't worry," he said. He circled the bed and Betty found herself trapped in the corner. He was talking to her as he approached. "I can help you a great deal with your career. A young girl like you needs all the help she can get in a man's world."

"I'm doing just fine on my own." She was almost desperate.

Kennedy kept coming. She moved along the wall and in the darkness bumped into a small washstand that supported a decorative ceramic basin and pitcher. Everything came crashing to the floor. In the silent house the noise was deafening.

"Shit!" Kennedy said curtly, and as lights began to go on in other parts of the house he headed for the door.

He left quickly leaving her bedroom door open. Betty moved to close the door behind him and could not resist a quick peek into the hall. There stood Joe Jr. in his pajamas, arms akimbo, his face expressionless. Betty gave him a helpless look but his blank look did not change. Without a word he returned to his room. Across the hall Jack's face appeared from the doorway of his room. Although his face was sympathetic, he too said nothing before disappearing back inside.

Betty locked the door to her room and sat in a chair by the window. Hours later, she drifted off into a troubled sleep.

The next morning at breakfast Joe Kennedy acted as if nothing had happened but Joe Jr. was conspicuous by his absence. Betty ate in silence, imagining that everyone, especially Rose, was staring at her, but each time she looked up only Jack was paying any attention to her at all.

"Where's young Joe this morning." Joe Kennedy asked as he speared another sausage from a huge platter. "Usually you can't get enough to eat when he's around."

"He's off sailing," said Rose. "He left early. Said he wouldn't be back until well after lunch."

Betty Donaldson felt her heart drop into her stomach and she bit her lip to prevent the tears she could feel welling up in her eyes. She wanted to run from the table but was afraid to make any move that would draw attention. She sat staring at her plate, trying to make herself as inconspicuous as possible.

Only Jack noticed her anguish.

After breakfast she went upstairs, hoping to pack and leave as quickly as possible. She threw her suitcase on the bed and dumped her clothes in a pile next to it. As she packed she tried to console herself. It had only been a foolish pipe-dream anyway. Joe Jr. could have his pick of a thousand gorgeous debutantes. Why would he bother with a girl who had no family background or fortune?

A knock on the door startled her and she held her palm across her chest to control the thumping of her heart.

"Who is it?"

"It's me. Jack."

She opened the door and Jack stood somewhat sheepishly on the threshhold. "My offer of sailing still stands," he said, his eyes taking in the suitcase on the bed.

She stepped back and he followed her into the room. "Thanks, Jack," she said, managing a poor excuse for a smile, "but I really have to get back to New York."

"Can I drive you to the station?" he asked.

"I can call a cab."

Jack Kennedy laughed. "We only have one cab in Hyannis. If he's busy you might be stuck with the Kennedys forever."

Betty smiled. "Then I'll take you up on your offer."

Jack did most of the talking on the way to the train station. He was at his humorous and charming best but Betty was mostly silent.

As she prepared to board the train Jack shook her hand and impulsively kissed her on the cheek. "I'm sorry about you and Joe Jr." he said. "You two would have made a smashing couple. Of course, I would have done my best to take you away from him."

"Do you know what happened?" Betty blurted.

Jack nodded. "You're not the first," he said. "My sister Kick won't bring any of her friends home from school. Sometimes Dad sleepwalks and winds up in the wrong room."

Betty raised an eyebrow and Jack Kennedy shrugged. "That's the official explanation," he said.

"Then why would Joe Jr. think—"

"We Kennedy boys compete against each other for almost everything," Jack said, "but we don't compete against Dad."

Betty nodded. "Well, Jack," she said, "I've got to go." She kissed him on the cheek. "Good luck in England. I envy you. There's a lot of history going to happen over there, and you're going to be right in the middle of it."

He smiled. "If it doesn't happen before September, it had better happen at Harvard," he said. "I'll be back for the fall term. You're the one I envy. Going off to Spain," he said. "I'd love to see the war."

"Soon enough," she said, "we'll all have our fill."

"Will you write me . . . from Spain?" said Jack. "I'd love to know what was going on over there."

"If you like," she said. "If I get there."

"Even if you don't," he said. "Write me anyway."

"If I don't get to Spain, you'll probably have a whole lot more interesting things to write about than I will."

"Fair enough," he said and they shook hands again.

She wrote him once from Spain. He wrote her once from Harvard. And although Joe Jr. was in Spain in 1939, Betty never saw him again.

That brief moment in the summer of 1938 seemed incredibly remote to her now. How naive and girlish she had been. Perhaps foolish was a better word. In two short years the world had aged and she had aged with it. That girl back in Hyannis in June of 1938 seemed like another person. She felt Joe Kennedy's eyes on her, pulling her from her reverie.

"I hope that you'll have dinner with me tonight," he said. "I feel we've got lots to talk about." He grinned, flashing rows of perfect teeth.

"That would be very nice sometime," she said. "I'd love to hear how your children are doing. But I'm afraid it's impossible tonight." She took out a cigarette and lit it with her Zippo lighter, took a deep drag, and blew a long exhalation of smoke in his direction.

Kennedy's smile faded. "Well, we'll have to make a date."

"Just as soon as I get settled and organize my story."

"Your story is about me, I hope."

"Partly, of course. But basically I'm after the answer that everyone in America wants to know."

"Which is?"

"Can the British hang on?"

Kennedy made a choking noise in his throat. "Not a chance," he said. "When they run out of money, which I estimate will be in about two months, it's all over. I've tried to tell Roosevelt, but he doesn't listen to me. He has ignored every recommendation that I have made during the past year and now we are paying for it."

"Will you support the President in the coming campaign?"

"Lots of people, including your boss, Henry Luce, would like to know that answer."

Betty had heard the rumors that Luce and other influential Republicans were trying to enlist Kennedy in the campaign against Roosevelt. "Has Mr. Luce asked you to endorse Willkie?"

Kennedy smiled. "He knows that I can deliver twenty-five million votes with my endorsement. The New Dealers are crapping in their pants thinking that I might hand the presidency to the Republicans."

"Willkie is claiming that the President is not telling the truth when he says there are no secret agreements between the U.S. and the British. He further claims that these secret agreements are guaranteed to bring the U.S. into the war on Britain's side as early as next spring."

"I fully intend to be back in the U.S. in time for the elections," Kennedy said. "At that time I will inform the

American people of everything I know about any 'secret agreements.' I'll let them make up their minds about Roosevelt and his New Dealers."

Betty Donaldson listened patiently as he went on. She knew that printing what he said about the President would be useless. Kennedy would only deny that he had ever said such things. He was almost legendary in his denial of statements that he had made about Roosevelt and the New Dealers who surrounded him.

Finally Betty interrupted. "You've been most helpful, Mr. Ambassador"—Kennedy made a face and she relented —"Joe. I'll also need you to help me get around the country—passes and the like. I'll want to talk to as many civilians, in and around London, as I can."

"No problem," Kennedy said. "I'll see to it that someone on the embassy staff takes good care of you."

"How about military installations? Can I get to them?"

"No problem. I'll have someone from our military attaché's office get to work on it. You'll need an escort. By this afternoon I should have someone for you."

"That's very kind of you. I'm sure Mr. Luce will appreciate the way you are taking care of one of his people."

The Ambassador grinned lecherously. "Screw Henry Luce, honey. I'm doing this for you. And I hope you won't forget it."

Betty stood up and shook his hand. "Don't worry, Joe," she said. "I have a long memory."

68

◆ CHAPTER 7 ◆

LONDON, Tuesday, August 13—The two men who sat on the park bench in Green Park did not look at each other while they talked. They contented themselves with observing the conduct of the strollers who were taking advantage of the remarkably beautiful summer weather. Once in a while one of them would look up at the barrage balloons which hung lazily in the blue afternoon sky.

To the two men the change in attitude of London's inhabitants was remarkable. Only seven weeks earlier the news from France had stunned the city. The unbelievable had happened and the hoped-for miracle was a dream of the past. France had fallen. The surrender had been signed, the disaster was now official. Hitler could look across the Straits of Dover and see his next victim. As the news of the French catastrophe spread, the city had become strangely quiet. Even the traffic had seemed quieted. Vendors hawked their wares with muted voices, and the usual bedlam at the Smithfield and Leadenhall Markets had given way to a restrained orderliness. Everywhere the faces were the same: grim, serious, troubled. The earlier determination had been on the verge of collapse. The news of disaster had brought uncertainty to the faces of millions.

But since that time, confidence and determination had returned. Hitler had wasted a precious opportunity for conquest, and while he waited and pondered his next move, the target of his insatiable lust grew stronger. In just seven weeks, hope had replaced despair.

The two men on the park bench did not share that hope.

"Look at them," said Sean Daly to the man who sat next to him. "They're finished. Their whole way of life is coming to an end." He was unable to keep a smile from his face. "And they refuse to accept it."

Josef Benke nodded once. "Yes," he said. He did not smile.

"I've waited a long time for this," Daly said.

"Yes, my friend," said Benke. "I know you have."

Sean Daly had been born in Dublin as Sean Ryan. He had been only two when his father was killed in what his mother referred to as "the troubles." When he was twelve, his brother, Patrick, who was nineteen, had been hanged by the British, with six of his confederates, in the aftermath of the Easter Rebellion. Expecting German aid, the Sinn Fein had attempted to seize Dublin and declare Ireland a republic. But the Royal Navy had thwarted German attempts at assistance and the uprising had been crushed.

Now, thought Daly, the time has come again. And this time there will be no stopping the inevitable. It had been a long time coming, but it was everything that he had hoped it would be.

Sean Daly was thirty-six. He was almost six feet tall, lean and sinewy, and although he had never worked the plow, he had the handsome, rough-hewn features of a peasant. His face, open and friendly, masked a sharp intelligence. Only his eyes, ice blue and penetrating, betrayed the forces that drove him.

Shortly after his brother's death, Sean's mother had married Thomas Daly, and the boy, at his mother's insistence, had taken his stepfather's name. His mother had been anxious to leave all remnants of "the troubles" behind them and hoped that a new life and a new name for her son would speed the process. The boy, however, would not forget. The family moved to Belfast and life in the British-dominated Northern Ireland made young Sean even more sullen and resentful. He had excelled in school and after graduation from the Queen's University of Belfast with a degree in engineering, he had gone to work for the engineering firm of Pitlock Brothers in Dublin. Four years later he had moved on to Harland and Wolff, the Belfast shipbuilders.

Quite by accident, documents that detailed a new electro-welding process used at Harland and Wolff and other British shipbuilders fell into his hands. The process, developed in England in 1932 and improved over the next several years, was less costly and more efficient than previous armour welding methods and provided British ships with more armor with less weight. During the years of the London Naval Treaty restrictions this saving in weight was of paramount importance to the Royal Navy.

On a trip to Dublin in 1936, Daly contacted the German Embassy and declared that he had something of value that he was willing to give them. The Germans assumed that he meant "sell" and were at first reluctant to meet with him, but when the naval attaché at the embassy got wind of exactly what it was that Daly had in his possession the Germans welcomed him with open arms. A deal was quickly consummated and Daly found to his surprise that the Germans were quite willing to pay for what he had offered for free. The sum was not insubstantial, two hundred and fifty pounds, but minuscule compared to the value of what had been purchased. Daly accepted the sum without comment.

The German naval attaché, Captain Bernhard Ritter, was also a functioning agent in the Abwehr, the German Military Intelligence Service operated by Admiral Canaris. Ritter was eager to establish a more permanent relationship with this new and perhaps important source of information. Daly agreed and over the next eighteen months passed several relatively unimportant pieces of information to the Germans. The Germans were always stingy with payments to those who provided information, but Daly did not care about the money. He accepted whatever was offered without protest or thanks, and Ritter noted that he usually put the money in his pocket without looking at it.

Captain Ritter was fascinated by Sean Daly's behavior.

As an intelligence operative, Bernhard Ritter found himself in an almost perfect situation. Assigned to Ireland, at that time called the Irish Free State, a nation with a long-standing adversarial relationship with Great Britain, he found it relatively simple to recruit spies and informants. The Irish Republican Army was eager to work with the Germans in almost any capacity against the British, but Ritter found them distasteful. He felt that the leadership of the IRA was dominated by Bolsheviks and that the membership was composed of lower-class hooligans, more interested in money than in revolution. As unpleasant as this was, Ritter was wise enough to realize that if and when war came between Germany and Great Britain, the IRA, with easy access to England, could play a vital part in the war effort.

Ritter, an astute observer of human nature, realized that unlike most of his other sources of information, Sean Daly was a man of pure intentions. Daly was not interested in money or the IRA's attempts to establish an independent and unified Ireland. He wanted only to hurt the British. Ritter assumed that there was some terrible grievance that stoked the fires of Daly's bitter resentment, but was wise enough not to inquire. It was enough to know that it was there. He could use a man like Daly. Hadn't Admiral Canaris himself told him that it is always easy to use a man with pure intentions?

In 1938, with talk of war growing daily, Ritter was transferred to the German Embassy in London and convinced Daly to leave Harland and Wolff and find a position in England. "When war comes," he said to Daly, "you will be much more valuable in England."

Somewhat reluctantly Daly agreed. He took a job with the engineering firm of Dowdswell and Davis in London, a company involved in construction projects in and around the city.

It seemed to Daly that his days of contact with the Germans were over. He could see little in his present position that the Germans could possibly find of value, but in due course he was contacted by Ritter.

"Just keep your eyes open," he was told. "Inform us of anything that you think might be of interest."

He did, passing along occasional information about new road-building equipment or construction projects that might be of some value to the German military. His new position seemed to provide Daly with less interesting information than had the job at the shipyards and Ritter seemed disappointed.

In the spring of 1939, however, as war hysteria gripped Europe, Dowdswell and Davis became involved in the design and construction of fortified gun emplacements on the Channel coast. Suddenly the Germans were very interested and

Daly was able to supply them with information about lines of fire, interior capacity, and concrete thicknesses at various points in the structures. The Germans were pleased and from then on Ritter had treated him with renewed respect.

When war came in September of 1939, the German diplomatic corps prepared to leave London. Daly's last contact with Ritter had been to inform him that now he could be of greater service to Germany and that he should await subsequent contact. The contact was not long in coming.

Within days of the German departure. Daly was approached by Josef Benke, the second secretary at the Hungarian Embassy. "You may," said Benke, "report anything of interest to me, and I will see that it gets to the proper authorities."

Benke was a small man, with dark hair and dark, sunken eyes. He had worked for the Nazis for more than five years, ever since he had been approached by Abwehr agents in his native Budapest. He had been assigned to the Hungarian Embassy in London in 1937 but knew that his time there was now growing short. There were forces in Hungary, sympathetic to Nazi Germany, that were about to drag Hungary into an alliance with Germany and Italy. The British, hoping to forestall the inevitable, allowed the Hungarian Embassy to operate with a somewhat diminished staff, but Benke knew that soon he and his fellow diplomats would be heading home.

The thought of leaving England saddened him. He had come to love this country, loved its traditions and its culture. His admiration was such that he even managed to effect the manner of speech and dress of the native Londoners. To Josef Benke, London was a city of light. He loved the theater, the art galleries, the parks. But Benke was above all a realist. He knew that before this summer was over, all that would change. Hitler would flatten this city and then invade. Occupation was all that his German contacts wanted to talk about. They were coming, and who could stop them? Perhaps it was better that he would not be here to see it.

"So what do you hear?" Daly said, interrupting Benke's thoughts.

"About what?"

"The invasion. When are they coming?"

Benke chuckled. "Our German friends do not confide such things to me. Perhaps, for a time, they wish to enjoy the fruits of their victory in France."

"If they landed tomorrow, they could be in London in three days," said Daly.

"Not to worry," said Benke sympathetically. "The day will soon be here." He shook his head. "Nothing can stop them."

"Every day that they wait will make the task more difficult," said Daly. His job with Dowdswell and David allowed him to travel freely about the countryside and he had seen first-hand the frantic efforts to fortify the coastal areas. The efforts were too little, and too late. At the present state of readiness the Germans could sweep them aside with ease. In his travels Daly had made notes as to the state of British readiness to meet the expected invasion. He summed up that state of readiness in one word: *nonexistent*.

"They shouldn't wait," Daly said. "They should come now. They should have come a month ago."

Benke shrugged. "The preparations for such a venture are enormous. Rest assured that when the day comes, the British Army will be overwhelmed. Until that time," he said without enthusiasm, "we must continue to do our work. Work that insures the inevitable German victory."

Daly nodded.

"The Germans are more insistent than ever about the correspondence between Roosevelt and Churchill," Benke said. "They are demanding more specific proof."

"What else do they want? If they intended to invade, they wouldn't need this nonsense."

"Perhaps, but can Marie acquire more of the documents?"

"Her contact is increasingly reluctant to provide more information."

"Does he suspect her?"

"I don't think so. He just seems to have grown leery of further involvement."

"She must press him for more."

Daly said nothing.

Benke also was silent, then, "Do you know Bletchley?" he asked finally.

"Yes. It's in Buckinghamshire, about an hour or so north of London."

"Something is going on up there. It might be important.

For the past two weeks people in my embassy have been monitoring a steady stream of couriers—on motorcycle —going from an estate in Bletchley to the offices of the Secret Intelligence Service on Broadway here in London."

"How did you find out about that?"

Benke hesitated then decided that there was no point in secrecy on such a matter. "We've had people watching Broadway for some time and it was noted that the same couriers arrived each day at about the same time. One of my men followed the courier to his point of origin and we discovered a monitoring facility of some sort in Bletchley. It is surrounded by barbed wire and guarded around the clock by an RAF regiment."

Daly's eyes narrowed. "Sounds important."

"Furthermore," Benke went on, "one of my men was able to acquire a recent map of the military installations in the region. It was quite detailed in its description of the facilities in southeast England, and I am sure that our German friends will find it most interesting. What is truly interesting about the map, however—" he smiled and paused for dramatic effect "—is that there is no mention, not even a dot, of any facility, of any kind, at Bletchley."

"What kind of monitoring facility do you suppose is there?" asked Daly.

"I don't know," Benke said. "But we must find out."

Daly looked sharply at Benke. "I hope you don't expect me to get in there. I don't mind reporting on the defensive installations along the coast, but I've no desire to be caught breaking into a military facility." He touched a hand to his throat. "The results of failure could be quite fatal."

Benke smiled. "Of course not, my friend. We would not wish to jeopardize your safety in any way. What I have in mind," Benke said, although the plan had actually originated at Abwehr headquarters on Tirpitz Ufer in Berlin, "is to use someone who is already privy to what is going on there."

"How do you intend to do that?"

"Right now I am in the process of selecting an appropriate target, someone with intimate knowledge of the facility." Benke did not say that he had at his disposal the Abwehr dossiers on many of those who worked for British Intelligence. "Once I select the right man"—he smiled wickedly —"it will be your job to convince the right woman to participate in our venture." Benke waited for Daly's reaction, but there was none. "Someone to entice our target into telling us what we want to know."

Daly's doubt showed in his face. "She won't like it."

Benke laughed. "My dear boy," he said, "you have always been able to convince her in the past."

"I'm not sure."

"Just remember: More secrets have been told to women in bed than have been revealed in all the torture chambers of history."

SPY RING SEIZED; PRO-NAZI GROUP PLANNED SABOTAGE

LONDON, AUG. 13

◆ *CHAPTER 8* ◆

August 13—"You must be daft," Marie Price said angrily to Daly when he proposed his idea to her.

"Keep your voice down," he snarled. "If anyone hears us we'll both hang."

They were in Daly's apartment, four rooms in a nice building in the Chelsea section of London.

She pushed her hair away from her face. "No, you keep your voice down," she said, her voice still angry, but quieter. "Just who the hell do you think you are?"

Daly smiled but said nothing.

"And what in hell do you think I am?" she continued.

"Marie, darlin'," he said, giving her his best Irish charm.

"Don't you Marie darlin' me, you bastard." When she was angry, her barely detectable accent was more pronounced.

The smile still on his face, Daly watched her carefully. She stood facing him, her hands, clenched into fists, resting on her hips. She was tall and slim and had silky blond hair, worn long to frame the perfect oval of her face. Even in anger, her lips curled in a snarl, she was beautiful, he thought. He gave her a long lingering look from head to toe. Men would do anything to possess that body—long legs, narrow waist, and breasts that made his throat dry at the thought of them.

He waited until she had calmed herself a little. "This could be our big chance," he said softly. "This war is going to be over in just a few weeks, and if we want to be on the side of the winners we have to show them that we can . . . can"—he groped for the right phrase—"can perform a service for them."

"Then why don't you perform the service? You get into bed with this . . . whoever he is."

Daly's eyes widened in distressed innocence. "Who said anything about getting into bed with anyone?"

She laughed derisively. "Shall I just make him tea, or blow in his ear? Perhaps a winning smile and he'll tell me where they've hidden the crown jewels?"

Daly put on the kettle for tea. She was calmer now and he knew that he could talk to her—knew that he could convince her—but for now he was content to let her talk herself out.

"I don't mind passing along bits of information," she said, "but I won't invite every Tom, Dick, and Harry into my bedroom to get it."

"Marie," Daly began, "if we're caught, it's the noose, as sure as we're sittin' here." His Irish brogue, usually nonexistent, was as thick as treacle. "How long can we last? A month? Two months? Sooner or later spies always get caught. The sooner the Germans get here, the better our chances are of escaping the hangman."

Marie swallowed hard, her hands at her throat. "Spies?" she whispered. She could feel the burn of the rope. "But I really haven't done anything."

The silence between them was punctuated by the whistling of the kettle. "I know that," Daly said. "A little bit here, a little bit there. Not very much that is important." He gave a sad smile. "But will the British know that?"

Marie had no answer.

"The Germans can save us," Daly said. "When they get here, we won't have to worry about anything." He took the kettle off the burner. "But we have to help them get here as quickly as possible."

She was nodding now. She could see the logic in what he was saying. Perhaps he was right. Helping the Germans was the only way. "It's just that I don't like being in bed with someone I don't know. And I don't like this American very much."

Daly spooned out the tea, letting her talk.

"And you promised," she said, "that it would only be this once."

He measured his words as carefully as he measured the leaves. "Let's not forget our young Sergeant Williams," he said softly.

"That was different," said Marie uncertainly.

"How was it different? You went to bed with him—he gave you information."

"He was after me. I didn't know he worked at Fighter Command Headquarters until later."

"It's the same thing."

"It was different. He was after me. He wanted to impress me with how important his job was."

He was relentless. "And he told you?"

"You know he did."

"After you'd gone to bed with him?"

"You wanted me to," she said helplessly.

Daly brought her her tea and sat next to her on the sofa. "And I want you to again," he said quietly.

She bit her lip and said nothing.

Daly touched her arm, running his fingers gently from elbow to wrist. "Don't pretend you didn't enjoy the young sergeant."

She looked at him sharply then softened. "He was nice," she said, a trace of a smile tugging at her lips. "Nicer than the American."

"I'll find someone just as nice for you this time."

She pulled away slightly. "I wouldn't think you'd want me with anyone else," she said.

"It makes me very jealous," he said. "I don't want anyone else to touch you."

"Then why?"

"It's also very exciting thinking about you and another man." He grinned lecherously. "You were never more excit-

78

ing than when you were describing how your young sergeant made love to you."

"You made me tell," she said pouting, her lips forming a perfect circle.

"But such detail."

She gave him a sly look. "This time I'll tell you nothing."

"You will tell me everything," he said, pulling her close to him and kissing her hard. "It excites me just thinking about it."

"Everything excites you," she said.

"But you excite me more than anything." His hand went to the buttons on her blouse.

"Stop it," she said, but made no move.

He opened her blouse. His Irish brogue was back. "Marie darlin', if you don't start wearin' a bra, you'll be the death of me."

They undressed quickly and she lay back on the couch. "So, who is he?" she asked as Daly efficiently hung his trousers over the back of a chair.

"Who?"

"The man I'm supposed to do this with."

Daly lay on top of her. "Don't know yet," he said into her ear. "But rest assured, he'll be someone you'll like."

"You promise?"

"Did I ever break a promise to you?"

They were moving together now and all talk of promises broken and kept were forgotten.

Daly lay naked on the sofa watching Marie dress. Although he had seen her naked many times he never tired of watching her. She moved like a dancer, he thought, always graceful and with never a moment's awkwardness or embarrassment. Hers was a body that quickened the pulse and revived the spirit. He had seen how other men watched her: sidelong glances, suddenly dry lips, embarrassed coughs as if she had aroused in them some passion that they had deliberately sublimated. If she were aware of her power, he knew he would be unable to control her. But she was an innocent, totally without guile. Such women, he knew, were meant to be used by men such as he. He felt no guilt in this. A woman like Marie would always have someone to take care of her. Soon it would be the Germans. Some officer would see her and she would become

79

his. But only until some higher ranking officer decided that his rank required that he possess such a beautiful trinket.

When Sean Daly first met Marie Price, he knew only that she was married to an English officer. He knew nothing of her first marriage or her earlier life. Daly had an intuitive suspicion that she and the departing German officer, Bernhard Ritter, had been in the midst of an affair, and had determined that he would pick up where the German had left off. To his surprise and disappointment, Marie Price had rebuffed his advances.

What Daly could not know was that Marie had tried very hard to make her second marriage work. In 1930 she had rather quickly accepted the proposal of Reginald Price, a man she barely knew, because she was desperate to escape the downward spiral her life had taken. Price had seemed kind and thoughtful and she had every hope that she could make him happy. At first things had gone fairly well but with each passing year, Reginald seemed more disenchented with their marriage. He was often angry with her for reasons she was unable to fathom, and she could only conclude that she had broken some rule that had never been explained to her. She had tried harder to please her increasingly remote husband, but was unable to do so.

In the spring of 1938 she had been contacted by Captain Ritter, a German she had known in Berlin during her days in the cabarets. He was eager to resume their former relationship, but she had refused him. Then, one night, soon after Ritter had contacted her, she had come home unexpectedly to find her husband and another officer dressing hurriedly in the bedroom. The nature of her marital problems had suddenly become clear to her. After that she had not let Price touch her, and he seemed glad to be relieved of the responsibility. She had contacted Ritter and he had been only too glad to console her. Her marriage to Price continued, if for no other reason than she did not know what else to do and Price seemed satisfied with the arrangement.

When Ritter left England, Marie had tried to right the course her life had taken. Unbeknownst to her, Ritter had "assigned" her to Sean Daly, telling him that she was of potential value as an agent for Germany. When Daly first saw her, he recognized her value immediately. He was determined to have her, but she had been just as determined to put her past behind her. With Ritter gone she would try to put her life back in order.

She had not counted on the persistence of Sean Daly. She had not counted on her own hunger.

Daly sensed that hunger beneath the quiet demeanor, and was determined to warm himself in the flame. His advances were at first subtle and made her smile, but when her husband was sent to France with the BEF, Daly resolved to make good use of his absence. His advances became more blatant and although she rebuffed each one he could sense that she was excited by his interest. She seemed flattered and intrigued by his relentless attempts at conquest, and he felt certain that her resolve was crumbling. He saw the anguish of uncertainty in her eyes, and could feel the heat emanating from her body. He was determined not to fail.

On the evening of May nineteenth, while Daly eagerly read the newspaper accounts of the German advances in France, there had been a knock on his door. When he opened it he found Marie. Without a word she walked past him into his apartment. She stood silently in front of the fire. He was wise enough not to speak.

After staring into the fire for what seemed like a long time she turned to face him. "He's dead," she said. "Reginald has been killed in France."

He managed to blunt his elation that the husband, whom he had assumed was his rival, had been removed from the field. He went to her and put his arms around her.

"I didn't know where else to go," she said.

"I'm glad you came to me," he said, turning her face toward his. He kissed her for the first time and she did not resist. He felt her body respond, moving into his. He knew then that her husband's death had released her from the obligation to refuse him. His hands moved to the buttons on the back of her dress.

"Don't," she moaned softly. "Please don't."

He ignored her plea, his hands moving confidently across her body. She shivered as each layer of clothing fell away, but she did not speak again until she stood naked in front of the fire.

"I feel wicked," she whispered.

"You are wicked," he answered as he fumbled with his clothes. "We are both wicked."

Now, as he watched her dress, he smiled. He knew that she would do anything he asked. He had never offered her anything more than what they had now, and if she was not satisfied with the arrangement she never complained.

She finished dressing and turned to face him. It gave her pleasure to know how much he enjoyed watching her. In a way it reminded her of the days when she had danced naked in the cabarets in Berlin. "Enjoy the show?" she asked.

"As always," he said, his erection huge again.

She laughed. "Look at you," she said. "Don't you ever get enough?"

"Come over here and find out," he said, sitting up on the sofa.

"I'm all dressed," she protested. "I have to be at work in a half an hour."

"For what I want, you don't have to take off a thing."

She hesitated then went to him. She knelt between his legs. "Don't take too long," she said. "I've got to get going."

He groaned a little as he felt the touch of her lips. "A little of this," he said, "and any man would tell you everything that he knew."

She looked up at him for a moment, but his head was back and he was staring at the ceiling. She gave a small sigh of resignation and went back to her work.

BRITISH BEAT BACK MASSIVE AIR RAIDS OVER
CHANNEL PORTS

LONDON, AUG. 13

♦ CHAPTER 9 ♦

August 13—Maxwell Munro stood up from behind his desk as Colonel Jackson entered his office.

"Captain Munro," said Jackson, "this is the reporter from *Time* I was telling you about."

Betty Donaldson entered Munro's office closely behind the Colonel. She wore a light flower-print summer dress that was cut low in front, revealing just a hint of cleavage. She stood in the doorway, taking in the room, and Munro, at a glance.

Jackson continued his introduction. "Miss Donaldson, this is Captain Maxwell Munro. He will be your official embassy guide during your stay in London. Captain Munro will expedite whatever official clearances you may require and accompany you on any excursions that you may wish to make."

"How do you do, Miss Donaldson?" Munro said. He could not help the surprised smile that streaked across his face nor the raised eyebrows as he eyed her from head to toe. Things were beginning to look up, he thought.

The look on Donaldson's face told Munro that she was not as pleased with the pairing as he was. She ignored his greeting. "I don't require a watchdog, Colonel," she said to Jackson. "I'm perfectly capable of getting around without the assistance of an embassy guard."

Jackson frowned. "Captain Munro is not an embassy guard, Miss Donaldson. He is a valued member of the

83

embassy staff." Jackson cleared his throat as if his lie had lodged there. Earlier that morning Ambassador Kennedy had provided Jackson with the perfect solution to the dilemma of what to do with Captain Munro.

"Jackson," Kennedy had barked into the phone, "there's a reporter here in London—from *Time* magazine—friend of mine. I want you to see that she's taken care of. She needs one of your military types to see that she gets access to any place that is considered off-limits."

"Of course, Mr. Ambassador," Jackson said. "I think I have the perfect person in mind."

"Never mind that," Kennedy had said. "I'd like you to put the Munro kid on this one. I think he'd be right for the job."

Colonel Jackson had smiled in surprise. It wasn't often that he and the Ambassador were of one mind. "Of course, Ambassador. I'll put Munro at her disposal right away."

"That may be true, Colonel," said Betty Donaldson, "but I'd still prefer to be on my own."

"I'm afraid we must insist, Miss Donaldson. The British are getting very leery of American correspondents wandering around. I think you'll find that Captain Munro will be of great value to you."

Betty nodded in resignation.

"Well, then," Jackson said, "I'll let you two get on with the arrangements." With a quick smile he was gone. What was perfectly clear to Munro was that the Colonel was using this opportunity to create busy work for him. Since his arrival at the embassy, Munro had sensed the tension that had been directed toward him by the other members of the military staff. Once again he was an outsider. The furtive glances, the conversations that suddenly stopped when he entered a room, the restrained greetings, the reluctant answers to his questions, all made it perfectly clear that he was not a welcome addition. He did not know why, but guessed that, as usual, it had something to do with his father. But if he were to be given busy work, it might as well be with a beautiful woman.

Betty opened a silver cigarette case, removed a cigarette, and tapped it against the case. "So, you're the embassy flunky."

Munro's eyes narrowed. "I'm not sure I follow you."

Betty held the cigarette to her lips. "This assignment," she said. "You're my baby-sitter. Do you think that's the kind of assignment that goes to"—she tried to remember the phrase—"'a valued member of the embassy staff?'"

"As I understand it," Munro said, "this was a personal request from your friend the Ambassador."

She seemed genuinely surprised. "Really?"

"So I'm told."

Betty removed a chrome-plated Zippo from her bag, flipped it open, and held the flame to her cigarette.

She looked at Munro rather closely for the first time. There was something familiar about the face, although she was positive that they had never met. "Aren't you a little young for such a position?"

"No."

It came to her in flash. "Munro," she said. "You're Senator Munro's son, aren't you?" She made a face as if she had detected a foul odor, and it was obvious that Senator Munro was not among her favorite politicians.

Max Munro nodded but said nothing. He was thinking that for a damn good-looking woman this Donaldson was a real pain in the ass.

"I remember reading about your assignment to the London Embassy earlier this year. Caused some controversy in Washington as I recall."

Munro's jaw was set, his teeth clenched. He had been over this story many times before. He had no desire to get into it again. "I will make myself available to you starting tomorrow."

"Was your father responsible for this plum assignment, Captain Munro? I seem to remember that a lot of people in Congress and at the White House made that charge."

"I have no desire to discuss either my father or my job." Betty Donaldson smiled as she watched Munro's face. It gave her pleasure to know that she had made him uncomfortable. That was a reporter's job. She had learned that from her father. If you can make the rich and privileged uncomfortable, he had often told her, then you must be doing something right. Betty extinguished her cigarette in the desk ashtray. "I meant it when I said I didn't need you," she said. "I'd prefer to be on my own."

"I'm afraid I have no control over that."

"Would a male correspondent be required to have someone from the embassy follow him around?"

"You'd have to ask Colonel Jackson. This is my first 'baby-sitting' assignment. But I might add that playing tour guide to a woman reporter is not quite what I had in mind when I came to the embassy."

The smile slipped from Betty's face. She could almost hear his father's voice in his words. "I suppose you think that women should stay at home and let men get on with the war."

Munro smiled a little. "I didn't say that."

"What happens if the war heats up a little?" she snapped. "Will your connections make sure you get home safely before the Germans arrive?"

"I imagine your connections are better than mine. I haven't been to see Joe Kennedy lately."

"My work got me here, not my connections."

"Really?" Munro said sarcastically.

"I was in Spain in thirty-seven," she said. "Poland last year. Belgium and France this spring."

"You obviously have more combat experience than I do."

"Don't feel bad," she said. "I've seen more combat than the U.S. Army."

"Do you take prisoners?"

Betty could not help her small smile. "Sometimes," she said. "Usually I prefer a firing squad."

Munro sighed. "Miss Donaldson, I don't know what you feel is going on here, but you don't have to convince me of anything. My commanding officer—at the bequest of the Ambassador—has told me to arrange for clearance for you from the British authorities. I intend to do just that. If you'd prefer another officer as your guide, I'm sure that could be arranged."

"I'm sure that won't be necessary, Captain," Betty said.

"Then when would you like to start?" he asked.

"Tomorrow," she said, then quickly added, "If that's all right."

Munro scanned one of two sheets of paper he had placed on his desk. "You'll need a few things." He read, "National Registration Identity Card, Alien's Certificate of Registration, Permit to Take Photographs, Official Pass and Identity Card for Foreign Correspondents."

"This used to be one of the most open societies in the

world," Betty said sadly. "Now you need a pass to go to the bathroom."

"Freedom has been suspended for the duration," Munro said, then went on with his list. "You'll also need a ration card for meat, sugar, eggs—most foods actually."

"I had dinner last night at my hotel, and breakfast this morning. No one asked me for any coupons."

"They won't in hotels or restaurants, but you'll need them if you go into the grocer's. Besides, you're entitled to them. If you don't need them, you can give them to someone. Makes a nice gift. People appreciate them."

"How long will all this take?"

"Not long. I'll have the embassy put in the request. You should have them by tomorrow—next day at the latest. Until then, we'll just stick close to London. No one will ask for any identification around here. Out in the countryside we might be challenged. If that happens it would be nice to have all our documentation in order."

"I guess so."

He passed her the second sheet. "This is the itinerary suggested by Colonel Jackson." He saw the wary look on her face. "This is just to get us started. Feel free to add to it or alter it as you see fit. Any changes will have to be approved by the Foreign Office—which can take a day or two—so I'd suggest that you make any changes as quickly as possible."

"I want to get out and talk to the people in the street," Betty said. "I want to hear how they feel about this war."

"If you don't have your credentials, someone is liable to take you for a German spy. The Local Defense Volunteers can get a bit nosy."

"That's where I'll need you, I suppose," she said.

"You'll need me especially if you want to get into someplace that's been declared off-limits, or if you want to roam around outside London."

"Perhaps I'll take my chances and talk to some people on the way back to my hotel."

"Suit yourself."

Betty got up from her seat. "Till tomorrow then."

"I'll send a car for you at eight A.M." Munro read her expression. "Nine if you prefer."

She smiled. "I would prefer nine," she said.

"No problem at this end."

When she had gone Munro sat for a long time staring into space. But the last thing he had wanted was to wind up as the escort to some pain-in-the-ass woman reporter. That was not why he had come to London. He took the sheet of paper from his desktop, crumbled it into a ball, and dropped it into his wastebasket.

WILLKIE CHARGES ROOSEVELT MADE SECRET AGREEMENTS WITH BRITISH; CHALLENGER CLAIMS PRESIDENT BRINGS U.S. CLOSER TO WAR

RUSHVILLE, IND., AUG. 13

◆ CHAPTER 10 ◆

August 13—Shortly after Betty Donaldson left his office, Max's phone rang. He looked at the instrument as if it were some strange, alien device. It was the first time his telephone had rung since his arrival at the embassy.

"Yes," he said.

"Captain Munro? This is Terrence Wymore, the Ambassador's assistant. The Ambassador would like to see you in his office as soon as possible."

Munro straightened his tie, combed his hair in front of the small mirror that sat on the wall near the door, and went directly to the Ambassador's suite of offices on the second floor. He was expected. The Ambassador's secretary, who sat at an ornate desk in the outer office, stood up and gave him a quick smile before leading him to the double oak doors that led to the Ambassador's office.

"The Ambassador is in a good mood this afternoon," she whispered to Munro before knocking on the door.

"Come in—come in," called Joseph Kennedy and the

secretary swung the door open and stood aside so that Munro could enter.

The Ambassador was in shirtsleeves, feet up on his desk, hands clasped behind his head, and smoking a huge cigar. He smiled as Munro entered.

"Good morning, Mr. Ambassador."

"Have a seat," Kennedy said.

Munro sat and Kennedy appraised him with a wry grin that made Munro slightly uncomfortable.

"Well, well," said the Ambassador after what seemed like a long pause, "young Mr. Munro." Kennedy puffed on his cigar. "So," he said, "how is your father, the Senator, these days?"

"He's just fine, sir," Munro said.

"I admire your father a great deal, you know," said Kennedy. "I think he's one of the great men of our era."

"Thank you, Mr. Ambassador," Munro said. "My father" —Munro struggled for the right phrase—"speaks highly of you, also."

Kennedy nodded and smiled.

Munro could have added that his father's opinion of the Ambassador had not always been so approving. But since the beginning of the war in Europe, Senator Munro had increasingly found the Ambassador's views to his liking.

The Senator was one of the leaders of a somewhat loosely knit, nonpartisan group of elected officials in Washington, labeled "the isolationists" by the press, who were determined to keep America out of any involvement in the European war. This group, comprising people like Senators Burton Wheeler of Montana and Wayland Brooks of Illinois, was virulently anti-Roosevelt and opposed to what they saw as his interventionist policies. Wheeler, in fact, had threatened to form a third party of dissident Democrats to oppose Roosevelt if the Democratic Party dared to re-nominate the President for a third term. Colonel Charles Lindbergh often attended this group's meetings and helped to promote their already strong fears of German military might with his tales of how the Luftwaffe had the capacity to reduce any European capital to rubble.

Other groups interested in keeping America out of the war

at that time ranged from the genuinely pacifist Quakers to the anti-Semitic Christian Front of Father Charles Coughlin to the openly pro-German America First Committee which could claim the support of Phillip La Follette, former governor of Wisconsin and a member of one of America's most distinguished political families. But the favorite speaker at America First rallies was that quintessential American hero, Colonel Charles Lindbergh.

"Lucky Lindy," first man to fly the Atlantic solo, had very early on become a fan of German resurgence and of National Socialism. Because of his involvement with the development of aircraft, Lindbergh, at the invitation of Hermann Goering, had visited Germany several times in the thirties and had been decorated by the Nazi hierarchy. Lindbergh had been greatly impressed with what he had seen in Germany, but what had impressed him most of all was the German aircraft industry. Lindbergh was one of those early proponents of air power who believed that the airplane would render all other forms of warfare obsolete, and his visits to Germany had convinced him that German air power was so superior to anything else in the world that resistance was pointless.

When war came, Germany's crushing victories in Poland and in France had cloaked Lindbergh in the mantle of the prophet. The isolationist press—the *New York Daily News,* the *Chicago Tribune,* the *Washington Times-Herald*—hung on Lindbergh's every word. His promise of a London devastated by German air power if Churchill did not accept Hitler's generous offer of peace was front-page news. Lindbergh demanded that America and Roosevelt stop encouraging the British to resist Hitler. Instead, he proposed that America cease all aid to Great Britain and extend a hand of friendship to the Fascist powers.

There were many others in America, even those sympathetic to Britain's plight, who wanted no confrontation with mighty Germany. They found solace in the words of men like Charles Lindbergh, Burton Wheeler, Senator Malcolm Munro, and Ambassador Joseph P. Kennedy.

"I thought," Kennedy said, "that it was time for us to have a little chat."

Munro nodded.

"How are things going with your new assignment?"

"Fine, sir. I'm really just getting settled in. It'll probably take me a little while to get—"

The Ambassador interrupted. "I mean with the reporter —Betty Donaldson."

"I've only just met her."

"What do you think?" The Ambassador was grinning.

"She seems . . . nice enough," he said.

"Nice enough," said Kennedy with an explosive laugh. "You don't find legs like that on most reporters, you know."

"I guess you're right, sir," Munro said.

Kennedy was still laughing, waving his cigar like a wand. "No, sirree, boy," he said. "She's quite a dish, that one." His laughter subsided and he pointed his cigar at Munro. "I wish you luck with her."

"Thank you, sir," Munro said.

"It was my recommendation that got you this assignment, you know."

"Thank you, sir," Munro said again. "I appreciate your interest."

"I don't miss much of what goes on around here," Kennedy said. "The word I get through the grapevine is that you've been getting the cold shoulder from the military types."

"I think so much has been going on here it's difficult to include a newcomer right away. I'm sure that things will be fine in a few days."

"What have they given you to do?" the Ambassador asked.

"For now I'll be checking lists of Americans who want passage back home. The liners *Manhattan* and *Washington* are due in next week and I'm to make sure that everyone who wants passage has a berth."

"Checking lists," Kennedy muttered and then his voice rose angrily. "Busywork," he said. "They just want you out of the way."

"I also have my assignment as tour guide to Betty Donaldson."

Kennedy did not notice the sarcasm in Munro's voice. "No thanks to them," he said.

"I'm sure things will get better once I've been here for a while."

Kennedy champed on his cigar. "Don't count on it," he said. "Most of the military types around here are hell-bent for getting us into this war. They don't think in terms of the human suffering involved. They don't trust anyone who might disagree with them." He shook his head sadly, as if the weight of the world were on his shoulders. "If I have my way, not one single American will ever have to worry about this ridiculous war. It's strictly a European fracas."

"My father has said that many times."

"Your father and I have a lot in common"—the Ambassador smiled—"at least when it comes to this war. Fine man, your father."

"Before I left for England," Munro said, "my father told me that I could learn a lot about international politics by studying your example." The quote was reasonably accurate. What the Captain had diplomatically omitted was that it had been excerpted from a parting argument between father and son.

"Damn fine man, your father. Knows what the hell he's talking about. When I was home, in December," the Ambassador said, "I had dinner with him. We met at Senator Wheeler's home. Senator Clark was there . . . so was Charles Lindbergh . . . and some others."

"He mentioned that."

"We had quite a long talk, your father and I. A nice long chat about the war and America's place in this conflict. I think your father and I agree on many things."

Munro reached into his log of complimentary things his father had said about the Ambassador. "He told me that if there were more Democrats like Joe Kennedy, he wouldn't be so fearful for our country."

The Ambassador was obviously pleased. "Did he, now?" He nodded approvingly, his face animated with a wide smile. "Damn fine man, your father." The smile slipped away and Kennedy leaned closer. "One of the things I tried to explain to your father, Max," he said, using Munro's given name for the first time, "was that I serve my country and my president to the best of my ability. I don't always agree with my instructions from Washington, but I am here at the discretion of the President and I must always carry out those instructions. Unfortunately, the best interests of our President and our country are not always the same."

Munro nodded and tried to look agreeable.

"It is no secret," Kennedy said, "that Roosevelt has surrounded himself with a bunch of left-wingers who are determined to run America into the ground. Not one —Roosevelt included—has an ounce of business sense. They haven't got the slightest idea of what made our country what it is."

Munro smiled. "My father has said the same thing many times."

Kennedy nodded. "And that is why your father thought it'd be a good idea to have a representative over here at this crucial time. Someone to let him know what is going on."

"Why didn't he just ask you, Mr. Ambassador?"

"Your father understands that I am loyal to the President and to my party. He would never ask me to betray the trust that has been given me. Nor would I ask it of him." He smiled, hoping that Munro would understand his position. "Politics is a strange business," he said. "If I were to betray my party—no matter how just the cause—I'd be a political pariah. My career in politics would be over." He sighed. "But I still have an obligation to do what is right for my country."

Munro was beginning to understand. "And that's where I come in?"

"The President is more concerned with his re-election campaign than with anything else." Kennedy's voice dropped almost to a whisper. "There are things going on over here that would shock the American people. Certain policies are being pursued that—were they known to the American electorate—would result in a landslide defeat for Roosevelt."

"According to some of the polls back home," said Munro, "he may lose anyway."

Kennedy chuckled. "There's enough evidence at this embassy to hand the presidency to Willkie on a silver platter."

The Ambassador went on. "Right now, staying out of this disastrous war is the most important thing in the world. More important certainly than whether or not Roosevelt gets his third term. More important than whether the winner is a Republican or a Democrat. Though, there were other Democrats with the strength and courage to do what has to be done."

Munro had little doubt that the Ambassador was talking about himself. "I'm sure you are right, Mr. Ambassador."

"I know I am," said Joseph Kennedy sadly. He stared at his cigar for a moment, then clenched it between his teeth. "Well, we've had our little chat, and I can see that we understand each other. For the time being I'm assigning you—on a temporary basis—to the code room. We're short-handed down there and this will be an emergency appointment until we can get some further help."

Munro started to speak but the Ambassador cut him off. "Don't worry about it. I'll clear it with Colonel Jackson."

"What about my other duties?"

"Don't worry about the passenger lists of the evacuees. They don't really need you for that. I'll take care of that for you." Suddenly he grinned. "I'm assuming that you don't want to give up your duties with our little reporter."

"Well . . . I . . . don't . . ."

"No problem. Take as much time with her as you need. Just try to spend a few hours a day down in the code room. I'm sure you'll find much to interest you down there."

"Yes, Mr. Ambassador. I'm sure I will."

Kennedy stood up and extended his hand across the desk. Munro stood and shook the offered hand.

"That's it, then," said the Ambassador. "Good luck . . . with both your assignments." Joe Kennedy gave a huge wink.

"Thank you, Mr. Ambassador."

In the hallway outside the Ambassador's office Munro breathed a sigh of relief. Talking to the Ambassador was like engaging a buzz saw in conversation. In that, the Ambassador was like most of the powerful men—including his father —that Munro had ever met. They left little room for argument in their discussions. As the object of the monologue, one was expected to nod a few times, occasionally grunt in agreement, and then, somewhere between bafflement and bewilderment, be shown to the door.

He took a deep breath and started down the hallway to the stairwell. At the top of the stairs he stood aside to make room for Captain Studwell and Lieutenant Commander Forbes, who were on their way up. Both gave him long withering stares. "Good morning, Captain," Studwell said pleasantly.

"Good morning, sir," replied Munro.

"Did you and the Ambassador have a nice long chat this morning?" Studwell asked.

Before Munro could answer, Studwell and Forbes stomped off down the hallway. It was obvious, Munro thought. Everyone here at the embassy knows that my father has had me assigned here to spy on them. The Ambassador knows it.

Studwell and Forbes know it. Even Colonel Jackson has a hard time meeting my eyes. He shook his head as he started down the stairs. "It didn't take long," he muttered, "for me to win the Embassy popularity contest." Just wait, he thought, until they hear that I've been assigned to the code room.

500 NAZI PLANES RAID BRITAIN; COASTAL AREAS, AIRFIELDS HIT

LONDON, AUG. 14

◆ CHAPTER 11 ◆

LONDON, August 14—It happened so suddenly that Winston Hamilton had no opportunity to brake his bicycle or avoid the collision. The woman stepped into the street from between two parked automobiles right into his path, and all that either could do was note the look of surprise on the other's face and accept the inevitable impact. Winston struck the woman a glancing blow and she spun around, her groceries flying, and flopped to the pavement. He managed to maintain his balance for a few yards and then tumbled from his bicycle. By the time he ran back to the woman she had raised herself on her elbows and was struggling to get to her feet.

"Are you all right?" asked Winston apologetically. The woman appeared shaken, her hair disheveled and her skirt hiked up to reveal a generous expanse of quite lovely thigh.

Winston looked away when he spoke to her. "I'm terribly sorry," he said. "How awfully clumsy of me." He ventured a look in her direction. She had pulled down her skirt and pushed her hair back from her face. She was, he thought, one of the most remarkably attractive women he had ever seen.

"Can you give me a hand?" she asked.

For a moment, transfixed by the partially unbuttoned

blouse, Winston was immobilized. "Of course," he said finally, and stepped forward to help her to her feet.

She brushed herself off as Winston scurried about gathering her groceries. "I'm afraid I've smashed your tea biscuits," he said sorrowfully.

She, attending to her clothing, paid him no heed.

"Good thing you didn't have eggs," he said.

"I suppose I should be grateful for the shortage," she said.

He was pleased by her brave attempt at humor. "Are you sure you're all right?"

"I think so," she said. "A few minor bumps and bruises. Nothing to be alarmed about."

"I'm glad," Winston said. "I really am sorry. I should be more careful. I'm afraid I must have been daydreaming."

She smiled. "You're very sweet to say so," she said, "but I'm sure it was entirely my fault." She paused and Winston thought that her eyes were suddenly damp. "I've been somewhat preoccupied lately . . . I"—her voice trailed away and she looked down.

Her apparent vulnerability touched something in Winston's heart, and he wanted to place a hand on her shoulder. Of course, he did no such thing. The whole scene had a fairly familiar ring, and the thought occurred to him that he might have been playing a part in one of those movies that he loved so much. He realized that he had not stuttered as he usually did when he talked with an attractive woman.

"Thank you for your help," said the woman. "You've been very kind." She dazzled him with a smile. "I'll be more careful in the future." She took her groceries from him.

"It's been a . . . a"—Winston was desperate for something to say—"a pleasure running into you."

She laughed, and he realized with a pleasant shock that he had made a joke.

"Well, yes, I suppose it has been," she said. "But I must be going." She smiled warmly. "Goodbye." She looked both ways, crossed the street and, as Winston watched her, disappeared around the corner.

He wanted to race after her, introduce himself, find out her name, ask her to dinner. But, of course, he did none of these things. Instead, he sighed, picked up his bike, brushed himself off, and, his thoughts full of this beautiful apparition who had streaked into and out of his life, pedaled home.

Two pairs of eyes watched him until he had disappeared at the end of the road.

"Well," said Sean Daly, "what do you think?"

Marie Price smiled innocently. "About what?"

"Will he do?"

"He's not terribly attractive." Marie saw Daly's eyes darken and quickly added, "But he seems quite nice."

"Do you think he was attracted to you?"

"What do you think?"

Daly's eyes went to the open buttons on her blouse. "I think he's probably drooling all the way home."

Winston Hamilton had been until quite recently a lecturer in German literature at Kings College. Last December the college dean, who had been involved in some secret work for the government since October of 1939, had, to Winston's surprise, asked Winston to join the project.

"We have a great need for those who are fluent in German, Winston," Dean Barker had said. "It's vitally important and we need good men now."

Tall, gawky, unathletic, and with a prematurely receding hairline, Winston Hamilton had never regarded himself as one of those "good men" who rush off to save their country in times of war. But with a war in progress, he could hardly refuse.

Much to his mother's dismay, Winston had been commissioned a second lieutenant in the Army, but when Iris Hamilton realized that her son's skills would keep him safe at home in England, she, along with Winston, was much relieved.

He was sent to a place called Bletchley Park in Buckinghamshire, some forty miles north of London, where he discovered that his colleagues were intercepting and decoding the German military's radio transmissions. The Germans sent these coded transmissions with the aid of a machine which looked much like a typewriter with revolving drums above the keyboard. The Germans called the machine Enigma and were apparently confident that their codes were unbreakable. The British, with the help of a stolen Enigma machine and with several machines which, incredibly, had been purchased before the war by the Government Code and Cipher School from the same manufacturer who supplied the machines to the Germans, had assembled a host of mathematicians, translators, and cryptographers in an attempt to prove the Germans wrong.

The original version of the Enigma machine had been invented in the early 1930s by a German engineer named Arthur Scherbius and was sold by his company to anyone interested in a device which could provide a method of secret communication. An operator typed a message on the sending machine, causing the drums to spin in a preset pattern. This pattern, which theoretically offered four hundred thousand permutations of the message, could then only be decoded by another operator with an identical machine and access to the coded preset drum patterns. It was estimated that a team of mathematicians might take more than a month to decipher a single drum pattern. If the codes were changed daily or even weekly it would be humanly impossible to decode the messages.

In 1938 the Wehrmacht, in desperate need of a device which would facilitate the instantaneous transmission and reception of secret messages, selected Scherbius's cypher machine as the method by which the German military would communicate on the field of battle. The Germans called the machine Enigma, from the ancient Greek word for puzzle, presumably because its variety of permutations was theoretically impossible to solve. They had the utmost confidence in Enigma's ability to conceal their secrets from any and all adversaries and manufactured the machine by the thousands. Each German military unit at or above battalion level possessed an Enigma and was instructed to use only this method of transmitting messages.

In 1939 the British Secret Intelligence Service had contracted with the Polish Secret Service to acquire a working model of the machine used by the Germans in all military transmissions. The Poles had succeeded beyond anyone's wildest dreams and provided not just a working model but a genuine Enigma machine actually manufactured in East Prussia. How the Poles accomplished this remarkable deed is unknown, but it is certain that this single action had much to do with thwarting Hitler's plans for a Nazified Europe.

Having the machine was one thing, breaking the codes that held the secrets to its mysteries was another. When war began the British gathered their greatest mathematical geniuses and put them to work deciphering the riddle of the drum codes. The mathemeticians soon realized that the Germans were correct; it was humanly impossible to solve the Enigma puzzle within the given time frame. By the time a drum code was broken the Enigma message was usually more than three weeks old. By now the Germans were changing the drum codes on a daily basis and the mathematicians realized that they would never be able to catch up. They also knew that if man could build a machine to encode messages, he could also build a machine to decode those same messages. And so at Bletchley Park in Buckinghamshire, the mathematicians abandoned their fruitless attempts to match wits with a machine. Instead they built what was believed to be the world's first electronic computer.

Once this remarkable achievement was completed, the computer, a tall column of twisted wires and flashing lights encircled by a bronze-colored casing, began the daily battle against the Enigma. By the summer of 1940, just as the German war machine was gearing up for the invasion of Britain, the British were able to intercept, decode, and translate virtually every message of consequence sent from one German military unit to another.

That's where Winston Hamilton, and a host of others like him, came in. Once the transmissions were decoded, swift and accurate translations were necessary and Winston Hamilton soon found himself immersed in a morass of German military data. In order to understand and accurately translate the intercepted data, the translators had to commit to memory a mountain of information about the Oberkommando der Wehrmacht. No detail was too large or too small. It was essential that the translators know the names and functions of all staff officers in the OKW and the location and function of all German military units on the Western front. Who was General Guderian or General Manstein? What forces did they command? Where was *Luftflotte 2* stationed and who was the commanding officer? What was the significance of movement orders for the 12th Panzer Division stationed at Birkenfeld?

The translators had to be able to make instant judgments as to which messages, out of the hundreds of mundane transmissions, might be of extraordinary importance. To the surprise of his superior officers—and even himself—Winston Hamilton had displayed an early ability to separate the significant from the insignificant. Sometimes it was in the phrasing, sometimes in the repetition of a key word, sometimes it was merely a hunch, but whatever it was, Winston Hamilton proved adept at discerning the meaning of Enigma.

What was required was a man with a keen eye and a faultless memory, who could train himself to think as if he were a German officer in the field. Winston Hamilton was such a man. For him it was an intellectual exercise, an opportunity to replay the games of his childhood. His toy soldiers were stretched across the map of Europe. But this time the stakes were real.

Winston had so totally immersed himself in the labyrinthian machinations of the German military, knew so intimately the minds of the commanders in the field, understood so thoroughly the intentions of the men at the headquarters of the Army General Staff on Bendler Strasse in Berlin, that he often imagined himself, in full Nazi regalia, standing next to von Rundstedt, Keitel, and Kleist while they explained to Hitler the necessity of an offensive thrust to the west.

The British and the French knew the thrust would come. The only question was when and where it would happen.

The logical answer was a German drive through Belgium, avoiding the French fortifications along the border between Germany and France and the impenetrable Ardennes Forest which straddled the French-Belgian border. An authentic set of German plans, detailing such a move, had fallen into Allied hands in January, leading the French to believe that a German assault on France through Belgium was imminent. Winston Hamilton, however, had earlier translated an intercepted message from General Guderian, the Commander-in-Chief of all Panzer troops, to General Staff Headquarters in Berlin. Guderian, it seemed, was arguing for an armored strike through the Ardennes Forest, and although no one on the general staff had given approval for such a move, Winston noted that no one had absolutely forbidden it. He brought his concerns to his superiors, who passed them along to their superiors, who mentioned the possibility to the French. For their part, the French were convinced that any such move could only be a diversion to draw them away from the real focus of attack in Belgium.

Hamilton had studied all of Guderian's messages, read his

book on armored tactics, found out all that he could about the man. The more he studied the more he became convinced that Guderian would indeed strike through the Ardennes. Hamilton had made a pest of himself, propounding his theories to all who would listen, but to no avail. The French were convinced of German intentions in Belgium, and the British were convinced that the French, who would bear the brunt of the assault, must know what they were talking about.

On Friday, May 10, the Germans attacked Holland and Belgium, and the British and French in anticipation of the move south moved their forces north to meet them. There were more than a few at Bletchley Park who cast a reproachful eye at Hamilton, more than a few who seemed pleased that his prediction had proved inaccurate.

On the morning of the thirteenth came the thunderbolt. Under cover of an early morning fog, General Guderian's armored divisions emerged from the Ardennes and crossed the Meuse River near Sedan. Guderian, with Rommel's 7th Panzer Division close behind, was in France, less than a hundred and thirty miles from Paris, and with the main body of French and British forces diverted to Belgium, he was virtually unopposed.

The rest was catastrophe.

Since then Hamilton had been elevated to a position of greater respect and authority. He had been transferred to London to the headquarters of the Special Intelligence Services on Broadway near the War Offices and St. James Park. Several times each day decoded messages were brought to those officers by motorcycle courier from Bletchley Park. At Broadway the decision about which messages were important enough to be passed on to the Prime Minister were made. Hamilton's job was to verify the translations and apply his special intuition to the significance of the messages.

This was the first job of any real significance for Winston Hamilton. More accustomed to the shenanigans of recalcitrant students than the vagaries of war, he was somewhat overwhelmed by his new stature. Tall and thin, and with a dismaying propensity for stuttering when under duress, Hamilton was, at twenty-seven, retiring. He had few male friends and, except for his mother, the only women he saw regularly were those who worked at SIS headquarters. His pleasures were few, reading German literature and weekly visits to the local motion picture show. Lately he had been so busy that he had hardly any time for relaxation at all. But as hard as he worked he could not eradicate from his mind the image of the young woman whom he had struck with his bike. He had never had a relationship with a woman. Long ago he had given up the hope that he would one day find someone who would look beyond his obvious physical inadequacies and see him for the person that he was, but there was something different about this woman. She had not looked at him as other women did, with that strange mixture of pity and disdain. She had looked at him as if he were a person, just like any other, and although it had certainly been an awkward situation, he had felt almost comfortable talking with her. He had even managed a joke and made her laugh. In his mind his brief encounter had grown progressively more significant until he began to imagine that this woman had actually been hoping that he would introduce himself. Gradually the encounter and his fantasy merged and Winston began to think that perhaps he had been quite suave. A hundred times since the event he'd imagined himself stopping her as she turned to walk away. "I'm Winston Hamilton," he would say to her, "and I would like to see you again." She would shyly look down. Then she would tell him her name—something like Cynthia or Daphne—and ask him to walk her home. It would be the beginning of a beautiful relationship. They would spend long winter evenings in front of the fire, she listening attentively while he read aloud from Schiller's *Würde der Frauen*.

She filled his thoughts, but he breathed not a word to anyone. Surely someone as devastatingly beautiful as his dream-woman would belong to someone else. What chance could he possibly have? He longed to see her again.

In his heart he knew that such things did not happen.

> 1000 NAZI PLANES HIT BRITAIN IN WAR'S
> BIGGEST RAID; LONDON DOCK AREA BOMBED:
> RAF CLAIMS 144 SHOT DOWN; BRITISH OFFER
> U.S. HEMISPHERE BASES FOR OLD DESTROYERS
>
> LONDON, AUG. 15

◆ CHAPTER 12 ◆

August 15—What was called the code room at the American Embassy was in actuality a group of three small, stuffy rooms in the embassy basement that were used for the reception, transmission and storage of all incoming and outgoing messages. All outgoing messages, no matter how mundane, were routinely coded before transmission. Several different codes, called color codes, were used, with "yellow" being used for those messages regarded as least important and "gray" used for those messages regarded as most secret and intended for the eyes of the President of the United States.

The first of the three rooms was the smallest and contained only a desk and a file cabinet used by the duty officer. Anyone entering the code area had to pass through this room, where he would sign in with the duty officer, who would enter the visitor's name in a log book. Beyond this room was the largest room, where the actual coding and transmitting took place. There sat the teletype machines with their coding disks and, under lock and key, the code books. The third room was the storage area, which contained a file cabinet for each of the different color codes. After transmission or reception the duty officer would place copies of each message in the appropriate file cabinet.

Several staff members had, at one time or another, commented on the lack of security procedures in the code room, but with the United States not being in an actual state of war, nothing was done about it.

Maxwell Munro had spent his first few days becoming familiar with the code room procedures. His job was relatively simple and required little of his time. Munro's shift as duty officer was from 8 A.M. to 12 noon. Because of the time differential this was the equivalent of a 3 A.M. to 7 A.M. shift in Washington, D.C., and was consequently the shift where relatively few, if any, messages were sent or received. Munro's duties consisted of logging in the infrequent visitor, making sure that the teletype machines were in the on position, and entering a record of any messages received.

His only companion during his shift was a young man named Anthony Sutton who was the code and cipher clerk. Sutton was in charge of the embassy code books, and it was his job to code and decode incoming and outgoing messages in the appropriate cipher. Sutton was a tall, handsome man in his late twenties who spoke only when spoken to and then gave only the briefest possible reply. After a few attempts at casual conversation, during which Munro discovered that Sutton was a Yale graduate, had been raised in New Jersey, and had been with the Consular Service for five years, Munro gave up and allowed Sutton the solitude he seemed to prefer.

During Munro's first three days on the job, there were less than a dozen messages received. If the duty officer on the previous shift hadn't established the procedure of filing only his incoming messages and leaving the outgoing messages for the next shift, Maxwell Munro would have had almost nothing to do.

It was almost inevitable that Munro would begin to read the messages before filing them. Most were in the form of reports by visiting American military officers—called Special Observers—on the status of the British war effort. Those messages that were regarded as most secret were stamped GRAY CODE: TOP SECRET to show that they had been encoded in the embassy's top priority code before transmitting. The gray coded reports might include the number of British fighter aircraft operational on any given day, or the number of antiaircraft guns available for use in certain locations, or the number of rifles required by the British Army to replace those lost at Dunkirk. The American officers were obviously getting their information from impeccable sources and many of the reports were sprinkled with the names of high-ranking military and government officials.

Munro picked up the small stack of messages that had been transmitted on the earlier shift. He checked the log book to make sure that each message had been entered, before walking through the teletype room. Anthony Sutton looked up from behind his desk as Munro entered the room, but he did not speak. Munro nodded wordlessly and continued to the file room, where he proceeded to file the documents. The first few messages were green coded and relatively unimportant. He placed them into the appropriate cabinet. The next was a gray code and Munro read it carefully.

FROM: LT. GENERAL DAVIES
TO: WAR DEPT, SECTION 15
SUBJECT: AIRCRAFT PRODUCTION
SOURCE: SIR A. SINCLAIR, SEC. OF STATE AIR MINISTRY

BR. AIR PRODUCTION AT CRITICAL PHASE STOP PRESENT
LOSSES 20 PERCENT GREATER THAN REPLACEMENT STOP
DESPERATELY REQUIRE U.S. P-40 FIGHTERS BOEING B-17
BOMBERS PRATT-WHITNEY ENGINES STOP SHORTFALL
TEMPORARY STOP CAUSED BY DAMAGE TO FACTORIES IN
BOURNEMOUTH DAGENHAM AND WEYBRIDGE STOP 30
DAYS BEFORE PRODUCTION NORMAL END MESSAGE

Munro whistled softly to himself as he filed the message. If the Germans could see that, he thought, they would be elated. Not only did the report reveal the desperate condition of the British aircraft industry, and the RAF's need for American replacements, it also confirmed the accuracy of the German attacks on the aircraft factories. Goering would run straight to Hitler if he could get his hands on it.

There were other messages, some as important, others not. Another gray code message caught his eye. It was longer than any of the other transmissions and addressed as SECRET AND PERSONAL FOR POTUS FROM FORMER NAVAL PERSON. The "Former Naval Person" was thanking POTUS for his "untiring efforts to give us all possible help," and seemed to suggest that POTUS would soon be sending U.S. Navy destroyers to the British to aid in the battle against German U-boats. The "Former Naval Person" then requested that the level of assistance continue at an even higher level. What followed was a long shopping list of military hardware that "Former Naval Person" required at POTUS.

Munro's eyes widened as he road. POTUS was obviously the President of the United States. Only Franklin Roosevelt had the authority to assign such a quantity of military weaponry to a foreign power.

It was immediately apparent to Munro that compliance with such a request would be a clear violation of the Neutrality Act and could place the United States in a position of great jeopardy. Compliance might even be constructed by Germany as an act of belligerence and result in an immediate declaration of war.

"Former Naval Person" was just as obviously Winston Churchill. The Prime Minister was a former First Lord of the Admiralty and the only person who could have such high level secret communication with President Roosevelt.

Munro opened the gray code file cabinet and flipped through the folders until he found the section headed POTUS-NAVAL PERSON. There were several dozen messages in the section. In addition to the messages between Roosevelt and Churchill, there were several from the British Ambassador in Washington, Lord Lothian, to Ambassador Kennedy. Munro gasped when he realized that the correspondence between Roosevelt and Churchill had begun even before Churchill became Prime Minister, and that it had been initiated by the President.

The earlier messages, when Churchill had been First Lord of the Admiralty, had been from "Naval Person." After May 10, 1940, when Churchill became Prime Minister, the messages to POTUS had been from "Former Naval Person."

Munro thought of the times his father had ranted about how the warmonger Roosevelt was determined to drag America into the war. Even Senator Munro was unaware of the extent of the collusion between Roosevelt and Churchill. Senator Munro was convinced that Roosevelt was giving Churchill as much aid and encouragement as he could without alarming the American people or diminishing his chances for re-election. The Senator, and other critics of the President, had often claimed that Roosevelt had encouraged the "war party" in Britain by ignoring the peacekeeping efforts of Prime Minister Chamberlain. Here was the proof. If Senator Munro knew that Roosevelt had circumvented Chamberlain and established contact with the Prime Minister's most vocal critic, he would ring the alarm bells all across America.

A sudden thought flashed through Munro's mind. What if this was the reason Ambassador Kennedy had had him assigned to the code room? If the Ambassador wanted to let the American people know what the President was up to, but did not want to personally be responsible for the revelation, what better way than to assign the son of a prominent critic to a position where he would have access to such damning information.

Munro's first thought was to close the file cabinet and forget that he had ever stumbled across the correspondence between the two leaders. Who was he to be privy to such information? Why should he know what others only imagined? Then it occurred to him that this information, even though it was classified top secret, must be known to anyone who worked in the code room. Although, theoretically, only the code room clerks who were in charge of the filing of gray code documents had access to the files, there were no security precautions to prevent anyone with access to the code room from reading the messages. He wondered how many others on the embassy staff were aware of what he had discovered.

Curiosity running rampant, Munro went through the files reading POTUS's answers to the messages from Former Naval Person. Each message was numbered, dated, and filed in chronological order so it was easy to follow the thought processes of the two leaders as they deliberated their course of action in the war against Germany.

What was immediately apparent from the early messages was that Franklin Roosevelt had been intimately involved in Churchill's strategy against Hitler. Fully nine months before Churchill had become Prime Minister, Roosevelt was engaging him in discussions usually reserved for heads of state. It was obvious that President Roosevelt had decided that Winston Churchill was the only man who could lead Britain. At one point in the early correspondence the American

President seemed to be suggesting a method by which Churchill could force Prime Minister Neville Chamberlain out of office and assume the prime ministership himself. This suggestion was made when it still seemed possible that Chamberlain would be able to negotiate a peace with Germany. In other messages the President advised Churchill to "stick some iron up Chamberlain's backside," in obvious reference to Chamberlain's cautious approach to almost every aspect of diplomacy. Later Roosevelt frequently advised Churchill to "get tough" with Germany, promising that the United States would provide all the aid necessary.

Munro withdrew messages at random, quickly read them, and moved on to others. Most of the messages were of the cheerleader variety, with Roosevelt calling on Churchill and the British to "hang in there" and "not to give up hope." Several times the President intimated that his hands were tied until after the election, but it was obvious from Churchill's response that he believed that Roosevelt would bring the United States into the war shortly thereafter.

Roosevelt's remarks, Munro told himself, were meant solely to offer encouragement to an old friend and a staunch ally, and that what Churchill perceived as a promise of a declaration of war was wishful thinking.

But there were other messages that filled him with doubt. One message from Churchill sent Munro scurrying through the files looking for Roosevelt's response. On the nineteenth of that month Hitler had made a peace offer to the British in which he had asked for nothing more than a free hand in Europe. Britain would be asked to forfeit nothing, only to "cease and desist in the continuation of the war against Germany." That was it. If the British accepted, the war was over. There were to be no reparations, no recriminations, no forfeiture of territory. It was a remarkable offer from a victorious nation to one on the verge of collapse. On July twentieth Churchill communicated the particulars of the peace offer from Hitler and asked for Roosevelt's advice. Munro recognized that this was a shrewd move. If Roosevelt wanted the war to continue he would have to make a commitment to the British. If not he could simply advise Churchill to accept Hitler's offer. Munro's hand trembled as he searched for the copy of Roosevelt's reply.

There was no reply. Roosevelt's message was missing.

In its place, Munro found a message from the British Ambassador in Washington that was addressed to Churchill. "Elated by President's response to your letter. Treasury Secretary Morgenthau reported to me this afternoon that FDR thinks that U.S. will enter war within ninety days."

The correspondence was dynamite and Munro knew that its revelation would cause a political explosion back home. Roosevelt had encouraged Churchill to refuse a peace offer from Germany. Roosevelt was also maneuvering to bring the U.S. into the war. What had begun as encouragement had become an offer of all-out support for the British. Republicans would have a field day with this information. Many would claim that were it not for Franklin D. Roosevelt, the war in Europe would be over. Munro could see the headlines in the *Chicago Tribune*: WARMONGER ROOSEVELT EXPOSED. Men like Clark and Wheeler and Lindbergh, and his own father, would scream "Treason!" from the rooftops. The polls, which already showed Willkie running even with Roosevelt, would show that Franklin Roosevelt's political career was over. Not only would Roosevelt lose the coming election, but it was very possible that Congress might begin impeachment proceedings against him.

Munro had in his possession a document that, if made public, could alter the course of history. An election forfeit, a war lost, a continent in perpetual darkness, a civilization in ruins.

He put the document back into its place in the file folder and slowly eased the drawer closed.

He casually walked through the middle room, expecting Sutton to make some comment about the time he had spent in the file room. But, true to form, Sutton said nothing when Munro walked past him.

600 NAZI RAIDERS BOMB LONDON AREA
AGAIN; RAF SHOOTS DOWN 140 ENEMY
PLANES; GERMAN CHANNEL BASES HIT HARD

LONDON, AUG. 19

◆ *CHAPTER 13* ◆

August 19—Each day, after his tour of duty in the code room, Munro returned to his office on the ground floor. He shared a secretary with the other assistant attachés and by the time he got to his office, she would leave on his desk any messages he had received while he was down in "the hole," as the others called the code room. His messages were few, and at a time when the military personnel at the embassy were increasingly overworked, Munro found he had little to do. When he complained to Colonel Jackson that he could make better use of his time, the Colonel coughed and told him that his primary duties were the code room and his escort duties with Miss Donaldson.

Munro had procured the required documentation and the obligatory gas mask and steel helmet for himself and her. She refused, however, to carry the helmet, saying that she would never "in a million years wear such a ridiculous contraption," and, despite Munro's warnings, would not bring it with her. The police either ignored or did not notice that she was sans helmet but, sure enough, on her second day without it a Local Defense Volunteer challenged her and threatened to report her to the local authorities if she did not return to her hotel and collect her helmet.

She had a list of places on her "must see" list, and Munro obtained any necessary permits, but most of the places she wished to visit required no special permission. For the most part she avoided the fashionable clubs, hotels, and shops in the West End, and concentrated on the working class areas of the East End. There, conditions were deplorable. In places like Canning Town and Silvertown near the Royal Victoria Dock, they found row upon row of ugly tenement buildings. Those ramshackle structures, built in the middle of the last century, housed the dockworkers, factory workers, and other laborers who were the lifeblood of the city. Their squalid homes provided little shelter and even less comfort. The scene was repeated in visits to Stepney, Poplar, Bow, and Whitechapel.

Betty shook her head sadly as they walked along the Limehouse Causeway, near the West India Docks. "This," she said, "is what I most despise about this country. The squalor in the midst of all the wealth and privilege. What do you think will happen to these people when Hitler drops a few bombs on this mess?"

"I don't know," he said seriously.

"I've seen places and people like this before," Betty said. "In Poland." She looked at the rickety, overcrowded buildings and her eyes narrowed in anger. "A few bombs and these miserable buildings will be instant rubble. And how will these people react? In Poland they panicked. Clogged the roads trying to escape. Made it impossible for the army reinforcements to get to the front. That's exactly what the Germans wanted—panic."

"Maybe," Munro said, "these people will be different."

"Why would these people be any different?" she said bitterly. "Look at these places. Why should they fight to preserve this?" This, she thought, was the kind of information President Roosevelt had to have. It was the kind of report that he would not get from his generals and politicians.

"They don't know," she muttered after listening to some Cockneys on Commercial Road in Stepney. "They think this is the worst of it. Wait till Hitler decides to turn Goering's Luftwaffe loose. Then let's see how they hold up."

"You sound," said Munro, as they walked back toward the embassy car, "as if you've been talking to the Ambassador."

Betty looked at him, her eyes narrowed. "Sometimes," she said, "even the Ambassador is right."

Munro watched her whenever she was not looking at him. She made no attempt at beautification. It was unnecessary. She wore little makeup and her clothes—baggy, men's-style

111

slacks and oversized shirts or sweaters—did nothing to accentuate her figure. Her hair was pulled back and pinned on top of her head and often hidden beneath a floppy hat, but she could not hide her beauty from him or anyone else.

Munro saw how others looked at her. At the markets men with hundred-pound sacks on their backs stopped to watch her pass, often giving Munro an appreciative nod or wink. Soldiers—especially pilots—emboldened by their proximity to battle, followed her on the streets, and she turned down enough dinner invitations in a day to feed every urchin in London.

Betty had an easy amiability that enabled her to get strangers to open up to her, and she talked to anyone and everyone. She stopped whenever she saw an interesting face, taking pictures of street merchants, asking questions of housewives on their way to market. Munro marveled at her style, her quick smile that immediately engaged her subject. Betty preferred to be on her own during her wanderings through London. She had needed Munro to help her acquire the required documentation and accepted the fact that he would accompany her on her first few trips into what she called "the real London"—the London of the shopkeeper and the laborer rather than the banker or the politician. But after she grew accustomed to the city, it was obvious that she considered his presence an inconvenience.

"I'd rather be alone when I talk to people," she said, "than have an embassy type watching over my shoulder. I want people to give me an honest reaction to how they feel about this war."

And so the "embassy type" began to spend most of his time alone. He ate lunch by himself because the other attachés rarely invited him to join them. Only Colonel Jackson insisted on including Munro in the luncheon discussions that were the norm at any one of a dozen restaurants close to the embassy. Unfortunately, Colonel Jackson was usually involved in luncheon meetings with officials from the Air Ministry or the Ministry of Information or some other government agency. When that was the case, Munro ate lunch alone.

After work he returned to his room at the Coleridge, a small, inexpensive hotel which was only a few blocks from the embassy. The room was small but clean and the hotel provided him with everything he required.

In the evening he wandered rather aimlessly about central London, marveling at the vitality of a city in the midst of a war and a people who lived under the constant threat of aerial bombardment and the imminent threat of invasion. Like everyone else he carried his gas mask with him wherever he went, a constant reminder of the havoc threatened from above. He ate at whatever restaurant he happened to find when he grew hungry. The restaurants were mostly gloomy, either barricaded with sandbags or shaded, after dusk, with heavy drapes across the windows so that one might have been entering a cave. But inside the mood was bright, even festive. Most of the men and many of the women were in uniform and their jovial spirit was infectious. In the nightclubs people danced and sang and drank as if there were no tomorrow, and indeed for some who wore RAF uniforms that would be the case. But the mood was gay, the attitude defiant, and the patrons toasted themselves and their comrades in a spirit of togetherness the likes of which Munro had never encountered. He, however, in this, as in everything, was an outsider, and the sense of camaraderie never touched him. It only made his loneliness more acute.

Every night Munro returned to his hotel, making his way through the dark streets of a city devoid of light. There were no streetlamps, and taxis and busses—which were almost impossible to find—wore shrouds over their headlights emitting only a wan, yellow light. Every night there were accidents caused by poor lighting, and pedestrians were warned to take extra care in crossing streets.

In his room, after making sure his blackout curtains were drawn, Munro read by a single lamp until early in the morning. When he was not reading he thought about Betty Donaldson. He pictured her in the flowered dress she had worn that first day in his office, her eyes sparkling in the bright summer sun.

He also thought about what he had discovered in the code room. Night after night he brooded about the implications of what he had read.

It was clear to Munro that none of the other military personnel at the embassy were aware of the secret correspondence between Roosevelt and Churchill. To a man they were pro-British and sorely disappointed that President Roosevelt was so cautious in his support. Only Jackson seemed even mildly appreciative of the material support that the President had authorized, and all were agreed that the President had not given the British enough moral encouragement.

Munro wondered what they would say if he told them that Roosevelt was "up to his neck in this war." He pictured their faces, saw the sudden smiles turn to looks of dismay when he also told them that he was going to put a stop to it.

Munro's fellow officers seemed pleased that he had been assigned to the code room because it confirmed their suspicions that he was working for his father and the Ambassador, and the time that he spent there was time that they did not have to be concerned about his snooping on them.

From late at night until early morning he sat in his chair, reading, thinking, brooding, sipping Scotch whiskey, until he fell asleep, fully clothed. His thoughts about the war were increasingly muddled. His sentiments had always been with the British, but he had hoped that they could defeat Germany alone. The more he learned, however, the more convinced he became that this would never happen and the thought that the United States was moving inexorably closer to involvement in the war filled him with an infinite sadness. There were few things on which he and his father agreed. Keeping America out of the war was one of them.

HEAVY CASUALTIES AS NAZIS BOMB LONDON
SUBURB AT RUSH HOUR; HITLER CLAIMS AIR
CONTROL, DEMANDS SURRENDER OR PERISH

LONDON, AUG. 21

◆ *CHAPTER 14* ◆

Wednesday, August 21—Winston Hamilton took the same route home every night that week, sometimes pausing at the spot where he and the woman had collided, but he did not see her again. Each evening the anticipation of encounter was deliciously tantalizing, but as the week progressed and his dream-woman did not reappear his trips home were more and more filled with sadness and resignation. On Monday, Winston waited for more than an hour on the corner where he had first seen her. What he would have done or said had she appeared he did not know.

On Wednesday evening Lieutenant Winston Hamilton was in a hurry to get home. There was a new moving picture opening at the Empire Cinema on Leicester Square that night and his mother had promised an early supper so that they could both make the early showing. Almost every Wednesday Winston and his mother would attend the same early show, but sometimes his job would keep him late and he would have to listen to her complain about the length of his workday. Usually he would just let her run on, but sometimes when he had quite enough of her complaining he would explode and say, "Please don't complain about my job, Mother. It is important." Then he would use the clincher. "I could be in North Africa or someplace equally nasty, you know." That would usually placate her.

Winston impatiently cleared off his desk, keeping an ear cocked for the sounds of the courier's motorcycle in the courtyard. If it didn't get here soon, he would not have time for the early show. He cursed the fact that the promised teleprinter between Bletchley and Broadway had not yet been installed. That installation would provide instant relay of intercepted messages and eliminate the necessity of waiting each day for the courier's arrival.

Just as he was about to give up his hope of leaving on time, the courier, his motorcycle snarling in the courtyard below, arrived. Winston gave a great sigh of relief. Perhaps he could make it after all. He needed the escape of several hours in a darkened theater, where the lives on screen seemed so much more real than his own.

When the Enigma intercepts were brought to his desk, he quickly ran through the translations, verifying their accuracy and noting that none of the messages seemed to augur anything out of the ordinary. It looked like Portsmouth was going to get it again, and several of the RAF airfields were due for another pounding. Other Luftwaffe elements would be patrolling the skies of southern England in a continuing attempt to draw the RAF into combat. It was all pretty standard stuff.

He initialed each page and then left everything in the in-file of his CO's desk where the material would be further analyzed, and within the hour sent to the Prime Minister's residence.

By five-thirty Winston was happily on his way home. When he reached Jermyn Street near the Piccadilly Arcade his heart skipped a beat but he did not allow himself to look either right or left. It was not that he had forgotten what he had come to think of as his magic encounter—if anything the memory of the moment was more vivid now than the reality had been—but such things as he had imagined happened, he was certain, only on the screen at the cinema. He accepted the hopelessness of his cause and pedaled grimly down the cobbled street.

His mother, happy to see him on time, put supper on the table while he had a quick wash-up, and in less than half an hour they were on their way to the movie house.

Mrs. Hamilton chatted incessantly along the way about the coming invasion. "You will let me know in time?" she said. "So that I can evacuate before Jerry arrives."

"If I can, Mother." Although he had never told her exactly what he did, his mother had astutely surmised that he was somehow privy to information that others were not.

As they rounded the corner, both were gladdened to see the relatively short queue in front of the Empire Cinema.

"Lovely," said Iris Hamilton. "Shouldn't be long."

Winston shook his head as if to clear his vision. His pulse was racing. He had seen her. Even though her back was turned to him he was certain that it was she. Near the end of the queue, about four or five couples ahead of him, was the woman he had dreamed about for more than a week.

She appeared to be alone.

Winston watched her, mesmerized by the way she moved, and as the line began to move forward he noticed that she was fumbling with her purse. As she reached the ticket window, she stepped out of the line and, a look of distress on her face, continued to rummage through the purse.

Just as Winston and his mother reached the ticket window the woman gave an exasperated sigh, pushed her hair away from her face, and looked up. Winston, caught staring, flushed in embarrassment.

"You again."

"Yes," he managed. "Me again."

She smiled but said nothing. He forced himself to speak. "Are you having a problem?"

"Apparently I've come out without any money. I suppose I'll have to go home and come back for the next show."

Winston cleared his throat. This was all taking place as if he had planned it. He even knew what to say next. "Perhaps," he said while his mother, mystified by all this, tugged impatiently on his sleeve, "you would allow me to pay for your ticket."

"I couldn't," she protested.

"It's no bother . . . really."

She sighed and he knew that she would accept. "Well," she said, "thank you. It would save me a great deal of bother, and I will repay you."

"No need," said Winston exultantly. It was almost as if he were following a preplanned script.

Iris Hamilton stood beside her son and gave him a nudge with her elbow. Her lips were tight and her eyes narrowed in

117

suspicion. She had detected the woman's barely perceptible foreign accent. She watched with interest as her son displayed a side of his character she had never seen before.

"Allow me," he said, "to introduce my mother. Mrs. Iris Hamilton." He gave a brief, almost elegant bow. "I am Winston Hamilton."

"And I am Marie Price," said the woman, extending her hand. She saw Mrs. Hamilton's eyes go to the other hand. "Mrs. David Price," she added.

Iris Hamilton nodded and, as Winston paid for the tickets, asked quietly, "Your husband, dear, is he in the forces?"

Marie closed her eyes for a moment. "He was with the BEF in France. He didn't make it back."

Iris Hamilton softened. "P.O.W.?" she said hopefully.

Marie shook her head, letting her hair fall in front of her face. She managed a small sniffle. "I'm afraid not. I've had a telegram from the War Office telling me that he'd been killed in action."

Iris Hamilton touched Marie on the shoulder. "Poor dear," she said. "You just come on in with us and forget your troubles for a while."

Inside they sat with Marie between Winston and his mother. Winston, sure that he was the envy of every man in the cinema, felt at least twice his normal size. When the lights went down and the movie began, he found it was impossible to concentrate on the screen. Marie's perfume filled his senses.

When Ronald Colman left for the front there wasn't a dry eye in the house, and Winston was overjoyed when Marie put her hand in his as she cried into her handkerchief.

When the show was over they emerged into a quickening nightfall and Iris Hamilton insisted that Winston walk Marie home. "You never know what you'll run into on a night like this," she said as she pushed them off together. "It's not like it used to be when I was a girl."

After their obligatory protests she watched them walk off together. Poor dear, she thought. She needs someone to take care of her—and so does my Winston. I won't be here forever. She watched them until they had disappeared around the corner, noting, before she crossed the street for the bus stop, that Winston seemed taller than he usually did.

Winston was silent for most of the walk to Marie's flat. On

the way he fantasized a little about what would happen when they arrived at her place. He would be strong and forceful, and she would invite him in for a drink or some tea. They would chat for a while and perhaps listen to some music. He wondered if she enjoyed classical. She looked more like someone who liked Swing. But, no matter. Whatever she enjoyed was fine with him.

When they arrived at the outside entrance to her flat, his fantasy was shattered in one blow. "Thank you," she said, offering her hand. "You've been very nice."

With great difficulty he was able to say, "I'd—I'd like to see you again."

She was silent and he steeled himself. It's too soon after her husband's death, he rationalized. His expression was a mixture of hope and despair.

Finally she spoke. "I haven't gone out with anyone since my husband was killed."

"I understand completely," he said, backing away.

"But I think it would be nice," she said, stopping his retreat. "I could use a friend—someone to be with from time to time."

Winston couldn't believe his ears. "That would be wonderful," he said.

"When?" she asked.

"When?" he repeated and then his eyes widened in comprehension. "Would Friday be too soon?"

"Not Friday," she said. "I'm busy on Friday." She smiled. "But Saturday would be lovely."

He grimaced. "I have the late shift on Saturday."

"Oh," she said, disappointment spreading across her face.

"I'll exchange shifts with someone," he said.

She brightened. "Promise?"

"I promise," he said. He had taken enough Saturday nights for others, he thought. Surely someone could exchange with him. "Perhaps we could have dinner?"

"That would be nice," she said.

Winston felt as if he were floating above the pavement. They said goodbye and he waited until she had gone inside before turning and walking away. He had not gone ten steps before he realized that he was whistling to himself. He had to restrain himself or else he might have broken into a happy trot.

Marie watched him from the second-story window. "Poor creature," she said over her shoulder.

"Never mind, poor creature," said Daly, who stood behind her. "What did you find out?"

She turned to look at him. He sat in her chair by the fireplace. "Not much," she said. "Other than that he lives with his mother and seems very lonely."

"I mean about his job. What he does at the government offices."

She shrugged. "He didn't say anything, but his mother told me that he had a very important job with the Army. I think she was trying to impress me."

"Never mind the mother. It's him we want to impress."

"He seems quite nice," she said. "Sad but nice."

"Looks like the kind who has trouble getting it up." Daly smiled wickedly. "This could be a real challenge for you."

"Don't worry about my part," she said confidently. "I'll find out everything he knows. You just worry about what you're going to tell your German friends when I do."

WILLKIE HOLDS GALLUP POLL LEAD; PRESI-
DENT TRAILS IN ELECTORAL VOTE; CHAL-
LENGER AHEAD BY 284 TO 247 MARGIN

NEW YORK, AUG. 23

◆ *CHAPTER 15* ◆

Friday, August 23—On Friday afternoon when Maxwell Munro returned to his office from the code room, he found an envelope on his desk and was surprised to find inside an invitation to dinner at the Ambassador's country residence in Sunningdale at Windsor Crest Park. This was the first word he had heard from the Ambassador since their conversation the previous week. There was no RSVP on the invitation so

Munro assumed it was expected he would appear at the dinner.

He was reading the *London Times* account of the massive German air raids of the previous morning and afternoon when Colonel Jackson knocked on the open office door. "Hope I'm not interrupting anything?" Jackson said.

Munro stood up. Even though neither man was in uniform, it was still customary to show respect to a superior officer. "No, sir."

Jackson came into the room. Do you mind if I sit down?" he asked.

"Please do," said Munro, waiting until Jackson was seated before he sank back into his seat.

"Well," said Jackson, "how are things going with you?"

"About as well as can be expected, Colonel."

Jackson sighed softly, "Yes, I'm afraid that things have not been ideal for you here. I haven't been very much help to you in that regard."

"You've been busy, Colonel. There is a war on."

"Yes, it seems that I'm always off to one government agency or another. I've been very busy escorting the military observers who arrived from Washington last week. The War Department never seems satisfied with the amount of information they receive about how the war is going."

Jackson got up, closed the office door and returned to his seat. "As you know," he said, "there is a great diversity of opinion here at the embassy about what role the United States should play in the war. I'll be direct, Captain. I would like to know where you stand on this question."

Munro could not keep the Roosevelt-Churchill correspondence from his mind and wondered how much the Colonel knew. "I'm not sure, Colonel. I find myself straddling the fence. Like my father and the Ambassador, I want the United States to stay out of this war. But unlike my father and the Ambassador, I want to give the British as much material assistance as we can without weakening our own defensive position."

Jackson smiled. "I don't think anyone here would quarrel with that position."

"I think the Ambassador might," said Munro.

"Perhaps the Ambassador doesn't know you as well as he thinks he does."

"I'm sure of that," Munro said. He held up his dinner invitation. "I doubt if he'd be inviting me out to his house if he knew that I don't share his position."

Jackson reached into his inside jacket pocket and pulled out his invitation. "Perhaps we can ride out together."

"Thank you," said Munro. "I assume that others from the embassy will be there."

"The high-level delegation of officers from the War Department, Admiral Ghormley and Generals Emmons and Strong, will be there. They are here to serve as observers and they will be the Ambassador's guests this weekend. David Carson, the Charge, will be there, and, I'm sure, some of the Ambassador's henchmen along with several other embassy staffers. The senior military attachés will all be there, but" —Jackson gave a stiff-lipped smile—"as far as I'm aware, you will be the only junior member of the military staff invited."

Munro looked at the invitation in his hand. "This ought to secure my position—or lack thereof—with the rest of the staff."

Jackson stood. "I'll have my driver swing past your hotel at about six," he said.

"Fine. Thank you. I'll be ready."

Jackson moved to the door. "I'm glad we had this talk, Maxwell," he said, and Munro realized it was the first time he had been addressed by his given name since he'd arrived at the embassy.

The Ambassador's country residence was less than an hour by car from London, and Munro, Colonel Jackson, and David Carson arrived at a little past seven. The entire ride had been consumed with conversation about the massive German air raids of the past week.

"I'm sure this is the big push the Germans have been threatening for some time," said Carson.

"Most definitely," said Jackson. "They've hit the airfields, hoping to knock out the RAF's ability to respond."

Carson went on. "I understand that the airfields at Middle Wallop and Martlesham were knocked out of action yesterday, and that Tangmere was a shambles after this afternoon's raid."

"I've got a friend out at Tangmere," Munro said. "College

pal who's with the RAF now. Maybe I should get out and see him."

"My information says that all the airfields will be back in full operation by tomorrow morning," said Jackson.

"The British are claiming over a hundred and sixty kills yesterday as compared to losses of only thirty-five," said Munro.

"Somewhat optimistic, I'd say," said Carson, puffing on his pipe.

Jackson agreed. "But even if they exaggerate by a factor of two, the loss ratios are more than the Germans can put up with."

When they arrived at the Ambassador's seventy-room mansion, they found that many of the other guests were already there. Predictably, the air raids continued as the main topic of conversation, with the recently arrived American military observers particularly interested in the RAF's ability to withstand the German assault. The Ambassador was already espousing his philosophy of doom.

"This is it," he was saying, standing in the middle of a circle of his guests. "This whole damn shooting match will be over in two weeks. That prick Churchill has been goading Hitler all summer, and now the chickens have come home to roost." The Ambassador turned as one of the servants led Munro, Jackson, and Carson into the huge drawing room, where the guests were having pre-dinner cocktails. "There you are," he said, addressing Jackson, a huge smile on his face. "What's happening in London? Churchill give up yet?"

Jackson's smile was minuscule. "Everything seems quite calm. The British seem quite confident of their ability to hold off the Luftwaffe."

"Let's see how they feel next week," Kennedy said.

He introduced his new arrivals to the other guests —Jackson, of course, already knew the American observers. There were no British nationals present. Munro had heard that dinner at Kennedy's estate was usually an occasion for British government and military officials to rub elbows with the American Embassy personnel. This evening, Munro thought, would be an all-American affair.

That thought was ammended when the Ambassador's aide, Terrence Wymore, walked into the room with a stunning blonde on his arm. The Ambassador's eyes lit up like a Christmas tree when he saw her. "And this," he said in a voice that demanded attention, "is Mademoiselle Maillaud. Until recently, Miss Maillaud was one of the top photographer's models in Paris."

Miss Maillaud gave everyone a sad-eyed smile and, Munro noted, a brief nod to the Ambassador. She was indeed beautiful—tall, angular, mysterious—with long blond hair that veiled half of her face. For a moment all conversation stopped as Miss Maillaud became the focus of attention.

"My friend Terry here," said the Ambassador, "was fortunate enough to make her acquaintance recently at a dinner we held for the Free French." Kennedy took the woman's hand, "It's so nice to see you again."

Munro, who, with the possible exception of Miss Maillaud, was outranked by everyone in the room, found himself a quiet spot on the arm of a chair next to the fireplace and settled down to watch what was happening. The Ambassador dominated the show, paying particular attention to the new observers. He would engage each one individually, but in a voice loud enough for everyone to hear. He emphasized his remarks with a finger poke to the chest of his target. The message, with minor variations, was basically the same to all. "This is a lost cause . . . the Germans can't be stopped . . . everything in England will go to hell just as it has in France . . . we've got to learn to accept the fact that the British Empire is finished . . . we can do business with Hitler."

More guests arrived. Kennedy introduced the Second Secretary of the Hungarian Embassy, Josef Benke, to the other guests. A beautiful young woman made her entrance, escorted by Anthony Sutton of the Embassy staff. She, too, Kennedy explained, worked for the Free French. Her name was Marie Price and Kennedy made a great show of kissing her hand. Munro saw Renee Maillaud's eyes narrow, ever so slightly, as she watched the Ambassador.

Marie Price seemed to be a young woman of great presence, thought Munro. She was beautiful in a way that, to his taste, Renee Maillaud's chiseled features could never match. There was a softness about her, a quiet dignity that, in contrast to Renee Maillaud's icy detachment, made her seem warm and approachable. She made the rounds, with Sutton, shaking hands, making eye contact, and smiling pleasantly when she was introduced to the higher brass. When she was introduced to Munro, her eyes widened slightly, as if, Munro thought, she seemed somehow surprised to meet him. She gave him a bold, appreciative look, and during the brief introduction, held on to his hand.

Just before eight Betty Donaldson arrived with Toby Graham, the air attaché. Graham immediately sought out Colonel Jackson and the two talked for a few minutes before Jackson went to the American observers.

While this was going on, the Ambassador's voice boomed across the room. "There you are," he called as Betty Donaldson entered. "I thought you would never get here."

Betty smiled pleasantly. "Colonel Graham was delayed by some business at the embassy," she said. "We got a late start."

Kennedy put his arm around her waist and drew her into the room. "This," he declared to the assembled guests, "is Betty Donaldson of *Time* magazine, the best-looking reporter on two continents."

Betty expertly disengaged herself from his grasp and went about the business of saying hello to everyone. "How are you, Admiral Gnormley? Nice to see you again. General Strong. We met at the White House last year."

"I remember it well, Miss Donaldson. Your little lecture on Poland, as I recall, was very informative."

With the exception of the women, Betty seemed to know almost everyone, and had something to say to everyone she saw.

Munro watched her. It was the first time he had seen her in a dress since that first day in his office, and she looked stunning. Her hair was down and it bounced as she walked. She wore a tight-fitting dress that clung to her lithe figure and emphasized her long thighs and delicately muscled calves.

At dinner the Ambassador continued his monologue against American participation in the war. He sat at the head of the long table and, in a crisp, clear, confident voice, delineated every aspect of the conflict.

The military observers, who were there to discover such things for themselves, sat in silence.

Munro watched Renee Maillaud, who sat across from him next to Terrence Wymore. Wymore was, as usual, enthralled by his boss's remarks, and was completely oblivious to the beautiful young woman by his side.

After dinner the Ambassador turned philosophical. "I've done as much as any man could do," he said, waving his cigar like a baton. "I've dedicated my life to keeping us out of this mess." For a moment he was pensive then went on. "In 1938, you know, we were on the brink of war. Hitler was ready to move into Czechoslovakia, and England and France were prepared to challenge him." He shook his head sadly and said, almost to himself, "Who the hell would go to war over Czechoslovakia?" Then looked up with a smile. "It was just before the Munich conference, and things really looked bleak. They were handing out gas masks and digging air-raid shelters in the parks in London." He paused, flicking his ash onto the floor and looking down the table at the row of attentive faces. "I sent for Charlie Lindbergh, who happened to be in Paris at the time. He flew in the next day and I had him give the British a blow by blow description of what they could expect if they went to war with Germany. Lindbergh talked about how the Germans could bomb any city in Europe into rubble at any time they wanted. Anyway, the next day Chamberlain flew off to Munich with a copy of Lindbergh's report in his briefcase and came back with an agreement that could have meant peace in our time." The Ambassador smiled. "I like to think that I had something to do with that."

"I'm sure that you did, Mr. Ambassador," said General Strong. "Too bad, it didn't last."

Admiral Ghormley chipped in. "It's very possible that Hitler construed Chamberlain's dedication to peace as weakness. It may have contributed to Hitler's aggressive behavior."

Kennedy's face reddened and his eyes narrowed. "You don't know Neville Chamberlain," he said, struggling to control his growing anger, "or you wouldn't say that. The man is the only Englishman that I have any respect for. I hate the rest of these goddamned Englishmen, from Churchill on down. He is a belligerent, drunken blowhard." He ground out his cigar in the ashtray as if squashing Churchill's image. "He's passed out until noon every day and spends his waking hours in a drunken stupor." He paused, looking into every face at the table.

The table was stunned into silence by the Ambassador's caustic remarks. Most were well aware of his propensity for intemperate statements, but, for once, he seemed to have outdone even himself.

Betty Donaldson was the first to break the silence. "Can I quote you on that, Mr. Ambassador?" She flashed a mischievous smile around the table, breaking the tension that enshrouded them like thick cigar smoke. They knew the unwritten rule, as well as she did, that private comments such as this were never reported without the speaker's permission.

Kennedy, his anger gone as quickly as it had come, gave her a huge grin. "Only if you want to see me on the carpet at the White House."

Everyone chuckled, thankful that an embarrassing moment had passed. Maxwell gave Betty an appreciative nod, but if she understood his gesture, she did not acknowledge it.

"I doubt that I'm going to be here much longer anyway," Kennedy said. "As soon as this war is over, I'm getting out of here."

Colonel Jackson spoke for the first time. "The British don't seem to think it will be over anytime soon." He spoke softly, but his words were almost a challenge.

The Ambassador stared at Jackson but the Colonel's eyes did not waver.

"Perhaps," said Kennedy, "when the bombing begins in earnest there will be a little less of this wishful thinking. I hope the British will be ready to face facts before the Luftwaffe turns London into rubble. In any event, I'm not going to sit around and get my ass blown to bits. After the first good air raid, I'll be on my way home." He looked around the table and said, "I've got a wife and a very large family to provide for. That's all I care about."

"It seems, Mr. Ambassador, that the President wants you to stay here," Betty said.

Kennedy laughed. "And for good reason. He wants to keep me out of the way until the election is over. He doesn't want the American people to hear what I have to say. I don't much care what he wants."

"Surely," General Strong said, "you must have some loyalty to the President?"

"Loyalty?" Kennedy said. "Let me tell you about loyalty. If it hadn't been for me, Franklin Roosevelt wouldn't be in the White House today. I financed his campaign. And at the '32 convention, when it looked like he was finished, I put together the votes that gave him the nomination. Me," he said, a finger poking at his chest. "No one else. And what did I get for it? A slap in the face and then, after cooling my heels for months, a bullshit job with the Securities and Exchange Commission." He pounded a fist on the table. "I should have been given a cabinet appointment. I earned it. Instead, the big jobs went to his do-nothing liberal cronies. They know more about loyalty in the wards in the East End of Boston than Roosevelt ever will. In Boston we don't turn loyal supporters into seventy-five-dollar-a-week errand boys."

When the gathering returned to the drawing room, Betty Donaldson approached Munro. "I have to talk to you about something," she said, then noticed that he still had his eye on Renee Millaud. "Munro," she said. "Don't you know who she's with?"

"Wymore."

"She's with Kennedy. Wymore is his cover. That's how they operate. It wouldn't do for the Ambassador to entertain his lady friends in public, so Wymore acts as his 'beard.'"

"I'll be damned," said Munro. "Who would figure it?"

"Look, I want to visit one of the airfields that have been hit hard by the Germans. American reporters aren't allowed to talk with the aircrews. Can you do anything? I'd need official permission and papers to get into the no admittance areas."

"I'll see what I can work out," he said.

They were joined by General Emmons and Colonel Jackson. Emmons seemed ebullient. "Well, Miss Donaldson, what do you think of our Ambassador?"

"He certainly speaks his mind," Betty said.

"Yes," said Emmons, "a real straight shooter. We could use a few more like him."

Jackson gave Munro a quick look. "The diplomatic service," he said, "is rarely known for its straight shooters."

Emmons raised his drink in salute. "They could use a few more smart fellows like Kennedy."

"What we need in the diplomatic service," said Jackson, "are ambassadors who are wise and show sensitivity to the great forces which are playing across the map of the world."

"Right," said Emmons. "Damn smart fellows, like Kennedy."

"Absolutely," Colonel Jackson said, a thin smile on his face.

They were interrupted by Terrence Wymore, who spoke to Jackson and Emmons. "The Ambassador would like to have a word with you both in his study."

Munro turned to see several other officers filing toward the door and Ambassador Kennedy making profuse apologies to the other guests.

"You must forgive me," Kennedy was saying. "I know it's rude, but I must speak to the military and embassy people about something that has just been brought to my attention. I promise we'll all be back in a few minutes." The Ambassador addressed the room. "Just have a seat and another drink. We'll be back shortly."

Those who remained were divided into several small conversational groups. Renee Maillaud sat by the fireplace, staring into the flames. Munro turned to Betty, who sat nearby. "Looks like it's just you and me."

"Colonel Graham told me that the Ambassador had assigned you to the code room."

"Which means," Munro said, grinning, "that I spend most of my time reading the newspaper."

While Munro talked briefly about his job, Betty looked around the room, coming to a halt when she saw Marie Price. The woman was astonishingly beautiful, she thought, and suddenly felt rather ordinary.

As Betty continued to watch her she noted that Marie was also scanning the room. Betty followed the direction of the woman's gaze and saw that Price had made eye contact with the Hungarian, Benke. Benke gave Price a brief nod, then quickly looked away, but there was something in that almost imperceptible nod that intrigued Betty Donaldson.

A few moments later Marie Price walked over to the fireplace near them.

Betty turned her attention back to Munro. "Your new job sounds interesting," she said.

"Actually rather dull—most of it anyway," Munro said.

"But," said Marie Price, speaking directly to Munro, "it is a very important job, and you get to read many things of great importance."

"Sure," said Munro.

"I envy you," said Marie. "Most of us must read the newspapers to find out what is going on in the world."

Betty wondered why Price was suddenly so interested in Munro. Maybe it was just her suspicious reporter's nature, but she couldn't dismiss that brief, silent signal between Marie Price and Josef Benke. She didn't like Benke, anyway. He was too smooth. For a Hungarian he was more English than most of the Englishmen she had met since her arrival. Look out, Munro, she thought.

Betty turned slightly in her chair. From across the room, his eyes narrowed in a stare, Josef Benke had his eyes fixed on Munro. The intensity of his stare was frightening.

Betty tried to get Munro's attention. "Can I talk to you about the visit to the airfields?" she said.

"Later," he said.

The Ambassador and the others came back into the room with profuse apologies to those who had been left behind.

Colonel Jackson approached Munro. "I'll be staying here this evening," he said. "The driver can take you back."

"What's going on?" Munro asked.

"Nothing really," Jackson said, his voice almost a whisper. "The observers will be meeting with the British Chiefs of Staff tomorrow and the Ambassador wants the observers and a few of the embassy people to stay the night so that we can have a kind of round-table discussion on how to approach the British. We'll be back in the city tomorrow afternoon."

The party resumed but had obviously lost steam. Those guests who were not staying the night began to make preparations for leaving. Toby Graham came over to Betty Donaldson.

She saw the apologetic look on his face. "Looks like you're staying," she said.

"Yes," he said. "I'll arrange transport for you."

She chuckled at the way he said "transport." It made her feel like a shipment of military supplies.

"You can come back with Carson and me," Munro offered.

"Carson's not staying?" she asked.

"No," said Graham. "He has business to attend to back at the embassy."

"Very well, then," said Betty. "I'll go with them." She turned and walked away.

The guests were leaving and the Ambassador was everywhere, talking with everyone, thanking them for coming, smiling jovially, shaking hands.

Betty returned in time to overhear Marie Price telling Munro about the wonders of Switzerland. "You would love it. It is the most beautiful country in the world."

"I'd like to see it sometime," he said.

"I would love to show you."

"Carson has sent for the car," Betty said.

They walked to the door, where servants were holding coats. Marie scrambled in her purse and removed a pen and a small piece of paper. She scribbled quickly and pressed a note into Munro's hand as she said good night.

He did not look at it until she was gone. When he did, he saw that she had written her address and phone number and a single word—*soon*. He grinned and turned to Betty Donaldson, who stood nearby. He held up the note and said with a wink, "Boyish charm, I guess."

In the car they rode in silence for a long time. Even the usually garrulous Carson seemed lost in thought. Munro watched the darkened shadows of trees rush past the country roads and wondered about Switzerland in the summertime.

"I've been thinking, Betty, about your visit to one of the airfields," Munro said.

"Really," Betty said. "I would have thought you'd be preoccupied with planning a trip to Switzerland."

"I have a buddy with 43 Squadron down at Tangmere. He's an American. We went to college together. I thought you might be interested."

"An American?"

"Yes. He's been with the RAF since May. Just went on active duty a month ago. Maybe we could ride out to see him on Sunday?"

"That might be a good story," she said. "Back home they love stories about Americans involved in the war."

"Well," Munro said. "Billy-boy is about as involved as you can get."

WILLKIE CAMPAIGN IN HIGH GEAR ACROSS
NATION; THOUSANDS CHEER CHALLENGER AT
MIDWEST RALLIES; ROOSEVELT'S FOREIGN,
DOMESTIC POLICIES DENOUNCED

RUSHVILLE, IND., AUG. 24

◆ *CHAPTER 16* ◆

Saturday, August 24—When Marie Price opened the door, she was wearing a blue bathrobe and matching slippers, her hair was in disarray, and she looked surprised to see Winston Hamilton standing on her doorstep.

The expectant smile slipped from Winston's face. "You've forgotten," he said. "We were going to have dinner this evening."

Price smiled. "I haven't forgotten. It's only that I've just this minute gotten home. I've been terribly busy today." She swung the door wide open. "Please come in. I'll be ready in no time."

Winston Hamilton stepped inside. The apartment was small but decorated in what he thought was quiet good taste. There was a small sitting room with a kitchen in one corner, and what was apparently a bedroom through a partially opened door to the left. From a second door Winston could hear the sound of running water.

Her eyes followed his look. "I was just about to take a bath," she said.

Winston's face reddened.

Marie sensed his discomfort. "Let me pour you a drink," she said, guiding him to the sofa, "and you can make yourself comfortable while I get ready."

"Perhaps," said Hamilton, "I should come back in an hour or so?"

She laughed. "Don't be silly. I'll be ready in no time." She tightened the belt around her waist, went into the bathroom, and turned off the water. In a moment she was back. "Now," she said, "what can I get you?"

"Whiskey," he said.

"That's fine," she said with a laugh. "That's all I've got."

While she poured his drink she chatted on aimlessly about her trying day. Winston half-listened as he tried desperately to acclimate himself to what was, for him, a completely alien situation. He had rarely been alone with a woman, never mind alone with a woman in her apartment. There had been that one girl in Leeds several years ago, he thought, but she was rather ordinary looking and almost as desperate as he. Marie Price had completely bewildered him from the beginning. For the first time in his life a beautiful woman—the kind he had dreamt about or watched on the screen in a lonely succession of darkened cinemas—had seemed attracted to him. She had quietly, but somewhat obviously, encouraged his attentions. If she had not done so he could never have mustered the courage to approach her. It must be the war, he thought. If the world were not turned upside down, a woman like this would never pay him a moment's heed.

With a sudden start he realized that she was standing in front of him, holding his whiskey. He took the glass from her. "I'm sorry," he said, "my mind was elsewhere."

She smiled forgivingly. "I'm sure you have lots on your mind."

Winston Hamilton sipped his drink as Marie Price cinched the belt on her robe as it began to slip open. Winston was suddenly, painfully aware that beneath the robe she was more than likely naked. The thought made him gasp.

"Too strong?" she said. She held out her hand. "Let me put some water in it."

"No. No. It's fine . . . really," he protested and took another sip to reassure her.

"I was telling you about my day," she said. "And I asked you about yours, but your mind was apparently on something else."

"I'm sorry," he said. "I do tend to drift off sometimes."

She sat on the arm of a chair across from him. She pulled the robe closed around her legs but not before he had been permitted a brief look at her bare thighs. "How was your day?"

Winston took a hefty drink from his glass. "Rather ordinary," he managed, but his mind was still on that fleeting moment of thigh.

"I'm sure that a 'rather ordinary' day for you would be rather extraordinary for almost everyone else."

"Not really," he said, and had another sip.

"Don't be so modest," Marie said. "From what little you've told me, I know how vital your work is."

Winston couldn't really remember telling her much of anything about his work, but it pleased him that she assumed that it was significant. It wasn't easy having an important position and not being able to tell anyone about it. He sipped at his whiskey. "Actually—even though it is essential—the work itself is rather boring."

Marie moved closer, sitting next to him on the couch. "You don't expect me to believe that?" she said, her hand resting on his knee for just the briefest of moments.

Electric shocks raced from his knee to every point of his body. He drained his glass.

She looked into his eyes and her voice grew soft. "I can tell when a man has an important job," she purred. "There's something about the way he carries himself. A kind of quiet confidence. A look in his eyes."

Winston's face was flushed. "Well, I'm not sure that I . . ."

She went on as if he had not spoken. "That look is what attracted me to you. Something that I saw in your eyes."

How marvelously perceptive of her, he thought. Not many women had ever looked beyond his admittedly ordinary exterior and been able to discern the singular person within. He could not keep the smile from his face. "What I do is important," he said. "It's not, however, the kind of thing one reads in the newspapers."

"I was sure of it," she said softly, not wanting to distract him.

"Just today, for instance," he said, "C himself told me that my work was absolutely essential to the war effort."

" 'C'?"

"Colonel Menzies—he's the man in charge." He saw that her face was a blank, so he added, "In charge of the Secret Intelligence Service . . . at Broadway . . . where I work."

"It all sounds so interesting," she said.

"I've probably said more than I should already." What amazed him was that his mother with all her prying had never been able to get him to say anything at all about his work other than the fact that it was important. This was the first time that he had ever told anyone where he worked. There really was no harm in it, he was sure, but somehow the revelation disturbed him. He looked into Marie's eyes and his doubts, although not forgotten, were pushed into the background.

"Of course, I wouldn't expect you to tell me any secrets. It's just that I find this sort of thing so terribly exciting."

Her eyes, incredibly blue—as blue, he thought, as the waters of a tropical lagoon—held him in their grasp, a grasp as firm as any predator's. She held him as surely as if she had reached out to embrace him, wrapping him in her arms, immobilizing him, squeezing him. The air in the room had quite suddenly vanished, and there was a buzzing noise in his brain.

With a smile Marie Price blinked and released him. He took in several long draughts of delicious air, feeling suddenly light-headed and bathed in a euphoric glow.

She watched him, assessing her power over him, smiling as his trembling fingers brought the empty glass to his lips. In her world life was a struggle for ascendancy. Just as she was powerless against Sean Daly and others like him, there were those, like Hamilton, who were powerless in her grasp. It was a game, much like the game played by nations, where the powerful took from the powerless, and the powerless took from the even more powerless. She would take from this one whatever she wanted and make him beg her to take more. She knew what he wanted from her—even if he himself was unsure of what that was. She would tantalize him, torture him, make him surrender his soul before she gave him what it was he craved.

There was a silence between them and for one fleeting moment Winston thought that something wonderful or terrible—or both—was going to happen, but Marie looked away and the moment passed.

She stood up, again cinching the belt of her robe. "I'd better take my bath now," she said softly, "or else we'll never get out of here."

She paused and stood quietly in front of him. Winston felt that there was an invitation in her words that he had only to act upon, but he was uncertain what that action might be. So he did nothing.

"Let me get you another drink," she said and before he could protest she had taken his glass from him.

She gave him his refilled glass and then disappeared into the bathroom. "I'll leave the door open a crack," she said, "so that we can talk while I'm in the bath. Help yourself to another drink when you're ready."

She left the door open about six inches and Winston could feel his heart start to pound. From where he sat he could look into the bathroom and even see part of the tub. He knew that he should look away, and for a moment he was able to force himself to do so, but his eyes found their way back to the opening in the door. When Marie Price passed in front of the opening and stepped into the tub, all he could see was a blur of flesh and hair—a bare arm, a leg, perhaps a naked back—but it was enough to make him shiver. She obviously was unaware he had been able to see her pass in front of the door.

He heard the water splash as she settled into the tub and then her voice through the door. "How delightful," she said. "There is really nothing like a warm bath to wash away the cares of the day—don't you think?"

Winston could only emit a strangled cough.

"What were we talking about?" she asked. "Oh, yes—how important your work is."

For a moment he heard only the splash of the bath water and caught a brief glimpse of her arm. Everything around him seemed painted in flesh-tones. He gulped down half of his drink.

"I'm sure that you could tell some wonderful stories about how exciting your work is."

"It's really not all that exciting," he said, trying to keep his eyes away from the door.

"You can't fool me," she said. "I can feel the excitement . . . it arouses me just to think about it."

He drained his glass, beginning to feel the effects of the liquor. The whiskey had made him sweat, and he wanted to loosen his collar. "I suppose that sometimes it can be rather thrilling," he said, getting up and pouring himself another drink. Better make it a short one, he thought.

He returned to the couch, his eyes glued to the bathroom door, all pretense of gentlemanly behavior gone. He wanted to see her. She was talking from behind the door, but he was barely able to comprehend what she was saying. It was as if all his other senses had shut down so that his eyes could concentrate on the tantalizingly narrow opening.

Suddenly she was there. Incredibly she stood in front of the opening, toweling herself dry while she made casual conversation. As she moved, various parts of her anatomy passed into and out of his view—a thigh . . . an arm . . . a breast . . . a shoulder . . . a hint of pubic hair . . . a leg . . . again a breast. Winston could barely breathe.

Then, so suddenly that he was taken by surprise, what he had most feared happened. She lapsed into silence, but he was too preoccupied to notice. He saw only that she was standing still, affording him a full-length slice of her nakedness. He greedily ran his eyes from her ankle to her thigh, saw a rounded hip, a flat stomach, a perfect breast, a shoulder, her face. Her face! My God, she had seen him watching her. It was for only a split second, then she lowered her eyes and moved away from the door, but she had seen him. She knew.

The door opened and the object of his pain and desire stepped into the room. She was barefooted, in her bathrobe, her hair wrapped in a towel. She did not speak, nor did she look at him. She let him dangle in the flames.

He put his glass down on the table next to the sofa. He started to speak three times before the words would come. "I'm afraid I must be going."

She looked at him without speaking, forcing him to look at her before she said softly, in a voice that was barely audible, "I thought you were a gentleman."

Her suffering was painful to him. "I've behaved despicably," he said.

Enjoying his pain, she let him suffer just a little longer before she said, "It was as much my fault as it was yours. "I should have known better. I know what you men are like."

He looked up at her, "But I never should have—"

She cut him off. "Why?" Her voice was almost sympathetic. "Because you take pleasure in the sight of a woman's body? I wouldn't find you so attractive if you didn't."

"But . . ." His voice trailed off.

She approached him and touched his arm. "Sometimes," she said, "I forget how reserved you English are about"—she hesitated—"such things." She took his hand in hers. "It is actually quite charming."

His naivete was almost laughable, but in some strange way appealing—even exciting. She had to admit that Daly was right. She did find this kind of seduction stimulating. For a moment she thought that she might guide Winston's hand inside her robe and place it on her breast, or simply lead him to the bedroom, but she knew instinctively that doing so would only frighten him away—if not this time, then the next.

As if able to read her mind, he pulled his hand away. "It is entirely my fault," he said. He shook his head, trying to shake away an awful memory. "Goodbye."

"I will let you go if you'll promise to come back."

He looked away, unsure that he could ever face her again.

"Promise?" she insisted, running her fingers across his cheek.

"I promise."

She smiled. "Then run along, you naughty boy," she said. She closed the door behind him. He really was a poor fool, she thought, but rather nice. It was a shame to deceive him so. But if things went as planned, before she destroyed him, she would give him more pleasure than he had ever dreamed possible. Before this war was over, a lot of people were going to die. It was good that some of them, at least, would find pleasure.

Marie was combing her hair in front of the mirror when there was a sharp rap on the door. She recognized the knock.

"It's open," she called.

Sean Daly entered and watched her for a moment as she continued combing. With her head cocked to one side, her long hair, still wet, hung almost to her waist.

"Well?" he asked.

"Well, what?" she asked. It was her turn to exercise some power over him.

"You know what. I saw him leave. How did it go?"

"It went well. I had the poor boy climbing the walls."

Daly looked toward the bedroom.

"Not yet, darling." She laughed. "It's too soon. We don't want to scare him off."

"Did he tell you anything?"

She told him about Broadway and Colonel Menzies and Secret Intelligence, making it sound like more than it really was.

"He's our boy, all right," Daly said. "When will you see him again?"

"Soon," she said.

"It had better be soon. We need this information before the Jerries take over. A day late and it's no use at all."

"Then they won't need it anyway," she said.

"Don't you understand?" he said. "This is for us. Not them. We need to give the Germans something of value. Something worthwhile. So that they can't ignore our contribution when this is all over."

"If you say so." This game was beyond her comprehension, but if it was what Daly wanted, it was good enough for her.

"When?" he asked again.

"Don't worry. He'll be crawling back soon. We must tantalize him first. Arouse his passions."

"Forget his passions," Daly said, his voice a threatening whisper. "Just get him to talk."

"Soon he will betray his mother to get what he wants."

Daly relented. "You are a wicked bitch," he said, smiling.

She swiveled in her chair so that she was facing him. Her robe was partially open, exposing one breast. "Why don't you come over here and let me show you how wicked I can be?"

Daly took off his coat and threw it on the sofa. "I thought I'd stop by for a nice cup of tea," he said, "but it can wait."

Marie stood up and let her robe slip to the floor. She was very glad that Daly had been waiting outside.

GERMAN BOMBERS STRIKE BRITISH AIRFIELDS;
LONDON AREAS HIT; FLAMES NEAR ST. PAUL'S;
MASS RAIDS ON THAMES DOCKS, CHANNEL
PORTS

LONDON, AUG. 25

♦ *CHAPTER 17* ♦

Sunday, August 25—The RAF fighter bases lay in a great ring around the city of London. The outer rim of the ring —Tangmere, Lympne, Hawkinge, Manston, Rochford—was near the southeastern coast, while successive inner rings drew closer and closer to the city itself. Each of these airfields had been under intense attack since August thirteenth, and most had incurred extensive damage. Goering had estimated that his Luftwaffe could put the RAF out of commission in just four days, but the airfields were still operational and the pilots and their planes still lay in wait.

Betty Donaldson and Maxwell Munro had left London that morning, Munro driving an embassy staff car, for the trip to Tangmere, near Portsmouth. The row houses of suburban London had soon given way to the single-laned roads of Surrey and then to the low lying hills of Sussex. All sign posts had been removed from the roads as a precaution against the threatened invasion and Munro had to make frequent stops to make sure that they were following the right road. Fortunately manhole covers were stamped with the name of the nearest town, and telephone kiosks gave their exact location on a label inside.

Betty Donaldson laughed when Munro pulled alongside the first kiosk. "Can't you just picture German panzer units stopping at each phone booth on their way to London? This is typical of the half-assed way the English do everything."

They were stopped at a roadblock thirty miles from the coast and were required to show their passes before they could enter what had come to be called the "forbidden zone." The young corporal who commanded the roadblock was bright and cheerful and when he looked at the passes called back to his men, "Coupla' Yanks," and waved them through.

The sun was bright, the day hot, and through the open windows of the car they could hear the wail of sirens in the distance. It was impossible to tell the exact direction of the sirens' wail and although Munro stopped the car several times and both stepped out to look up, neither saw any aircraft or heard the sounds of bombing.

"What do we do if there's an air raid in progress when we get there?" said Betty.

"I don't know about you," Max said, "but I look for the nearest shelter."

Shortly before 11 A.M. they were stopped at a roadblock at the end of a narrow, hedge-lined lane. An RAF sergeant stepped forward to demand their papers. He was unarmed, but behind him stood two others, a corporal and an aircraftman, who leaned casually on their rifles.

The sergeant inspected their papers carefully. "Americans," he said, surprised. "You should have been here yesterday. Jerry gave us a real going over."

"Anything today?" said Munro.

The sergeant shook his head once. "No," he said, "it's still early. He'll probably pop over for lunch."

They were waved through and soon came to the main gate of Tangmere Station, where they again had to show their papers to a gruff sergeant. He pointed to a red brick building off the road. "Park it over there," he said. "Someone inside will take care of you."

Inside they were greeted by a young man in a blue RAF uniform. "May I help you?" he said, a bright smile on his face.

Munro extended his hand. "Maxwell Munro, American Embassy. This is Betty Donaldson from *Time* magazine. We're here to see a friend of mine."

"Pilot Officer Wiggins," said the young man, looking at Munro's hand. "Sorry," he said, holding up his own right hand which was swathed in bandages. The fingers, bright red, protruded beyond the bandages. "Bit of a burn last week."

"I'm sorry," Munro said.

Wiggins smiled. "I'm the one who's sorry. Shot down over the Channel. Lost a rather valuable aircraft. We need all we can get right now."

Wiggens turned an appreciative eye on Betty Donaldson. "What can we do for you?" he said.

"We're looking for Bill Kimmel. He's an American who is flying with—"

Wiggens interrupted her. "Wild Bill," he said with a laugh. "Everyone knows Kimmel. He's quite the lad."

"Wild Bill?" Betty said, looking with disbelief at Munro.

Munro grinned. "I told you Billy-boy was something."

"He's out on the field right now," said Wiggins. "I can take you out there if you'd like."

They piled into a minuscule automobile. Wiggins steered with his left hand, steadying the wheel with his right elbow when he had to shift gears.

Munro watched him admiringly. "Looks like you'll soon be back up there," he said.

Wiggins looked at his hand. "Hope so," he said sadly.

He drove across a grass field and stopped in front of a ramshackle hut where a dozen pilots lounged in the sun in full flying gear. Several were in deck chairs, others in wicker, a few sat on the grass, backs against the wooden hut, faces toward the sun. No one looked up at their approach.

Munro jumped out before the car had stopped. "Billy Kimmel!" he yelled. "Where the hell are you?"

Heads snapped around in Munro's direction as he raced toward them.

Kimmel came out of the hut, a frown on his face. He was lithe and lean and moved with the confidence of an athlete. He looked around, pushing aside a shock of brown hair that hung in his face. As soon as he saw Munro, he let out a roar and his face was split in a wide grin. "Maxie!" he yelled. "What the hell are you doing here?"

"Came to see you," said Munro. "To find out what you're up to."

The two embraced and pounded each other on the back, and then Munro introduced Betty, who had stood back waiting for the rituals of reunion to be over.

"She's here to write a story about you, partner," Munro

said. "To let the folks back home know what a big hero you are."

Kimmel shook hands with Betty, his eyes catching and holding hers. He introduced them to each of the pilots around the hut. Betty was amazed at their youth; most of them were no more than boys. She pulled out her notepad and immediately began questioning them about their experiences of the past few days. To the last man they were confident that they could beat back the Germans.

Kimmel and Munro stood aside watching her work. "She yours?" Kimmel asked.

"No," Max admitted.

Kimmel grinned. "Glad to hear that. She's quite a woman."

"That's the truth."

The two old friends talked while Betty interviewed the other pilots. Finally she joined them. "That's quite a bunch of guys," she said admiringly.

"The best," Kimmel said. He invited them inside the hut for tea. "It's not much," he said, "but it's sort of like home."

The interior of the hut was spartan—open windows, a table and a few chairs. Against one wall was a small stove with a kettle perched on top. Next to the door, on the floor, was a telephone.

"This isn't so bad," said Munro kiddingly. "Sort of reminds me of the fraternity dorms back at school."

Kimmel laughed, but there was little joy in the sound. "Maybe after a bad Saturday night," he said.

"If you two college boys are finished reminiscing about how you broke hearts all over Minnesota," Betty said, "I came all the way out here to interview the one and only Billy-boy Kimmel."

Kimmel put on the kettle, set out three mugs, and then sat at the table. He offered Betty a seat across from him. "Go ahead," he said. "Ask me anything you want, but if that phone rings, don't be insulted if I leave without saying goodbye."

Betty put the notebook on the table. "First of all, why are you involved in this? Lots of Americans don't think this is our fight."

"Soon enough it will be. We can't avoid this one."

Munro sat at the table listening. When the kettle started whistling, he got up, poured the tea, and placed a mug in front of each of them.

Kimmel seemed different, he thought. He still seemed to be the same old devil-may-care Billy-boy of college football fame, but there was something else. He seemed older, wiser, more mature, more substantial. It was difficult to imagine that this was the same person who had created such havoc in college. Kimmel had once been voted "Least likely to grow up" during a Homecoming Weekend at which he had serenaded a ladies' dorm in his underwear during a driving snowstorm. Munro marveled at the change in him. His answers to Betty's questions were thoughtful, reasoned, and intelligent.

One thing hadn't changed, however, and that was Kimmel's touch with women. Betty fell into Kimmel's snare just as easily as had all those impressionable coeds back in Duluth. Munro could recognize the look—the head cocked to one side, the rapidly blinking eyes, the legs crossed, the nervous motion with the hands, the touching of tongue to lips. Betty seemed almost mesmerized. Kimmel, you bastard, he thought, you haven't lost your touch.

Kimmel must have read his thoughts. He turned to Munro and gave him a wink that reminded Munro of the old days.

"Let me ask you something for a change," Kimmel said to Betty. "I'm going to be coming up to London tonight, and I was wondering if you knew of a really good place to eat."

A smile played across Betty's mouth. "I know a few good places," she said.

"Maybe you'd like to show me one?" he asked.

"Tonight? I'm not sure."

"If you were English, it would be against the law to refuse an RAF pilot," he said.

"To refuse him anything?"

"Anything," he said.

Just then the phone rang and Bill Kimmel gave a start. He jumped up from his seat and his eyes found Munro. In that instant Munro saw the fear in his old friend, and in a flash of recognition he sensed the terror of the war in the air.

The squadron leader answered the phone before it could ring again. He listened for just a moment but everyone was in motion before he gave the word. "Jerry's on his way," he said and Munro saw the fear in the eyes of the men who gave him one quick look of envy—or was it reproach—before they ran to their aircraft.

"I'm at the Savoy," said Betty as Kimmel dashed for the door.

Bill Kimmel did not look back but he waved his hand over his head in a farewell gesture as he ran across the field with the others to the waiting Hawker Hurricanes.

Munro and Donaldson watched as the men climbed aboard the aircraft. The aircrews worked feverishly, starting engines, helping pilots into parachute harnesses, and strapping them into the cockpit.

By twos and threes the aircraft began to taxi toward the grass field, and then, engines snarling and growling like caged panthers, began the long run before the sharp climb into the sky.

In minutes they were all airborne and in minutes more had disappeared from view.

The silence was eery. One moment all had been chaos —phones ringing, men yelling, engines coughing to life with a great roar, planes flung into the sky—and then a silence descended on the place as if the world had suddenly gone deaf.

Betty broke the silence. "This is perfect," she said. "I can get one helluva story out of this."

"Not to mention a good dinner tonight," said Munro.

"Thanks for bringing me out here," she said. "And thanks for coming with me."

He grinned back at her.

"Should we wait here?" she asked. "Or head back to the gate?"

"Let's wait." Munro went back inside and plopped himself down in a chair.

"Where did you meet Bill?" she wanted to know. "What was he like in school? Why did they call him Wild Bill?"

Outside they heard a car horn blowing and some muffled cries in the distance. They went to the door and saw the car that had brought them out to the hut barreling toward them. Wiggins was waving his bandaged hand at them as the car weaved back and forth on the grass.

"Get in!" he yelled as he brought the car to a skidding halt in front of the hut. They jumped in and Wiggens wheeled the car around and headed back to the administrative building.

"What is it?" asked Munro.

"The Germans have broken through," Wiggins said.

At first Munro thought the invasion was on, but Wiggins made clear his meaning. "They've gotten past the fighters," he said. "And a large formation of bombers is heading this way." He was talking in a high-pitched voice that was strangely calm. "We'd forgotten that you were out there," he said, "then I noticed your car. Thought I'd better run out and fetch you. Wouldn't want to have you there when the bombers arrive."

The sound of the sirens was deafening as they made their dash to the shelters and Betty held her hands over her ears.

"This noise is worse than the bombs," she said.

Wiggins laughed. "Not bloody likely," he said.

Suddenly there was a loud crunching sound and the car rocked. Wiggens put his foot to the floor. "Here it comes!" he yelled above the noise.

Betty and Munro looked at each other as crunch followed crunch and one bomb after another walked across the field as if some gigantic farmer had sowed a straight row of explosives. The earth rose straight up around them and showered the car with debris. Wiggens kept on going.

He slammed the car to a halt in front of a low structure surrounded by sandbags. "Go! Go!" he yelled above the noise, and all three made a dash for the shelter.

Betty slipped as she jumped from the car. "Damn shoes," she yelled, but Munro had already yanked her to her feet and propelled her forward with a shove of his hand.

They dived through the door of the shelter, Betty stumbling down the stairs and Munro tumbling in on top of her. As they struggled to untangle themselves, they looked around and found themselves in the center of a circle of uniformed men and women who looked at them as if they might be visitors from another planet.

"I say," someone said. "It looks as if the Americans have arrived."

Betty looked at Munro and both burst into laughter. Soon, amidst the blast of explosions, the wail of sirens, the booming of antiaircraft guns, the entire shelter was rollicking with the sound of laughter.

It was over as quickly as it had begun, and soon the all-clear was sounding. The two Americans left the shelter with everyone else and, like everyone else, did a quick survey of the destruction. Other than some gaping holes in the airstrip and a single vehicle that burned in the distance, there did not seem to be much damage.

A young officer raced over to the group of officers with whom the Americans had shared their shelter, and pulled off a snappy salute. "Preliminary reports point to only minor damage, sir," he said. "Runway Two has a few large craters. The others were missed entirely. Relatively little damage to any structures."

The officer to whom all this was addressed seemed totally unconcerned. "Get some people out to Number Two and fill in those holes," he said. "Any injuries?"

"None reported, sir."

Munro and Donaldson watched the group of officers walk back to the administrative building. They seemed calm and in control. The sound of laughter drifted back to the Americans, who looked at each other in silent wonder.

"All in a day's work," Betty said.

Munro held up his right hand, trembling fingers out-stretched. "Not for all of us," he said.

Betty touched his hand. "Thanks for picking me up back there," she said. "I should know better than to wear heels."

"It was nothing."

"But," she said, smiling, "you didn't have to throw me down the stairs—"

Munro was laughing.

"—and then land on top of me." Betty laughed too.

"I guess I was in kind of a hurry."

Wiggins approached and stood politely by until their laughter had subsided. It was something he had witnessed often and felt himself a few times. The joy of survival was absolutely euphoric. After a battle or a raid, those involved who were fortunate enough to survive were often giddy with the sheer pleasure of their own existence. After a few such experiences the euphoria began to wear a little thin, but Wiggins was wise enough to stand back and let the Americans share a little of the joy of what was more than likely their first time under fire.

Wiggins wiggled his burned fingers. The pain reminded him

how false was this feeling of joy. The euphoria was merely the mind's misinterpretation of a sensation of intense relief. The pain was the reality.

"I can take you back out to the field," said Wiggins, when the laughter had faded. "The squadron should be coming back soon."

They stood by the hut and watched the Hurricanes circle the field and then one by one peel out of formation and drop low for landing. The Hurricanes, in their brown and green mottled camouflage, looked like great, ungainly birds as they swooped low, touched wheels to the grass, bounced momentarily back into the air, and then ran down the runway.

Before the last of the planes had landed, it was obvious that two were missing. Munro turned to Betty. She knew it, too, but, like him, she was too afraid to say anything.

When the last plane had touched down and taxied to a halt, the squadron leader jumped from his Hurricane and walked over to the hut. Munro noticed that he was not looking at them. His heart sank.

The squadron leader was a small man with a thin mustache and dark, slicked-down hair. "Wilson and Kimmel," he said flatly to Wiggins. "One-oh-nine's jumped us over the Channel."

"Any chance?" asked Wiggins.

The squadron leader gave Munro a quick look as if the American's presence made all of this very uncomfortable. "Wilson got out. His wingmate saw his chute. Kimmel never got out. I followed him down myself."

Betty Donaldson gasped. Munro put his arm around her shoulders.

"We pounced on a dozen or so Heinkels," said the squadron leader. "The escorts were nowhere in sight. We got three or four of them when all of a sudden all hell broke loose. Bill was on the tail of one of the Heinkels when a 109 got on his tail. Must have got him with the first burst. He went down immediately."

The British officers were quiet. Finally Wiggins said to Betty and Munro, "I'll take you back to your car, if you'd like."

As they reached Wiggins's car the squadron leader called to them. "If you write about Bill, miss," he said, "don't forget to say what a good fellow he was."

* * *

148

Munro drove for almost ten minutes without saying anything. Betty looked at him several times, but his eyes were fixed on the road and his thoughts were far away. She could only imagine what pain he was feeling. She had felt an instant attraction to Bill Kimmel, but had only known him for what seemed like a moment. He had flashed across her life like a streaking comet, and his departure had left her with an ache in her heart, but she knew that he had been such a momentary player in her life that the pain would drift away into forgetfulness.

She looked again at Munro. The pain in his face was awful. She touched him lightly on the arm. "I'm sorry," she said. "He was a wonderful guy."

The words were like blows and she saw his face crumple under their force. Munro pulled the car over to the side of the road, buried his face into his arms, and, very quietly, began to sob.

Betty put her hand on his shoulder. "It'll be all right," she said gently, over and over.

◆ *CHAPTER 18* ◆

LISBON, Portugal, August 25—Josef Benke steadied himself against the steady rocking of the motor launch and shaded his eyes from the bright afternoon sun. He scanned the long, low dock for any sign that someone would be there to greet him. The launch which brought him ashore from the flying boat, now floating gently in the harbor, carried him and the sixteen other passengers who had braved the trip from England. Several were diplomats, but most were businessmen, the representatives of neutral countries who did business with both of the warring sides. The war had been very good for business.

Although both Britain and Germany had declared a blockade zone around Europe, ships still made regularly scheduled crossings between Great Britain and Portugal, and the clipper flights of British Imperial Airways made biweekly flights between Lisbon and Poole. This commercial travel had remained unmolested by the combatant nations and enabled those with international concerns, both diplomatic and mercantile, to go about their business.

Benke carried a leather briefcase. At his feet was a small suitcase and a leather satchel. Neither item had been beyond his reach during the five-hour flight. The satchel, like the briefcase, had been registered as containing diplomatic mail and both had been sealed against the prying eyes of the British censors. Inside the diplomatic pouch was the diplomatic mail intended for his superiors in Budapest. In his briefcase were the more important messages. These were intended for Nazi Germany.

As usual, the car and driver were waiting for him at dockside, and as Benke slid into the back seat he instructed the driver to bring the pouch and the suitcase from the launch. They drove immediately to the Hungarian Embassy, where Benke reported to the Ambassador and turned over his valuable cargo.

The Ambassador was a small, rotund man named Andras Herczeg, who believed passionately in the destiny of Adolf Hitler and National Socialism. Five years earlier Herczeg had been a history professor at the university in Pecs, a small city of seventy thousand in the coal mining region near Yugoslavia. His slavish devotion to the ideology of the German National Socialists had brought him to the attention of the Hungarian government, which increasingly grew closer to an alliance with Nazi Germany. In 1939, at the personal request of German Foreign Minister Joachim von Ribbentrop, who realized how important Lisbon would become in the coming years, the Hungarian government had appointed Herczeg to the position of Ambassador to Portugal.

Ambassador Herczeg had done his best to serve his German masters.

In the sanctity of the Ambassador's office, Benke's briefcase was opened, and its contents transferred to a leather portfolio. The clasp of the portfolio was locked and then sealed by the Ambassador himself with an elaborate wax seal that he kept in a lower desk drawer.

This ritual completed, the Ambassador looked up with a smile. "And how are things in London, Ezredes?" he said, using Benke's Hungarian military rank. "The British getting a little nervous over the coming invasion?"

Benke began with a shrug, but then, noting the look of disappointment that had begun to spread across Herczeg's face, quickly changed gears. "There is near hysteria in the streets every day. People are making preparations to flee the capital on a moment's notice."

Herczeg beamed. This was what he wanted to hear. "Have some wine," he said. "We must celebrate." He pulled a sash by the window.

Benke resisted the impulse to look at his watch. He knew that Bernhard Ritter would be waiting for him to finish with Herczeg, and he was eager to meet with the German and pass along the latest information—information that was not in either of the diplomatic pouches. He was sure that Ritter would be particularly pleased about Joseph Kennedy's comments about Churchill and Roosevelt and about several interesting pieces of information he had picked up in conversation with the newly arrived American observers.

Josef Benke was a man who knew the benefits of serving many masters. In a world as insecure as this, one never knew when a man would need as many powerful friends as he could muster. He served his own country, he served the Germans, and he had developed a special relationship with the Abwehr —a relationship, he was sure, that would serve him in good stead in the years to come.

"It is pleasing to know," Herczeg said, "that you and I have played a small part in the elimination of the British Empire."

Benke nodded. One did not argue with fools like Herczeg.

"I am sure the rewards will be great," said Herczeg. "For both of us."

There was a knock on the door and a young man appeared. His name was Janos Bisku, and he was the Ambassador's personal aide.

Bisku gave a nod that was almost a bow as he approached the Ambassador's desk. "You called, Mr. Ambassador?" he said.

Benke eyed Bisku with disgust. Fawning sycophants like Bisku were everywhere these days.

Herczeg picked up the portfolio. "I want this delivered

immediately to the German Embassy. As always, it is to be given, with my compliments, to the military attaché, General Reitmann."

Benke coughed softly and Herczeg smiled. "Of course," he said, "you will inform the General that these documents have been delivered by Josef Benke, our able Second Secretary from the London Embassy."

"I will take care of this immediately, Mr. Ambassador," said Bisku, bowing as he backed toward the door. "Good day to you both," he added, but the two men in the room had already dismissed him from their thoughts. They were toasting the success of their mission, glasses raised in self-salute, as Bisku softly closed the door behind him.

Twenty minutes later Bisku was nervously pacing the floor of a small hotel on Duque de Loule Avenue, near the Edward VII Park and across the Avenue from the American Embassy.

As Bisku paced, Oswald Peterson of the British Secret Intelligence Service carefully removed the residue of wax from the clasp on the portfolio.

"You've got ten minutes," said Bisku. "If I don't arrive at the German Embassy in fifteen minutes, I'm in trouble."

"Relax, Janos," said Peterson pleasantly. "This won't take but a minute. If you really want to move things along, you can set up the light over by the table. As soon as I open this bloody thing, I'll start taking pictures."

Bisku immediately went to the table and began to clear a space.

Peterson fumbled with the lock pick. Bisku's nervousness was contagious, he thought. "Relax," he said again, but this time as much for himself as for his companion. "If anyone questions you, you've had car trouble. We've even got the garage mechanic down there with the car now."

"Please don't talk so much," Bisku said. "Just get this over with."

Peterson returned to his work, carefully picking at the lock so as to leave no trace that the mechanism had been tampered with. "When you've finished setting up the lights," he said, "you can get the wax and the seal ready. They are in that bag on the chair."

Bisku went to the bag, reached inside, and removed the seal. The handle was not as ornate as Ambassador Herczeg's, but the seal itself was a perfect copy that the British had made from an impression given them by Bisku.

Janos Bisku admired the workmanship in the copy of the Ambassador's seal and smiled for the first time since entering the room. He was thinking of how Herczeg's face would look when someday he found out how Bisku had made an ass of him. Slowly the smile slipped from his face. He hoped that he would still be alive when that day arrived.

Monday, August 26—A satisfied Josef Benke looked down from his comfortable window seat as the Tagus River and the city of Lisbon slowly fell away beneath the wings of the Clipper. The sharp reflection of the morning sun, bouncing off the river, made him turn away from the window. No matter, he had seen the view many times.

Another productive trip, he thought, another opportunity to solidify his position with the Germans before the inevitable invasion and occupation.

He was unaware that the man in the seat three rows behind him was carrying photographs of the documents that he had brought to Lisbon only yesterday.

BRITISH BOMBERS HIT BERLIN; NAZIS CONTINUE AIR ASSAULT

LONDON, AUG. 26

◆ CHAPTER 19 ◆

LONDON, Monday, August 26—The George was a dark, drab pub on Mortimer Street, close to Broadcasting House on Portland Place, that had become the watering hole of choice for the staff members of the BBC and the American radio and newspaper correspondents who sent their daily reports on the war back to the U.S. from the BBC studios. On any given evening the local patrons could rub elbows with Ed Murrow and the other American radio correspondents, the poet Dylan Thomas, the English radio comedian Tommy Handley, or John Barbirolli, the conductor of the BBC Symphony Orchestra. For reasons unknown, it was called the Gluepot by the regulars, and although the establishment may have been short on style and decor, its distinguished clientele gave it a certain enviable ambience.

Adjusting his eyes to the dim light and the thick cigarette smoke that hung across the room, Munro waded through the crowd at the bar. American voices were everywhere. He felt a tug at his sleeve and turned to see Betty.

"I see you found it all right," she said.

She had called him an hour earlier and invited him to meet her for a drink. He knew that she was concerned about him and how he had reacted to the death of his friend. "I don't think you should be alone," was what she had said.

"Follow me," she said. "I've got a table over here."

She led him to a round table that was already crowded. They squeezed in and Betty introduced him around the table to a group of newspaper reporters who were well into a discussion of the day's air battles. Betty was the only woman at the table.

"This how you spend your nights?" Munro asked.

"Sometimes," she said, laughing.

"She's here every night," chipped in one of the reporters. "Goes home with a different guy every night, too. Don't let her tell you differently."

Betty rolled her eyes. "Newspapermen," she said. "You can't believe a word they say . . . or write."

A waitress brought beers and Munro downed half a mug in one gulp. He raised his glass to Betty. "I'm glad you called."

"Everything O.K.?" she asked.

"I'm fine. I wrote a letter to Bill's mother today."

Betty reached across the table and squeezed his hand.

For a while they sat listening to the reporters arguing about the course of the war. Most of the discussion centered on the official figures of the number of German planes destroyed by the RAF. Typically, the American reporters did not believe much of the information that was given to them. One of them looked at Munro as if soliciting his support.

"Bill Talmadge," said the reporter. *"New York Times."* He extended a hand across the table to Munro. "Nice to meet you."

Talmadge was in his thirties. His face was long and lean, and his jet-black hair was combed straight back. He wore a brown jacket and a gaily colored bow tie.

"Max is with the embassy," said Betty.

"Do you guys get the same inflated kill ratios we do?"

"I think so," said Munro.

"Look at this," Talmadge said, reaching into his inside jacket pocket. He displayed a typed sheet which he had folded down the middle. "This is the daily handout from the Air Ministry. They claim 156 German planes shot down, and losses of only 27." He looked from Munro to Donaldson. "That's almost six to one."

"Sounds like a good day," Munro said.

Talmadge made a sound like steam escaping from a burst pipe. "A good day? All of their days have been like that." He snapped at the paper with his fingers. "If you can believe this stuff."

"And you don't?"

Talmadge looked around. What he was about to say could get him in trouble with the authorities. He leaned forward, closer to Betty and Munro. "Look," he said. "I think the RAF is pretty damn good—they're doing one hulluva job —but nobody is this good." He looked around again and moved closer, and for the first time Munro realized that Talmadge was a little drunk. "I've seen the Luftwaffe in action," he said. "In Spain and in Poland. They're top-notch. Nobody pushes them around like this." He leaned still closer, his beery breath in Munro's face. "These figures are bullshit."

Munro smiled. He had asked Colonel Jackson the same question. "Perhaps not," he said, repeating Jackson's answer. "You've got to remember that the Germans are sending over a mixture of bombers and fighters, while the British are engaging them exclusively with fighters. While the fighter to fighter ratios may be closer to one to one, the British are apparently decimating the German bomber forces." He had managed to quote Jackson almost perfectly and could see that

Talmadge, and Betty, were impressed with his grasp of the situation.

"So you think these figures are accurate?" asked Talmadge.

"I think you'll find that preliminary casualty reports are notoriously inaccurate in this type of situation, and while I don't think the British are being deliberately deceitful, you could probably reduce the kill ratios by a factor of two."

"Can I quote you on that?" said Talmadge. "American Embassy official says that British exaggerate German losses?"

Munro could imagine Colonel Jackson's reaction when he saw himself quoted in the *New York Times*. "I'd rather you didn't."

Talmadge shrugged. "No problem," he said, "but I'd really like to get to the bottom of these figures."

Munro turned to Betty. "Remember the Swiss girl from the Ambassador's party? Marie Price?"

"I remember," Betty said matter-of-factly.

"There was a note waiting for me at my flat when I got home today. She said that she hopes to see me soon."

Betty sighed. "Be careful with that one."

"Careful of what?"

"She seemed very interested in the fact that you worked in the embassy code room."

"Don't tell me you think she's a spy?"

"I don't know what she is," Betty said quietly. "I just know that I saw her making some kind of signals with that Hungarian."

"Benke?"

"Right. Benke. I don't trust either of them. There's something"—she paused—"something seedy about both of them."

"Benke, maybe," Munro said with a laugh. "I don't find anything seedy about her."

Betty felt foolish. She wished she had said nothing. "I've got to get going," she said. "I have an early day tomorrow."

"I'll see you home," Munro said.

"That's O.K. I'll grab a taxi."

"It's dark out there, and cabs aren't that easy to find. I'll walk with you till you find one."

She could see he would not be easily dissuaded. "All right."

The night was pitch black and while others made their way

through the darkened streets with the aid of the sickly yellow light from hooded flashlights, neither Betty nor Munro had thought to carry such implements. He took her arm, and together, like blind men, they groped their way down Regent Street. Occasionally a shape would come lumbering at them out of the darkness and they would stop until the other pedestrian had safely passed. At street corners they paused, and, like obedient children complying with a mother's parting advice, carefully looked both ways before scurrying across the street. The few taxis they saw were engaged, and buses drifted past them like abandoned hulks adrift on a moonless ocean.

They found themselves in a crowded but strangely quiet Piccadilly Circus. "I can get a taxi here," said Betty.

"We're more than halfway there. Let's keep walking." He smiled. "It's a nice night for a walk."

She laughed and said, "We might as well be in a cave."

As they passed the Windmill Theatre the door opened and two couples stumbled out into the street. The blaring sound of loud music rushed out behind them, to be cut off in mid-note as the doors swung shut.

"Don't they know there's a war on?" Betty said testily.

"This is the place where they have the nude show girls," Munro said.

"I imagine that you're a regular here, then," she said.

"Actually, I've never been inside," he said defensively. This was a lie. He had been there once, on one of his nighttime prowling expeditions. The nudes had stood motionless and, after the initial shock, were no more erotic than Greek statuary. He had found the high-kicking show girls infinitely more attractive.

They continued in silence, down Haymarket to Pall Mall and on into the Strand. They stopped in front of the Savoy.

"Here we are," she said.

"This, I guess, is where all the American reporters stay."

"Most of them, anyway."

"I've heard it's really jumping inside."

"Sometimes," she said. "Want to come in for a drink?"

He heard the reluctance in her voice and hesitated. "Maybe I'd better not. You said you have an early day tomorrow."

Betty shrugged. "O.K. Thanks for walking me home."

Munro mumbled a goodbye and turned away.

Betty watched Munro disappear into the darkness. She was angry with him for flaunting Marie Price's note, and surprised that she had allowed her anger to show. She trudged up the steps and into the hotel. "Shit," she mumbled as she passed the doorman, but he either did not hear her or, in typically English fashion, refused to believe he had heard correctly.

LONDON AREA POUNDED IN DAY-LONG AT-
TACK; HITLER THREATENS REPRISAL FOR BER-
LIN RAIDS

LONDON, AUG. 27

◆ *CHAPTER 20* ◆

CALAIS, France, August 27—Bernhard Ritter adjusted his navy blue greatcoat, flipped the remnants of his French cigarette onto the sandy beach, and crouched slightly to affix his eyes to the Zeiss-Nicon field glasses. The binoculars, a large, clumsy, long-range pair, supported on a wood tripod, were trained upon the English coast less than thirty-five miles away. The illusion of closeness was startling. Ritter felt he could reach out and touch the chalky cliffs of Dover.

"Enticing, isn't it?" said his companion, reading his thoughts.

Ritter moved back from the binoculars and turned to Major Karl List, who stood next to him in his pale blue Luftwaffe uniform. "So near," said Ritter, smiling, "and yet, so far?"

"Exactly," said List. He was not smiling.

As an officer of the Abwehr, German Military Intelligence, Ritter had the option of wearing the uniform of his former service while he was in the field, but this morning he did not choose to wear his navy uniform. Against the early morning chill he wore his naval overcoat over a dark gray suit.

Ritter had come to Calais directly from Lisbon after a meeting with Josef Benke, his contact in the Hungarian Embassy in London, and was on his way back to Berlin to report to Admiral Canaris. Like almost all first-time visitors to the German forward positions in France, Ritter could not resist the temptation to look at the English coast through one of the long-range binoculars that had been set up in observation posts along the French coastline.

List was a fighter pilot, a squadron leader of the 2nd Squadron of the Jagdgeshwader 26 Wing, stationed near Calais. JG 26 Wing was attached to the 2nd Air Fleet under Kesselring. Being the closest to the English coast, Luftflotte 2, as it was called, had the major responsibility for the destruction of the Royal Air Force as a preliminary to the invasion of Britain.

Karl List seemed young for such responsibilities, but amongst fighter pilots he was, at twenty-eight, already old. It showed in his face. There were deep lines around his eyes, his forehead was wrinkled in a perpetual frown, and the corners of his mouth were turned down in an expression of disapproval.

Ritter looked at his old friend and struggled to keep the look of dismay from his face. When last he had seen List, just after the fall of France, the younger man had been full of youthful enthusiasm, his eyes bright and dancing, his face flushed with the wine of victory. The Luftwaffe had swept all opposition from the skies and its pilots were the heroes of the Reich. Since that time victories had not come so easily. The RAF had regrouped from the debacle of France and was putting up fierce resistance. For the first time the Luftwaffe was faced with an enemy whose determination and equipment matched their own. List's squadron was losing pilots every day in combat and the strain was beginning to show.

Ritter put his hand on his friend's shoulder. "And what does the 'fat man' have to say about all this?"

List snorted in derision. "Goering? He says that we fighter pilots are not doing enough." He stuck his hands deep into the pockets of his trousers. "That we are not being aggressive enough. That we should already have cleared the skies of British fighters. He keeps talking about our numerical advantage. If that is true, I have yet to see it."

Ritter said nothing, knowing instinctively that the younger man needed someone to listen to his frustrations.

"We only have enough fuel for about eighty minutes in the air," said List. "Escorting the bombers, it takes us about a half hour to get to most of our targets. That gives us only twenty minutes over the target—even less if we are wasting fuel waiting for the bombers. And always, hovering like angry hornets, the Spitfires are waiting for us. You should have seen them go after the Stukas—like sharks after a wounded whale. Thank God, Goering had enough sense to remove the Stukas from service. I see the faces of the Stuka pilots in my nightmares. Every mission was a death sentence for them."

"It must be very difficult," said Ritter.

They were walking along the beach, the bright sun showing promise of another glorious day, but it was still early morning cool and the breeze off the Channel made Ritter clasp his coat closed against his chest.

"One to one we can take care of them," said List. "The Me-109 is still the finest combat aircraft in the world. Don't believe all this bullshit about the Spitfire. We can out-climb them, out-dive them, out-run them, and out-fight them. Their only advantage is that we have to come to them, but in head-to-head combat our results are exceptional. Two to one, at least. They avoid us as much as they can and go after the slow-moving target or the cripples."

"I have heard," Ritter said, "that their radio detection system enables them to anticipate our every move."

"Hardly."

"I don't understand, then," said Ritter. "The information we have in Berlin is that this radio detection system allows them to anticipate each offensive thrust made by the Luftwaffe. Goering has already told Hitler that if not for this early warning, the British would have already been defeated."

"If this system is so wonderful, why is it that when the fighters go in alone we almost always catch the British by surprise with their fighters on the ground? It is only when we are burdened with the bombers that the RAF has enough time to scramble their fighters and lie in wait for us."

Ritter thought about that for a moment. What List was telling him was contrary to everything that he had been told about the radio detection and ranging system the British had perfected and used against the Luftwaffe. Stories had begun to circulate around the Bendler Block that the British detection system was an impenetrable screen that instantaneously gave warning of any German strike. According to List, the system only worked against slow-moving bombing operations. If that were the case, then perhaps the system was not as infallible as he had been led to believe.

"Explain to me," said Ritter, "how this works."

List looked around, picked up a stick, and then squatted in the sand. He scratched two parallel lines in the sand. "England," he said, pointing to one. Then the other, "France." He touched the stick between the lines. "The Channel. We scramble here," he said, pointing to a spot behind the French line. "The bombers here. We rendezvous here." He touched a spot close to the middle of his imaginary English Channel, then traced a line toward the other coast. "It takes us more than thirty minutes to get from one coast to the next. By that time they are waiting."

"What about diversion?"

"Tried it," said List. "The day before yesterday, for example. Luftflotte Three sent a bomber group with fighter protection to hit Portsmouth, then we sent a larger group out one hour later. We headed for Portsmouth hoping that they'd think it was a follow-up to the earlier raid, but at the last possible moment we veered north to hit Canterbury." He shook his head and dropped his stick to the sand.

"And?" said Ritter.

List stood up. "They were waiting for us." He slapped sand from his palms. "Just like someone had phoned them our plans."

Ritter's eyes narrowed at List's phrase.

"I guarantee," said List, "that if we had made a straight run in with fighters only, we'd have caught them with their pants down."

Ritter was thinking of something that Josef Benke had told him at yesterday's meeting, something Benke had overheard at one of the many parties he'd attended in London. "The British," Benke had said, "have decided to oppose only bombing raids. They are quite willing to allow the fighters to roam freely." If this were true it would account for the apparent ability of the fighters to get through the radio detection screen. It would not, however, account for the RAF leaving planes on the ground when the German fighters crossed the Channel alone.

"What difference is there," Ritter asked, "other than speed, between the fighter raids and the bomber raids?"

"None."

"There must be something. Are the orders any different?"

"Only in that for pure fighter operations we issue our own schedules. For bomber raids, in order to synchronize the schedules, the orders are relayed from Berlin to group headquarters and then to the individual fighter wings."

"And how are the orders transmitted?"

"Through the Enigma decoding devices," said List. "Don't worry, we thought of that possibility, also. The device is absolutely secure."

Ritter nodded, but as far as he was concerned nothing in the intelligence field was certain.

"Two weeks ago, on Adler Tag," List said, "we threw everything we had at them. We should have destroyed the RAF. It should have been within our power to do so."

"Do you doubt that it is?" asked Ritter.

List looked at him carefully. It was a question that could only be asked between close friends. "Sometimes I wonder," he said. "Theoretically we have the numerical superiority to render their air force impotent in a relatively short time. And yet . . ."

"And yet?" encouraged Ritter.

"And yet they keep coming. Their defense is as effective as one would expect from an air force of two or three times its reported size. They always seem to be in the right place at the right time."

How, Ritter wondered, was it possible for an enemy to always be in the right place at the right time?

List looked at his watch. "I must return to my squadron," he said. "There will be target briefings before we begin."

"Do you know yet what your targets will be?"

"No. Only the Fliegerkorps Commanders know the actual targets until about an hour before takeoff."

"I wish you luck and good hunting," Ritter said.

The prospect seemed to cheer List. "Good hunting," he said. "I like the sound of that."

Wordlessly the two made their way back across the beach

toward the waiting staff car. When Ritter dropped List at his airfield, he had the feeling that he was saying goodbye to his old friend for the last time.

By the time Ritter had bid his friend goodbye, Bletchley had already received and translated the Enigma messages declaring the targets for the twenty-seventh of August. Two hours before the target assignments had been given to the Luftwaffe pilots, the information had been distributed to those staff officers who had Ultra clearances, and the squadrons were put on the alert. Reinforcements were brought up from reserve units and Fighter Command dispersed the squadrons to positions from which the most effective defense could be devised.

Just as Major List had predicted, the Royal Air Force was ready and waiting for the Luftwaffe to arrive.

FLORIDA DEMS BOLT PARTY: STATEWIDE GROUP TO SUPPORT WILLKIE OVER THIRD-TERM ISSUE

WASHINGTON, AUG. 28

◆ *CHAPTER 21* ◆

BERLIN, August 28—Number 319 Potsdamer Strasse in the Zehlendorf section of Berlin was the city residence of Herbert von Dirksen, the former German Ambassador to Great Britain. Since leaving the Foreign Service with the outbreak of war, von Dirksen had been absent from Berlin and the halls of power. He had spent most of his time at his country estate in Groditzberg, Silesia, where he was ignored by the Nazi hierarchy whom he had served so well. His relationship with Foreign Minister Joachim von Ribbentrop, whom

Dirksen had succeeded as ambassador to Britain, had never been good. He would be the first to admit that he had only himself to blame for this turn of events. He had made no secret of the fact that von Ribbentrop's noble prefix had been fraudulently acquired, and he had often refused to use that appellation. He had badly misjudged von Ribbentrop's abilities, had always treated him with thinly disguised contempt, and had been as surprised as anyone that this miserable excuse for a German had somehow captured the confidence of the Führer and made rapid progress through the minefields of National Socialism.

Von Dirksen regarded himself as a victim of the vicious political in-fighting that was an integral part of National Socialism. Through a combination of miscalculation and arrogance, he had alienated Ribbentrop, the eventual victor in the Foreign Ministry sweepstakes, and unwittingly relegated himself to the backwaters of German history. Von Dirksen was a man without a patron, and, in Nazi Germany, that meant he was a nonentity. He had been rendered invisible by disfavor.

Ten days ago he had received a cable from Admiral Wilhelm Canaris of German Military Intelligence asking if he would be good enough to make himself available to the Abwehr in a matter of considerable importance to Germany. Von Dirksen had leaped at the opportunity. At last, he had thought, someone is wise enough to realize the value of my knowledge.

He had come to Berlin immediately and informed Canaris that he was at his complete disposal.

Nothing had happened for a week. Today, a telephone call had informed him that an Abwehr officer would call on him that very afternoon. Von Dirksen had been miffed at the cavalier way he was treated, but decided to say nothing. He had been too long ignored to risk the wrath of anyone who might possibly hold the key to his reinstatement.

When the doorman led Bernhard Ritter into von Dirksen's study, the former ambassador was at his desk, busily at work on a stack of correspondence. In a frame, displayed prominently on the desk, was the Iron Cross (Second Class) that von Dirksen had been awarded in the Great War. He looked up absently as Ritter entered, as though his busy schedule had led him to forget their appointment. He allowed a look of recognition to spread across his face, as if he had only then remembered that he had agreed to meet someone from the Abwehr.

Ritter hid a half smile behind a short nod of his head. He was well aware of von Dirksen's position and assumed that the correspondence on the desk was either fake or nothing more important than letters to family or friends.

The two greeted each other formally, Ritter offering the profuse thanks of Admiral Canaris, who was sorry that he could not be there personally. Von Dirksen ushered Ritter to a comfortable seat in front of his desk.

"Well, Captain," von Dirksen said, returning to his chair at the desk, "how may I be of service to the Abwehr?"

"We are," Ritter began, "interested in your personal evaluation of the American Ambassador in London, Joseph P. Kennedy."

Von Dirksen beamed. "Kennedy and I were quite close when I was in London. I was able to use that friendship to the advantage of Germany on several occasions."

"How so?" asked Ritter.

"During the Czechoslovakian crisis in '38, for example, Kennedy, who was very close to the British Prime Minister, told me that Chamberlain had absolutely ruled out the possibility of a direct confrontation with Germany over this matter. I was able to inform the Foreign Office that Germany was free to dictate whatever terms the Führer deemed appropriate without fear of English interference." He smiled. "That, of course, is exactly what transpired. With the benefit of my information, the Führer was able to send Chamberlain back to England with his hat in his hand."

"Did you ever discuss with Kennedy the benefits of supporting Germany?"

"Such a thing is not done between gentlemen," von Dirksen said. "Besides, it was hardly necessary. He was very free with political and military information, and very sympathetic to the German position in most things."

"Did he ever speak of German territorial ambitions?"

"He said that Germany should have a free rein in the East."

"It has come to our attention that Kennedy is contemplating a break with Roosevelt over the matter of aid to England. Is this consistent with what you know about the man?"

"Most assuredly," said von Dirksen. "He spoke disparagingly of Roosevelt many times, saying that he was poorly advised on Germany because of the influence of the Jews and the liberal clique. Kennedy is no admirer of Roosevelt. He did, however, show great admiration for the Führer and expressed a desire to meet him."

Ritter could barely conceal his excitement. Everything that Benke had told him about Kennedy was confirmed by von Dirksen. "You think then it is likely that there will be a break between Kennedy and Roosevelt?"

"Without doubt. Kennedy told me that he had put Roosevelt in the White House, and he could put him out any time he wanted to. He said that he controls the votes of twenty-five million Catholics who would vote for whomever he tells them to."

"Wonderful," Ritter said. "Absolutely wonderful." He clasped von Dirksen's hand. "If this comes to pass, and we have every indication that it will, the Americans will no longer be a threat to us. The British will have no alternative but to sue for peace. We can consolidate our gains on the continent without fear of interference."

"And," said von Dirksen, rising from his chair, "rid ourselves of the Jews."

The euphoria drained from Ritter's body. Von Dirksen had reminded him that there was more on the German agenda than conquest. "Yes," he said uncertainly. "There is that."

"Then we can turn to the East. The Russians must be dealt with before long."

"I must be going," Ritter said. "You have been most helpful, Herr Ambassador."

Von Dirksen followed him to the door. "You will tell the Admiral that I have been of some service?"

"Of course. As soon as I get back to the office."

"Do you think that the Admiral will report to Foreign Minister von Ribbentrop?"

"I'm sure he will," said Ritter.

Von Dirksen called to Ritter as the Abwehr officer slid into the back seat of his waiting staff car. "Tell them that I am willing to serve Germany in any capacity," he said. "Germany has need of men such as I."

Ritter slammed the door shut. "Drive," he snapped to the driver.

Ritter did not look back.

RAF AGAIN HITS BERLIN; HEAVY DAMAGE REPORTED; BIGGEST YET ON NAZI CAPITAL; RAID ANGERS REICH

LONDON, AUG. 29

◆ CHAPTER 22 ◆

BERCHTESGADEN, Bavaria, August 29—Even the majesty of the Bavarian Alps had failed to assuage the anger of Adolf Hitler. He had come here to his mountaintop retreat, three hundred and fifty miles from the tribulations and petty concerns of Berlin, to find the physical and spiritual rejuvenation that he required before deciding upon the most momentous undertaking of his political and military career. Hitler needed the tranquility of his beloved snow-capped mountain peaks. It was here that he could devote all of his considerable energies to devising the plan for the invasion of England.

He was well aware that his generals had given his plan only their lukewarm approval, but these were the same men who had been unreceptive to his plans in Poland, Belgium, Norway, and France. After his incredible successes they had rushed to congratulate him and assure him how certain they had been that his tactics would succeed. He had come to Berchtesgaden to escape the advice of such fools.

Instead, he had been driven to a fury by the news that he had received from Berlin.

On the night of August 26, British bombers had raided the German capital. The raid had been small and the damage of little consequence, but the news had had a galvanizing effect on the Führer. His promise to the German people that they were safely beyond the reach of any and all enemies had been broken. He, Adolf Hitler, had been proved wrong.

Only a week earlier, at a meeting of the German High Command in Berlin, Reichsmarschall Goering had assured his Führer that the Royal Air Force was little more than an empty shell that was on the brink of collapse. Goering had even gone so far as to repeat a joke he had made months before. "If an enemy bomber ever reaches Berlin, my name is not Hermann Goering," he said, and then, remembering the anti-Semitic punchline that had made the joke famous in Germany, he added, "You can call me Meier!" The others in attendance, Keitel, Jodl, Brauchitsch, and Halder, were not confident that the Luftwaffe had indeed destroyed the RAF as a fighting force, but, as usual, no one had been able to summon the courage to tell the Führer what he did not wish to hear. Hitler, certain of victory, had planned the invasion for September 15 and had so informed his generals.

By the afternoon of August 27, a furious Hitler had ordered his High Command to assemble at Berchtesgaden on the morning of the twenty-ninth. Over the telephone, a whining Goering had pleaded for understanding from his Führer. "It was a total surprise," said the Reichsmarschall. "A final desperate blow from a dying enemy. Now that we are aware that they would attempt such despicable tactics, we will be prepared to repel them with all the means at our disposal."

Later Hitler had regretted his display of temper. Perhaps Goering was right. Who would have believed that the British would have the criminal audacity to bomb Berlin? Only a monster like Churchill would attempt to involve the innocent civilians of Berlin in what should be a soldiers conflict. Hadn't he given explicit orders that London was to be untouched? Hadn't he offered them the most magnanimous terms that any conqueror had ever offered? He had been a gentleman about this entire conflict. It had never been his intention to engage the British Empire. He had always expressed his deep admiration for the British race and had hoped to encourage them to give up this fruitless struggle before needless blood was shed. Besides, this conflict only diverted his energies from his interests in the east. It was time, once and for all, to bring these hostilities to a close. Negotiations had proved fruitless. Invasion was the only answer. But even now he would prove to the world that he would not be provoked by such barbarity as Churchill's bombing of Berlin. Even in the face of such provocation, he would refrain from retaliation.

On the night of August 28, while Hitler's generals were on their way to meet with the Führer, the RAF again struck at Berlin. This time the raids were larger and the damage more severe. Bombs fell near the Reichstag Building and in the Tiergarten section.

Hitler was awakened at 1 A.M. by his adjutant, General Schmundt, and informed that the raid was in progress. The most powerful man in the world spent the rest of the night sitting at his desk, staring at the moonlit mountain peaks beyond his window. Throughout the night, General Schmundt brought the dispatches from Berlin and quietly set them in front of his brooding Führer. Schmundt's hands trembled uncontrollably each time he entered the room. He had never seen Hitler so angry.

Hitler's anger had not abated by morning. He was served his normally spartan breakfast of bread and fruit and a cup of tea alone in his bedroom. His valet laid out his field marshal's uniform on the bed, but Hitler did not move from his position by the window.

At 10 A.M. General Schmundt knocked softly and entered the room. He waited for Hitler to acknowledge his presence before making his announcement, but after a few minutes he realized that his Führer's thoughts were elsewhere. He cleared his throat. "The generals and Admiral Raeder have arrived, my Führer."

Hitler's head slowly turned away from the window. "Goering is here?"

"Yes. Everyone."

"I shall be there presently." Hitler's hands were clenched into fists. "Let them wait."

One hour later Hitler entered the downstairs dining room that had been converted into a conference room. The soldiers leaped to their feet, startled by Hitler's sudden, unannounced appearance. In addition to Grand Admiral Raeder, the others were: Wilhelm Keitel, Chief of Staff of the High Command of the Armed Forces; Alfred Jodl, the Chief of the

Operations Staff; Franz Halder, Chief of the Army General Staff; Walter von Brauchitsch, Commander-in-Chief of the German Army; and Hermann Goering, Commander-in-Chief of the Luftwaffe, President of the Reichstag, Prime Minister of Prussia, and the second most powerful man in Germany.

Hitler stared coldly at each man in turn, saving his last, most withering look for Goering. "Good morning, Meier," he said, his words hurled like cobra venom at his corpulent Reichsmarschall. "How are things in Berlin this morning?"

Goering turned crimson. He tried to speak, but Hitler cut him off with a chopping gesture of his right hand. For the next hour, Hitler berated his commanders in a shrieking diatribe that had all of them shaking. His wild gestures—slashing, punching, swinging—were like physical blows battering them into submission. Even when he paused, to wipe the spittle from his lips or to take a sip of water, no one dared move an inch.

At one point Keitel dared a glance at Jodl and both motioned with their eyes toward Goering, who was gasping for breath from fear and exhaustion. The man they called "Der Dicke"—Fatty—was loathed by the German High Command. He was responsible for this outrage. A genuine hero of the first war, Goering had used his contacts with German industrialists and the aristocracy to help bring Hitler to power. He had then used his position with Hitler to accumulate a vast fortune. The generals despised Goering's craving for wealth and power and ridiculed his tremendous bulk and even greater appetite.

When he was finished, Hitler ordered his generals to sit. Suddenly he was calm. He pointed a finger at Goering. "I want it remembered," he said, "that I tried to do the honorable thing. It was not my intention to bring civilians into this conflict. But if that is what Churchill wants, then by God that is what he will get."

Goering swallowed. He knew, but could never have told Hitler, that on the night of August 24, German bombers of Luftflotte II had mistakenly dropped several tons of bombs on central London. Knowing the Führer's explicit directive that London must not be bombed, Goering had neglected to inform Hitler that an error had been made. The British bombing of Berlin was, he suspected, in retaliation for the earlier German bombing.

"My men and planes are ready to do your bidding, my Führer," Goering said.

"Then prepare them well," Hitler said. "The people of London will soon beg their criminal government for an end to these hostilities."

Goering beamed. From the beginning these were the orders he had craved. No longer would his planes have to be content with dropping bombs on grass airfields or ships in the Channel, finally they would be able to do what they did best—spread terror. Goering, like Hitler, understood that the tactics of terror could do more damage than mere physical destruction. His Luftwaffe had destroyed the will of the Poles, and in France, with five million men still in the field, the French government had begged for peace rather than suffer the wrath of his marauding air force. So would it be in London.

Goering had regained his confidence. He looked around at the others, a superior smile on his face. "The Luftwaffe will not fail you."

Hitler's eyes were darts that impaled his Reichsmarschall against the wall. "There will be no more failure," he said quietly. "They will submit, or be destroyed."

REICH ADMITS "SLIGHT" DAMAGE TO BERLIN;
NAZIS SAY WAR ENTERS NEW, DANGEROUS
PHASE

BERLIN, AUG. 29

◆ *CHAPTER 23* ◆

August 29—"You are quite certain then," Admiral Canaris said, "that Kennedy is ready to denounce his own president."

Bernhard Ritter said, "Nothing, Herr Admiral, is certain in war, but—"

Canaris interrupted his subordinate. "I need no reminder of the vagaries of war, Captain," he said.

They were in the Admiral's office on the top floor of Abwehr headquarters. The office was surprisingly small and simply furnished. The Admiral sat behind his desk, his pet dachshund in his lap. Ritter sat across from Canaris. He was in full uniform.

"I meant, of course, that Kennedy is as unpredictable as the weather."

The Admiral's long face revealed nothing of what he was thinking. "I would still like to hear the forecast, Captain."

"I believe that in the very near future Ambassador Kennedy will make a complete break with Roosevelt and the policies of the Roosevelt administration."

"Before the election?"

"Absolutely. That way he will maximize the impact of the breach. If he waits until after, he will merely be another disgruntled politician. The Republicans are waiting to welcome him with open arms."

"And this defection will influence the election?"

172

"Decisively," said Ritter. "The opinion polls show Roosevelt and Willkie almost neck and neck. Any major disruption in the Roosevelt campaign will be enough to throw the election to Willkie. Kennedy's defection would be a disruption of major proportions comparable to one of the Führer's closest political allies—Goering, Himmler, or Hess —declaring that the Führer's policies are immoral."

Canaris suppressed a smile. He scratched the dachshund behind the ears but said nothing.

Ritter went on. "Rumors of the collusion between Roosevelt and Churchill are rampant in the American press, and Willkie has based his campaign on his opposition to those secret agreements. Kennedy could destroy the Roosevelt campaign by declaring his knowledge of, and his opposition to, Roosevelt's criminal behavior in this matter."

"And when Willkie is President, what can we expect? I've heard it said that he too is sympathetic to the British."

"Sympathetic? Possibly. But it would be politically impossible for him to do anything about those sympathies. His election campaign is based on noninterference in Europe. His backers are isolationists who wish only to stay out of the war and rid themselves of Roosevelt. Willkie's hands are already tied. As president, he will be unable to do anything."

"But," Canaris said, "all of this depends on Kennedy's doing what you say he will do. And you have already noted how unpredictable he can be."

"That is true," Ritter said, "but the facts are clear." He counted them on his fingertips. "Kennedy despises Roosevelt. He feels that Roosevelt has insulted and belittled him and he wants to make the president pay. He admires the Führer and has called him the greatest genius of the century. He agrees with our Jewish policy and has said that Germany should have a free hand in Europe. He despises the British and would welcome a German victory. He has at his disposal the means to accomplish all that he wants and he is a man who usually gets what he wants."

Canaris was silent for a long time. He returned his pet to its customary spot in his lower desk drawer, using this delay, as he usually did, to collect his thoughts. He drummed his fingers on the desk. "There are those in the SS," he said finally, "Heydrich and others, who feel that we can be more certain of the outcome if we let Kennedy know that Germany would look favorably upon his intervention in this matter."

"That," said Ritter, "would be exactly the wrong move. If Kennedy feels that we are attempting to manipulate him, there is no telling how he would react. The man is so perverse that he is likely to reverse himself and support Roosevelt. The best thing to do is to wait for him to act."

"But we cannot wait too long. The SS will have our heads if we wait for Kennedy and he does nothing."

"According to Benke, Kennedy wants to get home in time to determine the outcome of the election by making a personal appeal to the American people. If he is not on his way home before the election, we can leak the information about the Churchill-Roosevelt agreements. Coming from us, though, it won't have half the impact that it would coming from Kennedy."

"Then we wait," said Canaris. "You will closely monitor the situation so that the opportunity does not pass."

"Yes, Herr Admiral."

"You realize, Captain, that if we fail, the SS will want a sacrifice. You will be lucky to wind up behind a desk in Poland. I will be unable to intervene."

Ritter smiled. "But if we succeed?" he said.

"Ah, yes," said Canaris, a smile breaking across his face. "If we succeed, the world is ours."

They sat quietly, basking in the glory of it. There was little else to say. Together they had orchestrated a scenario that would save Germany from a long and fruitless struggle—a struggle whose outcome was by no means certain. With Roosevelt out of the picture, the British would have to withdraw from the war. There was no other viable option. Oh, perhaps Churchill would attempt to save face with a lot of bellicose rhetoric, and refuse to make an official end to the conflict for some time, but it did not matter. Without American help, the British lion was toothless. If Kennedy performed as predicted, the war between Britain and Germany, for all intents and purposes, was over. Germany could then consolidate her European Empire and begin to build the foundation for the thousand year Reich.

And they—Ritter and Canaris—would have done it.

All that remained now was to sit back and wait for the final chapter to unfold.

1500 NAZI PLANES BLAST TARGETS; CITIES,
DOCKS, AIRFIELDS BOMBED; RAIDS CONTINUE
THROUGHOUT NIGHT

LONDON, AUG. 30

♦ *CHAPTER 24* ♦

LONDON, August 30—When the telephone rang, Max
Munro had been drinking for over an hour and was well on
his way to a pretty good buzz. He had a glass of Scotch in one
hand and in the other a document that he had surreptitiously
removed from the code room that afternoon. The document
was a long letter from Franklin Roosevelt to Winston Churchill. He was lost in thought, rereading the letter for what must
have been the hundredth time, when the jangling phone
ended his reflection.

" 'lo," he said.

"Max? Is that you?"

It was Betty. The sound of her voice cheered him considerably. "Yes," he said, making an effort to speak clearly, "it's
me."

"You O.K.?"

"I'm fine," he lied. He was surprised to hear from her.

"I just wanted to check up on you—see how you were."

"I'm fine," he said again, wishing that his brain weren't so
clouded.

"What are you doing?"

He looked at the glass in his hand. "Just sitting around."

"You alone?"

"Yes."

"How about meeting me for a drink?"

"Sure," he said. "When and where?"

"I've got a story to file. Give me an hour and then meet me at the Pillars of Hercules on Greek Street. It's a pub—just off Manette Street, below Soho Square."

"I'll find it." He felt almost sober now.

"One hour."

"See you there."

His elation over her call evaporated when he saw the document on the table by his chair. In the letter Roosevelt talked about the political difficulties involved in transferring fifty or sixty U.S. Navy destroyers to the British. Such a transfer would be in obvious defiance of the Neutrality Act and an incredible provocation of Germany. Roosevelt, however, left no doubt that he intended to supply the ships to Great Britain. The President intended to bring the United States to the brink of war and defy the Germans to do anything about it.

Munro was certain now that the President was maneuvering the United States into the war against Germany. He wondered how his father would react to this direct evidence of what he would call "Roosevelt's treason."

He was startled by a sudden knock on the door. Until that moment he had deluded himself into thinking that his removal of the document from the embassy was not theft, but his reaction to the knock on the door had shattered his illusion. Quickly he slipped the paper back into the folder he had used to carry it from the code room and slid it under the small sofa in his sitting room.

Munro opened the door. Standing in his doorway was a very attractive woman.

"Hello, again," she said.

His eyes widened in surprise. "Miss Price," he said.

"May I come in?" she asked.

He stepped back and she walked past him, trailing the subtle fragrance of her perfume. She wore a light summer skirt and a white blouse and had her hair tied back. She looked incredibly beautiful.

"Excuse the mess," he said, picking up things from the chair.

Marie sat down. "Don't worry," she said, "I don't mind a little mess. I like to know if a man has anything to hide."

Almost reflexively his eyes went to the sofa where he had hidden the Roosevelt document.

Her eyes sparkled with mischief as if she and Munro shared some exciting secret. She looked him up and down boldly and ran her tongue across her lips. "Are you surprised to see me?"

"Frankly, yes."

She laughed. "I am a creature of surprises," she said. She crossed her legs, managing to reveal a sizable portion of thigh in the process, then looked at the bottle of Scotch on the table. "Aren't you going to offer me a drink?"

"I was just getting ready to go out when you arrived."

She looked at him questioningly and he realized how disheveled he must look.

"I meant that I was about to get dressed to go out."

She smiled. "I'll have that drink while you get dressed."

He went to the kitchenette and returned with a glass. "Would you like some water with this?"

"No," she said, taking the glass. She looked up at him. "You aren't going to make me drink alone, are you?"

He hesitated, then poured into both glasses.

Marie sank back into the chair. "Cheers," she said, raising her glass to her lips.

He drank. Talking with Betty had almost made him sober, but this drink leapfrogged him beyond where he had been. Momentarily the room moved beneath his feet. He made it to the sofa and sat down heavily.

Marie got up and sat next to him, brushing her legs against his. "You seem warm," she said, touching his forehead then running her fingers across his cheek.

Her face was only inches from his, and he found himself mesmerized by her incredibly blue eyes. Her lips parted and he saw the tip of her tongue. Suddenly his mouth was on hers.

Her tongue snaked into his mouth and she pressed herself against him. His free hand reached under her skirt, moving up the inside of her thigh.

Marie took his glass from him. "Let's get rid of these," she said, placing both glasses on the lamp table behind the sofa. She draped herself across him, pinning him to the sofa as she kissed him hungrily.

His hands were inside her blouse, stumbling fingers struggling with the clasp of her bra. She laughed and reached behind her. With one swift motion she released the clasp. Marie stood up. "Is that your bedroom?"

He nodded and she walked into the bedroom. Munro picked up the Scotch, the two glasses, and followed her inside.

She was already naked from the waist up when he entered the room. She turned to face him with a smile, her large breasts swinging in unison, and threw her blouse on the floor. She reached behind her, unbuttoned her skirt, and in one smooth motion slipped out of the skirt and panties.

She had a dancer's body, he thought as he watched her, long smooth legs, flat stomach, and firm breasts. His throat was dry and someone had apparently removed most of the oxygen from the room. He stood frozen in the doorway.

"Are you going to join me?" she asked. She ran her hands up her body, her fingers pausing tantalizingly over her hips and then her breasts. Then, hands behind her neck, she lifted her long blond hair on top of her head and held it there.

Munro walked over to her. She took the bottle and the glasses from him and placed them on the bedside table while he fumbled with his shirt.

"Let me," she said, and quickly undid the shirt buttons.

He looked down as she opened his shirt. "Magic," he said.

She undid his belt buckle. "If you think that's magic," she chuckled, "wait till I get the rest off."

Marie Price was an expert, an artist of the bedroom. She was ravenous, exhausting, exhilarating, and Munro found himself responding as he never had before. When he thought he had no more to give or take, she spurred him on to new heights of effort and satisfaction. She talked constantly, whispering in his ear, or crying out in the midst of her pleasure.

Once or twice, Munro was vaguely aware that the telephone was ringing, but every part of his conscious self was engaged with Marie Price. There was no room for anything else.

Finally she allowed him to sleep, and he fell into a shallow slumber. He was aware that she had covered him with a blanket and felt the warmth of her body as she snuggled next to him. As he drifted in and out of sleep he gradually became aware that she was no longer next to him. He heard noises —slight rattles, minute scrapes, small thumps.

The phone rang again and his brain ached in protest until the ringing stopped. He was almost awake now. He lay on his

178

back, eyes partially opened, his arm across his face. The noises had stopped.

The door opened slowly, and he saw Marie, silhouetted in the doorway. She peered into the darkened room, watching him quietly for a moment. He did not move.

"Max, darling," she whispered. "Are you awake?"

He watched her, through partly closed eyes.

She called again. This time a little louder. "Max?"

When he did not answer, she quietly closed the door.

He listened. In a moment the noises were back—the scraping, the rattling, the thumping. It was obvious, he thought, she was going through his drawers and searching his closet. What the hell was she looking for? Money? That didn't make sense. What the hell else did he have that she wanted? He had nothing that she could possibly—with a start he sat up.

Jesus Christ, he said to himself, the letter is under the couch. If she finds that . . . He jumped up, banging his toe against the corner of the bed. Ignoring the pain he hopped to the door and yanked it open.

Marie sat on the couch. She wore only Munro's open shirt. "Awake at last," she said cheerfully, holding up a water-filled glass. "I was thirsty and you were dead to the world. Sit," she said, patting the cushion next to her.

"I'd better get dressed," he said. She couldn't have known about the letter, he told himself. So what was she looking for?

There was a knock on the door.

"Get into the bedroom," Munro ordered.

Marie did as she was told and Munro raced to the bathroom to grab his robe.

The knocking at the door turned into a pounding.

"Coming. Coming," Munro called as he slipped into the robe. He pulled the door open and there was Betty and a man who looked vaguely familiar.

"I called several times," Betty said. "No one answered. I was afraid something had happened to you."

Munro grimaced, remembering he had promised to meet her.

"You remember Bill Talmadge," Betty said. "He was good enough to come with me when I thought that . . ."

Munro pulled at the belt that held his robe. "I must have fallen asleep . . . forgotten the time."

At that moment Marie Price called from the bedroom. "Who is it, darling?" she asked.

"Excuse me, Munro," Betty said coldly. "I didn't mean to interrupt your evening in Switzerland."

Betty turned quickly and walked down the hall.

Talmadge winked at Munro. "It's been a pleasure," he said, grinning wickedly, then followed Betty.

Munro closed the door. He didn't want to look at Marie, who had now emerged from the bedroom.

"Your girlfriend?" she asked impishly.

"Hardly."

"She certainly acted like your girlfriend."

"I was supposed to meet her."

"Perhaps I should be going?" Marie said, and when Munro did not answer she went into the bedroom.

As soon as she had disappeared, Munro reached under the couch and found the folder. He withdrew it and checked inside. There, undisturbed, was the letter. He breathed a sigh of relief and slid the folder back out of sight.

Why had she come here in the first place? He found it difficult to believe that a woman as beautiful as Marie found him so devastatingly attractive that she could not keep away from him. What was it that Betty had said about her?—that she seemed very interested in the fact that he worked in the code room at the embassy.

He pulled out the folder and looked at the letter again. He had been a fool to remove it from the embassy. If the letter fell into the wrong hands, the results would be devastating. He would return it to the files first thing tomorrow.

He slid the folder back underneath the couch and listened to Marie humming to herself as she dressed. She appeared in the doorway, buttoning her blouse. "I had a lovely time," she said. "Let's do it again."

Munro, feeling drunk and foolish, managed only a nod.

Marie headed for the door. "Sorry about the girlfriend," she said.

◆ *CHAPTER 25* ◆

BERLIN, August 31—Because of its proximity to Gestapo Headquarters, the restaurant in the House of Flyers on Prinz Albrecht Strasse was a favorite of many of the SS officers who worked next door in the gray, grim building that housed the offices of the Geheime Staatspolizei. It was the same restaurant where Admiral Canaris often dined with SS Obergruppenführer Heydrich in what both liked to call "Kameradschaftsabende,"—evenings of comradeship. It mattered little that each despised the other.

SS Obersturmbannführer Otto Kaufmann lifted his briefcase from the floor and placed it on the empty chair between him and Captain Bernhard Ritter.

"This, I suppose," Ritter said, indicating the briefcase, "is the reason for the luncheon invitation?"

Kaufmann giggled. He was a small, red-faced man, lost in his black SS dress uniform. Ritter resisted the impulse to reach across the table and squash Kaufmann like an overgrown cockroach. That would have been dangerous, as the Obersturmbannführer was a man to be feared. Kaufmann was a favorite of Reinhard Heydrich, the man who headed the vast security apparatus of the German Reich. Kaufmann's credentials had been earned during the first weeks of the war when the Einsatzkommandos under his command in Poland had established an enviable record of extermination of Jews and other undesirable Poles. This former grocery store clerk was now second in command at the newly formed Department VI, the foreign intelligence section, of the Reich Security Administration.

Bringing his laughter under control, Kaufmann reached his fat, baby fingers into the briefcase and withdrew a small stack of typed pages. "I thought you might like to look at these," he said casually, placing the papers on the table.

Ritter leaned forward. His eyes widened as he looked at the first page.

Kaufmann noted his reaction with great satisfaction. "You will find," he said, "that the other pages are just as startling."

Ritter leafed quickly through the papers. To his amazement he was looking at copies of the information that Benke had delivered to him only a week ago, and that he had delivered to Admiral Canaris only three days earlier. Obviously, Reich Security had spies within the Abwehr. "Interesting," he said.

Kaufmann snorted. "Quite. Photographic copies of messages between Roosevelt and Churchill taken from the American Embassy in London. The originals, I assume, have been returned to a safe place in the embassy code room."

Ritter was suspicious. "Why show these to me?"

Kaufmann giggled. "So there will be no illusions about the eventual victor in the struggle between our respective agencies. And to impress upon you the need for cooperation."

Ritter's suspicions grew. The SS cooperated with no one, unless it was to their own benefit. "How can I be of assistance?"

"We can be of assistance to each other," said Kaufmann, putting the papers back into his briefcase. "We, in Department VI, are aware that the Admiral hopes to save his position with this information."

Ritter's thoughts flashed to Admiral Canaris, whose hope of saving the Abwehr from being assimilated into the Reich Security Administration had just been dealt a mortal blow. Perhaps he had misjudged Kaufmann's abilities. "I must take off my hat to you, Herr Oberstrumbannführer," he said. "This is a remarkable piece of intelligence work." Ritter's praise was genuine.

Kaufmann nodded graciously.

All around them black-uniformed officers, the pride of the Gestapo and other related agencies of the Reich Security

Administration, sat ramrod straight at their tables. The din of their combined conversations was like a murmuring wave that washed over Ritter. The lives—and deaths—of millions, Ritter thought, are being decided in this room, over venison and sauerbraten. The clatter of cutlery on china was like a drum roll.

"What made you decide to make your career with the Abwehr?" said Kaufmann, his voice conversational. "Rather than the Gestapo or the Sicherheitsdienst?"

Ritter would have liked to say, because those organizations are filled with thugs and perverts. Instead, he said, "The Admiral asked me to join him when he took over the Abwehr in 1935. I had great respect for him as an officer."

"Sometimes such decisions can affect a man's whole life."

"I'm not sure I understand."

"It is well known that the Admiral has lost the confidence of the Führer, and that the Abwehr will soon come under the control of the Reich Security Administration. It is difficult to say what will happen to those Abwehr officers who cling to their previous loyalties."

"A desk in Poland perhaps?"

Kaufmann smiled. "Somewhere in the backwaters of the war, to be sure. Those who wish to share in the coming glories must be willing to make their decision early. The earlier the better."

Ritter understood. The Admiral was in trouble, and Ritter did not intend to go down with a sinking ship. It might be wise to play both sides of the street for a while. "I have always believed that a man's loyalty should be, first, to his Führer . . . and then to himself."

"I can see why Obergruppenführer Heydrich himself considers you a man worth cultivating."

Ritter was extremely pleased. "Heydrich has mentioned my name?"

"Several times, I assure you. He is particularly impressed with your small group of agents in England. At a time when it is exceedingly difficult to get information into and out of England, you seem to be one of the very few who can."

"I did not know that the Obergruppenführer was aware of my agents in England."

Kaufmann removed a small piece of paper from his pocket.

"Oh, my, yes," he said, reading from the paper. "Benke, Daley, and Price. Quite a nice assortment. Well placed and apparently quite good."

Kaufmann and Heydrich knew much more than Ritter or Canaris had imagined. "Not as good, it seems, as the people who acquired those messages." Ritter pointed to the briefcase.

"Informants are everywhere. Men such as you are more difficult to find."

Ritter said nothing. This, he knew, was the moment he had waited for. Kaufmann had not invited him to lunch to flatter him for an hour. The man wanted something.

"I would like to know about your man inside the embassy."

"He is unaware that these documents are going to Germany. He wants only to discredit Roosevelt. He thinks that the documents are being given to American journalists. However, he is balking at turning over any more documents. He believes he has found a better way to make use of this information."

"How?"

"Through an American politician's son who also works at the embassy. Our man is certain that the son is collecting evidence of Roosevelt's perfidious behavior and passing it along to his politician father."

"Who is this American politician?"

"Senator Maxwell Munro?"

Obviously the name meant nothing to Kaufmann.

"Senator Munro is one of the most influential men in Washington," Ritter explained. "If he had this information, Roosevelt's political career would be over."

"Then why don't we have it delivered to him?"

"And have it dismissed as German propaganda? As a forgery intended to discredit Roosevelt and influence the presidential elections? Coming from us, this material is immediately suspect," said Ritter. "None of the material is in the handwriting of, or signed by, the principals—it is typed on an embassy machine. Even if we turn it over to American journalists it would be regarded with suspicion. To have the required effect, the documents must be delivered by an unimpeachable source."

"Such as?"

"Senator Munro or"—Ritter looked around the room—"Ambassador Kennedy himself is a very real possibility," he whispered. "That is what I have been trying to accomplish."

"Very well," Kaufmann said. "We'll do it your way for now, but in the meantime we would like to continue gathering the messages from the American Embassy. The General Staff finds them most informative."

"My people have already taken steps to make contact with Munro."

"My department would expect to see any information first," Kaufmann said. "Before it goes to Canaris?"

"Of course," said Ritter. "I understand."

"And anything else that your people in England come up with."

Ritter thought quickly. There was little profit in giving Kaufmann everything. After all, Admiral Canaris just might prevail. Then where would he be? He was certain that Kaufmann was unaware of Price's involvement with Hamilton of the British Secret Intelligence Service installation at Broadway. That operation was potentially as important as this business at the American Embassy. He would hold on to that secret for now. There might be rainy days ahead and a man in his position might need all the secrets he could muster. "Of course," he said. "You will be the first to know anything."

Kaufmann giggled and offered a clammy hand to seal their bargain.

"Enter," called out Admiral Canaris in answer to the sharp knock on his office door. He put his dachshund back into his berth in the lower drawer and waved Colonel Hans Oster, the Admiral's chief of staff, into the chair in front of the desk. "What is it, Hans? You said it was a matter of some urgency."

Oster nodded. He was fifty-one, of average height and build, with blond, thinning hair. "I think we may have a problem with our good friends at Prinz Albrecht Strasse."

The Admiral sighed. "There is nothing new in that." He too was always concerned with Heydrich's encroachments, but Oster seemed unable to accept the fact that the Reich Security Office and its Gestapo functionaries were an irreversible fact of German life. Oster despised Hitler and what his National Socialist German Workers Party had done to Germany.

In April of 1940 Oster had warned the Allies of Hitler's plans for the invasions of Norway and Denmark. In May he had warned of the coming German thrust into the Low Countries. Throughout the war he continued as a central figure in the small German resistance movement. In 1945, with the guns of the advancing Allied armies rumbling in the background, Hans Oster would be executed for his efforts.

"It's Ritter," said Oster. "He's been seen with Obersturmbannführer Kaufmann. Passing documents back and forth."

Canaris's face darkened. "Do you think Ritter has gone over to the other side?"

"Difficult to say." It was not unusual for Abwehr officers to request transfers to the larger, more dynamic Security Administration. "Rats will desert the sinking ship."

"We're not sinking yet," Canaris said.

Oster did not apologize. "Not yet," he said.

"What do we do about Ritter?"

"I can assign a few men to keep an eye on him. Perhaps my informant has been overzealous."

"I want you to take care of this, Hans," Canaris said. "I don't want to get involved in a messy squabble with Heydrich . . . or Kaufmann."

"As you wish, Admiral," said Oster. He looked at his chief with a mixture of revulsion and regret. There was a time when he had thought that the Admiral was one of the most admirable men in Germany, but now he saw a man whose pathological fear of Hitler and his gang had turned him into an empty shell of his former self. The Admiral was only two years older than his deputy, but the strain of his position made him appear much older. He was, thought Oster, a man who detested what he and his country had become, but could not summon the courage to do anything about it. What Oster did not know was that the Admiral was well aware of his anti-Nazi activities or that the Admiral himself had established contact with the British Foreign Office through intermediaries in Switzerland, and was in fact working cautiously for the overthrow of the Hitler regime. Canaris's only fear was what defeat would mean to Germany. That fear caused him to move carefully in the dangerous and deceitful world in which he lived.

In the end his caution would not save him from the Gestapo. He and Oster would die, side by side, on a chilly April morning in 1945.

In the heady days of 1940, however, that chilly morning was far beyond the comprehension of either man. "See that this is taken care of, then," Canaris said, returning his attention to his pet dachshund. "I leave it entirely in your hands."

Oster nodded and rose from his chair. "As you wish, Admiral."

◆ CHAPTER 26 ◆

LONDON, August 31—Munro sat in the lobby of the Savoy Hotel and watched the well-dressed patrons exit their limousines in the courtyard approach to the hotel, and make their grand entrances. They either went directly to the Grill or were directed to the Lounge for a drink while their tables were prepared. The Savoy was one of London's oldest and most prestigious hotels, and along with the Grosvenor House and the Dorchester in Park Lane, it had become the focus of much of the night life in London's exclusive West End. Everywhere Munro looked there were uniforms, tweeds, and furs. Occasionally he recognized one of the American press contingent, but for over an hour there was no sign of Betty.

Munro stood up when she entered the lobby. She was looking over her shoulder, laughing at something that Bill Talmadge, who followed her through the swinging doors, had said. She turned, saw Munro, and the laugh disappeared.

He approached her. "I've got to talk to you."

Betty shook her head. Talmadge stood protectively behind her. "Bill and I are about to have dinner."

"This can't wait."

There was an awkward moment of silence between them which was finally broken by Talmadge. "Why don't I go upstairs and change? I'll meet you in the salon in half an hour."

"Thanks, Bill," Betty said, touching Talmadge lightly on the arm. "This won't take long." She turned back to Munro as Talmadge walked to the stairs. "Well? What is it?"

"Not here," he said. "Can we go outside? Walk for a bit?"

"This way," Betty said, and led him to the rear of the hotel, past the American correspondents' bar, which was packed as usual. They exited the Savoy through the Embankment entrance, and crossed Savoy Place to the small park between the hotel and the river.

She kept walking. "Go ahead. I'm listening."

"For starters," he said, "I'm sorry about last night."

"Forget last night," she said. "What you do with your time is your business." Her pace quickened. "Just tell me what it is that's so important."

"I think you were right about Price and Benke. Last night Marie Price was searching my place when she thought I was asleep."

"Searching for what?"

He hesitated. "I'm not sure."

"Why don't you call the police?" she asked finally.

"I would rather not."

They reached the Victoria Embankment, crossed, and stood at the railing looking down into the Thames. The Waterloo Bridge was to their left and off in the distance to their right was Westminster. The barrage balloons hung lazily in the slate-gray sky of early evening.

"You're leaving something out," she said.

"What makes you think that?"

"You've come to me instead of going to the police or your boss, Colonel Jackson. That's what you should do."

His back to the river, Munro leaned against the railing. He looked down at his shoes.

"What was she looking for?" Betty asked.

"I can't tell you that."

"Why can't you go to Colonel Jackson?"

He was silent.

Betty flicked the cigarette over the railing. The glowing ash made a scarlet spiral to the river below. She looked at her watch. "I've got a date for dinner," she said and headed across the street.

Munro called to her. She stopped and looked back. "I took something from the Embassy," he said. "I had it in my apartment."

"Had?"

"I returned it this morning, but I can't tell Jackson that I took it."

"What was it?"

"A letter," he said. "I can't tell you any more than that. I don't want to read about this in next week's *Time* magazine."

"What if I promised not to file the story?"

"What if it was the biggest story you'd ever had? A story that could topple empires and presidents? How good would your promise be then?"

"You've found it, haven't you?" she said quietly.

"Found what?"

"What everyone's been looking for. The proof."

"I don't know what you're talking about."

"The proof of what Willkie and the Republicans have been saying all along. What Wheeler and Clark and your father have charged all summer. What Lindbergh's been ranting about for a year. Roosevelt's going to bring us into the war, isn't he?"

He was silent. He looked down the river toward Westminster and Big Ben.

"What else would topple empires and presidents?" Betty said. "If I filed that story—and could prove it—Roosevelt would be a sure loser, and without him in office the British would be unable to continue the war."

Both looked into the Thames as if afraid to face each other. Betty was lost in thought for a long time before she said, "I wouldn't file that story."

He looked at her questioningly.

"I wouldn't want to see Hitler and his goddamned cut-throats parading up Whitehall. This country would be finished . . . and we'd be next." She turned her back to the river and looked at Munro. "I don't get it," she said. "Your father would give his right arm for this information. Joe Kennedy would like nothing better than to wrap this around Roosevelt just before the election. Why don't you give it to them?"

"Maybe I don't agree with the Ambassador on what the world is all about. Maybe I don't agree with my father on anything. Or maybe I just don't want to see Hitler and his cutthroats parading up Whitehall, either."

"Do you want my help?"

"Yes."

"We're going to have to keep an eye on Benke and Price."

"How do we do that?"

Betty smiled and aimed a thumb back over her shoulder at the Savoy. "We've got a pack of reporters in there who don't have anything to do all day but wait for the Ministry of Information to distribute the fact sheets. The rest of the time they sit in the bar and drink. I know that some of them would welcome a little detective work."

"I don't want to involve anyone else in this."

"They don't have to know why they're tailing Benke and Price. They'll do it because I ask them to."

"You're sure?"

"No problem. When we get the goods on these two, we can turn them over to the authorities. We can leave out the part about your little excursion into espionage." She touched him lightly on the arm. "I'm glad you came to me," she said, looking up at him. "I think I may have misjudged you after all."

"You wouldn't be the first," he said softly, his eyes across the river as if he were remembering the other times.

Betty put her arm through his and rested her head on his shoulder. "Nice night," she said finally, after a long silence.

The first stars were beginning to twinkle through the gathering darkness, and the barrage balloons had become vague dots against the evening sky. "Yes," he said. "Nice night."

She looked up at him. "I can get rid of Talmadge," she said. "He's just a friend."

"O.K.," he said. He felt better than he had in a long time, as if a great weight had been lifted from his shoulders.

She squeezed his arm. "Let's get back. We've got a lot to talk about."

◆ *CHAPTER 27* ◆

LONDON, September 1—The effect of the August 29 meeting at Berchtesgaden was almost immediate. Goering took personal control of the air fleets and began sending a flurry of Enigma signals from Berlin to his air-fleet commanders in France and Belgium. It was immediately apparent to the decrypt-analysis teams at Bletchley Park that something big was in the offing, and the word went out on the newly installed teleprinter between Bletchley and Broadway that the Germans, apparently, were preparing another massive engagement similar to that of August 15.

Winston Hamilton had never seen so many signals. The teleprinter had been clacking away most of the morning and on into the afternoon. After the messages were removed from the machine, several secretaries made copies for distribution to the various departments. Winston took his copies, separated them into individual messages, and tacked them to the cork board that he kept in his office. Each message went under a heading assigned to the various squadrons of the three huge German air fleets that ringed the southeastern coast of England.

The messages told Winston that the German bomber and fighter wings were being brought up to full strength, and that Goering was in the process of committing much of his reserve forces to whatever action he had planned. Winston's excitement grew. This was going to be a repeat of "Der Adler Tag," the big day in August that signaled the beginning of Goering's attempt to sweep the skies clear of RAF planes and pilots.

Thanks to Ultra intercepts, the RAF had been in possession of Goering's plans a week before Eagle Day arrived. Forewarned by Ultra, and often given specific German targets, the RAF had been able to prevail, but the losses had been so great that those in authority doubted that the RAF could afford another "victory" like those four incredible days in August.

The air crews were exhausted, and replacements did not begin to equal the losses suffered. Aircraft and equipment were in a dangerous state of disrepair. Slowly but surely the Luftwaffe's tactics of attrition were having the desired effect.

Winston surveyed his board. What he saw was not reassuring. "They just keep coming," he whispered, "as if there were no end to their supply of men and planes." At that moment his thoughts were the same as those few others who had access to the Ultra intercepts. "Can the RAF withstand one more massive assault?" The issue was very much in doubt.

ROOSEVELT TRADES DESTROYERS FOR BASES; IGNORES CONGRESSIONAL CRITICS, ACTS ON OWN AUTHORITY; BRITISH JUBILANT, OPPONENTS ANGRY

WASHINGTON, SEPT. 3

◆ CHAPTER 28 ◆

Tuesday, September 3—"I don't believe it," Joe Kennedy said. His face was red with anger. He held up a piece of paper for all to see. "Even though I have the proof in my hands, I still don't believe it."

He had called the key members of the Embassy staff to his office as soon as he had arrived in the building that morning. Most of them were already aware of the reason for his anger.

"Last night—after midnight—I was informed by the State

Department that President Roosevelt has decided to transfer fifty U.S. Navy destroyers to the Royal Navy. Roosevelt has done this on his own, without the permission of Congress." The Ambassador paused, expecting the others to mirror his disbelief.

No one said a word.

Kennedy's eyes widened. "This is an act of war."

Colonel Jackson remembered that today was the anniversary of the British declaration of war against Germany and that he had been with the Ambassador when they had learned of the impending declaration. Kennedy had called Franklin Roosevelt on the transatlantic phone. It had been 4 A.M. in Washington and the President had been roused from his sleep to listen to his Ambassador, who was close to hysteria and tears. "It's the beginning of a new Dark Ages—the end of the world!" he had cried. "It's the end of everything."

"The Congress and the American people would never have agreed to this," said Kennedy. "That's why he's done it on his own."

David Carson was the first to dare speak. "According to many of the sources I speak to, Mr. Ambassador, the President is firmly within his rights to make such a—"

The Ambassador cut him off. "Where are those sources, Carson? At the British Foreign Office? Or Churchill's Cabinet perhaps? We're as good as in this war now, by God."

"Mr. Ambassador," Jackson said. "I doubt very much that Mr. Hitler will be in any hurry to declare war on the United States over this move. He has the British isolated and alone, and I think he would prefer to keep it that way."

"Then you agree with what the President has done?" Kennedy said.

"I am a soldier, sir," Jackson said. "It is not for me to debate political questions."

"Typical military cop-out," snarled Kennedy. "I wouldn't be surprised if Hitler steps up his invasion plans, so that he can finish off the British before Roosevelt can drag us into the war. Now that the British have bombed Berlin, we can expect that the Germans will begin bombing London. They should never have challenged Hitler like that."

"Mr. Ambassador," said David Carson, "the German's bombed London more than a week ago. The British raids were in response to—"

"Small stuff," Kennedy said. "The British should have ignored it and hoped that it wouldn't happen again."

"The bombing of London is almost inevitable," Toby Graham said. "With the failure of the Luftwaffe to eliminate the RAF, Hitler has only two choices—give up, or expand the scope of the war. He doesn't appear to me to be the type to give up."

"I'll tell you one thing," said Kennedy. "After the first air raid, I'll be on the next plane for New York. My house in Prince's Gate doesn't have an air raid shelter and I won't sit and wait to be bombed to hell. I've been spending my weekends at my country house and I recommend that we put the embassy staff on a shortened work week—say Tuesday through Thursday—so that we can spend long weekends outside the city."

The staff looked at each other in amazement. "Mr. Ambassador," said David Carson, "if things are going to be as bad as you think they are, then we will have more work to do—not less. There are several thousand Americans still in London who may need the services of the Embassy."

"We tried to get all Americans out of the country when this mess started," Kennedy growled. "They didn't want to go. I hope you don't expect me to sit around and get blown to bits trying to arrange passage home for these bastards."

Carson was shocked. "I will certainly be here," he began.

"You do what you like," the Ambassador said. "I'm going to spend as little time here as I can."

The staff sat in stunned silence. Most, especially the military men, could hardly believe their ears. As far as Colonel Jackson was concerned, the Ambassador was abandoning his post in wartime, and to his mind there was no greater disregard of duty.

◆ CHAPTER 29 ◆

September 3—Betty was breathless when she arrived at the small pub on Berwick Street in Soho where she had agreed to meet Max for lunch. "Sorry I'm a bit late. I had a few things to tend to."

"I just got here," he lied.

She eyed his near-empty beer mug, smiled, gave him a kiss on the cheek, and sat down across from him at the small table he had managed to save.

"You've heard, of course?" she asked.

"Roosevelt finally bit the bullet and gave the British what they've been clamoring for."

Betty lowered her voice conspiratorially. "Just as you said he would."

"I'd begun to hope I was wrong." He motioned to the barmaid for two beers. "According to Ambassador Kennedy, by this evening the United States could be at war with Germany. He's been bellowing like a wounded bull all morning. He's close to hysteria. Says that Roosevelt has destroyed everything."

"I think Hitler's got enough to keep him busy right now."

"I hope you're right."

She touched his hand. "It's inevitable anyway, Max. One way or the other, it's going to happen."

They ordered lunch when the barmaid brought their beers.

"Got some other news for you," Betty said, smiling. "About your little Swiss friend."

Munro tried to ignore her sarcasm. "Let's hear it."

"It seems that you're not the only one she's after," she said. "She also has her lovely fangs in a British officer named Hamilton."

"How did you find that out?"

She smiled. "I told you that reporters are pretty good at detective work. Besides, it wasn't that hard. Talmadge tailed her to her apartment the night before last. Hamilton showed up, riding a bicycle and carrying a big bunch of roses."

"Then what?"

"Judging from what happened when she was at your place, I've got a pretty good idea that Hamilton got his money's worth for the roses."

Munro winced. Betty wasn't about to let him forget his escapade with Marie Price. "I mean after this guy left."

"Talmadge followed him home. It was easy. The guy is on a bike and Talmadge had a car."

"So we know where Hamilton lives?"

"Better than that," Betty said. "I went there this morning."

"You what?"

"I just wanted to get a good look at him. I figured I'd just say that I worked for *Time* magazine and was interviewing Londoners about the war."

"What happened?"

"He wasn't there. But I talked with his mother."

"His mother?"

"He lives with his mother. I gave her the *Time* magazine patter, and she invited me in. Nice old lady. Gave me a nice cuppa' tea, as she put it. She was only too glad to talk about her son. Very proud of him, apparently. Former college professor. Languages." Betty lowered her voice to a whisper. "Fluent in German."

"What does he do?"

"That's the interesting part. His mother doesn't know—or, at least, says she doesn't. Top secret, she said. He works for some secret military organization. Of course, according to his mother, Hamilton is winning the war all by himself."

"What do we do next?"

"Tomorrow I'll get someone to follow Hamilton from his house—his mother says he leaves every morning at seven-thirty—to wherever he works. If we can find out where he works, and who he works for, we should be able to figure out how important he is."

◆ *CHAPTER 30* ◆

BERLIN, September 5—The crowd had gathered early on a gray, overcast day in Berlin to cheer on the great man. Stettiner Station in the center of the city was bedecked in Nazi banners and a Party functionary was there to see that there was an ample supply of flags to be waved by the cheering throng. A buzzing ran through the crowd when the first in a long line of black Mercedes staff cars pulled up to the front of the train station and the Luftwaffe band began to play. The cheering and flag-waving began before the car had pulled to a stop between the two lines formed by the Nazi honor guard.

The door was opened and out stepped Reichsmarschall Hermann Goering, the beloved Commander-in-Chief of the Luftwaffe. The crowd went wild, and Goering, beaming from ear to ear, gave them his bent-elbowed version of the traditional stiff-armed Nazi salute. The arrivals and departures of the Nazi elite were always attended by pomp and circumstance, but only the appearance of the Führer himself could outdo the displays of affection accorded to Goering. He was, at this moment, the most popular man in Germany. To the average German, Goering seemed more a man of the people than any of the other leaders of the nation. To many, Hitler seemed remote, even godlike. His piercing, hypnotic eyes, while able to cast spells over the masses, were unable to project warmth. Goering, on the other hand, was as at home in the beer halls as he was in the Reichstag.

As Goering made his way between the cordon formed by the honor guard, a young girl stepped into his path. She presented Goering with a dozen roses—roses conveniently provided by the same Party functionary who had provided the flags. It did not matter. The crowd roared its approval when the Reichsmarschall took the roses and planted a kiss on the forehead of the girl. Only those in the front row were aware of the difficulty that Goering had in bending that far.

Reichsmarschall Hermann Goering boarded his private railroad car, *Asia,* shortly before noon. In the early afternoon, after a sumptuous lunch, Goering and his entourage of military aides and journalists from the German and foreign press set off for France. The journalists were certain that they were about to witness the long-promised invasion of Great Britain.

Goering was in an ebullient mood. His Führer had given him a second chance to complete the job begun in August, and this time he would personally spur on his air crews to new levels of sacrifice. He was well aware that his air force had suffered serious damage. It was whispered in some quarters that barely fifty percent of the Luftwaffe's aircraft were still serviceable, but Goering was certain that his men had inflicted even more damage on the enemy. If his Luftwaffe was injured then the RAF, he was sure, was mortally wounded.

Goering wore his sky blue Luftwaffe Field Marshal's uniform that he had designed himself. He was the ultimate poseur, changing uniforms at least five times a day and always conscious of the trappings of rank. Although his official portraits—several of which hung in the railroad cars —showed a handsome and miraculously slim Hermann Goering, he had not earned the nickname "Der Dicke" for nothing. He was grossly overweight and his private railroad cars had been custom refitted to permit his great bulk to pass comfortably through the doors. Goering, a showman who loved the grand entrance, had several times been embarrassed by the comic spectacle of his bloated body firmly wedged in a doorway, while his aides frantically struggled to push him through. One of his aides was now responsible for checking the width of doorways through which Goering would pass so that the Reichsmarschall could avoid public ridicule.

Goering's private railroad cars—three of them—were the most opulent in Europe. They were certainly more ostentatious than the private cars of Adolf Hitler whose tastes were more spartan than his Reichsmarschall's. Those who traveled with Hitler had to content themselves with plain food and unornamented furnishings. Hitler was a vegetarian who considered food little more than a biological necessity, and his diet was at least partly responsible for the uncontrollable flatulence with which he plagued his followers. More than one of his entourage had found himself persona non grata after wrinkling his nose in his Führer's presence.

Traveling with Hermann Goering, however, was like being on holiday. The food was marvelous, the wine excellent, and the great man himself, unlike Hitler, who preferred solitude, was always at the center of attention. Goering was a marvelous storyteller who enlivened his yarns with wild gestures, funny faces, and knee-slapping, and the journalists —particularly those from the German papers—were having a wonderful time. This was a grand adventure, and they were part of history.

Hermann Goering was a born braggart, a man of extravagant tastes who enjoyed all of the excesses that his position within the Nazi hierarchy allowed. He fancied himself a Renaissance man, a connoisseur of good food and fine art. He was able to satisfy his love for art by plundering the art collections and museums of occupied Europe. In 1940 he was forty-seven, his body a bloated caricature of the swashbuckling air ace he had been in 1918. His morphine addiction, a vice only whispered about in the Reichstag, had already begun to rob him of the mental acuity of his earlier days.

An aide pushed his way into the circle of reporters who surrounded Goering, waited patiently until his boss had finished another one of his funny stories, and then handed Goering a message which had just been received in the communications car.

Goering looked at the message and smiled, and then, his eyes twinkling, he addressed the reporters. "As you are well aware, last night aircraft of the Kampfgeschwader II, under Field Marshall Kesselring, bombed London for the first time." He held up the note he had been handed. "I have here the Luftwaffe reconnaissance reports on the results of that raid." He glanced at the note. "Severe damage inflicted upon several factories and docking facilities along the Thames . . . fires burning out of control throughout the night and still smoldering as of four o'clock this afternoon." He looked up. "These raids are our response to the British bombing of Berlin several days ago, but I wish to assure you that, in contrast to the RAF's indiscriminate destruction of civilian lives and property, the German Air Force will strike only at targets of indisputable military value." His smile broadened. "I can also assure you that this is only the beginning. These raids will continue and increase in intensity until Churchill realizes the futility of resistance." He crumpled the paper into a ball. "Churchill will rue the day that he ordered his pilots to attack Berlin."

The Reichsmarschall lifted his great bulk out of his specially reinforced chair and announced to the reporters, "You will have to excuse me, gentlemen. I must attend to my duties."

The reporters filed out of the car, some whispering to each other that the war must surely now be in its final stages. When the last of them had gone, Goering rang for an aide and sat down to scribble a quick message to Kesselring.

Goering liked to give orders. Consequently he bombarded his commanders in the field with communiqués and directives. He might have used the telephone for many of these messages, but he was afraid that these landlines, stretching across Europe, were not secure. The perfect answer to this problem was the Enigma coding machine, that the Luftwaffe called "Glowlamp." He could send as many orders as he wished without worrying that they might fall into enemy hands. Goering, to the delight of the cryptographers at Bletchley Park, used the Enigma device more than any other German commander.

His aide entered and Goering finished writing before he looked up and gave him the message. "Take this to the communications room," he said. "Have them encode the message for immediate transmission on the Glowlamp machine."

The aide nodded and left immediately. Goering smiled with satisfaction. He had just ordered the beginning of the destruction of London. He was glad that Hitler had finally lifted his ridiculous directive forbidding the bombing of the city. How was he, Goering, to succeed when he could not attack his enemy's weakness? If Hitler had let him have his way, London would be in ruins by now, and the war would be over. Sometimes, he thought sadly, the Führer was too kind-hearted.

Goering thought of the preparations already underway. Everything would be in place by the time he arrived in Calais. He would add a few personal touches, shake a few hands, pose for some photographs for the press, and send his pilots off to destroy London. He would remain long enough to greet his returning warriors, pose for a few more photographs, and then reboard his train. He sank back into his chair, imagining the hero's welcome that would await him in Berlin. It was entirely possible, he thought, that the war would be over before his train returned to Stettiner Station.

In the communication room Oberfeldwebel Heinz Gurtner switched on his Glowlamp machine. He waited for the glow of the ready light to come on before opening his code book. He ran his finger down the page until he found the designated drum code for that day and then set the drums to the corresponding lettering. Only then did he look at Goering's message. He whistled softly to himself as he read. It's about time, he thought. He'd had enough of this war already. Maybe a good dose of German explosives would bring the English to their senses.

As he began to type the message into the machine, Glowlamp instantaneously regrouped the letters into an indecipherable jabber. He wrote:

FROM: REICHSMARSCHALL HERMANN GOERING,
LUFTWAFFE HQ (TRANSIT)
TO: GENERALFELDMARSCHALL KESSELRING, LUFTWAFFE
HQ CALAIS-MARK
5 SEPTEMBER   1830 HOURS

CONTINUE AS PLANNED WITH LIGHT BLOWS AGAINST
ENEMY STOP I WILL ARRIVE YOUR HQ TOMORROW TO TAKE
PERSONAL COMMAND STOP PREPARE COORDINATED HEAVY
STRIKES AGAINST LONDON DOCK AREA FOR AFTERNOON OF
FOLLOWING DAY STOP HEIL HITLER END MESSAGE

The coded message was plucked out of the air by Field Marshal Kesselring's Glowlamp operator at Luftflotte II headquarters in Calais-Marck. The machine began the process of rearranging the letters into the form of the original message.

At almost the same moment the RAF intercept station at Cheadle gathered in the same scrambled message. Within seconds the transmission had been relayed by cable to Bletchley Park, where the clacking keys of the X-3 machine signaled to the operator that another message had been received. At the conclusion of the transmission the message was taken from the decoding room to Hut 3, for the translation from German into English. Once translated, the message was relayed by teletype to SIS headquarters in Broadway. The whole process took less than six minutes.

At Calais-Marck, General Field Marshal Kesselring was in conference with the commander of Lehrgeschwader 2 - 1 (j) Gruppe, the Messerschmitt 109 squadron stationed at Calais-Marck, when the message was delivered to his adjutant. When he was finished, Kesselring read the message. The prospect of having Goering breathing down his neck for a few days did not please him.

By the time Kesselring had read the message it had already been given to Air Marshal Sir Hugh "Stuffy" Dowding, Commander-in-Chief of Fighter Command, at his underground headquarters at Stanmore, and to Stewart Menzies, chief of the Secret Intelligence Service, at his office on Broadway, and was on its way to Prime Minister Churchill at 10 Downing Street.

This latest piece of information was the final, and perhaps most important, indication that the war was about to take a dramatic turn. Since August 31 reconnaissance aircraft of the RAF Coastal Command had been able to document an alarming increase in the number of barges and other small craft in the ports and estuaries of France and Belgium. On August 31, for instance, there were eighteen barges in the port of Ostend in Belgium. By September 5 there were more than two hundred. These figures were duplicated up and down the coast. This fact, coupled with the tremendous increase in Wehrmacht activity near the French coast and, now, the Ultra intercept of Goering's orders for September 7, led the British military authorities to the inevitable conclusion that the Germans were now, at long last, prepared to make the final leap across the Channel. The military authorities recommended that the government order Invasion Alert 2: Attack probable within three days.

ANGRY HITLER THREATENS MASS DESTRUCTION OF BRITISH CITIES; BERLIN BOMBINGS, DE-STROYER DEAL INFURIATE CHANCELLOR

BERLIN, SEPT. 6

◆ *CHAPTER 31* ◆

LONDON, September 6—The air was electric and the city that soon would be under siege was alive with activity. The invasion alert had stirred the military into an even greater frenzy of activity and all morning long trucks and men and materials had rolled past gaping onlookers. In the parks of the central city the Royal Engineers were busily at work preparing positions for the soon to arrive antiaircraft guns. Everywhere, while curious spectators stopped to gape, sergeant-majors bellowed orders to their sweating charges. Sounds of, "Look lively there, lads" and "Put your backs to it, boys" resounded throughout the city.

Sandbags were put in place, antiaircraft guns rolled into position, barrage balloons laboriously inflated and hoisted aloft. Every now and again a dark Humber staff car would pull up next to a group of sweating soldiers. Out would step an officer and stir them on to an even higher level of effort. As soon as the staff car disappeared the men would grumble their complaints, and more than a few voiced their protest against such inhuman treatment. Inevitably their protests fell on the deaf ears of their sergeants, and the air of urgency, which surrounded the men like an electric current, kept them at their tasks.

At the south entrance to St. James's Park, Winston Hamilton walked past a group of sweating soldiers, glad that his position did not necessitate such herculean labors. It pleased him to note that in the midst of all the activity the huge bed of dahlias at the entrance to the park was untouched and bloomed as magnificently as ever. It would have been unthinkable—totally un-English—for him to have imagined that these beautiful flowers might be replaced by some implement of war. He noted, with a smile, that whoever had positioned the gun emplacement which was now under construction had seen to it that the dahlias would go undisturbed, and he wondered if German soldiers would be as thoughtful. He doubted it very much.

Winston would have liked to tell the grumbling soldiers that their efforts were not in vain. Twenty-four hours from now, he thought, the skies over London would be dark with aircraft, and, although Ultra had not yet disclosed the intelligence, it was entirely possible that Hitler's armies would be on their way across the Channel. He added his own silent, 'Bend your back to it, boys.'

The park was only a short walk from his office which was part of the huge complex of government buildings known as Whitehall that ran from Trafalgar Square to Great George Street. Marie had promised to meet him today at the small bridge that bisected the St. James's Park Lake. She had promised to meet him there on Wednesday, also, but, for some undisclosed reason, she had been unable to do so. He had waited for almost an hour before trudging wearily back to his office, where he had tried in vain to get in touch with her at the Free French headquarters at Carlton Gardens.

Getting through to someone at de Gaulle's headquarters was probably more difficult than telephoning Churchill—the place was absolute chaos. How, he wondered, did they expect to do business in England when the people who answered the phones spoke only French?

His heart sank when he reached the bridge. She was not there yet.

He waited for fifteen minutes, pacing back and forth as if he were on guard duty, then crossed to the other side. All of his doubts about himself, well hidden these past few weeks, were let loose from the dark places in his soul. Why had he allowed himself to think that Marie could find something in him that other women had not? She could have anyone she wanted—why would she pick him?

She saw him pacing, head down, hands thrust in pockets. She almost laughed at the sight of him. Poor fool, she thought. She had played him perfectly. Men like Winston Hamilton were terrified by sexually aggressive woman, so she had played the part of a lady with just a slight promise of seduction lurking in the background. He had told her everything he knew, which turned out not to be very much.

She wondered why Sean Daly had picked him. He obviously didn't know anything of any great importance. Trying to impress her, Hamilton had told her all about his job. He had told her about his boss, Stewart Menzies, and about the important people that he met during the course of his workday. These important people, according to Winston, were always praising him for his good work, but his work seemed to be little more than translating relatively unimportant documents that had only some peripheral connection with the war.

Daly had hoped for more—much more. What the hell. It wasn't her fault. If Winston had known anything, he would have told her. It was Daly's fault for choosing such a nonentity.

It was time, she thought, to get rid of Winston. To send him back to his mother. Her new assignment, Munro, had, in more ways than one, much more interesting possibilities. The switch in assignments pleased her.

Winston saw her approach and felt his heart soar. She had been delayed. That was all. Nothing more. He loved to watch her. Her hair bouncing with every step; her legs, long and slim; her body, lean and taut, were delights beyond his imagination. This past week had been like heaven for him. She had linked her arm through his when they walked down the street, and young officers—some of them RAF pilots —had looked at him with the kind of respect that men give to one another in recognition of some marvelous accomplishment.

She kissed him lightly on the cheek. "Hello," she said.

"I've missed you," he blurted out. His pain was palpable.

Marie ignored his suffering. "I can't stay long," she said, looking at her watch.

That one casual, thoughtless motion told him everything he had feared and more than he wanted to know. She was dismissing him from her life. Perhaps there was already someone else. Of course there was. Probably a high-ranking officer or a government official. She thrived on the feeling of being with someone important—he knew that. He had tried, without revealing essential details, to make his job sound as significant as possible. She was always pestering for details about his work and about the people he encountered. But without telling her about Ultra he could never make his job important enough to satisfy her.

"I've got a very busy day," she said. "I've been asked to find housing for many of the French refugees in the city. It isn't easy."

"Will I see you"—he almost said "again." Instead he said, "tonight?"

She looked away from him, her eyes on the lake. "No," she said simply. The best way was to end it quickly. No need to let him linger.

"Perhaps tomorrow, then?"

"I'm going to be terribly busy for some time with this housing thing. I'll be all over the city today and tomorrow until late in the day. No telling how long it will take."

"Can I call you, then?"

Why did he have to make this difficult. "I don't think you should bother," she said. Marie looked at her watch again. "Well," she said, "I have to be in Holborn by one o'clock. I must be going." She left no room for protest. "Goodbye, then," she said and walked off.

Winston was numb. He could not bear to watch her leave. He turned away and looked across the lake. Looming in the background, above the trees, were the buildings of Whitehall. Behind them, hidden from view, was the Thames. Beyond, less than three miles from where he stood, lay the docks and factories, and the surrounding houses, that Hermann Goering had targeted for destruction. If Hitler and Goering made good their boast, the whole area could be leveled tomorrow.

"Houses," he said aloud. Hadn't Marie said she would be

all over the city looking for houses? Surely she wouldn't look in the East End. His heart was thumping against his chest. But what if she did?

He raced after her, sprinting like a madman.

Marie hadn't gone a hundred yards on Birdcage Walk when she heard him calling to her. She turned, more surprised than angered at first, but the sight of him, legs churning, arms waving wildly, actually infuriated her. She had cut him off, gently but firmly, and here he was racing after her. What a fool! Arms akimbo, she turned to face him. "What do you want," she said crossly.

"Where did you say you were going tomorrow?" he asked, his breath coming in painful gasps.

"I didn't," she said. "Where I'm going is none of your business."

"But you said you were going all over the city."

"And?"

"Not to the East End?"

She had no intentions of ever going to the East End. It was vile and dirty and even the French refugees would refuse to relocate there. "And if I am?" she said defiantly.

"You mustn't," he pleaded. "Promise me that you will not be there tomorrow."

Her eyes narrowed. "Why not?"

He was still gasping for breath after his sprint. "I can't tell you," he said. "I can only tell you not to be there tomorrow."

She thought quickly, unsure of what was happening. "But I have an appointment there," she lied.

"Don't go. Whatever you do don't go."

"I have no choice." She was almost enjoying this now. "I have to go."

"When is your appointment?"

"Afternoon," she guessed. Jackpot! She saw his face crumple. "Sometime in the afternoon."

He was taking deep breaths. "I can't explain to you," he said, one deliberate word at a time, "and you must never repeat what I have told you, but you must not be in the East End tomorrow afternoon."

"You'll have to give me more reason than that."

"I've said too much already."

Marie saw the panic in his face and tried to question him

further, but Hamilton turned and ran in the direction from which he had come.

Marie Price watched him for a moment before she continued on her way. What was happening in the East End tomorrow that Winston wanted her to avoid? She couldn't, for the life of her, imagine.

"Strange and foolish man," she muttered.

NAZI RAIDS INTENSIFY, LONDON HIT; P.M.
SCOFFS AT HITLER'S THREAT; CHURCHILL
CLAIMS, "WE CAN TAKE IT"

LONDON, SEPT. 6

◆ *CHAPTER 32* ◆

CALAIS, Saturday, September 7—The cameras clicked, and Hermann Goering maintained his pose for just a little longer. His hands were on his hips and his face towards the sky. He stood alone on the forward observation post on the cliffs of Cap Gris-Nez, his entourage of staff members conveniently out of camera range. No one would steal this moment of triumph from the Reichsmarschall.

Above him swarmed V-shaped formations of aircraft in row after perfect row. The steady drone of engines, like a million angry hornets, was an awesome spectacle that silenced even the usually ebullient press corps. They watched, mouths agape, as the cream of the German bomber forces, Junkers, Heinkels, Dorniers, gained altitude and joined their fellows in a steady stream of swastika-winged aircraft aimed directly at the enemy's heart.

Goering clapped his hands in almost childish glee and pointed to the south. The spectators turned in the direction that Goering had indicated. Formation after formation of smaller craft rushed in to join the bombers. "Messerschmitt," said Goering needlessly, as the fighters dipped their wings in salute to their commander-in-chief.

It was the greatest air fleet ever assembled, more than a thousand aircraft strong, and more than twice as large as the air fleets that had devastated Warsaw and Rotterdam. Against them the RAF could not hope to muster an equal force. Although Goering had underestimated the fighting strength of Fighter Command, there were still fewer British fighters available for combat than the Luftwaffe had in the air at that moment. The RAF pilots were near exhaustion. The Germans had put an almost constant pressure against them for close to ten weeks and pilot losses to the smaller British force had reached a critical level. Even if aircraft production were able to match losses, it was impossible to replace the pilots. The "few" were becoming fewer.

September 7 was a glorious day for the Reichsmarschall. He had evaluated the failures of August and determined that the problems had been caused by a lack of coordination between bomber and fighter groups. The fighter pilots were free spirits who preferred what they called *freie Jagd*—free chase—to the less exciting but vitally important role of defending the bomber groups. Consequently, the British, with vastly inferior numbers, had been able to concentrate their efforts against the slower and more vulnerable bombers, while refusing combat with the free-roaming fighters. As a former fighter pilot with twenty-two victories to his credit and his country's highest award for valor, Goering understood the feelings of the fighter pilots. Goering had been the last commander of the Richthofen Fighter Squadron and saw himself as the last of the warrior knights, but knew that the air war could not be won using the outmoded standards of individual combat of the last war.

As his vast air fleet, now almost a mile high and ten miles deep, droned toward England, he turned his attention to the horizon. A thin sliver of white, the chalk cliffs of Dover, hovered in a light mist. He shaded his eyes with one hand and squinted trying to bring the English coast into sharper focus, but the mist and the light played tricks with his eyes and the coastline seemed to hover above the Channel like some ethereal castle suspended in the clouds.

Goering snapped his fingers impatiently and an aide rushed forward with field glasses. The Reichsmarschall raised them to his eyes and pulled the Dover coast into full view.

The photographers moved positions so that they could include the English coast in the background with Goering. The cameras clicked, the newsreels whirred, and Goering, ever the showman, strutted back and forth in a stance that reminded some of Mussolini.

Again he looked skyward. The angry black cloud that was his air force still passed overhead. By now the leaders of the formations were halfway across the Channel. In less than ten minutes they would cross the English coast, and twenty minutes after that they would wreak havoc on London.

This time, he thought, there will be no stopping them. The juggernaut would continue until London lay in ruins and Churchill begged for peace.

Goering sucked in his belly and gave the photographers his best profile. The cameras clicked furiously and he knew that tomorrow his photograph would be on the front page of every newspaper in the world. He chuckled, thinking how Hitler hated the fact that Goering was more popular than he, and had often chided his number two man for using the press to promote that popularity. Well, thought Goering, wait until tomorrow, my Führer. When I bring the war to a close, the German people will give me a welcome such as Berlin has never seen.

The plotting room at the RAF Fighter Command Headquarters was already a bustle of activity. Coastal radar stations had picked up the gathering German forces while they were still over France and the huge table map that filled the room displayed the counters that represented the growing numbers of German aircraft. The table map showed the English and French coasts and the Channel between them. At opposite ends of the table, holding the long-handled, croupier's rake with which they advanced the counters, stood the young women of the Woman's Auxiliary Air Force. The WAAFs wore headphones and listened intently to the instructions which detailed the number, direction, altitude, and speed of the approaching German aircraft. When the attackers reached the coast where their type and number could be identified by the Ground Observer Corps, the WAAFs would differentiate between bombers and fighters on the map.

Every few minutes or so, one of the young women would advance the counters on the board while another would take more counters from the trays that circled the table and add them to the growing numbers over the Pas de Calais. Across the table, another WAAF would advance the counters that represented the RAF's response to the German thrust.

Watching the proceedings from a balcony that encircled the room was the duty controller. Leaning on the railing, he watched with growing unease as the German numbers grew. He had never seen anything like this. Moments before he had sent an assistant to inform Air Chief Marshal Dowding that a large attack was forming. In just those few moments the numbers had increased drastically and he was anxious for his chief to appear.

The women on the plotting-room floor quietly attended to their duties. Like croupiers at the gaming tables they nonchalantly pushed forward their chips. Their motions were sure, unhurried, and emotionless, but as the numbers grew, the women began to steal furtive glances at each other. No words were needed, the glances were enough. This was it.

The staff at Bentley Priory, Stanmore, headquarters of Fighter Command, was well aware that this was going to be a special day. All morning long a steady procession of RAF bigwigs had been arriving and early that afternoon Air Vice-Marshal Keith Park had flown in from Group Command Headquarters at Uxbridge. There was enough Air Force brass crowded into the Air Chief's small office to let everyone know that something was in the air. The rumors spread like wildfire. It was common knowledge, of course, printed in newspapers the world over, that the Germans had massed their invasion barges along the French and Belgian coasts. Many were aware that Invasion Alert 2 had been announced. The world watched and waited as the drama unfolded. But no one knew better than the staff here at Bentley Priory how dangerously thin the RAF's defenses had become. They knew, better than anyone dared to admit, that the RAF was within an eyelash of extinction.

Dowding and his entourage appeared at the railing. The commander-in-chief took in the situation at a glance, and imperturbable as ever turned to Air Vice-Marshal Park. "Here it is," he said softly.

The duty controller gave him the most recent information. "Observer Corps is reporting a large number of fighters accompanying the bombers, sir. Looks like a two to one ratio."

"How many aircraft on the board?" asked Dowding.

"More than six hundred—and still growing."

Dowding turned to Park. "What do you think?"

Park gave a tight-lipped smile. "Hermann's finally learning," he said. "Heavily escorted bomber formations to tempt us into combat."

"All of 11 Group is on alert," said the controller. "Half the group is already in the air, the rest awaiting the call."

"Let's get them up, then," said Dowding. "But hold them over their sector stations, prepared to move in when the Germans make their target selections."

The duty controller frowned, but said nothing. Dowding, apparently, was planning to hold his fighter squadrons in defensive formations over their stations anticipating that the Germans were once again attacking the airfields. But, by this time, the Germans had usually dispersed into smaller groups to attack their individual targets. This time they were remaining in formation, obviously heading for some other target. The duty controller looked at the table map. It was becoming apparent what that target was. He cleared his throat. "They don't seem to be breaking up," he offered.

Dowding nodded, but said nothing. Air Chief Marshal Sir Hugh "Stuffy" Dowding was more responsible for the existence of Fighter Command than anyone. In May of 1940, when the War Cabinet had been persuaded by the French to send ten additional fighter squadrons to France in hopes of stemming the German tide, it had been Dowding who told Churchill and his Cabinet what they did not want to hear. The ten squadrons, said Dowding, were too little and too late. If they were sent to France they would be lost for the next and more important battle. Those ten squadrons could spell the difference between defeat and victory.

Dowding's view, to the great consternation of the French, had won the day. The RAF had lived to fight another day.

The duty controller was growing nervous at Dowding's

continued lack of response. "11 Group doesn't have the machines to match up with this force. Shall I call in 12 Group?"

"Not yet," Dowding said calmly. "Let's see what develops."

The counters on the map table converged as the first units of 11 Group made contact. Undeterred, the black swarm of German counters plowed on toward London.

On the plotting-room floor the activity had grown more frantic as more and more RAF squadrons moved in. Several of the WAAFs, knowing what the results of such one-sided contact must mean, wiped away tears as they continued to move the counters across the table. Inexorably, like a bulldozer pushing aside everything in its path, the swarm pressed on.

The duty controller stole a quick glance at Dowding. The Air Chief gripped the railing, his knuckles white, his teeth clenched. What the hell is he waiting for, wondered the duty controller, and then it came to him in a flash like summer lightning. Dowding had no intention of committing his remaining forces to the battle because he did not think they could survive. If Fighter Command did not exist, then the war was as good as over. Just as he had held back his fighters from the French when they were desperately needed, he was now holding them back from his own people. London would have to make it on her own.

◆ CHAPTER 33 ◆

Saturday, September 7, 1940—Max Munro was in his office at the embassy when he heard the first thin wailing siren somewhere off to the east. Such sirens usually meant little. German bombers crossed the English coast every day and sirens went off all over the place. Usually the bombers were intercepted by RAF fighters somewhere over Kent or Sussex and that was the end of it. He put the sound out of his mind and went back to work.

He had stopped by the embassy to clear up some paperwork that he did not want to leave for Monday. He was planning to spend Monday escorting Betty to a few military installations in the countryside. He had already ordered a picnic hamper from Fortnums, and intended to take advantage of the magnificent weather. He and Betty could make a day of it.

Another siren went off. Closer this time. Not more than a minute later another siren began wailing. Closer still. And then several in unison, making a great caterwauling wail. He got up and went to the window. Traffic had not yet stopped, but pedestrians were looking up as if trying to gauge the direction of the ominous sounds. A policeman appeared, stopped traffic, and began directing passengers and pedestrians to the nearest shelters. That, thought Munro, would probably be up by Marleybone Arch. The embassy had its own shelter for embassy personnel.

He went back to his papers.

More sirens joined in until, he thought, every siren in the city must be wailing. The sound was disconcerting. No matter how many times one heard it, no matter how many false alarms there had been, there was always a disquieting impulse to head for cover. Just as he decided that perhaps he should head for the embassy shelter, the door opened and Colonel Jackson walked into the room, carrying field glasses.

"It's a raid," he said calmly. "Looks like a big one."

"Are you going to the shelter?"

"I thought I'd go up to the roof and watch," he said. "I was wondering if you'd like to join me."

The roof was the last place Munro wanted to be during an air raid. "Sure," he said. "Sounds great."

They took the elevator to the top floor and then the stairs up to the roof. Jackson led the way to the rear of the roof where they could look east toward the docks. Munro looked down at the immense marble courtyard that formed the embassy's backyard and involuntarily rested an arm on the railing that encircled the roof.

The day was magnificent. A late summer sun bathed the city, and the reflection of a million sparkling windows sent slivers of light cascading across the rooftops. Straight ahead, less than two miles away, the dome of St. Paul's loomed protectively above the surrounding buildings. To the right

—the southeast—the Houses of Parliament were clearly visible, with Big Ben thrusting into the clear, blue summer sky. Here and there, slivers of greenery punctuated the mass of red brick and gray granite that stretched as far as the eye could see. In the distance, between the rows of buildings, Munro caught glimpses of the Thames glistening in the sunlight.

"There!" said Colonel Jackson, pointing to the east.

Munro shaded his eyes. There, high to the east and slightly south, he saw the vapor trails of the bombers stretching out like long chalk marks across the blue chalkboard sky.

Jackson had the field glasses to his eyes. "Good God," he said. "They're still in perfect formation. It's as if they've made it through untouched. Where the hell were the fighters?"

Jackson gave the field glasses to Munro, who looked briefly. "You're right," he said. "It looks like a parade."

The rumbling started like distant thunder or muted kettle-drums, but they could feel the vibrations as the bombs hit. Almost immediately black clouds of smoke mushroomed skyward as if to touch their tormentors. Explosion followed explosion in such quick succession that the sound was as one long continuous reverberation.

Colonel Jackson had the glasses again. "They're after the docks," he said matter-of-factly.

Now the underside of the black smoke glowed a dull red, while white hot flashes, like photographers' bulbs, illuminated the billowing cloud from within.

The first wave of aircraft banked in unison to the right, and for what seemed like minutes the awful din was silent. Only the roar of the city and the clamor of its traffic could be heard above the siren's wail. Then, close on the heels of the first wave, followed the second, and the thunder began anew. That wave, and the next, and the next, simply dumped their destruction into the swirling conflagration below.

"This is what it has all been leading up to," Jackson said. "There's no end to it now."

When the first siren sounded, Marie Price had just emerged from a butcher shop on John Street in Islington near the Chapel Street Market. Her travels had taken her to the northern sections of the city and before returning home she

215

had decided to purchase some ground beef. With all the talk of scarcity, she was amazed that meat still seemed to be plentiful in the butcher shops around the city.

As she walked toward the bus stop on Pentonville Road the sirens became more insistent and many of the pedestrians had stopped to look up. Like the others, Marie looked up into the clear cloudless sky. The weather had been beautiful, warm and sunny, without a drop of rain for over a month. This had been the most marvelous summer in recent memory. Then she saw them. Small, dark specks, leaving misty white trails across the sky.

People streamed out of nearby shops to see what was happening. Many began to point toward the specks in the sky.

The sirens were wailing all around them now, but the planes seemed so far away and so high in the sky that those watching had no real sense of danger. Traffic moved passed them as if nothing was out of the ordinary, and many watched the spectacle in the air for a short time then and went on their way. Marie was transfixed, remembering.

There was a distant, incongruous rumbling of thunder on the clear, summer day. Low in the sky several thick columns of smoke began to rise slowly above the city.

"Looks like they've got the docks," someone said.

"The whole East End's getting it pretty bad," said another.

Marie walked hurriedly toward the bus stop, wondering if the buses would still run in the middle of an air raid. She had to get in touch with Sean Daly. Hamilton had told her to stay away from the East End in the afternoon. He had given her a warning so that she could avoid the bombing. He had known all along that this was going to happen.

She had to find Daly. She had to let him know.

The London docks, from Bermondsey to West Ham, were ablaze. For mile after mile, from London Bridge and beyond, the East End of the city was enveloped in a thick pall of smoke. Row after row of ancient tenement houses collapsed beneath the force of the explosions or were consumed in the rapidly spreading flames. Houses, families, neighborhoods disappeared.

Max Munro and Colonel Jackson stayed on the roof for over an hour watching wave after wave of German bombers appear over the city and drop their bombs on dockland. The skies were clear of British planes and the Germans, in flying circus formations, flew unmolested to their targets and turned for home.

After leaving the embassy roof, Munro tried to get in touch with Betty at the Savoy. But the lines were either overloaded or out of order. He wasn't worried—so far the raids had been confined to the East End, and if the Germans decided to bomb the West End, the Savoy was reported to have the best air raid shelters in London. He decided to stay at the embassy, at least until he could get in touch with her. The embassy shelters were safe and certainly more comfortable than anything he might be forced to use if he were caught in a raid on his way home.

By seven o'clock he had grown more concerned. He still was unable to get through to the Savoy and the air raids continued. Then his phone rang. It was Betty.

"I've been trying to phone you," he said as soon as he heard her voice. "Are you OK?"

"I'm fine," she said. "The phone's were out of order here for a while. They just came back on. I've been in the basement bar. You should see the setup downstairs here. It's like a night club."

"I'm glad you're OK." He could hear music in the background.

"I need your help," she said.

"Sure. What is it?"

"Can you get a car?"

"I can get an embassy car. But the traffic is tied up for miles. What's up?"

"Try to get over here as quickly as you can," she said. "I'll wait for you."

He took the smallest car in the embassy garage, a two-door Austin. The traffic around Grosvenor Square was a nightmare. It took him more than fifteen minutes to get to the end of Duke Street and onto Grosvenor. The street was jammed with abandoned buses and cars. He fell in behind a taxi driver who obviously knew his way around. Several times Munro followed him onto the sidewalk and around an immobilized obstruction. At Davies Street the taxi turned north and Munro followed knowing that Oxford Street, a wider thoroughfare, was dead ahead. They zipped past Claridges, and the taxi turned right at Brook Street, but Munro went

217

straight. At Oxford the traffic was moving—at a snail's pace. At Oxford Circus he peered down Regent Street but traffic was backed up as far as he could see. Everywhere he went, emergency vehicles—fire engines, ambulances—were angrily clanging bells and howling sirens at the motorists who blocked their way, and the police were ordering cars to pull over. Munro squeezed the Austin through the tiny space between two abandoned cars and spun into a side street. Several times he had to drive on the sidewalk but eventually he made it through to the next wider street where he was able to move east then swing back south onto Oxford again.

At St. Giles Circus he pulled onto Charing Cross Road and luckily fell in behind a fire engine. He made good speed for five minutes but even the fire engine slowed near Leicester Square. The police cleared a path for the fire engine but would not allow him through. He showed his embassy card, but was given only a blank stare by a young constable who had neither the time nor the inclination to discuss international protocol with a pushy American.

Finally the traffic moved and he zipped the Austin onto the Strand. An hour and a half after leaving the American Embassy he pulled into the courtyard at the Savoy.

Betty was waiting for him, with two men, Bill Talmadge and someone else. They all carried their gas masks and helmets. "What took you so long?" she asked.

As he started to explain about the traffic, she yanked open the door and the two men climbed into the back seat.

"This is Dick Underwood," said Betty getting into the front. "He's with the *Herald Tribune*. Talmadge you know."

"What's going on?" Munro asked.

"We can't find a car anywhere," said Betty. "Not a taxi to be had, and we want to get to the East End to find out what's going on over there."

"You guys have spent too much time in the reporter's bar at the Savoy," Munro said. "The East End is an inferno."

"We're reporters," Betty said. "We've got stories to write."

Munro thought for a minute. Obviously she was determined to do this. "I'll go on one condition," he said.

"Name it," they said in unison.

"If I decide that it's getting too dangerous, we turn back with no arguments."

"Agreed," said Betty. "Let's go."

As Munro put the Austin in gear, a man raced toward them from the Savoy. He leaned in the window on Betty's side. "You going where I think you're going, Betty?"

"You bet," she said.

"Got room for one more?"

Betty laughed. "I didn't know you radio people actually went out and got stories," she said. "I thought you just copied your stuff from the newspaper."

"Most of the time we do, but once in a while we like to see what it's like to travel with real reporters."

Betty opened the door. "Climb in," she said and the man scrambled into the back seat. "This," she said to Munro, "is Ed Murrow. Works in radio."

Murrow said, "Can somebody light my cigarette for me? It's so crowded back here I can't get my lighter out of my pocket."

Munro eased the Austin back out into the traffic on the Strand. If we're lucky, he thought, the police will stop us before we get blown to kingdom come.

To Sean Daly the flames were like the festive bonfires of childhood celebrations. He, like thousands of others who came to watch, was drawn like a moth to the flame. They lined the walkways and bridges along the Thames on the outskirts of the flames and watched in morbid fascination as a major part of their city was consumed in the great fire. Some were shocked, others were angry. Daly was blissful.

In the early evening he had found a position on the Victoria Embankment, near the Charing Cross Station. It has finally come, he thought, his eyes dancing with the reflection of the flames. This could only be the beginning of the end. Soon the Germans would be here.

Rumors raced through the throng as quickly as the spreading fires across the river, gathering momentum with each new telling. The Germans had landed at Dover . . . thousands were dead but still they kept coming. An old woman, munching on an apple, told Daly that German parachutists had landed in Kent and captured several unspecified RAF airfields. Her companion insisted that the night raids had actually been launched from one of these captured airfields. A middle-aged man in a dark business suit announced that he

219

had heard a BBC report that a Panzer unit, apparently landed under cover of darkness, had been spotted in West Sussex. The most prevalent rumor was that the Germans were only hours from London and that some advance units had actually reached the outskirts of the city.

Daly was ecstatic. He wanted to savor the moment. He wanted every part of it etched into his brain forever. The only thing lacking was someone with whom to share his ecstasy.

Being alone with his thoughts was like being alone on New Year's Eve. He was the single reveler at the funeral. He wanted to scream at the top of his lungs. "This is what you have been asking for!"

He had to share his joy with someone. It was out of the question to contact Benke. What better person than Marie Price? He would find some champagne and go to her flat. Together they would celebrate the coming of the liberators.

None of the rumors were true. What was true was that in the face of the German assault, the army had issued the code word *Cromwell,* which was the signal to ring the church bells across the nation. The tolling bells signified that the nation had gone to Alert Status 1—invasion probable within twelve hours.

Across the coastal regions of southern England the populace gathered weapons—old hunting rifles, shotguns, pitchforks, clubs—and awaited the arrival of the first invading army since William the Conqueror.

As night fell the fires burned unabated, glowing like beacons through the burgeoning smoke. While the Auxiliary Fire Service struggled desperately to contain the flames, and the Air Raid Wardens dug into the rubble in search of survivors, the bombers of Generalfeldmarschall Hugo Sperrle's Luftflotte III followed the beacons that brightly illuminated the undulating River Thames and dropped their bombs into the chaos below.

◆ *CHAPTER 34* ◆

Munro nosed the Austin onto the London Bridge. From there he and his passengers could look down the river toward the docks.

"My God," someone whispered as Munro slowed the car to a crawl.

Both sides of the river were in flames. The sky glowed as bright as day over the Surrey Docks and looking east they could see Tower Bridge, which stood silhouetted against an orange backdrop of flames that roared as with a million voices and rose to incredible heights. In there somewhere was Bermondsey, Millwall, Poplar, Deptford, West Ham.

"Silvertown," said Betty softly to Munro.

He looked back and nodded. It seemed only yesterday that they had toured the squalid slum area. Silvertown had been teeming with life—children, street vendors, workmen, shoppers. Now it burned brighter than any other area.

"I think the raid is over," Talmadge said. "I haven't heard any explosions for well over an hour."

"There hasn't been any 'all clear,' either," said Munro.

"We're close to the Surrey Docks," Murrow said. "Let's see if we can get that far."

Across the bridge Munro turned onto Tooley Street and headed east. Once past Tower Bridge they were in the heart of dockland. They were stopped several times by police or firemen but were always able to talk their way forward. Often they were forced to back out of streets that were blocked with debris or bomb craters and find another route. Finally on the Lower Road they were stopped by an Air Raid Warden who would not allow them to continue. No amount of pleading would change his mind. Munro turned the car around.

"Pull over here," Betty said. "We can leave the car here and walk the rest of the way."

They got out and Talmadge, needlessly, reminded everyone to bring their helmets and gas masks.

They put on the helmets and Betty giggled. "I hope I don't look as silly as the rest of you," she said.

"Don't count on it," Murrow said.

Munro adjusted the strap on his helmet so it would not come loose.

"Let's go," said Talmadge, heading in the direction from which they had just come. The others followed.

They threaded their way down streets of smoldering ruin, backtracking when blocked, climbing over rubble, weaving around obstructions. Everywhere they looked was chaos —firemen fighting desperately to contain the spreading flames, screaming children searching for parents, policemen blowing whistles ordering everyone off the streets, air-raid wardens ushering others to the shelters.

They were walking down a deserted narrow street that was illuminated by a still burning tenement. The flames cast their shadows, long and sinister, across the width of the street and up the opposite wall. Halfway down a voice cried out, "You lot. Where in bloody hell do you think you're goin'?"

They found themselves accosted by a tiny, middle-aged man who wore a helmet and the arm band of an air raid warden. Murrow tried to explain that they were American reporters, but the warden would have none of it. "There's a UXB on this street," he said. "Didn't you see the ribbons?"

"UXB?" said Munro.

"Unexploded bomb," the warden said slowly so that none of them would misunderstand. "Right over there." He pointed at a building across the street. "Now get your arses off this street before I arrest the lot of you."

They retreated quickly and wandered rather aimlessly for a few minutes.

"Does anybody know where we are?" Munro asked.

Murrow smiled. "Most of the local landmarks seem to have disappeared."

They crossed another in a succession of unfamiliar streets. Betty stopped. "Wait a minute," she said, pointing down the middle of the street to where a small crowd had gathered. "Something's up." She headed down the street. The others followed.

The small crowd, mostly women, stood across from a collapsed building watching as two men scampered across the rubble. They were eerily quiet as the reporters approached.

"What's happening?" asked Betty bluntly.

"There's a child lost in there somewhere," whispered a young woman, herself no more than seventeen. "They're tryin' to locate her."

Betty noticed that one of the women was whimpering softly. The other women had formed a protective cordon around her, and Betty assumed the woman was the child's mother.

The men across the street picked their way carefully over the face of the rubble, pausing frequently to press their ears against the gaps in the granite. Suddenly one man raised his hand. His head disappeared inside a small hole as the crowd held its collective breath. The man jumped to his feet. "I hear her," he called. "She's alive."

With a great whoop the crowd surged forward leaving the Americans on the opposite side of the street. "What are we waiting for," Betty said and ran across to join the others, who were already attacking the debris of the collapsed building.

"Carefully, carefully," the man who had discovered the child was saying. "This lot could collapse at any minute."

They formed a human chain, passing the rubble hand over hand and dumping it into the street. Soon the hole was large enough for someone to crawl inside.

"Let me," said a boy of about twelve, and he began to scramble up the pile.

Munro clamped a hand on the boy's shoulder. "Let someone else do it, son," he said.

The boy shrugged his hand aside. "It's me sister in there."

He was lowered into the hole and while the rescuers waited two policemen and an air raid warden approached and demanded to know what was happening. There was a heated discussion and the policemen and the warden demanded that the crowd wait until the Rescue Service could arrive. "The whole bloody thing could collapse, and then where would you be?" said the warden.

Just then the boy emerged from the hole. "She's stuck under a pile o' bricks," he said frantically. "I couldn't move her. I think her legs is broken."

The mother began to wail and then, as if in sympathy, so did the sirens.

"Oh, Christ," said someone, "they're comin' back."

"Better get to the shelters," said the warden.

The wailing woman sprang forward, attacking the rubble as if she could bore a tunnel to her child. The crowd hesitated and then, against the protests of the warden, went to her assistance.

Close by, the first explosions reverberated. Unlike the distant rumbling of the afternoon, these were the distinct detonations of individual bombs. Each explosion seemed louder than the one before as the bombs advanced on their position.

The diggers worked frantically as the noise grew in intensity. The policemen raced to help them. "No sense standing around," Munro said and quickly got back into the line that was passing the debris down to the street. He looked back and Betty and the others were at his side.

The noise was all around them now. Every explosion made them jump, but they kept at it. The hole was widened and two of the men crawled inside. In minutes one returned and someone gave him a crow bar. He disappeared inside again.

A bomb hit somewhere at the end of the street and the blast, like a furnace-hot tornado, knocked the crowd flat. Before they could get up another hit collapsed a building at the opposite end of the street with a great crashing sound and showered them with dirt and debris. A great tongue of flame shot up from nowhere as if the earth had opened up and released the fires of hell.

The warden was screaming at the top of his lungs. Hysteria rushed at them with the blast and danced its fiery fingers around them. Suddenly the men inside the rubble reappeared and called for help. Hands reached in and a cry of joy went up as the child, a girl of about three, was passed out into the arms of the waiting rescuers.

Someone carried her gently down and handed her to her mother. Betty threw her arms around Munro and hugged him as if he alone had been responsible for the child's rescue. "We did it," she said and then, suddenly aware that she had singled him out for special mention, hugged each of the other reporters in turn. "All of us."

The noise of the bombs had moved on, bringing terror to some other street, but for now this neighborhood had battled and won.

Talmadge asked one of the policemen for directions and they headed back to the car.

It was dark and Dick Underwood was out in front. Suddenly there was a yell and Underwood disappeared. The others raced forward to find that Underwood had fallen into a deep hole that was either a bomb crater or where a part of the street had collapsed.

They pulled him out, unharmed, but complaining about the condition of the London streets.

Ten minutes later they found the Austin, covered in dust, but undamaged. They jumped in and drove off, heading back towards Tooley Street and London Bridge. The bomb blasts were behind them now, and they drove on through deserted streets.

"Everyone else," said Talmadge, "has the good sense to be in a shelter."

When they reached the bridge they looked back. Downriver the fires still burned brightly and it seemed impossible to imagine that they had been there, in the midst of all that, and emerged unscathed.

As they crossed to the comparative safety of the other side of the bridge, Underwood asked if anyone felt like singing "London Bridge is falling down."

No one did.

It was almost midnight when Marie Price heard the banging on her door. Her first thought was that it must be the police, but then she heard Daly's voice.

"Open up!" he called. "It's me."

She yanked the door open and he almost fell into the room. He had a bottle of champagne under one arm and a sheepish grin on his face.

"You're drunk," she said in amazement. She had never seen him like this.

He closed the door. "I've been celebrating."

"Celebrating? I've been trying to find you since late this afternoon. I wanted to tell you something Hamilton told me yesterday."

"Hamilton?" Daly frowned. "I told you to get rid of him."

"I did, but—"

"Good," Daly said, working on the champagne cork. "Get some glasses for the bubbly."

"But this could be important."

He laughed drunkenly. "Important? What's going on outside is important. What's happening on the invasion beaches is important."

Her eyes widened. "Invasion? You've heard something?"

He chuckled. "The news is everywhere. The Germans will probably be in London tomorrow."

"But I've been listening to the radio. No one has said anything about—"

He held up the bottle. "Tonight we celebrate. Tomorrow is the day of reckoning." He slipped an arm around her waist and pulled her close.

Marie resisted momentarily, but he was insistent and she could feel the urgency in his body. His need was transmitted to her and soon she forgot what it had been that she wanted to tell him. She opened her mouth, then moved forward, thrusting her body against his. She arched her back and began a slow undulation. "If it's celebration you want," she whispered in his ear, "you've come to the right place."

The Austin pulled into the Savoy courtyard and slipped into a small space between a parked Bentley and an idling Rolls. The tiny car was covered in dirt and dust and looked decidedly out of place next to its posh neighbors.

The doors opened and the grimy occupants tumbled out. They looked equally out of place.

"Can't wait to get into a bath," said Underwood.

Murrow brushed the dirt from his suit and carefully lit another cigarette. "I'm going to freshen up," he said, "and then get right over to Broadcasting House. I want to file this story while it's still fresh in my mind." He shook hands with Munro. "Thanks for the ride," he said with a grin. "It was great fun."

They shook hands all around and then Murrow, Underwood, and Talmadge left Munro and Betty alone.

Suddenly she felt self-conscious. "I must look a sight," she said, pulling her hair back from her face.

He grinned. Her face was dirty and her clothing disheveled. "You look wonderful," he said.

She stepped forward and kissed him lightly on the lips. "Liar," she whispered.

He laughed out loud and pulled her closer.

"What are you going to do now?" Betty asked.

"A bath sounds good right about now."

She stepped back and eyed him from head to toe. "Maybe," she said, "you'd like someone to scrub your back?"

Munro grinned. "I'll do yours, if you'll do mine."

"You've got yourself a deal," she said.

Arm in arm they went into the hotel, drawing stares from the well-dressed guests who were arriving from some of the city's elegant clubs—places like the Café de Paris, a favorite haunt of the Free French, the Café Anglais, Quaglino's, the Apertif, Prunier's, or Dunhill's. Places where the champagne flowed, the bands played the latest dance music, and the sound of sirens and distant bombing only added to the ambience and gave the evening a special sparkle.

Max and Betty waked through the lobby, oblivious to anything but each other.

All night long the mayhem continued. While the inhabitants of the more fashionable areas of the city, Mayfair, Kensington, Hammersmith, and Ealing, listened to the sirens, and the alarm bells, and the sound of distant explosions, the slums of the East End, Silvertown, Poplar, Plaistow, and Mile End Road were pummeled throughout the night. It was as if the Germans had decided that the poor of the city were responsible for the war and must therefore be singled out for special punishment.

From the air the world was a dark place with one brightly shining beacon of light. From the ground the world of the East End was an inferno.

Marie awoke to the dull sound of a distant voice. She reached across the bed to find Daly. He was gone. She could still hear the voice and imagined that Sean must be talking to someone in the other room. She got out of bed, slipped on a robe, and padded barefooted toward the sound of the voices.

Daly was sitting at the kitchen table, his head in his hands. He wore only his trousers. He was listening to the radio.

"What is it?" said Marie. "What has happened?"

He looked up, his eyes sad. "Nothing has happened," he said. "Absolutely nothing."

"But the bombing. You said it was the beginning of the invasion."

"I know what I said," he snapped. "But they didn't come."

Marie sat at the table across from him. "After last night," she said, "it can only be a matter of time."

"I'm beginning to wonder if they will ever come. Everything that we have risked has been for nothing. We've wasted our time on fools like Hamilton, and risked being hanged into the bargain."

"Hamilton," she said, brightening.

"What about him?"

"That's what I wanted to tell you last night. That's why I tried to get in touch with you all day. On Friday, when I met with Hamilton, he wanted to know where I would be on Saturday."

Daly shrugged, "So?"

"He told me not to go anywhere near the docks on Saturday afternoon."

Daly's eyes narrowed. "What you're thinking is impossible."

"He knew when and where the Germans would bomb."

"But you said he knew nothing."

"He fooled me," she said. "I still can't believe it myself, but he did not tell me everything he knew."

"If this is true . . ." he said, his excitement growing. "I must tell Benke right away. Do you know what this means?"

"Tell me," she teased.

"Either that someone very high up in the German military is revealing German plans to the British, or the British are somehow able to read the German military's codes. It all fits," he said. "This place in Buckinghamshire, where they send the messages to Hamilton's office, is bristling with all sorts of radio antennae. They must intercept German radio messages there and ship them off to London. What did you say that Hamilton did before the war?"

"Language professor," she said, smiling happily. "German."

"It fits. They get the messages and he translates them. That's how he knows."

"I didn't think he had it in him."

"It would also explain," said Daly, "how the British have been able to outmaneuver the Germans. You've got to contact him again. Today! We've got to find out how they do it."

"You told me to get rid of him. I'm supposed to see Munro tonight."

"Forget Munro for now. This is more important."

"So how do I make him tell me what I want to know?"

"You don't," he said. "I will."

"I don't understand."

"We don't have time for finesse," he said. "It's now or never for the invasion. You will bring him to me and I will make him tell us."

"Are you sure there is no other way?"

"If we are to influence the course of the war, it must be now."

She knew what that meant for Hamilton, but she could see that Daly was right. Time was short. There was no other way.

1500 NAZI PLANES POUND LONDON; CAPITAL SHAKEN, HUNDREDS DEAD; RAF DOWNS MANY RAIDERS

LONDON, SEPT. 7

◆ CHAPTER 35 ◆

Sunday, September 8—Munro was in Colonel Jackson's office at the embassy when Ambassador Kennedy called from his refuge in the country.

"Everything is fine here, Mr. Ambassador," Jackson said. "The East End had a bad night, I'm afraid. The radio is reporting more than four hundred killed and perhaps as many as fifteen hundred injured." He listened. "No, I don't suppose there is any need for you to come in to the city today. . . . Tomorrow? Tomorrow there is a luncheon at Claridge's for the American observers and the Air Ministry staff. . . . Yes, sir, I believe you're expected. . . . Yes, I suppose that Carson could fill in for you, Mr. Ambassador." Jackson listened, his face grim. "Then I will explain to the British that you have been"—he searched for a delicate phrase—"detained in the country for a day or two." He thumbed through his desk calendar. "Well, Tuesday is rather light, sir, so I don't suppose that you will be missed, but on Wednesday King George is giving a luncheon at the Carlton for the observers and some of the embassy staff. . . . Yes, sir, I do think your attendance is required. In my opinion, Mr. Ambassador, it would be undiplomatic for the American Ambassador not to be at a function given by the King expressly for an American contingent." Jackson listened for a long time. "You may, of course, be right, Mr. Ambassador, but I'm quite sure the President has carefully considered the ramifications of his actions." Jackson pinched the bridge of his nose, as if stricken by a sudden headache. "Yes, Mr. Ambassador," he said, "I'm sure you will let the President know your feelings when you get home."

He said a pleasant goodbye and very gently placed the telephone on the cradle. "Roosevelt's fault," he said.

"Beg your pardon, Colonel?"

"The Ambassador thinks that Roosevelt is to blame for the bombing of London. He thinks that the destroyer deal has convinced Hitler that the President wants to get into the war, so Hitler is trying to finish off the British before the Americans can arrive. He says his first obligation now is to get home as quickly as possible and let the American people know the real truth about what is happening in Europe." Jackson looked down at his desk and shook his head. "I'm all for giving the British everything they need," he said. "What was it Churchill said? 'Give us the tools and we will do the job'? I hope they can. But I'm not optimistic that they can do the job on their own."

"Will the Ambassador make it to the King's luncheon?"

"He will be there reluctantly. I think Mr. Kennedy would

prefer to spend the rest of his time as ambassador in the country as far removed from the bombing as possible."

Jackson changed the subject. "How are you getting along with that reporter you were assigned to?"

"Quite well, actually."

"Rather choice assignment, I'd say. She's a remarkably good-looking young woman. In my day," Jackson said, sounding as if he were ninety years old, "reporters chewed cigars and wore rumpled suits. She's quite an improvement. Will you see her today?"

"Yes."

"Anything special on the itinerary?"

"Well . . ." Munro didn't want to say that his "itinerary" consisted of rushing back to the Savoy where he hoped to find Betty Donaldson still in bed where he had left her. "Nothing special, actually."

"Splendid," Jackson said looking at his watch. "Then why don't I take the two of you to lunch, and then you both can accompany me on a little trip to the country this afternoon. I'm sure it's the sort of thing she'd be interested in. I'm being taken on a tour of one of the Local Defense Volunteer organizations—I suppose they call them Home Guards now—by General Wills, who is chief of staff to General Paget."

"I'll check with her."

To Munro's disappointment Betty was enthusiastic about the trip.

"Sounds great," she said over the phone. "When and where does Jackson want to meet?"

They lunched at Claridge's, close by the embassy, and Munro could see that Betty was enjoying herself. She obviously found Colonel Jackson an informative and interesting host. Munro sat silently while the two of them discussed the course of the war and America's involvement.

"I believe," said Jackson, "that this week and next will be crucial for both sides. Hitler must invade before next week is over. After that time, his chances of success diminish daily."

"I understand that the Ambassador was out of town last night and missed the raid," Betty said.

Jackson shot a questioning look at Max Munro.

"It's all over town," said Betty quickly. "One of the reporters from the *New York Times* told me this morning that the Ambassador is being referred to as 'Jittery Joe' at the Foreign Office."

"I don't think it does anyone any good to question the Ambassador's courage," Jackson said.

"Colonel, the *New York Times* is reporting that the Ambassador is anxious to get home before the elections in November."

"I wonder if your sources mention that your publisher, Henry Luce, along with many others of influence, is trying to get the Ambassador to abandon the President and endorse the Republican candidate?"

"I guess," Betty said, "your sources of information aren't too bad, either."

Jackson looked at his watch. "I think we should be on our way. The General will be waiting."

The General turned out to be a rather stuffy, middle-aged man with a red face and a large belly. It had obviously been some time since he had seen combat. He picked them up in his Humber staff car, and with Munro up front with the driver they set out for Sandwich, a small town near the Dover Straits.

The trip took more than an hour, and on the way General Wills extolled the virtues of the Home Guards. "The Jerries will be in for a bit of a surprise," he said. "I think they'll find the Home Guard regiments well-armed and ready for combat."

Although Colonel Jackson knew these units were poorly armed, he was reluctant to contradict the General. The regular army had only recently been armed with American rifles, and many of the Home Guard units had no weapons of any kind.

Betty was not so reticent. "What kind of defense could they put up against crack German troops?" she asked. "Aren't they mostly middle-aged men, too old for the army?"

Wills seemed startled by her frontal approach. "You'll see," he said. "Jerry will be in for a surprise."

The Home Guards unit was waiting in a field on the

outskirts of town, a rather motley collection of farmers, shopkeepers, and others, all too old for the regular army. There were about sixty of them, all with weapons from the last war and with uniforms mismatched and ill-fitting. They were led by a Colonel Wharton of His Majesty's Household Cavalry—retired, who looked as if he might have seen his last cavalry charge at Waterloo.

The men were enthusiastic and when General Wills arrived they formed two straight lines so that he and Colonel Jackson could pass down the ranks in review. Then they marched in formation, gave a demonstration of their marksmanship, and took up defensive positions behind the stone walls that lined the surrounding fields.

Colonel Jackson nodded his head and pretended that he was impressed.

Munro and Betty stood a small distance apart from the others. He whispered, "If the Germans land near here, these men are supposed to hold them until the regular army units can move up."

"Fat chance," she said, thinking of Poland. "The Germans will roll through as if these men weren't even here."

After the demonstration, Colonel Wharton took his visitors to his home to meet his wife. She was a delicate woman, close to seventy, who served them tea and homemade pie. She sat with Munro and Betty while the others chatted about the inevitability of invasion. She talked mostly about her garden and the unusually magnificent summer they were having. "I remember a few summers like this one," she said, then added with a smile, ". . . when I was a young girl."

Betty listened and smiled and then, after a polite interval, asked the inevitable question. "What will you do if the Germans come through here?"

Mrs. Wharton looked surprised, as if the question had never occurred to her. "Do?"

"Yes. Do you have an evacuation route planned?" Munro asked.

"Heavens, no," said Mrs. Wharton. "I'll stay here with the Colonel until the Germans are driven back into the sea."

Betty Donaldson gave Munro a quick sidelong glance and then sipped her tea. She cleared her throat several times.

Mrs. Wharton smiled. "I know what you're thinking, Miss

Donaldson. How in the world does this old fool think that these old men, led by her even older husband, can withstand the German Army? I know we can't, and I'm well aware that we will probably all die here. But the Germans will know that there are people here who are willing to die to defend this island." Mrs. Wharton sipped her tea. "You can tell that to your readers back in America."

"I will," said Betty. "You can be sure of that."

The trip back was quiet. Even General Wills seemed more subdued than earlier. "There have been no reports of bombing today," he said. "Maybe Jerry has changed his mind about the invasion."

They heard the sirens as they approached London. By the time they reached the city it was almost dark and the bombing had begun. A dull red, rosy glow lay ahead of them and the sound of muffled explosions filled the warm summer evening.

"The docks again," General Will's driver said grimly.

They kept to the outskirts of the city, entering from the north, so as to avoid the bombing. Once again the East End bore the brunt of the raid.

At the Savoy, Munro got out with Betty. "I'll just see Miss Donaldson safely inside," he said, "then I'll make my own way home."

Wills and Jackson bid them farewell and the car drove off into the darkened streets. Betty and Munro waited in the Savoy courtyard. Both were reluctant to go inside.

"We can have dinner downstairs in the shelter," Betty said.

"I'd like that," he said, "but you know I'm supposed to meet Marie Price tonight."

Betty made a face.

"We agreed," he said defensively, "that I'd string her along to find out what she's after."

"I know what she's after," said Betty. "I'm following Hamilton around, and you're having a good time with this floozy."

He grinned. "Do I detect a note of jealousy here?"

She punched him lightly on the arm. "Damn right you do."

"Tell you what. I'll have a drink with her, find out what she wants, get rid of her, and come back here as soon as I can."

"OK. I'll get something to eat, and I'll wait for you in the downstairs bar."

He pulled her close and kissed her. "Now I'm the one

234

who's jealous," he said. "Thinking of you sitting around with all those horny reporters."

"You better hurry back," she said. "I might just pick the best one I can find."

"Then I'd better get going." He kissed her again and she watched as he walked out into the Strand to hail a passing taxi.

In the background the thumping of bombing went on.

FIRES RAGE IN LONDON AS NAZI AIR FLEETS
CONTINUE SAVAGERY; 400 DEAD IN NIGHT OF
TERROR; GOERING DIRECTS AIR BATTLE

LONDON, SEPT. 8

◆ CHAPTER 36 ◆

The vibration of the distant bombing rattled the jars on Marie Price's dressing table. She looked toward the curtained window before returning to combing her hair. With each long brushstroke she thought about Max Munro, who by this time was probably waiting for her at the club. The evening would have been a lot more fun with him than it would be with Winston Hamilton.

According to Daly, Benke had been intrigued by her information about Hamilton's apparent foreknowledge of the German air raid on Saturday and had demanded that she contact Hamilton immediately. She was glad that Benke had refused to permit Daly to beat the information out of Hamilton. Benke had insisted that Daly allow her to try to find out how Hamilton had known about the German bombing.

She put down her brush and inspected her face carefully in

the mirror. There were lines around her mouth and a perceptible puffiness below her eyes. She was no longer young. The years and the hard life were beginning to take their toll and she wondered how many good years she had left. It was time, she thought, to find someone who could take care of her. Daly was too unpredictable. After the invasion, she would have to find herself a German officer in a position of authority who would appreciate having a beautiful woman by her side.

She put a dab of French perfume behind each ear and on her throat. It was her last bottle of precious French perfume, and it seemed a shame to waste even a drop on the likes of Winston Hamilton, but soon there would be plenty again. She smiled as she imagined Hamilton's reaction to the note she had had delivered to his flat by some filthy urchin she had seen in the street. "I must see you again. I know now that it would be a mistake to forget what we have meant to each other. Come to my place tonight at eight. With all my love, Marie."

In the street below, Winston Hamilton, barely able to contain his excitement, fiddled with his tie and checked to see that his shoes had a proper shine. To reassure himself, he touched Marie's note. He had reread it over and over again, savoring each line, discovering new meaning with each reading. He went inside, mounted the stairs, and, after a brief pause, knocked.

The door swung open almost immediately. He drew in a sharp breath at the sight of her. She wore a white blouse, opened to reveal ample cleavage, and a tight-fitting skirt that clung to her body. She was magnificent, he thought.

She took his hand and drew him inside. "Winston," she purred, "how foolish I was." She closed the door behind him, moved into his arms, and kissed him.

Her perfume was overwhelming, her lips incredibly soft. Her body molded itself to his, and each point of contact was like fire.

Her mouth was against his ear. "I'm so grateful to you," she whispered. "How can I ever thank you?"

"What for?"

"You saved my life yesterday. If it hadn't been for you, I might be like those poor devils in the East End."

His eyes widened. "You must never mention a word of what I told you," he said. "It could be disastrous."

"Now, now," she said soothingly, taking his hand. "You don't have to worry about any of that. Your secrets are my secrets." She smiled teasingly. "I'll tell you a secret."

"What?"

"I've been thinking about you since yesterday. Wondering what I could do to show you how much I care."

Winston gulped air. "Yes?"

She led him to the bedroom. "Don't be shy," she said, slipping his jacket over his shoulders and letting it drop to the floor. "It's time for us."

She sat him on the bed and loosened his tie, then went to the other side of the bed and quickly undressed. He felt her on the bed moving toward him. Then, from behind, her arms were around him. He sensed that she was naked.

"You want me to undress you?" she cooed into his ear. She removed his tie and unbuttoned his shirt, stripping it from him while he sat in silence. Now he could feel her nakedness brushing against his. She pressed herself against him, her tongue moving around his ear. He could feel her breasts against his bare back, her nipples like two hot coals against his skin.

"Stand up," she whispered.

He obeyed, his back still to her, and she unbuckled his belt and pulled his trousers to the floor. He gave only a whimper as she slipped his shorts down and let them drop around his ankles.

She pulled the covers back and slipped beneath them, then invitingly held them open for him. Winston slid in beside her. She moved closer until their bodies were against each other, then lightly ran her hands across his chest and down his belly. He was on fire.

"Can I tell you a secret?" she asked softly. "I have waited for this moment since the first time we met."

"I was afraid to even dream of this," Winston said.

Marie rolled on top of him, letting her breasts dangle down in his face. "No more fears," she whispered, reaching between them and guiding him inside her. "No more secrets between us." Her mouth was against his ear. "Say it," she whispered as she quickened her movements. "No secrets."

237

"No secrets," he groaned.

"That's it," she said as her pace intensified. "No more secrets."

Mesmerized by her words, her motions, and his longing, he could only repeat her words. "No more secrets."

The Apertif club on Jermyn Street was alive with activity. The dance floor was crowded and each table was packed beyond capacity. Young men in uniform were everywhere.

Prominently displayed at one end of the smoke-filled room was a large cardboard sign, clearly visible to all, with the words of the popular song "We're Gonna Hang Out the Washing on the Sigfried Line." Every ten minutes or so the band would strike up and everyone would break into a joyous chorus. Few needed the sign to remind them of the words, but it hung there as a constant display of defiance.

Max Munro stood next to the bar watching couples whirling on the dance floor. He had long since surrendered his small table to four RAF flyers who had made the trip in from their airfield somewhere south of London. If this night were their last they would enjoy it to the hilt. With very little effort they had acquired four girlfriends from other, less dashing soldiers, and proceeded to turn the nightclub into their personal playground. They led the group in songs of their choosing, helped themselves to drinks from any and every table, and danced with almost every woman in the place.

No one begrudged the four their childish pleasures. Everyone was eager to please them, to be near them, to somehow bask in their glory. The male patrons gladly offered them drinks and food, and, Munro was certain, the four girls were sure to offer them whatever else they might require.

He looked at his watch for the tenth time.

The bartender grinned. "Women certainly can be unpredictable, can't they, sir?"

Munro raised his glass in a salute to the contrary nature of the opposite sex. He drained the glass and headed for the door.

Monday, September 9—"But, I tell you," said Josef Benke, "he is beginning to tell the girl what we want to know." Benke had come to Daly's flat to get a progress report.

238

Daly slammed a fist into his open palm. "But it is not working fast enough," Daly said. "I still say, let me have him for an hour and he will tell us everything."

"Sean, my friend, you must learn to be more patient."

Daly exploded. "How can any of us be patient? Every day the Germans delay the invasion, their chances for success diminish."

Benke shook his head sadly. "These things take incredible amounts of planning, Sean."

"Don't you read the reports I give you for the Germans?"

"Of course I do."

"Then you must know that British aircraft production already outstrips combat losses, shore defenses are strengthened daily, and the influx of American equipment has almost totally resupplied the British Army."

"I know what you are saying, my friend, believe me, and I will take this up with my German contacts in Portugal as soon as I can."

"When?"

"With all this air activity, it is next to impossible to get a flight out of England, but I may be able to leave tomorrow or the next day."

"Hamilton holds the key to how the British have been able to withstand the German air attacks. He has already told Price that they have advanced knowledge of German intentions. He talks about an 'Ultra secret,' but whether it is a device or a code name for someone who gives them the information, we don't know."

Benke was silent. Daly, he knew, would never be satisfied until the Germans had occupied and subjugated the British homeland. He wanted revenge. As for Benke, he would be satisfied to have this damn war over with. Why couldn't the British make peace with Hitler and let the Germans do what they wanted on the continent? That way everyone would be happy.

"I must be going," Benke said. "You can be sure that I will relay your concerns to my contacts in Lisbon."

Daly made a rude noise with his mouth.

◆ *CHAPTER 37* ◆

Sunday, September 15—During the long drive from Berlin, Admiral Canaris had been quiet, and Bernhard Ritter had settled back in his seat to enjoy the early morning. The sunlight flickered through the dense, green forests of Brandenburg as the staff car wound its way through the narrow roads. Occasionally they would break out into a high clearing and Ritter was able to see for miles in any direction. This, he thought, was Germany at its most beautiful—sparkling lakes, thick pine forests, rolling hills—a land untouched by war. It was easy to understand why Reichsmarschall Goering had selected this area for his hunting lodge.

Karinhall was the sprawling country estate that Hermann Goering had commissioned in 1934. The mighty structure was a tribute to the success, both past and present, of the second most powerful man in Germany. With the full approval of his second wife, the German actress Emmy Sonneman, Goering had named the grandiose structure of rough-hewn beams and native stone after his first wife, the Swedish noblewoman Karin von Kantzow, who had died of tuberculosis in 1931.

Karinhall was only one of several grand residences owned by Goering. There was his home in Berlin, the Leipzieger Palace, where Goering and his wife held court; the Reichsjagerhof in the Rominterheide in East Prussia, which, although magnificent, was a true hunting lodge that had been built from huge tree trunks and topped with a thatched roof;

his estate in Veldenstein, stocked with every conceivable native species of fish and game. But Karinhall was the Reichsmarschall's favorite residence.

Here Hermann Goering indulged his every fantasy, from his wine cellar, his private cinema, his bowling alley, to his elaborate model railroad that filled the huge attic of Karinhall. The model railroad was Goering's pride and joy, and he took delight in watching the amazed expressions of his visitors when they first gazed on his favorite toy. At the flip of a switch, Goering could send model airplanes, suspended on hidden wires, zooming across his miniature landscape, and then his raucous laughter would fill Karinhall as he dropped miniature bombs on the tiny houses that dotted the model railroad.

Karinhall was both pleasure palace and shrine. Upon its completion, Goering had disinterred the body of his first wife and placed her in a vault in one of the gardens. Visitors were often required to spend a few moments there with the Reichsmarschall, who, every day that he was in residence, placed roses on the grave.

When Canaris and Ritter arrived at the outer gates they were stopped and closely scrutinized by two of the soldiers of the 120-man security force that guarded the estate from intruders. After their credentials had been accepted, they were instructed to follow a guard on a motorcycle who led them down a two-mile-long avenue to the house. Each side of the wide road was flanked by marble lions in various poses, and Ritter gaped in wonder like a starstruck child on his first visit to the circus.

Canaris looked straight ahead. His doleful expression never wavered. He had been summoned to Karinhall this morning for a confrontation with his nemesis, Reinhard Heydrich of the Reich Security Office. The continuing dispute between the Abwehr and Heydrich had finally reached unmanageable proportions and Reichsmarschall Hermann Goering had been called in to arbitrate their differences. Canaris did not feel hopeful that the dispute would be resolved in his favor.

Their car circled the courtyard and stopped in front of the huge double-doored entrance. They were led inside to a large high-ceilinged room off an entry foyer, and found that Heydrich and Kaufmann were already there. Canaris and

Heydrich greeted each other with facile pleasantries. Ritter and Kaufmann pretended not to know each other and waited to be introduced—a fact that did not go unnoticed by Canaris.

"Well," said Heydrich pleasantly, "I am sure that the Reichsmarschall will be able to resolve our little dispute."

"Most certainly," Canaris agreed.

Heydrich turned his attention to Ritter, who was looking at the hunting trophies that filled each wall of the huge room. "And you, Captain Ritter," said Heydrich. "I hear only good reports about your involvement in this matter."

"Thank you, Herr Obergruppenführer," said Ritter.

"It is unfortunate," Heydrich said to Canaris, "that our dispute could not be settled without resorting to a higher authority."

"Yes," said Canaris, "it is unfortunate."

"That is why," Heydrich went on, "all espionage activities should be placed under a single jurisdiction."

Canaris smiled. "Yours, of course, my dear Heydrich?"

At that moment Hermann Goering entered the room. "Good morning, gentlemen," he said breezily as the others jumped to their feet. Goering went to the gramophone in the corner of the room and selected a recording. Soon the room was filled with strains of Auber's "Fra Diablo." "The French," he said, "make marvelous music."

He winked at Canaris. "Our friend Heydrich, I am sure, prefers German opera."

The others laughed politely at Heydrich's expense. Goering was one of perhaps three men in Germany who would dare to make a joke at the expense of the Obergruppenführer.

As he often was at Karinhall, Goering was dressed in civilian clothes—a white shirt, silk tie, and brown slacks. "Be seated, gentlemen," he said. "Let's get to the bottom of this matter quickly."

Goering sat down heavily in an ornate, hand-carved chair while Canaris and Ritter sat on a sofa to his right, Heydrich and Kaufmann on a similar sofa to his left.

"The Führer has asked me to arbitrate this dispute," Goering began, "because of Reichsfuhrer Himmler's obvious conflict of interest in this matter."

Heydrich's face hardened. He had hoped that his boss,

Himmler, would be able to decide in his favor, but Canaris had protested to the General Staff and the resultant furor had led them to Goering.

"As I see it," said Goering, "we are faced with two problems here, and both sides offer different solutions to each."

Canaris marveled at the Reichsmarschall's lucidity this morning. He seemed like the old Goering. Perhaps the rumors that he had broken his morphine addiction were true. What the Admiral could not know was that Goering's doctors had prescribed paracodeine as a morphine substitute and the Reichsmarschall was gamely attempting to keep his consumption of the new drug to thirty capsules a day.

"The first problem," said Goering, holding one pudgy finger between the thumb and forefinger of his other hand, "is the situation at the American Embassy. The question is, can we influence the American presidential elections? In the short term this is the least critical problem, but in the long term, perhaps the most important. We are in possession of documents that, if released to the press, could perhaps injure Roosevelt's chances for re-election."

"Not perhaps," said Heydrich. "Most certainly."

Goering ignored the interruption. "The Abwehr is of the opinion that the American Ambassador is on the verge of doing our work for us. That would, obviously, be a far more effective method of influencing the election than any attempt by us to warn the world of Roosevelt's criminal intentions. But only if Ambassador Kennedy performs as the Abwehr hopes he will."

"The second problem," Goering said, holding a second pudgy finger, "is of more immediate concern. The Abwehr reports the disturbing possibility that the British have somehow obtained advanced knowledge of German military intentions, especially those of my own Luftwaffe. Admiral, this is an especially dangerous charge. It means that someone on the General Staff—possibly a high-ranking Luftwaffe officer—is guilty of treason."

"Not necessarily," said Canaris. "Captain Ritter, whom I have brought with me this morning because he is the officer assigned to this case, feels that the problem is one of signal interception."

"I believe, Herr Reichsmarschall," Ritter said, "it is possible that the Enigma system has been somehow compromised."

Goering's face darkened. "I have it on reliable scientific authority that such a thing is impossible."

Heydrich was well prepared. He opened a leather portfolio and removed a letter. "If I may, Herr Reichsmarschall, I would like to show you this document. It is a reply to an inquiry I made to Karl Bensmann, professor of mathematics at the Kaiser Wilhelm Institute at Dahlem."

There was a knock on the door and Goering looked at his watch. "Enter," he called.

The door opened and Goering's valet, Robert Kropp, entered carrying a silver tray on which was a crystal water goblet and a small pillbox. "Time for the Reichsmarschall's medication," he said.

Goering opened the pillbox and removed a single capsule, placed it delicately in his mouth, and drank some water. He returned the glass to the tray, then waved his hand impatiently at Heydrich. "Tell us the essential details of the letter."

Heydrich waited for Kropp to leave the room before he continued. "According to the professor, it is mathematically impossible for anyone to break the Enigma codes. Even if an Enigma machine were to fall into the hands of an enemy, and he intercepted all of our signals sent on such machines, it would take fifty top-notch mathematicians three months to decipher the first message. According to Bensmann, there are no more than thirty or forty mathematicians in all of Britain with the ability to undertake such a task."

"Would breaking the first message enable them to decipher subsequent messages?" Goering asked.

Heydrich smiled. "Because of the nature of the Enigma machine, one message has absolutely no bearing on any other. Those fifty mathematicians would have to start over again, from the beginning, with the second message. One day's Enigma transmissions would keep the best mathematicians in England busy for more than twenty-five years. These calculations are based on absolutely verifiable scientific fact. There is no doubt."

Goering turned to Ritter. "Well?" he said sternly.

"Our agents in the field have isolated a British officer who translates intercepted German signals. He personally warned one of our agents that the bombing of London was to begin on Saturday afternoon. September seventh, and, furthermore, identified the target area."

"If this is true," Heydrich interjected quickly, "it proves only that there is a traitor in the chain of command—not that Enigma has been compromised."

"We must have definitive proof," Goering said.

Canaris said, "The Abwehr proposes that we perform a test of the Enigma system. Select a target—something that has not been touched before—put out the details on the Enigma machine, and wait to see how the British respond."

"A waste of time," snapped Heydrich. "We already know the Enigma system has not been compromised. I say drastic action is required."

"Such as?" said Goering.

Heydrich smiled. "The Abwehr knows who this officer is who supposedly has information about German intentions. Make him talk."

"That," said Canaris, "was our first thought, but such action could jeopardize our entire spy network in England."

"Spy network?" Heydrich laughed sarcastically. "I would hardly characterize your small list of agents as a network."

"I did not realize, Reinhard," Canaris said calmly, "that I was summoned here to be insulted."

Once again Goering was the mediator. "Gentlemen, gentlemen, please. There is no time for this. I agree with Obergruppenführer Heydrich that something must be done quickly."

"Then, I will instruct our agents," said Canaris reluctantly, "to conduct a more vigorous investigation of this man."

Heydrich sneered. "Herr Reichsmarschall," he appealed to Goering, "those Abwehr people in England are amateurs. They are incapable of conducting a proper interrogation."

"What are you suggesting?" Goering asked.

"I will send a team of Gestapo interrogators to do the job."

"To England?" said Canaris.

"Of course not, Admiral. To Ireland. The Abwehr, supposedly, has strong contacts with the Irish Republican Army. The Abwehr claims to move agents in and out of England, through Ireland, all the time. It would seem a simple matter to kidnap this English officer and, with the help of the IRA, bring him to Ireland. There, the Gestapo under the direction of Obersturmbannführer Kaufmann, can conduct an interrogation." Heydrich grinned wickedly. "Believe me, gentlemen, in a very short time, he will tell them everything he knows. Of course, if the Admiral feels that the Abwehr is incapable of completing this task, perhaps—"

"The Abwehr is capable," snapped Canaris. "It seems, however, inordinately risky—"

"Risky?" interrupted Heydrich. "Surely the Abwehr is not afraid of risk?"

"Enough," said Goering. "I have decided that this plan will be implemented immediately. Admiral, your people in England will be ordered to take this officer to Ireland, where he will be interrogated by the Gestapo."

Heydrich and Kaufmann looked triumphantly at each other.

"As you wish, Herr Reichsmarschall," said Canaris, realizing the futility of protest. "We will begin at once. The Abwehr is always pleased to cooperate with the Reich Security Service."

Heydrich said to Goering, "And now to the matter of the American Ambassador. The Abwehr prefers to play a waiting game, but I feel that this is too risky. If we wait we may lose our chance to influence the American elections. I say we must release the information we have now. Let the world know that Roosevelt and Churchill have conspired against Germany."

"And have the American press dismiss it as German propaganda?" said Canaris. "Captain Ritter has every reason to believe that Ambassador Kennedy will denounce Roosevelt on the eve of the election. Such a pronouncement would be devastating to Roosevelt. He cannot possibly win without Kennedy's support."

"There is no guarantee that Kennedy will oppose Roosevelt," said Heydrich. "Furthermore—"

Goering raised his hand for silence. "Well, Captain Ritter, you seem to be the man in the middle. What do you have to say?"

"My contacts with Ambassador Kennedy are certain he will return home to denounce the policies of his president. He has already demanded that he be allowed to return home before the presidential elections."

"Probably to vote for Roosevelt," said Heydrich.

Goering gave him a sharp look and motioned for Ritter to continue.

"The Hungarian second secretary, Josef Benke, who is very close to Ambassador Kennedy, was shown a copy of a letter that Kennedy had sent to the American Secretary of State, in which Kennedy states his grievances against Roosevelt, and condemns Roosevelt's interventionist policies. He accuses the American President of conspiring to bring his country into the war on the side of the British. He also warned that if he were not permitted to return home before the elections, a copy of the letter would be given to the American press."

"And Kennedy showed this letter to Benke?" Goering said.

"It was shown to Benke by the Ambassador's principal aide—a man named Terrence Wymore."

Heydrich was disbelieving. "Why would Wymore show the letter to Benke?"

"Because he is eager to let us know, through the Hungarians, that Kennedy wants a stable business relationship with Germany. He has certain lucrative business contracts in England that he wishes to keep intact after the invasion."

"Let him know," said Heydrich, "that if he denounces Roosevelt, he can have all the damn contracts he wants."

"Kennedy is fiercely independent—what the Americans would call a maverick," Ritter said. "If he felt that Germany was encouraging him to turn against Roosevelt, he might refuse to cooperate. Our best hope is to wait and allow him room to operate on his own."

"Wait," Heydrich hissed. "Herr Reichsmarschall, this is a time for action. While the Abwehr waits, we let a golden opportunity pass us by."

Goering stood up and walked to the window. This was a difficult decision, he thought. He was a daredevil by nature and preferred action to inaction. Heydrich's plan had more appeal for him than Ritter's, but there were several aspects that still had to be considered. The first and foremost was that he fully expected the invasion of England to begin in another week. Once underway, there was nothing Roosevelt could do to stop it. And once England was occupied, the Americans would be powerless to oppose Germany. A few minor feints into South America would keep the United States busy while Germany gobbled up the rest of Europe. The second consideration was that, unbeknownst to any of the others, the Reichsmarschall had his own plan underway for the defeat of Roosevelt. He had already spent millions of American dollars in an intense effort to influence the American elections. The money was disbursed through an American oilman, William Rhodes Davis, who had sold Mexican oil to Germany, and who had excellent contacts with the American labor leader John L. Lewis.

If he accepted Heydrich's plan and it failed, all chance of defeating Roosevelt would probably be gone. On the other hand, if Heydrich's plan succeeded, and Roosevelt lost the election, Heydrich would reap all of the credit. Goering turned away from the window and faced his guests. Heydrich had the confident air of a man who knew that sooner or later all good things must come to him. Goering smiled. Perhaps it wasn't such a difficult decision after all.

"I have decided," said Goering, "that in this instance, the Admiral's caution is well warranted."

◆ CHAPTER 38 ◆

**UXBRIDGE, HQ, 11 Fighter Group, Sunday, September
15**—To the surprise of everyone at Air Vice-Marshall Keith
Park's headquarters, Winston Churchill arrived unannounced
shortly before eleven. There were those at 11 Group HQ who
thought it uncanny that the Prime Minister should arrive just
as a major attack was getting underway. Already the radio
detection stations on the coast had picked up the increase in
Luftwaffe activity on the French side, and it was apparent
that another big day was beginning. Churchill had, of course,
been informed by Ultra intercepts that Goering would make
another massive effort to destroy the RAF and had decided to
come out to Hillingdon House, where Park maintained his
operational center, to watch for himself.

Churchill accompanied Park down into "The Hole," the
bombproof rooms fifty feet beneath the rolling fairways of the
Hillingdon Golf Course. In the Ops Room, the WAAF
plotters had already begun tracking the advance of the
German aircraft. While Park quietly explained the situation
to the Prime Minister, the red bulbs on the panels across the
room indicated that every available squadron was either in
the air or standing by.

The duty controller nodded to Park and the Prime Minister
as they joined him on the balcony above the huge table map
and returned his attention to the colored disks that the
WAAFs pushed across the map. Every few minutes he spoke

quietly into one of the six telephones that connected him to each of his sector stations, and another light would go on in one of the panels.

In less than half an hour all the lights were on and the controller turned to Park. "All squadrons are airborne. We'll have to call in 12 Group for assistance."

Park nodded.

Churchill peered over the railing at the map below. The counters, representing the German aircraft, seemed to form a solid line across the Channel, but still the WAAFs added more to the steadily growing number. "How many of the bastards?" he whispered to Park.

"Close to a thousand, Prime Minister."

"And more coming?"

Park nodded.

"Will you commit your reserve forces?"

Park kept his face expressionless, but he could not look at his Prime Minister. "Everything we have is in the air, Prime Minister. There is no reserve."

Churchill's body sagged momentarily as if he had been struck a blow to the midsection, but he recovered before anyone noticed. He clamped his jaws around his cigar and without a word went back to his seat.

Savoy Hotel

The underground shelters at the Savoy were packed. Since the eleventh of September, the West End was no longer immune to German attack, and the residents now rushed to the shelters at the first sound of the sirens. On the thirteenth a bomb had hit Buckingham Palace, signifying that the war had, indeed, come to all. Now the long nights of the Blitz were shared by everyone.

At a little past noon the first wave of German bombers broke through the fighter defenses and showered their rain of destruction across central London.

To the American reporters in the Savoy shelters, the raid was a good excuse to get an early start on the drinking day. The Savoy was at the center of the action in London, and some of the reporters rarely ventured more than a mile in any direction. Since the bombing had started in earnest, some almost never left the premises. One portion of the downstairs River Room had been maintained as a restaurant and had become one of London's hottest night spots. Another portion had been divided into cubicles so that the hotel guests could spend the night in safety and comparative comfort. Below this level were more rooms which had been converted to shelters; one was reserved exclusively for the Duke and Duchess of Kent.

"Pleasant way to spend a Sunday afternoon," said Betty Donaldson, raising her glass to Max Munro, who sat across from her at the tiny corner table they had managed to secure.

The music and loud conversations drowned out the sound of the explosions, but the vibrations were transmitted through the floor.

Munro nursed his Scotch and water. "Ambassador Kennedy doesn't think that London can take another day of this."

"Looks like we're going to find out."

"He's convinced the country is on the verge of collapse. I understand he's told the President to prepare for imminent catastrophe."

Betty looked around the room. In addition to the American reporters there were many English couples enjoying lunch. "If everyone in England is as calm as the people here, I don't see any possibility of that."

"Anything new with Marie Price?"

"I should ask you," Betty said.

"I haven't heard from her since last week."

"Apparently you've lost out to the English officer she's been seeing. It seems they are—as the gossip columns would say—an item." She grinned mischievously.

"Do we know anything about him?"

"Not yet. Kind of a mystery man. I was hoping that you could find out something."

"How?"

"Ask Colonel Jackson if he knows what goes on at fifty-four Broadway. If we knew what Hamilton did, we might know what Price is after."

"Jackson has excellent contacts all over this town. I'm sure he'll know something."

"In the meantime," said Betty, shaking her empty glass, "I'll keep after Price. Something is bound to show up."

Munro waved to a waiter. "You're enjoying this, aren't you?"

She grinned. "I can see the headlines now. 'American Reporter Cracks Nazi Spy Ring.'"

"What if she's just a broad on the make?"

Betty was suddenly serious. "Call it reporter's instinct, call it woman's intuition, that little bitch is up to something."

Sunningdale

Terrence Wymore knocked once on the door of his boss's study and waited until he heard Joe Kennedy's voice before entering. The Ambassador was on the phone, feet up on the desk. He waved Wymore into a seat as he listened intently to whoever was on the other end. "How bad is it?" he asked. He listened for a short time. "Well, keep me informed. I'll be here for the rest of the day. If things get as bad as I think they are going to, we can abandon the Embassy and use my house here as temporary quarters . . . Well, you do what you think best, but I don't think the Germans can tell which is the American Embassy from twenty-thousand feet."

Finally the Ambassador said goodbye and hung up. His face was ashen. "This is it, Terry," he said. "The biggest raid of the war is taking place right now over London, and the word I get from contacts at the War Office is that the invasion is on for three o'clock today."

"You've said all along, boss, that the Germans were gonna pound the shit out of these guys."

"We'll stay here until the shooting is over. After the surrender we can arrange for passage home. Damn it! I knew I shoulda got the hell out of here last week."

Wymore nodded sympathetically.

"As soon as the Germans started bombing London, I knew it was the beginning of the end. If Roosevelt wasn't so damn set on keeping me out of the election I would have been home already. Now who knows how long it will take?"

The Ambassador reached for a cigar. "Talked with Beaverbrook yesterday," he said as he held a match to the cigar. "He told me that British aircraft production in August exceeded German production." Lord Beaverbrook was the

Minister of Aircraft Production and a close friend of the Ambassador's. "I told him he was full of shit. Where does he get figures for German aircraft production?"

"Beats me."

"They make them up," Kennedy said. "I told him that according to my information from Charles Lindbergh, the Germans have barely begun to utilize their available aircraft. Beaverbrook claims that the German Air Force is hurting." He laughed. "I wonder if he's looked out his window today?"

"Do you want me to contact Benke again?"

"You showed him the letter?"

"Last week. He said that he would include mention of it in his report to Budapest, and that it was certain to be brought to the attention of the Germans."

"Just so long as they know that Roosevelt and I don't see eye to eye on this war."

"The letter went out in the diplomatic pouch four days ago. It probably arrived in Washington on Friday."

Kennedy grinned. "That'll give old Franklin something to think about. I also told Beaverbrook that I was seriously considering endorsing Willkie."

"And Beaverbrook will tell Churchill, and Churchill will tell Roosevelt," said Wymore.

"News travels fast in political circles."

Abwehr Headquarters, Tirpitz Ufer

On the long ride back to Berlin, Canaris had been silent. Ritter, assuming that his boss was disturbed because Heydrich and Kaufmann had taken control of what, initially, had been an Abwehr operation, tried to console him. "We still control the Kennedy operation," he pointed out. "And the initial stages of the second operation are under our jurisdiction."

Admiral Canaris was certain that his subordinate had betrayed him to his most feared enemy. "I assume that we can contact Benke by radio, if we so choose," he said.

"Yes," said Ritter. "The Hungarian Embassy is well equipped to receive radio messages."

"A message that only Benke will receive."

"He is equipped with an Afu set, but only for the gravest emergencies. The risk of capture is too great." The Afu was the compact, but powerful, German radio that was generally used by agents in the field.

"We are under orders from the Reichsmarschall. Inform Benke of the plan to bring the English soldier to Ireland. He will proceed immediately and inform us—by Afu—as soon as the plan is in motion."

Once he was back in his office, Canaris summoned Colonel Oster. When Oster entered the Admiral's office, Canaris was bent over a large map of the English Channel which he had spread across his desk. He had a pencil in his hand and was tracing a line along the English coast.

"How did the meeting go?" Oster asked.

"Not well. Heydrich convinced Goering that the Enigma machine could not possibly be compromised. It is typical of Heydrich to believe that there is a traitor somewhere in the General Staff."

Oster breathed a silent sigh of relief. "Goering won't even use your suggestion to test the Enigma system?"

"They think it's a waste of time. They'd prefer to find traitors." He threw the pencil down on the table. "A traitor couldn't possibly relay such information to the English so quickly. The problem has to be somewhere in the lines of communication."

"It does seem impossible that the Enigma codes can be broken," said Oster.

Canaris smiled. "True," he said. "But it's that kind of overconfidence that leads to carelessness. Every move we make is relayed through Enigma. If the British are reading those messages, they can stay one step ahead of us. How else do you explain their survival in the face of such odds?"

"What do you want to do?"

Canaris returned to the map on his desk. "Even if Goering won't test the Enigma system, we will." He pointed at a spot on the English coast. "Here," he said, his finger resting on East Suffolk, "Leiston. Far removed from where we might be expected to strike. I want to send an Enigma message to the commandant of the Brandenburg Division in Holland." The Brandenburg Division was one of a group of commando units that was under the direct control of the Abwehr. "Tell him to prepare for a paratroop assault on the town of Leiston on the morning of the seventeenth."

"Surely, Admiral you don't intend to—"

"I want you to go to Holland, where you will personally countermand the order. We will conduct an aerial reconnaissance of the area before the order is given and another just before the mythical assault is to take place. If the British have reinforced this sleepy hamlet, we can begin to assume that they have somehow managed to read our Enigma signals. You alone will have knowledge of what we are doing. You will report personally to me by the morning of the eighteenth."

"As you wish, Admiral," Oster said. "I will proceed immediately."

As Oster headed for the door, Canaris called to him, "I would suggest that you order the reconnaissance over the telephone. If the British are reading the Enigma signals, we could lose a pilot."

Oster nodded and closed the door behind him. His heart was pounding as he went to the elevator. If Heydrich and Kaufmann were trolling for traitors, he thought, they might inadvertently turn him up in their net. That was a risk he had always taken, but suddenly he could feel Heydrich's hot breath on the back of his neck.

◆ *CHAPTER 39* ◆

BERLIN, Monday, September 16—Evening in Berlin. No
sirens. No bombing. Except for the blackout it might have
been any other evening in any other year. The occasional
bombings were of little more than nuisance value, intended to
remind the Germans that they too were vulnerable. Of late
the raids had done very little damage, and most Berliners,
who were well aware of the savage pounding inflicted on
London by their Luftwaffe, could only smile and shrug at the
Royal Air Force's lack of effectiveness. Theaters and cinemas
were as popular as ever, restaurants and cabarets were
crowded, and except for the fact that there was a scarcity of
young men on the streets, Berlin and its people had hardly
been touched by the war.

Adolph Hitler was strangely calm. The officers of his High
Command, who had been summoned to his Reichstag office
that evening, expected the Führer to rant and rave about the
terrible news from the skies over England. All were already
aware that the Luftwaffe bomber forces had been decimated
by a fighter force that, according to Reichsmarschall Goering,
was on the verge of extinction. The Kampflieger had suffered
a major defeat, so many bombers lost or heavily damaged
that almost a third of the bomber force was out of action.
Obviously it would take some time to recover from such
horrendous losses.

But Hitler had said little of the catastrophe in the West. He
had greeted his generals warmly, and although he seemed
somewhat subdued, had managed to conduct the meeting

with his usual forceful style. Only near the end of the meeting—almost as an aside—when he passed around a handwritten directive so that his generals might read his words, did any of his old fire return.

While Generalfeldmarschall Keitel read the directive, the Führer, uncharacteristically, explained his thinking to the others. "As I have said, previously, we require ten days after the destruction of the Royal Air Force to implement the details of the invasion. I have postponed the operation several times waiting for these conditions to be met. But now, in the middle of September, there is not enough time to assure a successful landing before bad weather in the Channel makes the problems of supply even more difficult." The Führer sighed heavily. "Therefore, I will instruct my commanders in the West to disperse the invasion barges and dismantle the air loading equipment."

The generals gaped in amazement.

"I have decided," said Hitler, "to postpone the invasion —indefinitely."

The generals, most of whom had opposed the invasion plans in the first place, greeted the Führer's pronouncement with a mixture of relief and dismay. Most, while secretly relieved that the invasion was off, were flabbergasted that Hitler could so cavalierly dismiss plans that had cost Germany so dearly.

Keitel began with a mild protest. "But, Führer—"

For the first time that evening, Hitler's voice was sharp. "This is my irrevocable decision," he said. "There will be no discussion."

Silence fell across the room until Hitler, his calm demeanor returning quickly, proceeded. Soon the meeting was over and Hitler bade his generals good night. After they had gone he sat quietly at his desk listening to the sounds of traffic in the streets below. On his desk, fashioned as a crude paperweight, was a molten chunk of metal, taken from the instrument panel of a downed British bomber. The paperweight had been a present from Hermann Goering. The molten metal was attached to a plaque which said, "Such is the fate of all who attack the Fatherland."

Adolf Hitler picked up the paperweight and threw it the length of the room.

* * *

At that time Hermann Goering was in the midst of a furious tirade directed at his commanders who had been summoned to Karinhall for an evening conference. Oberst Theo Osterkamp, the regional Fighter Commander at Wissant, bore the brunt of the Reichsmarschall's fury.

"Once again," Goering bellowed, "the fighters failed me! I gave them the responsibility of protecting the bomber forces and they failed me."

"But, Reichsmarschall, because of their limited range, the fighters were unable to accompany the bombers all the way to the target. As it is, almost a third of our losses come not from enemy action, but from aircraft crash-landing after running out of fuel."

"Excuses, excuses!" roared Goering. "I have had enough excuses."

Gamely Osterkamp continued. "Reichsmarschall, intelligence reports claimed that RAF Fighter Command should have had less than one hundred fighters operational yesterday. The reports of our pilots put the figure at closer to seven hundred."

"Preposterous!" Goering bellowed. "Fighter Command no longer exists as a fighting force." He slumped, exhausted, into his chair. The reality of the situation slowly dawned on him. It was over. Riding in triumph through London and the hero's welcome in Berlin. All gone. But how? How was it possible that an inferior force had thwarted the most powerful air force in all the world? His eyes narrowed and he looked at the faces of his commanders. Was it possible? Was Heydrich correct? If there was a traitor, none would be more devastating to Germany than any of the men in this room.

Washington, D.C.

The President of the United States was engaged in one of his favorite activities—mixing after-dinner cocktails. His close advisers, who were now with him in his upstairs study, had long ago ceased to be amazed that Franklin D. Roosevelt, who, in all other things, claimed the prerogatives of his office, derived such pleasure from serving his guests. While they chatted amongst themselves, the President busied himself with the ice bucket and bottles that sat on the tray next to his wheelchair.

Even though the late summer evening was warm and the men gathered in the President's upstairs study were in shirtsleeves, no one thought to request that the air-conditioning be turned on. Thanks to the previous tenant, the President's office, bedroom, and second-floor study were air-conditioned, but Franklin Roosevelt, who felt that the recently developed cooling device aggravated his sinus condition, never used it.

The President had a copy of that day's *New York Times* in his lap and knew that sooner or later the talk would turn to events in the newspaper. As always, Franklin Roosevelt let the others talk until he decided what had to be done. Tonight, as usual, the talk was about his re-election chances.

There were five of them in the room with the President this night. Secretary of State, Cordell Hull, was almost seventy, and had served the President in the same capacity since Roosevelt's first cabinet. Harry Hopkins, twenty years younger than Hull, and the former Secretary of Commerce, was a close confidant of the President—in fact, he lived at the White House—and was known simply as a presidential adviser. Harold Ickes, sixty-six, Secretary of the Interior, was Roosevelt's top political strategist. He also had been with the President since the first term. Also present were Stephen Early, the President's press secretary, and his assistant, Peter Anderson.

Harry Hopkins held up a copy of the offending *Times*. "How the hell can they print crap like this?" he said to Press Secretary Stephen Early. He read, " 'Willkie says that Roosevelt promoted Munich pact.' Now what kind of nonsense is that?"

"They're not saying that the President did promote the Munich pact," Early explained. "They're just saying that Willkie says he did."

"Same thing," Hopkins protested. "You ought to have a talk with those people."

The President smiled as he listened. This had been the typical tenor of the after-dinner conversation at the White House for the past month. It was about time, he thought, for Harold Ickes to chip in with the latest poll results.

Right on cue the Secretary of the Interior, Ickes, interrupted his colleagues. "The latest Gallup Poll shows that the President has picked up strength in two more states."

"Yes," Hopkins said, "but Willkie is still leading the President by a substantial margin."

It always amazed Franklin Roosevelt that people could talk about "the President" as if he were not in the room. "It's not all bad news," he said cheerfully, holding up his copy of the newspaper. He read the front-page headline, "'British down 185 German planes in day of fury.'" The President's eyes sparkled. "Now, that's what I call a good day's work."

Hopkins would not be mollified. "We're in trouble here, Mr. President. Willkie is turning out to be a helluva campaigner. While you're worrying about the war in Europe, he's out there drumming up votes. He's hit a responsive chord with the voters on keeping us out of this war."

"Staying out of war always appeals to the voters."

"You've got to say it as often as he does, Mr. President."

"I say it every time I give a speech. Every time a reporter asks me a question."

"Willkie is now saying that if you are elected to a third term you would be an American dictator," said Hopkins.

A smile flashed across Roosevelt's face. "Wouldn't I look swell in one of those ludicrous uniforms, having tea with Mr. Hitler and Mr. Mussolini?"

Everyone laughed and the President seemed pleased at his little joke. "Doesn't anyone have any good news for me today?" he asked.

"Well, Mr. President," said Cordell Hull, the Secretary of State, "on page eight of today's *Times* it says that Ambassador Kennedy's house in London doesn't have an air raid shelter."

"Now, that is good news," said Roosevelt, laughing. "If I could only persuade my fellow dictator to direct a few well-aimed bombs in that direction, we'd have one less source of irritation to deal with."

"I doubt they would find him home," said Ickes. "The word I'm getting from London is that Joe hasn't spent much time in London since the bombing began."

Hull nodded. "They're calling him 'Jittery Joe' now."

"Jittery Joe," Roosevelt said, laughing.

"I'm afraid he's no laughing matter," said Hopkins, ever the pessimist. "He could cost us the election. He keeps hinting that he's ready to support Willkie."

"He's bitter about the third term," said Ickes. "Felix Frankfurter told me that Kennedy said he expected to be the compromise candidate for president this year. He was miffed when the President decided to run again."

Hopkins looked at Ickes. "And this is the man you were pushing as a candidate for vice-president?"

Ickes's face reddened. "If Garner had made a deal with Farley, we would have needed a Catholic on the ticket to secure the nomination. That's the only reason I offered his name. He's the last person I'd want to see in any office."

Roosevelt interceded before the two could get into a heated argument. He had noticed a tendency lately for Ickes and Hopkins to get under each other's skin. "Now, now, boys," he said jauntily. "Let's not worry about what's in the past. What do we do about Jittery Joe now?"

"Let him rot in London," said Hopkins. "Out of sight, out of mind."

"That would be fine," said Roosevelt, "but he has sent a letter to Secretary Hull, threatening to reveal all he knows about my correspondence with Churchill if we don't allow him to come home before the election."

"Who the hell does he think he is?" said Hopkins. "Threatening the President of the United States."

"It's no idle threat," said Cordell Hull. "If he leaks word of that correspondence, everyone will say that Willkie's charges of secret deals are true."

"And," Ickes said, "Arthur Krock would make sure that his master's words were splashed all over the front page of the *New York Times*."

"Henry Luce would make it a cover story in *Time* magazine."

"Speaking of Henry Luce," said the President to Peter Anderson, who had managed to become part of the woodwork while the discussion swirled around him, "I had another letter from Miss Donaldson, today."

"Yes, sir?"

"I've found her letters most informative," Roosevelt said. "They confirm my feelings about the character of the average Englishman. She indicates that the general populace is quite prepared to go it alone if they have to. Suggesting her for the job was an excellent idea, Peter."

"Thank you, Mr. President," said Anderson, barely able to contain his delight at such praise from his chief.

That small detail taken care of, the President returned to the subject at hand. "What do we do about Kennedy?" he asked. "If he tells what he knows, how do we cover ourselves?"

No one had an answer.

"I'd prefer the voters heard it from me, before Kennedy gets the chance," Roosevelt said. "I'll tell the American people that any deals I made with Churchill were to protect the vital interests of the United States."

"They don't want to hear that," said Hopkins.

"Sooner or later," the President said, "they'll understand that it's the truth."

"The only thing the voters will understand," said Hopkins, "is that you lied and Willkie was telling the truth. Better to keep Kennedy quiet."

"How?" asked the President.

Ickes said, "Perhaps we can reason with him."

"Reason?" said Hull. "The man has no scruples. His mind is as blank as uninked paper."

"Appeal to his loyalty," said Ickes.

There were chuckles all around and Stephen Early said, "Joe Kennedy never did anything without thinking of Joe Kennedy."

Just as the session threatened to deteriorate into a contest of who could tell the worst Joe Kennedy story, the President cleared his throat and brought a silence to the room. "I think I understand Joe better than any of you," he said. "He feels that we've exiled him, and he's bitter that we have ignored his counsel. I'm going to let him stew in his own juices. We'll tell him we're trying to arrange for his departure from the Embassy, but that we need some time to find a replacement."

"And if he insists on coming home?" asked Hopkins.

"We'll bring him home, but we'll wait until a few days before the election. The less time he has to do damage, the better."

The faces in the room were glum. Roosevelt grinned. "Don't worry, boys," he said. "I've been handling Joe Kennedy for years. I don't see why I can't take care of him this time."

"Henry Luce is dying to get that endorsement for Willkie," Hopkins said. "If he does . . ." his voice trailed off as if he were unable to articulate such a horrendous thought.

Roosevelt chuckled. "There are worse fates than spending one's declining years at Hyde Park," he said.

No one seemed to appreciate the President's humor.

LONDON IN FLAMES AS NAZI BOMBERS POUND CITY; 10TH CONSECUTIVE NIGHT OF HEAVY BOMBING RAIDS

LONDON, SEPT. 17

◆ *CHAPTER 40* ◆

LONDON, September 17—The offices of the Special Intelligence Service were housed in a rather unattractive nine-story office building within easy walking distance of St. James's Park and Winston Churchill's underground war rooms at Storey's Gate. To those who worked there, the building, and the establishment for which they worked, took their names from the street—Broadway.

On the morning of the seventeenth of September, two Enigma messages had electrified the normally placid atmosphere at Broadway. The first message was from the German General Staff to the Army and Luftwaffe commanders in Belgium and Holland, where the invasion preparations had been most intense. According to the message, Hitler was ordering his commanders to disperse the equipment that had been so laboriously gathered over the last few months. The air-loading equipment was to be dismantled and the invasion barges themselves were to be returned to their ports of origin for other duties.

The news was like a thunderbolt. If accurate, it could mean

263

only one thing—Hitler had abandoned, at least for this year, his plans for invasion. Those at Broadway who were privy to this information could barely conceal their elation. The long, desperate hours waiting for the inevitable hammerblows were apparently over. In the midst of the jubilation a message was prepared for the Prime Minister, and provisions were made to deliver what, at that moment, was felt to be the most important Enigma transmission ever deciphered.

Before that task could be completed, however, a second message was delivered from Bletchley to Broadway. This message, also from the German General Staff, ordered a parachute landing at Leiston by Commando units of the Brandenburg Division. Jubilation turned to consternation and Stewart Menzies, chief of the SIS, called in his key staffers for a hurried conference.

Menzies's office was on the upper floor of an office building on Queen Anne's Gate, a narrow street behind Broadway. Although his office had a different address from the Broadway Building, the two structures were actually back to back and connected by a rear passageway.

"Well," Menzies said, "it seems we find ourselves in somewhat of a dilemma." He picked up the first message. "On the one hand—the invasion is off." He picked up the other. "On the other—we should expect a parachute landing tomorrow morning. What are the possibilities?"

"Mix-up in communications?" ventured a senior staff member.

"But which is the accurate message?"

"It doesn't really make any difference," said a voice in the back row.

All heads turned to look at the speaker, a young lieutenant named John Bishop, who was relatively new to the inner workings of Broadway.

Menzies had already come to the same conclusion, but was interested in how Bishop had arrived at his decision. "Perhaps you'd like to explain your reasoning, Lieutenant Bishop."

"Well," Bishop began, "we can hope the first message is accurate, but we must act as if the second is. If the Germans do plan a parachute assault, we must be prepared to repel them."

"And what if," said a senior staffer, "this message is a trap to determine if we have broken the Enigma system? If we reinforce Leiston, it could be a dead giveaway."

Menzies said, "Well, Lieutenant?"

"If this were a test, I doubt that it would come in conjunction with an order that appears to cancel the invasion. That only serves to confuse matters. Anyway, I don't see that we have much choice."

"I'm afraid," said Menzies, "that I must agree with the lieutenant. We have no choice. Even if it is a test we must respond. I shall recommend to the Prime Minister that we regard the parachute landings as a possibility, and that as unobtrusively as possible we send reinforcements to the area."

"What about the other message?" someone asked.

"Its accuracy will become self-evident in time. If the Germans start removing their invasion barges from Holland and Belgium, then we will know that this message was correct. If nothing happens at Leiston, we will also know that, in all probability, our Ultra secret has been compromised."

"Get him to Ireland?" said Marie Price. "It's sheer madness. They'll catch us. They'll hang us."

"Be quiet," said Sean Daly sharply. They were in Marie Price's flat. Daly had arrived with the news from Benke only moments before. "Let me think," he said. "I can make the trip to Ireland easily by myself, but how do I get Hamilton there?"

"Tell them it's impossible," said Marie. "Tell them I won't do it."

"You," said Daly, "will do as you are told. This is a direct order from Germany. We have no choice."

It was a relatively simple matter for him to get back and forth to Ireland even though travel between the two countries was severely restricted. Ireland had remained neutral in the conflict and the Germans still maintained an embassy in Dublin. The British were justifiably suspicious of traffic between the two countries.

He would have preferred to do the job alone, but every scenario he could think of included Marie. He looked at her. Christ, he thought, this isn't going to be easy. She was already scared out of her mind. If she didn't calm down, she would be the death of both of them.

He sat down next to her. "Look," he said. "This is probably the best thing that could happen to us."

Her face registered her disbelief.

"We get Hamilton to Ireland," he said, "and we stay there until the war is over. We'll be absolutely safe. In a few weeks, once the Germans occupy England, we can come back." He smiled reassuringly. "You'll be safe until this is all over."

"But how do we get him there?" she asked.

"You leave that to me," he said. "I want you to persuade Hamilton to take some leave. Even thirty-six or forty-eight hours."

She nodded. "Then what?"

"You tell him you want to get away to some romantic spot where the two of you can be alone." He grinned. "I'll be waiting for you," he said. "You're seeing him tonight?"

"Yes," she said.

"Good. Start tonight. Tell him you want to get away for a few days. Let him know how wonderful it will be."

"I know what to tell him," she said. "What happens to him when they are finished with him?"

"They'll probably take him as a prisoner of war," he lied.

Marie closed her eyes. She knew what would happen to Winston Hamilton when the Germans had finished with him. "I'll talk with him tonight," she said.

"I knew that I could count on you," Daly said.

◆ *CHAPTER 41* ◆

ANTWERP, September 18—Colonel Hans Oster had been scheduled as the only passenger on the Fokker Tri-motor, on the trip from Antwerp to Berlin, but the commander of Kampfgeschweder 3, Oberst Gliszinski, had prevailed upon him to allow some of the wounded to accompany him.

Sixteen wounded and four nurses had joined him just moments before the scheduled take-off. As the engines of the Tri-motor roared, the wounded were loaded into the rear of the aircraft where the seats had been removed to make room for cots. Several of the wounded were burn victims and Oster found their constant moaning terribly depressing. The others lay quietly.

The moaning reminded him how much he despised those who had been responsible for the war. He had opposed Hitler and his thugs from the beginning. He had given warning of Hitler's intentions to the British and the French, but they had been too weak-willed to stop Hitler when he could have been stopped easily. Now one was gone, the other hanging on for dear life. It was like a nightmare from which there was no waking.

The only thing worse than a German defeat would be a German victory which would solidify Hitler's iron grip on Germany and Europe. Hitler was only fifty-one, thought Oster. If he could defeat England, he, and the perverted thugs he had gathered around him, might rule for another thirty years. The thought made him shudder.

He removed the large manila envelope from his briefcase

267

and removed the photographs. He looked at them for the hundredth time in the past three hours. The story they told was always the same. To the untrained eye they showed little, but Oster knew that the photographs, taken by reconnaissance aircraft of Luftflotte 2, stationed in Belgium, might mean the difference between defeat and victory. The first set had been taken on Tuesday morning, the second set on Wednesday afternoon.

After inspecting both sets, the Photographic Evaluation Officer of Kampfgeschweder 3 in Antwerp, had pointed out that the British were moving several armored units into the area around the small town of Leiston. "Not only that," said the young Oberleutnant, "there seems to be an increase in infantry strength." Camouflaged trucks had appeared since the Tuesday photographs. "Something is going on," said the Oberleutnant. "I can't tell you what, but it looks like they're expecting something."

Oster put the photographs back in the envelope. There was no way he could keep this from Canaris or the General Staff. Other tests, of course, would be done, but to Oster the message was clear. The British had intercepted and decoded the Enigma transmission he had sent two days ago.

The mystery of the failure of the Luftwaffe had been solved. The RAF had read every message sent between Goering and his commanders, known every move the German forces would make. Now, without this advantage, how long would they be able to survive?

Oster realized this revelation would revive the seriously sagging fortunes of Hermann Goering. Der Dicke would be exonerated from his disastrous failures and returned to his preeminent position as Germany's second citizen. In many ways, Oster hated Goering as much as he hated Hitler, and here he had in his hands the instrument of the fat man's salvation.

The battle that had been lost over the skies of England would, in all probability, be rejoined with renewed vigor. The hope that the madness would come to an end was gone forever.

From the rear of the plane came a shriek of pain from one of the wounded men. The sound was like a knife in Oster's belly.

* * *

"It's absolutely the perfect place," said Marie, echoing what Daly had told her. "It's quiet, secluded—romantic."

"Sounds wonderful," Winston Hamilton said, "but don't you think Scotland is a little far to go on a thirty-six-hour pass?"

"Not at all," she said. "We can leave London on Saturday and be back early on Monday morning. That gives us two nights alone, away from all this . . . this . . . noise."

What she referred to was the bombing that had hit London every night since September 7.

Winston smiled. "I'll see what I can do," he said.

Even though it was only 4:30 in the afternoon, the crowds were lining up at Dickens and Jones department store on Regent Street in anticipation of the evening's raid. It was a ragtag army of old men and women, and mothers with babes in arms and children in tow. The queue, ten deep and half a mile long, threaded its way along Regent Street and around the corner of Great Marlborough Street. Most, it seemed, had all of their personal belongings with them, carried in baby prams, or old suitcases, or simply wrapped in a sheet and carried over the shoulder. They had come, a stream of frightened humanity, from the devastated East End, to what they hoped would be the relative safety of the West End, and to the major department stores of the city that had opened their doors so that they might find shelter.

With the exception of the big raid of the fifteenth, the Germans had given up on daylight raids—the costs were too high—but every night the sirens sounded at around 7:30. The all-clear did not sound until four or five in the morning, and Londoners, most of whom had to get to work each day, were exhausted.

It was a scene that reminded Betty Donaldson of the frightened peasants in Poland who had gathered their belongings and fled in the face of the advancing German Army. "Out of the frying pan, into the fire," she said. "Things are just as bad here in the West End as they are in the East End."

"Better shelters over here, I guess," Munro said.

They were walking across Maddox Street, towards Savile Row, the upper part of which was still closed due to an unexploded bomb from last night's raid. Parts of Bond Street were roped off, and looking down the street they could see that many of the storefronts had collapsed leaving the innards exposed. They turned north towards Brook Street. Everywhere the scene was the same—buildings collapsed and piles of rubble in the streets.

"You must have had quite a night," said Munro.

"You're lucky you missed it."

Munro had accompanied Colonel Jackson to send off two of the American generals who had been in London as observers. Both generals knew Munro's father and had requested that Max make the trip with them. They had spent the night in Bournemouth, gone to Poole in the morning, where they had seen the generals off on the *Clipper*, and returned to London that afternoon.

"How was the trip?" Betty asked.

"Jackson spent most of the time trying to convince the generals that the British can hold out through the winter, and that the Ambassador doesn't know what he's talking about when he says they can't."

"Were they convinced?"

"I'm not sure. General Emmons kept saying what a great guy Kennedy is."

"Easily impressed."

"The other thing the Colonel seemed concerned about was the sensational coverage given to the bombing in the American papers. He feels it's bad for morale and hoped the generals would inform the American public that things aren't as bad over here as some of the more sensational reporters are leading them to believe."

"I wonder what the good Colonel would have said if he'd been here last night."

They turned into Oxford Street, one of the main shopping thoroughfares in London. Gutted buildings lined both sides and several of the major stores showed only their skeletal remains. Rubble had been pushed into huge piles to open the street to traffic and demolition crews were at work, bringing down the remnants of buildings too damaged to remain standing.

"Further down the street," said Betty, pointing, "Selfridge's was hit, and a bomb hit the Marble Arch Underground Station which was crowded with people taking shelter."

"How many dead?" he asked.

"No official tally yet, but it looks like lots."

"I thought the damn undergrounds were supposed to be safe."

"Apparently the bomb hit outside, bounced once and rolled down the stairs before exploding."

They walked on in silence for a while until Munro said, "I need a drink. Is Claridge's still open?"

They went down Davies Street to Brook Street and found a table in the lounge at Claridge's. They ordered drinks and sat in silence until they arrived. Munro took a long drink from his glass. "Bastards," he muttered to no one in particular.

"Did you ask Jackson about the building on Broadway?"

"Yes, as a matter of fact. It seems that it's one of the places maintained by British Military Intelligence. Jackson has no idea what's going on over there."

"Military intelligence," Betty murmured. She grabbed his arm, her eyes sparkling. "I knew there was something going on with that girl friend of yours. I followed her and her boyfriend last night. They went to the movies."

"And you followed them?"

Betty nodded. "About ten minutes into the movie the air raid warning went off and we had to leave. I followed them to the Underground Station at Piccadilly and stood right next to them. She spent most of the time trying to get him to agree to go somewhere with her. He kept saying it was too far and that he could only get a thirty-six-hour pass. She's after something. I've seen the way she looks at him. There's no love there. She's with him because she wants something that he has."

"Now what?" Munro asked.

"I want to know where she's taking him that's so far away. I want to know what she's after." She looked at her watch. "Let's get back to the Savoy before a raid starts. We can get a bite to eat and"—she batted her eyelashes playfully—"if you like, we can stay there tonight. Air raids are so much more comfortable," she said, "when you're in your own bed."

WILLKIE WARNS OF AMERICAN DICTATORSHIP IF ROOSEVELT WINS; CHALLENGER CALLS ELECTION "THE BATTLE OF AMERICA"; MUST FIGHT TO SAVE DEMOCRACY, HE TELLS SUPPORTERS

COFFEYVILLE, KANS., SEPT. 19

◆ *CHAPTER 42* ◆

BERLIN, ABWEHR HQ—Admiral Canaris looked across his desk at Colonel Oster. "Well, Colonel," said Canaris, "it looks like Captain Ritter was correct in his concern for the safety of the Enigma system."

"I'm sure his new masters at Prinz Albrecht Strasse will be glad to hear that."

"The General Staff will be most pleased with our efforts. I believe this is a feather in the Abwehr's cap. What do you think this revelation will mean to the war effort, Hans?"

"Probably an intensification of the air-war against England. Only this time, I believe, the Luftwaffe will prevail."

"And then?"

"Invasion. Occupation," said Oster, and then in a moment of recklessness added, "God knows what else."

Canaris masked a thin smile behind a cough. "And that prospect does not please you?"

After his indiscreet comment, Oster was determined to be careful. "I am always pleased when I can serve Germany."

"You realize, of course, that if Heydrich's plan succeeds, the Reich Security Office will also be aware that the Enigma system has been compromised."

Oster nodded.

"If that happens, the credit which belongs to this office would go to Heydrich." After a pause Canaris said quite casually, "The only way to prevent that would be to let the British know about Heydrich's plan."

"Forgive me, Admiral," Oster said. "I am not quite sure I understand what you mean."

Canaris leaned forward, his elbows on the desk. "I am well aware of your activities against this regime. I too have contacts with the other side, Hans," he said gently. "And I make it my business to know what my own people are up to."

Oster knew that if Canaris decided against him, he would be dead before morning. "I am at your mercy, Admiral," he said.

"Please," Canaris said. "Your secret is safe with me. There are many who sympathize with your goals."

Oster noted that Canaris did not include himself in that number. "I serve Germany as well as I can," he said.

"As do we all. Can your contacts at Prinz Albrecht Strasse get you the details of the operation in Ireland?"

"Yes, Admiral."

"I have several contacts in Switzerland," Canaris said casually, "who would see to it that such information got to the British. If we knew the name of the English officer who is the target of this operation, it would simplify matters somewhat."

"Yes, it would," said Oster, "but I'm not sure I understand why you have decided to assist me in this. Only a week ago you seemed pleased at the prospect of British capitulation."

"My sources within the General Staff tell me that the Führer has decided to attack Russia after England is defeated. That prospect terrifies me." He closed his eyes, envisioning a million corpses in the snow. "But, if England survives, the Führer could not possibly turn to the east. The General Staff would not permit an attack to the east as long as England remained in the war."

Oster did not share the Admiral's faith that the General Staff could contain Hitler, but he saw no other option.

"How long will it take to find out about Heydrich's plan?"

"Not long," said Oster. He was surprised that the Admiral did not ask for his source and wondered if the crafty old bastard was aware that it was Heydrich's adjutant who fed him his information. "Certainly within a day or so."

"We'd better act as quickly as possible," Canaris said. "The information won't do the British any good if it's too late to stop the kidnapping."

Oster knew that they had embarked on a course that could easily lead them both to the gallows—or worse. Traitors were rarely dispatched quickly in Nazi Germany, and there were those in the SS who were expert at administering a slow death. He had been on that course for some time now. It was nice to know that he would have exalted company. "I will begin immediately," he said, rising from his chair.

As Oster left the room, Canaris lifted his dachshund out of the lower desk drawer where his pet had been taking a nap. He waited until Oster had closed the door and then scratched his pet under the chin. "You know, my little friend," he whispered, "I am getting much too old for this sort of thing." The dog looked up at his master. Canaris imagined that he saw sympathy in the animal's face. "Who will take care of you when they catch me," Canaris said sadly. He was certain that one day he would be caught. As usual, he was quite right.

Euston Station was crowded with travelers and Betty Donaldson marveled at how easy it was to follow Marie Price without being noticed. She had been following her for more than an hour and the only difficult moment had been when Marie had decided to take the bus. Betty got into the queue several places behind and hoped that she would not turn around and notice her.

Before that it had been easy. Marie had never looked back. Betty's only fear was that Price would turn quickly, see her, and remember her face from Ambassador Kennedy's party. She doubted, however, that Price would remember her at all. Marie Price had not really paid much attention to anyone at the party, until Munro had mentioned his work in the code room.

Betty wore a tweed coat and hid behind a floppy hat, and she felt positively dowdy in contrast to the flamboyant good looks of the woman she followed. The station was a bedlam of activity. There were soldiers, sailors, and airmen of every description, and their wives or lovers were there to see them off or to welcome them home. Children who were about to be evacuated to safer locales played together while their distraught mothers, burdened with battered suitcases, called for them to stay put. Some of the young men in uniform seemed young enough to be candidates themselves for evacuation.

The noise was deafening—train whistles, departure announcements, screaming children, weeping mothers and wives—but the confusion made it simple for Betty to continue her pursuit.

Marie approached a ticket window and Betty fell in line behind her. At the window Marie spoke through the hole in the glass to a woman inside, and after a brief conversation, which Betty could not hear, she exchanged money for two tickets.

Betty turned aside to let Price past and then stepped up to the window. "That was my friend who was just here," she said.

The woman stared at her blankly.

Betty pointed a thumb over her shoulder. "The gorgeous blond?" Betty said. "The one my husband can't stop talking about."

The woman nodded knowingly. "Can I help you?" she said.

"I'd like two tickets on the same train," Betty said.

The woman hesitated and Betty jumped in with, "Our husbands both have leave, and we're all taking a little vacation together."

The woman smiled and said, "Two tickets to Dumfries."

As Betty looked in her purse for the fare, the woman lowered her voice to a friendly whisper. "If my man was home on leave, I don't think I'd want him anywhere near her."

Betty slipped the money under the glass and took the tickets. "What time is that train leaving?" she asked.

"Twelve noon."

"Tomorrow?"

The woman eyed her strangely. "Saturday," she said.

"Of course," Betty said quickly. "Today is only Thursday. I don't know what I'm thinking about lately."

"It's the war," the woman said. "Nobody knows what they're doing."

"Dumfries!" Munro bellowed. "That must be"—he calculated quickly—"Four or five hours from here."

"Five," Betty said. "We'll get there before five o'clock."

"And then what?" Munro asked.

"I figured we'd just follow them to wherever they were going."

275

"The whole thing sounds silly to me. They're probably going off to shack up for the weekend."

Betty grinned. "The worst thing that could happen is that we'll do the same."

"We don't need a ten-hour train ride to do that," said Max.

Betty smiled. "Oh, yes, you do," she said.

"Actually," he said, "I quite enjoy train rides. Some of my most wonderful moments as a child were spent on trains. I'm certainly looking forward to this one. Where did you say we were going—Dumfries? Wonderful. I hear it's lovely this time of year."

She laughed. "It'll be fun. And exciting, too."

"I know the kind of excitement I'm looking for," Munro said.

Betty touched him on the arm. "Something is going to happen there. I can feel it. She's not dragging him all the way up there just to play house."

Munro pulled her into his arms and kissed her tenderly, then again, harder, more insistently. He could feel her body respond. "I don't think I can wait," he said. "Saturday is too far away."

16 NIGHT RAIDS KILL HUNDREDS IN LONDON;
HEART OF CITY BEARS BRUNT OF BOMBING

LONDON, SEPT. 20

◆ *CHAPTER 43* ◆

Friday, September 20—Munro was at work in his office on Friday morning. The telephone call took him by surprise. It was Marie Price, and she sounded close to hysteria. "I must see you right away," she said. "Please. It is a matter of life and death." They agreed to meet in Green Park in twenty minutes.

She watched him approach, and wondered if she had done the right thing. She could not go to the British authorities. They would hang her. If Daly ever found out, he would kill her. What had started as an exciting game had turned deadly serious. This planned kidnapping was sheer madness.

Munro stopped in front of her and waited for her to speak. She sat down on the bench and wordlessly he sat beside her.

"I need your help," she said.

"For what?"

"I need a visa. I want to go to America."

"Half the people in London want to go to America."

"Can you help me?"

"That's not really my department," he said. "You'd have to apply at the embassy. I can tell you who to talk to, but—"

She interrupted him in mid-sentence. "When could I leave?"

He could hear the fear in her voice and tried to be gentle. "There are over a thousand Americans who thought they would stay in London. The bombings have made most change their minds, and the embassy is swamped with visa applications. Our first responsibility is to American nationals. It's not just giving authorization to leave," he explained, "it's arranging passage. There aren't too many ways out of here at this point."

"Then you can't help me?"

"Not with this," Munro said, "but if you tell me what it is that is troubling you, I might be able to help."

She looked at him, and for a moment he thought she might disclose the problem, but then she looked away. "I'm afraid," she said, "that no one can help me now."

She stood up and Munro stood with her. "I know you're in trouble," he said. "Let me help you."

"It's all right," she said, looking away. "I'll be fine."

Betty was right, Munro thought. Marie was involved in something important. "Don't do it," he said as she started to leave.

She looked at him in puzzlement.

"Whatever it is that you're planning to do—don't do it."

She smiled sadly. "I envy people who have choices."

She turned quickly and walked away. Despite her purposeful stride, she seemed lost. Munro watched her until she had disappeared among the trees that lined Queen's Walk.

Neither had noticed the man who watched them from behind his morning paper. When Munro started back to the embassy, the man folded his paper carefully and followed him out of the park.

Munro spent the rest of the morning and most of the afternoon working on a list of American weaponry the British government was interested in acquiring. Colonel Jackson had dropped the list on his desk that morning, saying it had to be kept under lock and key. Munro found it difficult to concentrate on anything but his meeting with Marie. Every thirty minutes he called the Savoy to speak with Betty, but she was out and the clerk had no idea when she might return.

When Betty finally did get back to him, it was late in the afternoon, and she could barely contain her glee about what had happened. "I told you," she said. "I knew she was involved in something."

"Now, apparently, she wants to get uninvolved."

"What we have to do," said Betty, "is find out what it is that she wants to get uninvolved from."

278

"Maybe it's time that we talked to the authorities," Munro said.

Betty was adamant. "I'm going after her and her boyfriend tomorrow," she said. "This could be one helluva story. Are you coming with me?"

If he went to the authorities now she would never forgive him. "Yes," he said.

"I knew I could count on you."

"Can we have dinner later?" he asked.

"If we are going away for the weekend, I have to file a story by tomorrow morning. I'll probably be at it most of the night."

"OK," he said, but she could hear the disappointment in his voice.

"We've got the whole weekend together," she said. "We'll have plenty of time for each other."

"I suppose you're right," he said without conviction.

She could hear the skepticism in his voice and moved quickly to dispel his doubts. "It's going to work out fine," she said. "Trust me on this. I know what I'm doing."

He wasn't so sure about that.

"We'll meet at Euston Station before noon tomorrow."

He sighed. "Don't worry, I'll be there."

279

◆ *CHAPTER 44* ◆

Saturday, September 21—Lieutenant John Bishop stared in
disbelief at the papers he had spread across his desk. He
looked at the man who had brought them to his office and
who now sat in the chair on the other side of the desk. "Why
the hell wasn't this brought to our attention sooner?"

Wilfred Russell smoothed his mustache and said calmly, "I
suppose, John, because no one really thought it was in your
jurisdiction."

Bishop was a tall man with jet-black hair, a thin mustache,
and dark, dangerous eyes. He was at least twenty years
younger than Russell. "I realize that domestic surveillance is
your province," he said, "but we are sister agencies, and
there is supposed to be communication between us."

"That's why I'm here, old boy." Russell was in his mid-
forties and slightly overweight. "To communicate."

"Someone should have brought this to us sooner."

"No need for recriminations, old boy," Russell said. "As
soon as it crossed my desk, I thought to myself, now here is
something that the boys over at MI-Six should know about."
He smiled. "Got myself right over here to let you know about
it."

Bishop realized that Russell was right. There was no need
for recrimination. Besides, it would have done little good.
The fault, he knew, was in the system. In 1939 British
Military Intelligence had been reorganized so that the branch
entrusted with counterespionage—MI-5—had been placed
under the jurisdiction of the Home Office, while the branch

entrusted with espionage—MI-6—had been renamed Special Intelligence Service and placed under the jurisdiction of the Foreign Office. The resultant split in the services had caused some unfortunate gaps in communication. This, Bishop knew, was one of them.

"All right, then," Bishop said, "this Benke fellow has been passing information to the Germans. Your boys have followed him twice to Portugal, where he met with representatives of Germany. I must say that this is where your people should have turned this over to us."

"Technically, John, the man was engaged in espionage in this country. That places his activities wholly within our jurisdiction. Now, I agree that you should have been informed. That's why I'm here now."

It was senseless to argue. Interdepartmental rivalries would have to be solved by others. Bishop returned to the report. "Others are involved with him, I see."

"Yes. Our boys have been following him for about a month—since around the nineteenth of August. Quite a careful fellow, actually. Nothing out of the ordinary for some time. Then on the eighth of September, he was observed meeting with one Sean Daly. Daly is an Irishman who works with an engineering firm, Dowdswell and Davis, here in the city. Quite a lot of government work involved. Some of the information that Benke passed to the Germans apparently came from him"—he leaned across Bishop's desk and pointed at one of the pages—"You'll find it right there," he said.

"Naturally, we put some people on Daly, hoping to find whoever else was involved before we had him arrested. Not much luck until just a few days ago. We followed him to the home of Marie Price, who is registered as French, but is believed to be Swiss. She works with the Free French at Carlton Gardens, doing whatever it is that crowd is doing over there."

"Why haven't you arrested them?"

"We were about to," Russell said, "but it gets a bit sticky at this point."

"Sticky?"

"Some of the information that Benke is delivering to the Germans could come only from the American Embassy —news, for instance, that Ambassador Kennedy wants to go home in time for the elections, or that he and Roosevelt are at odds over the President's policies."

"That information is available in the daily newspapers."

"Not with this kind of detail," Russell said. "There were certain things that had never been reported to the newspapers, certain conversations between Churchill and Roosevelt. It was all very puzzling until yesterday when Price was observed meeting with an American from the embassy—an assistant to the military attaché. We feel that he must be Benke's source."

"So now you can arrest the lot of them."

"Well," Russell said, "the Home Secretary wants us to move very carefully with the Americans. We don't want to do anything which might disturb our relationship with Roosevelt."

"These people are spies," said Bishop. "The Hungarian and the American should be kicked out of the country, and the others will hang."

"It isn't quite that simple," said Russell.

"Why not?"

"The American is the son of a very influential senator who is an opponent of Roosevelt's. An arrest might cause a backlash of American opinion and hurt Roosevelt's chances in the coming election."

"I don't think we can be concerned with that," said Bishop.

"I'm very much afraid the Home Secretary does not agree with you. I am to inform you that unless the situation deteriorates drastically, we are to delay the arrest of any Americans involved in this case until after the American elections."

"I don't like it," Bishop muttered. "It stinks of politics."

"Quite right," Russell said, "but I'm afraid that you will have to let us handle this from our end."

"I assume you have these people under twenty-four-hour surveillance?"

"We have four men on the job."

"Four men to watch four people?"

"All four are rather predictable. All work somewhat regular hours. The Home Secretary felt that four men were enough."

"We'd be glad to lend a few extra men," Bishop said.

"I don't think that will be necessary, thank you," said Russell coolly.

"Seems that you don't need us at all on this," Bishop said. "I'm surprised you bothered to let us know about it."

"Actually," Russell began, "the reason I came over was to discuss a problem that you might find hits a little closer to home."

"What problem is that?"

"Miss Price has several gentlemen with whom she shares her favors, including one of your people."

Bishop got to his feet. "Who?" he asked.

"We're not sure yet, but he was followed to this building the day before yesterday." Russell was apologetic. "As soon as I saw that in the report, I rushed over to let you know."

"We'll have to arrest all of them immediately," Bishop said almost to himself.

"I say, old boy," said Russell, "I thought I had explained the Home Secretary's position on this matter."

Bishop glared at Russell, who realized that what they whispered about Bishop was true. It was said that Bishop did not belong behind a desk, that he would be happier in the field, slitting German throats with the knife he was rumored to carry in his inside jacket pocket.

"If someone in this building has been compromised," Bishop said, "and the information gets to the Germans, you may just as well forget about winning this war."

He walked out of the room, leaving a stunned Russell to wonder what in hell was going on here at Broadway.

Colonel Menzies appeared to take the news calmly, but inside he felt a deep sense of foreboding. "I think," he said, "that we can count on the Americans for some sort of cooperation. I can't say the same for the Hungarians. They're practically allies of Hitler's already."

"What do you suggest, sir?" Bishop said.

"We have to arrest everyone right away. And we must find which one of our people has been turned."

"What about the Home Secretary's instructions about the American?"

"There will be diplomatic problems, of course, with the American and the Hungarian, but I'll speak to Lord Halifax at the Foreign Office about this right away. He'll straighten it out with the Home Office. This is going to be bad," Menzies said. "Very, very bad."

The clock on the wall read 11:30 and Max Munro was finishing his morning's work when Colonel Jackson came into his office. The look on Jackson's face quickly told him that something was wrong. Jackson hesitated for a moment and then said, "Max, I'd like you to come down to my office for a minute."

"What's up?" Munro asked.

Jackson did not look at him as they went down the stairs. "Some people in my office would like to speak with you," he said.

There were four men waiting in Jackson's office. Two were seated in front of Jackson's desk, two others stood near the door. As Munro and Jackson entered, the two by the desk stood up, and one of them took two steps toward Munro.

"Captain Munro?" he asked. Munro nodded. "My name," said the man, "is Wilfred Russell. I am with British Military Intelligence—Security Service. These two gentlemen"—he indicated the two men at the door—"are with the Criminal Investigations Division of Scotland Yard." He turned to the fourth man. "This is John Bishop, also with Military Intelligence."

"Why do you want to see me?" Munro asked.

"Are you familiar with the Second Secretary to the Hungarian Embassy—Josef Benke?" Russell asked.

"I met him at one of the Ambassador's parties. About a month ago, I'd say."

"Have you seen Mr. Benke since then?"

"No." Munro looked at his watch. There was no chance now that he was going to get that train. Betty would be upset, but it wasn't everyday that one was dragged in front of the Security Police.

"What about an Irish national named Sean Daly?"

"Never heard of him," Munro said.

"Do you know of a woman named Marie Price?" said Russell.

"I met her at the same party where I met Benke."

"Have you had occasion to see her since that evening?"

Munro hesitated as every pair of eyes in the room bored

into him. He could feel the accusations in their stares. Just before Russell could repeat the question, he said, "Yes, I have seen her since then."

"Would you be so kind as to tell us the particulars of those subsequent meetings?"

"Perhaps if you told me what you were after, I might be able to help you," said Munro to Russell.

"Very well, then," said Russell. "We would like you to tell us what kinds of official documents you gave to this woman so that she and Josef Benke could give them to Germany."

"I never gave official documents to her or to anyone else." Munro looked at the stark accusing faces. Only Jackson seemed sympathetic to his plight. "I don't think I had better say anything else until I talk with the Ambassador."

"The Ambassador has been sent for," said Russell. "He's on his way in from the country."

Jackson spoke for the first time. "Then perhaps we should wait until he arrives. I must remind you that Captain Munro is an American citizen with diplomatic status, and as such cannot be held for any crime in your country."

"I haven't committed any crime, Colonel," said Munro.

"Very well, then," Russell said. "Captain Munro will not leave this building, nor will he attempt to contact anyone on the outside. One of our men will remain on guard at the entrance."

"We are perfectly capable of insuring that Captain Munro does not leave the building," Jackson said.

Russell was about to protest but thought better of it. "Very well," he said. "I will leave him to your care. We will return when the Ambassador arrives."

Jackson remained in the room while the others exited. Hands thrust deep in his pockets, he paced in front of the window.

"Colonel," Munro said, "I just want you to know that these charges are baseless."

"I want to believe that's true, Max," Jackson said. He closed the door behind him, leaving Munro alone.

Outside the embassy Bishop looked back as if reluctant to leave, then moved toward the waiting car. Russell held the car door open and Bishop slipped into the back seat. "Now what?" asked Bishop.

Russell looked at his watch. "I don't expect Kennedy back

for several hours. I think we can go over to Carlton Gardens and pick up Miss Price."

"She'll be there on a Saturday?" Bishop wondered.

"Followed her there myself, this morning," said one of the CID men in the front seat.

"No rest for the wicked," said Russell.

The platform was all but clear now as the conductor walked the length of the train slamming shut each compartment door. Each slam was like the ticking of a loud clock that reminded Betty how little time was left. Marie Price and Winston Hamilton had boarded at least ten minutes earlier, and all that remained were a few late souls who dashed across the platform to scramble aboard. Amidst the shriek of whistles and blasts of steam, Betty stood immobilized by indecision, unable to will herself to climb aboard the waiting train.

Where the hell was he? She was angry and worried.

The station sounds seemed far away—the whistle blasts, the slamming doors, the babble of voices, the farewell cries, the hiss of steam—as Betty, hoping that Munro would appear at the gallop, kept her eyes trained on the far end of the platform.

A voice spoke from behind her and she turned to see the conductor. "I'm afraid he's not coming, love," he said sympathetically, and she could tell that he had imagined that she was waiting for someone to see her off. "If you're coming with us, you'd best be getting on board."

She gave a smile of thanks and the man's good-hearted face broke into an immense grin. He took her one suitcase and helped her climb into a compartment. "You have a lovely trip, love," he said, slamming the door shut.

She had no sooner sat down than the train lurched forward, then stopped, then, to the sound of a wailing whistle that echoed through the quiet spaces of the cavernous station, moved forward again. As the train slowly picked up speed, Betty looked back along the platform, but it was empty now, and she knew that she was alone.

◆ CHAPTER 45 ◆

The door flew open and Ambassador Kennedy burst into the room with Colonel Jackson following closely behind. The Ambassador wore a blue blazer over a tennis sweater, white slacks, and tennis shoes. It was obvious what he had been doing when he had been recalled to the embassy. He was puffing furiously on a cigar and stood, with hands on hips, in front of the seated Munro, as if to dare him to deny the charges.

"I didn't do it," Munro said simply.

Kennedy rolled the cigar around in his mouth. "For your sake," he said, "I hope not."

Colonel Jackson stepped forward. "I think the British are making a mistake," he said. "The whole thing seems rather circumstantial to me."

"I want to speak with Munro," Kennedy said. "Alone."

Jackson's face fell, but he left the room without comment.

The Ambassador waited until they were alone, then pulled up a chair beside Munro. He removed his cigar from his mouth and leaned forward. "All right," he said, assuming a fatherly tone, "you can tell me what happened. You've got diplomatic immunity. I can have you shipped home tomorrow. The British can't touch you, no matter what you've done."

"I haven't done anything."

"I'm told the Price girl was in your apartment. She wasn't

287

there to discuss the price of coffee. I might tell her a few secrets myself," the Ambassador chuckled. "She's quite a dish."

"I didn't tell her any secrets."

"C'mon," Kennedy said. "You had the opportunity. When I assigned you to the code room, I never imagined that you'd turn this stuff over to the Germans."

"Who did you imagine that I'd turn this 'stuff' over to?"

Kennedy's eyes narrowed. "What is that supposed to mean?"

"I think you put me there so that I'd let my father know what's been going on between Roosevelt and Churchill."

Kennedy chewed on his cigar. "If that was my purpose, young man, why wouldn't I just do it myself?"

"I don't know. I'm sure you've got your reasons. But I do know one thing. If you wanted this correspondence kept secret, I was the last person you should have put in the code room."

Kennedy stood up. "So you did tell the Germans?"

"That's not what I said."

"That's what it sounds like to me," the Ambassador said as he moved toward the door. "I will recommend to the State Department that we rescind your diplomatic immunity. If we were at war, I'd recommend that you be shot."

Before Munro could respond, the Ambassador slammed the door and was gone.

Jackson came in immediately. "What happened?" he asked.

Munro told him everything, leaving out only that he had taken documents home with him. "I wish that you had come to me about this earlier," Jackson said. "Were you and Donaldson really going to follow those two all the way to Scotland?"

"Yes, sir," Munro said. "It was Betty's idea."

"Where is she now? It would help if we could get her to verify your story."

"Probably back at the Savoy."

"I'll pop over there and talk with her. Maybe we can have this whole thing straightened out by the time the British get back here."

* * *

Betty Donaldson watched the green English countryside slip past her window. The man in the seat across from her was eating a huge chunk of some foul-smelling cheese, breaking off bite-size pieces with his penknife. The pungent aroma filled the compartment, permeating everything, and Betty was certain that she would have to take a bath to get the smell out of her hair and her clothing. No one else seemed to mind.

Next to the man with the cheese sat a young soldier who obviously felt that his uniform made him irresistible. Every time he caught Betty's eye, he gave her a gigantic wink. Next to him was another soldier, fast asleep and snoring loudly. He had slumped over so that his head rested on the shoulder of an elderly gentleman who sat next to him. The old man seemed uncomfortable, but since it would have been unpatriotic to protest, he did nothing.

On Betty's side of the compartment was a middle-aged man in a business suit who had buried himself in his newspaper. Next to him another sleeping soldier and nearest to Betty, a young woman who announced to one and all that she was on her way home from a visit with her husband who was "with the RAF" somewhere south of London. This revelation, Betty supposed, gave the woman some sort of special standing with the other passengers.

Betty pretended preoccupation with the view and was thankful that she had been able to get a window seat. She had convinced herself that Munro would not have left her waiting at the station unless he had a perfectly good reason, and she was worried that something might have happened to him. What would he think when he discovered that she had gone on without him?

Once she found out where Hamilton and Price were heading, she would call him at the embassy. That thought made her smile. Munro would insist that she wait for him and probably be on the next train. He might even be following her right now in hopes that she would wait for him in Dumfries.

She closed her eyes and rested her forehead on the window, letting the feel of the cool glass transport her from the stuffy compartment. Soon they would be across the border into Scotland, and soon after that, Dumfries. After that her course was a blank. She could only watch, and wait, and follow.

* * *

Russell's composure wilted under Bishop's relentless stare. "How were we to know that she was about to run?" he snapped.

They had returned to Bishop's office after two fruitless hours outside the Free French headquarters at Carlton Gardens, where they had awaited the return of Marie Price, who, according to a woman who worked with her, had stepped out for a half hour to take care of some errands.

"Perhaps she spotted us outside, waiting for her," said Russell defensively.

"Perhaps," Bishop said, without conviction.

"I've got men covering her flat," Russell said. "When she comes back we'll nab her."

"What about the others?"

"I have a man outside Benke's flat in Half Moon Street. He is still inside, and we are awaiting confirmation of an arrest warrant. His diplomatic status makes the search warrant rather sticky, but he is not going anywhere without our following. The Americans are being extremely cooperative. Ambassador Kennedy has given us authority to search Munro's rooms, and the Home Office has prepared a deportation order which requires only the Secretary's signature. In addition, the Ambassador has given us carte blanche to use search warrants on any of the other personnel at the American Embassy—in case others are involved."

"Rather decent of him," said Bishop. "He could've made things difficult for us." He thought for a moment. "I think we should take him up on his offer. Particularly regarding anyone working in the embassy code room. That's where the leaks had to originate."

"Quite right," said Russell. "I'll get on it right away before word gets out that we are holding Munro. If anyone else is involved with him, we wouldn't want to give them the chance to destroy evidence." Russell offered Bishop a cigarette, then tapped his against his silver case before lighting.

"And what about Sean Daly?"

"I'm afraid that he hasn't been seen since yesterday."

Even though Russell was his senior, Bishop could no longer hold his anger. "Good God, man," he said. "This is incredible."

"We've had one of our best men on him for almost two

290

weeks. Followed him night and day. I can show you the reports. Yesterday he was followed from early morning. He took a bus to Kensington Road and walked through Hyde Park. He doubled back several times and seemed to be in no hurry or to have any particular destination. He exited the park at Bayswater Road and went directly to the Lancaster Gate Underground. My man hurried after him, but by the time he got to the station, Daly had gone."

"So, both Daly and the woman have disappeared?"

"I'm afraid so," Russell said reluctantly. "But we still have the American—and Benke. Unfortunately, both have immunity. They do not have to tell us anything."

A grim smile drifted across Bishop's face. "Don't worry about that," he said. "They'll tell us everything we want to know. I'll see to that myself."

Russell found that kind of talk exceedingly distasteful. He was from the old school, where goals were attained through a combination of stealth and guile. Young upstarts, like Bishop, who had no experience in intelligence work before the war, thought that the ends justified any means, no matter how reprehensible. Whatever happened to the English tradition of fair play, he wondered. Why, in many ways some of these fellows were just as bad as the Germans. That would never do.

Betty was used to traveling light. As the train pulled into the Dumfries station, she had the strap of her duffel bag over her shoulder and stood ready to exit the compartment as soon as the train pulled to a stop.

The Dumfries station was a typical small-town railroad station, consisting of a single building and a street-level platform that was not elevated to the height of the compartments so the passengers were forced to make two steps down onto the concrete. The station was indistinguishable from most of the others that the train had passed through on its journey north.

Betty was one of the first to step down to the platform. She kept her eyes on the compartment two cars ahead. Sure enough, Hamilton was the first to appear. He was carrying two small valises which he put down to offer a hand to Marie Price.

Betty noted that the first thing Marie did was look up and down the platform, and she had the distinct impression that Marie was looking for someone. Hamilton picked up the bags and, with Marie Price holding his arm, started down the platform toward the street.

Betty waited, looking around as if expecting someone, and then, from a safe distance, followed Hamilton and Price.

Parked on the street, next to the station, were two buses and a single taxi, and Betty's heart sank as she realized that if they took the taxi she might lose them for good. She hurried, hoping at least to hear their destination, but Hamilton and Price walked past the taxi and approached the buses.

The bus drivers stood next to the open doors of their vehicles and Hamilton stopped at the first one. "Bus for Portpatrick?" he asked.

The driver, an old man with a cigarette dangling from his lips, aimed a thumb in the direction of the next bus. Hamilton and Price moved past him and Betty followed closely.

"Portpatrick?" said Hamilton to the second driver.

"Aye," said the driver, a man younger than the first but still well into his sixties, "that's me last stop." Despite his age he eyed Marie appreciatively. "In ye go, laddie," he said to Hamilton. "Have yer fare ready when asked."

Betty watched them clamber aboard the bus. Portpatrick, she thought. Where the hell is that? She wanted to get to a telephone and let Munro know where she was heading. She approached the driver. "Excuse me."

"Aye, lassie."

"I want to take this bus to Portpatrick, but I need to make a telephone call first. Is there a public phone I can use?"

The driver pointed across the street to the red kiosk. "Right there," he said, "but if ye don't get on board noo, y'll no get a seat on this bus."

Betty saw the bus was indeed filling rapidly. She looked toward the station. Others were heading this way. "Could you save a seat for me?" she asked.

The driver made a face as if she had asked him for a hundred pounds. "That I couldni do, lassie. Furst come, furst served. But there wull be anither bus for Portpatrick in two oors."

Betty decided quickly. "When will we get there?"

"Y'll be there by half past seven," the driver said proudly, and added, "on the dot."

Betty sighed and stepped aboard the bus.

Sean Daly climbed aboard right behind her.

◆ *CHAPTER 46* ◆

LONDON—At the same time that Betty was finding a seat on her bus, officers of British Military Intelligence, accompanied by detectives of Scotland Yard, and armed with search warrants, were spreading across London. Their immediate targets were those American Embassy employees who were assigned to the code room. The Ambassador had been confident the British would find nothing. So far he had been correct.

Just before six o'clock, Anthony Sutton, Max Munro's code room shift mate, returned to his flat. He had been out walking, inspecting the bomb damage in the neighborhood. The sight of the shattered buildings and rubble-strewn lots had made him more certain that America must, at all costs, avoid this madness. He put on the kettle to make some tea, and turned on the radio. Vera Lynn, the "Sweetheart of the Forces," was singing "A Nightingale Sang in Berkley Square." Sutton scowled. Not much chance of nightingales in Berkley Square this summer, he thought. He turned off the radio. All one heard was a succession of patriotic drivel anyway. The songs, the programs, the news were all the same. All designed to let the poor unsuspecting saps think that they had a chance to win the war. Better that they should be told the truth.

Although it was still light, Anthony Sutton had drawn the blackout curtains in his small third-floor flat in Belgravia. His two rooms were small and sparsely furnished—a bed and double dresser in the bedroom, and, in the other, a table and two chairs near the gas stove and a couch and stuffed chair next to the fireplace that provided the apartment's only heat.

On the mantelpiece, above the fireplace, was a photograph, the only personal touch in an impersonal room. It showed a young man, tall and thin even then, standing next to Charles Lindbergh. Lindbergh looked straight ahead into the camera, his eyes bright, his shy smile somehow charismatic. The young man, Anthony Sutton, had eyes only for Lindbergh. His head was turned toward his hero, and his eyes were aglow with adoration.

Just as the kettle started to whistle, there was a sharp knock at the door.

"Just a minute," called Sutton and took the kettle off the gas. "Who is it?" he called.

"Police, sir," said an exceptionally polite voice. "We'd like a word with you, if we may."

A second knock, louder this time, forced him to act. He went to the door and opened it. There he saw two plainclothed policemen and behind them, looking rather sheepish, one of the aides to the chargé d'affaires of the embassy.

"May we come in, sir?" said one of the policeman.

Sutton hesitated. The aide gave him an embarrassed smile and said, "They have a warrant to search your flat."

"Authorized by whom?" Sutton said sharply.

The policeman smiled. He didn't mind his job so much when they got nasty. "Authorized by the Home Office"—he paused dramatically—"and by your own Ambassador."

Sutton stepped back and the three men entered his flat.

"Why don't you have a seat, sir," said the policeman. "We'll be as neat as we can about this business and take up as little of your time as possible."

Both policemen kept up a constant chatter as if the search was secondary to their conversation. When they emerged from the bedroom and started looking through the sitting room, Sutton closed his eyes, feigning boredom, and listened to the rattle of the dishes and the clatter of the pots as they went through his small kitchenette.

He opened his eyes after there had been silence for a short time. One of the men was looking under the kitchen sink. He didn't see the other one. He looked around the room, but saw only the embassy aide, who sat quietly in one of Sutton's kitchen chairs gamely trying to detach himself from the proceedings.

Then a voice called from the other room. "I think you'd better have a look at this, Inspector."

Sutton knew it was over.

In a short time both men were back in the room. "Can you explain these documents?" said the older policeman, and Sutton noticed that, for the first time, he did not call him sir.

"Just some work I brought home from the embassy."

The policeman turned to the embassy aide. "Perhaps you could identify these documents, sir?"

The aide took several of the documents and looked them over carefully. "I'd say they came from the code room," he said. "They are stamped with the time of transmission or reception."

"Well, there's a box full of 'em in there," the policeman said. "Must be hundreds of 'em."

The news of Anthony Sutton's arrest spread quickly throughout the embassy. As Colonel Jackson was telling Munro the details, Terrence Wymore came into the office.

"The Ambassador has asked me to inform you," he said to Munro, "that the British Secret Service, for the present, see no further need to detain you." The dour expression on Wymore's face made it evident that he did not concur with that decision. "The Ambassador suggests that you pack your things and prepare to leave the country before they change their minds."

"I'm not going anywhere," Munro said.

Wymore scowled. "Perhaps the Colonel can talk some sense into you."

"Unlike others," Jackson said, "a soldier does not desert his post in time of war."

"I assume you are referring to the Ambassador," Wymore said.

"You may assume as you wish," said Jackson.

Wymore spun on his heels and left the room.

"This gets you off the hook," Jackson said.

"What about Betty? You haven't seen her yet?"

"She wasn't at the Savoy. I left a message for her to call the embassy as soon as she returned."

"I'd better find her," Munro said.

"Max, you don't think there's any possibility that she went after them without you?"

"She wouldn't do that," Munro said confidently.

"She does seem like a rather headstrong young woman. I'm not sure that I'd put anything past her."

"She's probably out working on a story. I'll find her, even if I have to sit in the lobby of the Savoy all night."

The two men shook hands and Munro, glad to be released from his temporary confinement, quickly left. He planned to go to the Savoy and talk with Talmadge or one of the other reporters who were always hanging around in the bar. Someone must have some idea where Betty had gone. He would find her and explain what had happened. She'd be the first reporter to get the news about Sutton's arrest.

Sutton was talking, telling everything that he knew. His admission could not, however, be labeled a confession. As he responded to the questions of his British interrogators, he displayed the righteous indignation that had led him to steal the documents in the first place. He had no remorse for what he had done, even when told that the information had gone, not to sympathetic reporters, but to the Germans. All of this was offered in the insolent tone of one who knows that he alone has done the right thing.

"I wasn't going to stand by and let you and Roosevelt drag America into this war," he snarled. "I still won't."

There were four men in the room with him. Two from the Criminal Investigations Division of Scotland Yard, whose job it was to question Sutton, and John Bishop and Wilfred Russell, who sat behind the prisoner and observed the interrogation. Bishop gave an exasperated sigh and the two interrogators looked to him with apologetic shrugs. It wasn't easy to get cooperation from someone like Sutton. Besides, according to British law, he had done nothing wrong, and he knew it. He had taken documents which belonged, not to the British, but to the American government. Even though the documents were potentially harmful to Great Britain, and of benefit to Germany, Sutton could only be held accountable to his own government. He held diplomatic immunity and the British were limited to expelling him from their country.

"You've actually done me a favor," he said, laughing.

"Now there isn't any need for me to operate in secret. I can do what I should have done from the beginning—let the American people know what's going on here. Roosevelt and his warmongers are as good as finished."

Bishop leaned over and whispered into Wilfred Russell's ear. "I don't see how we can let him go."

Russell saw the look in Bishop's eyes and his own eyes widened in horror. "Surely you don't mean . . ." he stammered.

Bishop smiled. "Perhaps you'd better talk with the Home Secretary," he said. "This man has to be silenced somehow."

Russell gathered his things. "I'll be back soon," he said. His eyes were pleading. "Don't do anything until I get back."

Bishop nodded and, when Russell had gone, broke into a wide grin. These old-timers, he thought. Full of good intentions and the English sense of decency. Of what use were good intentions when the Germans were planning a victory march up Whitehall?

The ancient bus rolled into the town of Portpatrick, down the narrow, cobbled main street, past weatherbeaten buildings which had stood for centuries. In other Septembers the town might have been enjoying the last of the summer visitors, but in this, the first summer of the war, Portpatrick was as dead as winter.

Portpatrick lay on the coast, on the North Channel that separated the Irish Sea from the Atlantic. On the other side of the Channel, the northern coast of Ireland was less than 35 miles away. The town had once been a thriving seaport, but with the widening of the River Clyde in the last century the big ships had moved upriver to Clydebank and Glasgow. Portpatrick, now a fishing village and a seaside summer resort for the families of the men who worked in the shipyards and the docks in the industrial cities of the Scottish Lowlands, had long since begun to settle into a slow but steady deterioration.

Most of the bus passengers had been dropped in a succession of small towns between Dumfries and there, and by the time the bus arrived in Portpatrick there were only seven passengers left on board. As was his usual practice, the driver stopped in front of a small inn called the Purple Heather, where he would leave his bus overnight and begin his journey back on the next morning.

"End of the line," he said as he applied the hand brake.

"Isn't it charming?" Marie Price said as she looked at the inn from the bus.

"Looks rather decrepit to me," said Winston Hamilton.

"That's part of the charm," Marie said, laughing.

They exited the bus, and Betty Donaldson waited until they had gone inside before she gathered her things and followed. Sean Daly observed her movements with great interest. He had sat behind her and across the aisle, and had noticed that she seemed inordinately concerned with Price and Hamilton's conversation. She was American, he was sure, and that intrigued him even more. Of what possible concern could these two be to her? Perhaps he was imagining things, but, just the same, he resolved to keep an eye on her.

The war really was beginning to have an effect, thought Sir Duncan Sommers as he looked around the dining room of L'Escargot. Here it was, a Saturday evening and the restaurant had only a handful of patrons. Damn shame, he mumbled to himself. People shouldn't let these bloody Germans disrupt their lives. But even he had been shaken from his usual routine. Normally he dined at the Dorchester, but since last week's bombing, the service and the food had been rather below their usual standards. One would hope that a hotel with the tradition of the Dorchester wouldn't allow minor bomb damage in the dining areas to so effect the quality of service. He sighed, and sipped his martini. He supposed that there would be many such disappointments before this was over.

As usual, Sir Duncan dined alone. He was not the kind of man who made or encouraged friendships, and since the death of his wife almost twenty years ago he had come to enjoy his solitude. He was a rather portly gentleman in his early sixties, known to his associates for his keen intelligence and unflappable demeanor. He had worked in British Military Intelligence for more than thirty years and was, at present, the Deputy Chief of the Secret Service.

Sir Duncan had just finished his pâté de foie gras and was awaiting the arrival of his next course—a filet of Dover sole—when he spotted Alec Henderson, one of Lord Halifax's aides at the Foreign Office, in conference with the maître d'hôtel at the entrance to the dining room. He saw both men turn and look in his direction. Obviously his quiet dinner was about to be interrupted. He nodded slightly toward Henderson—acknowledging that it was permissible for the younger man to approach his table.

"Terribly sorry to disturb you, Sir Duncan," Henderson began, sitting across from Sommers. "But something rather important has come up, and I thought SIS should be informed right away." Henderson was in his middle thirties, slightly balding, and plagued with nervous gestures. He was the sort of man whose capabilities did not impress a man like Sir Duncan Sommers.

Sir Duncan raised his hand ever so slightly from the table, and Henderson was silent as the waiter brought the filet of sole. "Perhaps you'd care to join me?" asked Sommers. Henderson politely refused but accepted the subsequent offer of a martini. When the waiter departed, a brief nod granted Henderson permission to proceed.

"I tried at first to contact Lord Halifax," said Henderson, "but it seems that both he and Sir Stewart are in conference with the Prime Minister over this nasty business at the American Embassy."

Sir Duncan was well aware that his chief, Sir Stewart Menzies, was with the Prime Minister. He said nothing, hoping that his silence would encourage Henderson to get to the point of this interruption.

"This evening we received an intriguing report from our legation in Bern. It is purported to be from the same source within German Military Intelligence who has previously given us some exceptionally accurate information."

Sir Duncan, his interest piqued, put down his fork. This source, who could only have been someone with impeccable contacts within the German intelligence services, had indeed given vital information in the past. It was Sir Duncan's belief that the source was Admiral Wilhelm Canaris of the Abwehr, or, at the very least, one of his top aides. He had met Canaris before the war and had found him to be a man with little regard for the Nazi regime. Canaris had taken great pains to point out to Sommers that only his fear of communism allowed him to give his support to Hitler, who he felt was the only man in Germany who could save his country from that particular disaster.

"The message," said Henderson apologetically, "is almost

too incredible to believe, but too important to dismiss: the Germans are preparing to kidnap, right off the streets of London, one of your people at Broadway."

Sommers raised a single eyebrow. "I don't suppose your source tells us who this victim will be?"

"Unfortunately not, but he does provide a clue as to why."

Sir Duncan went back to his Dover sole. Perhaps, he thought, he might try the roast pigeon for his next course. "Go on," he said to Henderson.

"The message says that the Germans have reason to believe that we have penetrated something called the Enigma system. I'm not sure what that could be, but I imagine it's some sort of secret weapon or perhaps a military code." Henderson did not notice that the color had drained from Sir Duncan Sommers's face. "The kidnapping, apparently, is to put to rest all doubt about this situation. It sounds utterly fantastic, of course, and most unlikely that the Germans could actually do such a thing, but . . ."—he looked at Sommers, who seemed to have discovered something horrible in his fish—"Are you all right, Sir Duncan?"

Sir Duncan pushed his plate aside. "I'd like to have a copy of that message in my office within the half hour," he said.

"Of course, Sir Duncan. I'll see to it immediately."

Sommers looked at his watch. "Perhaps it would be better if you met me at Storey's Gate."

Henderson stood up. He, of course, knew that Storey's Gate was the entrance to the underground war rooms where Churchill, Halifax, and Menzies were meeting at that very moment. "I can be there in less than fifteen minutes," he said.

Sommers saw the look of panic in young Henderson's face. He smiled reassuringly. "Yes, my boy," he said. "I'm afraid that we are going to have to interrupt that meeting with the Prime Minister after all."

◆ CHAPTER 47 ◆

Munro was waiting in the Savoy American Bar when the air raid sirens began to howl. Most of the patrons in the bar did little more than make annoyed faces or mumble a quiet obscenity into their drink. The Germans had, with Teutonic punctuality, arrived at this time every evening, and after fourteen consecutive nights of bombing, no one was surprised or even particularly worried.

The bartender announced that the bar was closed, but that service was, of course, available in the downstairs bar. Amidst a great deal of grumbling and complaining, the patrons gathered their drinks and headed for the shelters. Munro was in no mood to move downstairs, so he downed his whiskey and soda and decided to go for a walk. None of the reporters had seen Betty or Talmadge.

Outside, the evening sky was alive. Great searchlight beams crisscrossed the twilight canopy, illuminating the heavy cloud cover; antiaircraft guns boomed and their shells exploded somewhere above the clouds. It was obvious to Munro that the guns were mainly to bolster civilian morale. The gunners couldn't possibly hit anything under these conditions. Off in the distance, perhaps around Victoria Station, he could hear the rumble of the bombing and the reply of the gunners. Around him the streets were quiet and almost deserted.

He walked up to Shaftesbury Avenue and down toward Piccadilly, stopping to read the theater billboards along the way. At the Apollo, the play was *Margin For Error* with Margaretha Scott, and next door at the Globe, Michael Redgrave was appearing in *Thunder Rock*. He passed a movie theater which advertised the latest John Garfield film, *Dangerously They Live*, and chuckled at the irony of the title.

Piccadilly Circus, with the statue of Eros removed and in storage, seemed an unlikely spot for prostitutes, but they were out and roaming the near-deserted streets. A few approached him, but Munro plowed on, lost in thought. As he passed one of the nightclubs a door opened and the sound of voices singing filled the night air. Munro, unconsciously, took up the refrain and found himself mumbling the words of the "Lambeth Walk."

He circled back down Haymarket, across to the Strand, and was back at the Savoy as darkness finally enveloped the city. He went inside and down to the River Room where an air raid party was in full swing. Someone had started a conga line and young and old had joined in the fun, snaking their way around the room, stepping gaily and kicking their legs in time with the beat.

The incongruity struck Munro—somewhere men and women and children were dying, and here grown men and women played like children. He watched them briefly and then went back upstairs.

As he crossed the foyer, he saw Bill Talmadge coming in the front door, alone. Talmadge saw Munro at the same moment and both stopped dead in their tracks.

Talmadge spoke first. "I thought you went off for the weekend with Betty."

"I couldn't get to the station on time," Munro said, feeling vaguely apprehensive. "I thought she might be with you."

"I haven't seen her since she left for the station this morning. I'm sure she didn't come back to the hotel."

For the first time Munro allowed himself to think it was possible that Betty had gone after Price and Hamilton by herself. He muttered an obscenity.

"What's going on?" asked Talmadge. "Is something wrong?"

Munro mumbled an incoherent reply and started for the door. As he hit the street a taxi pulled into the Savoy courtyard and he raced ahead of an elderly gentleman and his wife who were making their way toward the approaching vehicle. He did not hear the shouted protests as he jumped into the taxi and ordered the driver to take him to the American Embassy.

It was obvious that Winston Hamilton had had too much to drink. His loud laughter filled the small dining room of the Purple Heather. What was equally obvious to Betty as she watched them from her table across the room was that Marie Price was trying to get Hamilton drunk. They had been joined by another customer—Betty wasn't sure but she thought the man might have been with them on the bus from Dumfries—and he was buying Hamilton drink after drink.

There were only two other patrons in the dining room of the small inn, and they appeared to be local people out for a quiet evening. Betty ate her simple meal slowly, sipping her beer, casually observing the three across the room with what she hoped would appear as only casual interest.

Earlier, after unpacking in her small, upstairs room, she had used the public telephone at the inn to try to contact Munro at the embassy, but had been told that he was out. She had left the name and telephone number of the inn and was hoping that he would soon return her call. She wasn't quite sure what she ought to do next and hoped that Max might have some ideas.

After her meal Betty took a seat by the large stone fireplace that dominated the room. She sat by the fire, sipping a drink, reading a book, and watching the noisy threesome. Once, when Hamilton staggered off to the toilet, the other man and Marie Price put their heads together in deep conversation. He made forceful, insistent gestures and, at one point, thumped his fist on the table. Marie nodded, but she seemed frightened, and she looked around the room as if exploring avenues of escape.

When Hamilton returned the man rose from his seat and shook his hand. Betty heard him say something about an early rise the next morning and watched him leave. Hamilton and Price sat for a while, talking and drinking, and then Marie stood and tried to encourage a reluctant Winston Hamilton to do the same.

"It'll do you good," Betty heard her say. "It'll do us both good. The night air will clear your head."

Hamilton mumbled something and then laughed as he tried to get up from his chair. Marie Price helped him to his feet and into his coat, and together they staggered toward the door.

Betty waited. She could hear Hamilton's drunken chuckle as he and Marie moved past the window of the inn. She gave them a few minutes, then put on her coat and went outside. The sea air was cold and Betty buttoned her coat and held the collar up around her neck as she huddled in the doorway, waiting a moment before she went after them.

Portpatrick was a ghost town. Never a bustling hub, after dark the village center was devoid of activity. Betty listened to the silence. Under the restrictions of the blackout, the village appeared abandoned and darkened buildings lined the winding, narrow streets. The streets themselves were dark, an unlit movie set of a Scottish village, awaiting a director's call to "lights, camera, action."

Her eyes accustomed to the darkness, Betty crossed the deserted, cobblestoned street and headed in the direction that Hamilton and Price had taken. A sliver of moon gave enough light for her to see and before long they were directly ahead of her, Hamilton singing softly and leaning heavily on Marie.

They were heading for the beach; Betty could hear the sound of waves lapping against a sea wall and the distant cries of gulls. She ducked into a doorway as they paused and then, when they had disappeared around a corner, she hurried after them. Cautiously she peered around the corner. They were at the other end of a short, narrow street. Ahead of them she caught a glimpse of moonlight reflecting off the surface of the sea.

At the end of the street Betty stopped and again looked around the corner. Hamilton and Price were thirty yards ahead of her walking alongside the sea wall. The tide was high and the moon traced a silvery streak across the choppy waters of Portpatrick Harbor. Betty was about to follow when something made her stop. Two men were approaching Hamilton and Price from the opposite direction. Their hands were thrust deep in their pockets and they were whistling a jaunty tune, but there was something about them that made Betty wait at the corner.

The men drew abreast of the two she was watching and walked past without so much as a nod. Just as Betty was about to step out the man closest to Hamilton whirled and Betty saw the glint of something in his hand. She heard a dull thud, like a palm smacked against an overripe melon, as the man struck Hamilton across the back of his skull. Hamilton dropped in a heap to the pavement. Marie gasped, but made no other sound or attempt to run away. The men lifted Hamilton to a standing position, then draped his arms around their shoulders. They dragged him off, looking like two friends bringing home a drunken comrade.

Marie watched them go in silence, then turned back in the direction from which she had come. As Betty turned to retreat quickly, she crashed into a man who stood directly behind her.

It was the man from the inn. He clamped a hand across her mouth to prevent the scream that had started in her throat. Sean Daly flashed a knife close to her face. "Scream," he said, "and I will kill you." He released her mouth but held her pinned against the wall with his forearm. "Who are you?" he said. "And what business do you have here?"

Betty's eyes were wide with terror. She tried to speak but could not.

"It's the woman from the inn," said Daly when Marie rounded the corner. "I told you she was following us."

Marie's eyes widened in recognition. "I know her from somewhere," she said. "I'm sure of it."

"I'm an American newspaper reporter," Betty managed.

"What do you want with us?"

"I wanted a story," Betty said.

"A story? What kind of story?"

"She knows," Marie wailed. "She knows."

Daly clamped his hand across Betty's mouth again and she felt the knife at her throat. "Now someone will write your story," he said.

Betty felt the knife dig into the soft flesh of her throat. She squeezed her eyes shut and prepared to die.

"No!" Marie screamed and grabbed Daly's arm. "I won't let you do this."

"And what do you suggest we do with her? Leave her here to tell the authorities?"

"No killing," said Marie. "I won't stand for it."

"There's no other way," said Daly.

"No killing," Marie said again. "Bring her with us. When this is over, we can let her go."

The next few seconds were the longest in Betty's life. Daly released his grip. "All right, she comes." He put his face close to Betty's and she could smell the liquor and cigarettes. "But if she gives me any trouble, I'll kill her. I promise you."

Betty's knees buckled and she almost fell to the ground. Marie helped support her.

"You do as you're told," she said, then added, "please."

"I'll take her to the boat," Daly said. "You get back to the inn and pick up your things. Hurry," he snarled. "We leave in ten minutes."

Marie hesitated, afraid to leave Betty alone with Daly, but then began to move quickly back up the street toward the inn.

They watched her go, Daly holding Betty's arm in a viselike grip. "You're very lucky," he said. "Instead of a trip to hell, you get a trip to heaven." He chuckled then pulled her viciously close. "Be careful," he growled in her ear. "Hell still waits."

London

Lieutenant John Bishop listened in astonishment as Maxwell Munro told him what had happened. Next to Munro sat Colonel Jackson, who confirmed Munro's incredible story.

After Munro had been unable to reach Betty at the inn in Portpatrick, Colonel Jackson had suggested that he go to Bishop and let him handle it. Jackson had made the necessary phone calls and despite the lateness of the hour had accompanied him to Bishop's office at Broadway, where they had been kept waiting for the better part of an hour until Bishop appeared, apologizing for the delay, blaming some important work on which he and others were working.

Halfway through Munro's story, Bishop, who had seemed uninterested at first, sat bolt upright in his chair. "You are absolutely positive that the man's name is Hamilton, and that he works in this building?" he had asked. When Munro gave his assurance, Bishop excused himself and left the room. He returned to inform them that he had ordered the local police to find the three and hold them in custody, then told Munro to continue with his story.

"You mean," said Bishop, when Munro had finished, "that you were just going to follow those two and see where they led?"

Munro nodded sheepishly.

"You should have told me this earlier," said Bishop.

"I didn't think it was important. Besides I had my own troubles at that point, I couldn't very well say, 'Excuse me, I have a train to catch,' could I?"

"And you've called this inn"—Bishop looked at a note he had made—"the Purple Heather?"

"As soon as I got the message. The woman who answered said that she had gone out and hadn't come back."

"And the other two were there, also?"

"They had gone out and hadn't come back."

"The local police—such as they are—will get on this immediately. I have also ordered Special Branch units of the Glasgow Police to be in Portpatrick before morning."

"I'm sure they'll have no trouble finding them," Jackson said.

Munro said to Bishop, "There's something else, isn't there? Something you're not telling us."

"Earlier this evening," Bishop began, "we received word from one of our very reliable sources on the continent that the Germans would attempt to kidnap someone who works in this building."

"Hamilton?"

"It seems to fit," Bishop said.

"But why take him to some remote spot in Scotland?" asked Jackson.

"Portpatrick is less than thirty miles from Ireland," said Bishop. "They probably intend to get him across and into the Irish Republic."

"Now that you know," said Jackson, "you can stop them?"

"If they succeed in getting him across to Northern Ireland, it will be very difficult—next to impossible—to prevent them from taking him south."

"What does this man know that makes him so valuable to the Germans?" asked Munro.

"Obviously I can't tell you that," Bishop said, "but Hamilton is one of a rather select group of individuals who is in possession of a secret that is more valuable to Britain then a fully equipped army."

"What about Miss Donaldson? Do you think she is in danger?" asked Colonel Jackson.

"Let's just hope that she doesn't follow them very closely. If they tumble to her, she could be in serious difficulty."

After eliciting a promise from Bishop to keep them informed, Munro and Jackson left Bishop's office. The Lieutenant went down the hall to the antiquated elevator that would take him to the ninth floor where his chief was presently in conference with other members of his staff.

"Well?" asked Stewart Menzies simply when Bishop entered his office.

Bishop brought him, and the others, up to date.

"So, you think Hamilton is the target?" Menzies asked.

"Yes. All the pieces seem to come together."

Menzies looked at the men who circled his desk. Each nodded his agreement with Bishop's appraisal. "Well, then," said Menzies, "if the Germans are to take a personal hand in this, as the message seems to indicate, they will either have to bring personnel into Ireland via submarine or parachute or use someone from their embassy in Dublin. We can increase the number of our people assigned to keep tabs on the German Embassy, and, at the same time, get word out to our Irish network to be on the lookout for any unusual activity. Have I left anything out?"

"I'd like to go after them," Bishop said.

"Follow them, you mean?"

"Yes."

Menzies shook his head. "I know it's difficult to just sit back and let this thing play out, John, but I think we should wait for word from the field before we go racing off on a wild goose chase. Anything else?"

This time it was Sir Duncan Sommers. "I'd say let's bring in the Hungarian fellow, Benke. He seems to know as much about this business as anyone."

"I agree," Menzies said, looking at his watch. "Let's wait a bit and get him out of bed. Perhaps a knock on the door at midnight might upset him enough to start him talking."

◆ CHAPTER 48 ◆

The escape from the British mainland, thought Betty
Donaldson, had been well planned and remarkably simple. A
motor launch had awaited them at the end of one of the
decaying piers in a quiet cove just outside Portpatrick, and
taken a quick trip several miles into the waters of the North
Channel. Just when the water had started to get rough and
Betty began to fear they were expected to make the trip in this
small boat, they were hailed by a passing trawler. A transfer
had been rapidly accomplished, and the small boat, piloted by
the two men who had assaulted Hamilton, turned back
toward Scotland.

Winston, still unconscious, was sprawled across a bunk in
one of the lower cabins in the fishing trawler. Marie sat next
to him, stroking his hair and wincing each time she touched
the large bump on the back of his skull.

"Poor thing," she said to Betty, who sat on the bunk across
from them. "They didn't have to hit him this hard."

Betty looked at the cabin floorboards. She was thinking
that was not the worst that would happen to Hamilton.

Marie guessed at what she was thinking. "It's not my
fault," she said. "I didn't know it would be like this."

"You should have told Munro your problem," said Betty.
"He could have helped you get out of this situation."

"He couldn't help me. I tried . . ."

Just then Daly entered and looked suspiciously from one to
the other. "You ladies seem to be getting along rather well,"
he said.

"She saved my life," Betty said.

"Not yet, she hasn't," Daly said. He looked at Hamilton.
"How is he?"

"How does he look?" said Marie angrily. "Those fools
could have killed him."

309

Daly rolled back Hamilton's head. Hamilton groaned. "He'll be all right." Daly chuckled. "Don't worry. The Germans will take good care of him." He placed a small bottle of brown liquid on the small shelf at the head of the bunk. "When he wakes up, give him two drops of this in a small amount of water. It'll keep him unconscious for three or four hours at a time."

"Don't you want me to take it, too?" Betty asked belligerently.

Daly looked at her, letting his eyes linger on her breasts before they moved down her body to her legs, which she had tucked beneath her. Betty tugged at her skirt to cover her knees. She felt naked and was instantly sorry that she had goaded him.

"I'd rather have you awake," said Daly menacingly. "Besides, I need to keep Hamilton alive. If you give me trouble, I'll kill you."

"Leave her alone," Marie said.

"Don't worry," Daly said. "I have more important things to be concerned with."

"What happens to me when this is all over?" Betty asked.

"That's up to you," said Daly. "I may let the Germans decide." He drew his finger across his throat, then smiled wickedly. "Or I may decide to keep you with me for a while."

"I'd prefer the Germans."

Daly laughed. "Suit yourself," he said, and left.

"Pig," Marie muttered.

"What happens next?" Betty asked.

"We will be picked up in a smaller vessel a few miles off the Irish coast just before dawn. Someone will be waiting to drive us across the border into the Irish Republic. After that, I don't know."

Hamilton groaned again and Marie Price looked at the small bottle that Daly had left. "Will you help me prepare the drink for him?" she asked.

Betty lay down on the bunk, turning so that she faced the wall. "Sorry," she said, "you'll have to do that by yourself."

Obersturmbannfuhrer Otto Kaufmann prayed that the nightmare would soon be over. His stomach had long since emptied itself of everything he had consumed, and he now was racked with the pain of endless dry heaves. For the past three hours he had confined himself to the claustrophobic cabin provided by the U-Boat captain. He knelt on the floor, his head in a wastebucket, and prayed for the feel of solid land beneath his feet.

The first part of the trip from the new submarine base at Saint-Nazaire on the Bay of Biscay had been uneventful and, except for the cramped quarters and ever-present smell of grease and oil, had been reasonably pleasant. During the daylight hours they had run submerged to avoid the numerous British naval patrols that lay in wait like hungry dogs. In the evening they ran on the surface, and as the boat plowed through the rising swell Kaufmann felt the first stirrings of queasiness. Once the submarine entered the open waters of the Atlantic and began the northward run up the western coast of Ireland, the boat had bobbed like a cork in a bathtub, and Kaufmann's stomach distress had begun in earnest.

There was a knock on the bulkhead outside the curtained opening which led to the passageway. Kaufmann did not respond but the knock was repeated. "Come," he said reluctantly.

The curtain was pulled back and Korvettenkapitan Albert Strasser stepped into the tiny cabin. He wore a white cap with a leather visor and a battered peacoat over a heavy sweater, and held a rolled-up map. He looked at Kaufmann and wrinkled his nose in barely disguised contempt. He was young but worry lines had aged him beyond his years. He did not shave while at sea, and in the tradition of the U-Boat captains, his uniform was studiously unkempt. Like most German professional soldiers and sailors, Strasser openly detested the men of the SS. They were, he thought, like Kaufmann, unfit for combat duty. Already the rumors had run through the Kriegsmarine about the atrocities committed by the SS in Poland. As soon as Strasser had laid eyes on Kaufmann he'd suspected that the rumors were probably true.

"How are we feeling?" said Strasser cheerfully. He was enjoying Kaufmann's discomfort. "Any better?"

Kaufmann shot him a venomous look from over the bucket. "How much longer must I suffer the confines of this damn boat?"

Strasser's eyes flashed with anger. If this war were to be won, it would be by "damn" boats like this one and not weasels like Kaufmann. "Eighteen hours, perhaps." He unrolled the map and held it flat on the bunk in front of Kaufmann. "The navigation officer estimates that we will arrive off the western coast of Ireland"—he pointed to a spot on the map—"by six o'clock this evening. We will lie on the bottom until we have the cover of darkness. Then we will surface and you and your men will go ashore in rubber rafts."

Kaufmann's stomach flopped at the thought.

Strasser scratched at his stubble, hiding a smile behind his hand. "The cove is well protected from the sea, and you and your men should have no trouble getting ashore."

Kaufmann examined the map carefully. The Irish coast seemed dominated by jagged, rocky fingers reaching out to sea. He imagined them as witches claws ripping at the bottom of the flimsy, rubber boat. "I'm sure there will be no problem."

"My orders are to remain in position, submerged, watching for your signal, for twenty-four hours," Strasser said.

If Strasser expected Kaufmann to show some appreciation of the danger to his boat and crew, he was disappointed. It did not occur to Kaufmann that Strasser was responsible for anything other than to see that he, and his SS cohorts, made it safely home to Germany. "Good," he said matter-of-factly.

"You have familiarized yourself with the method of signaling?" asked Strasser.

Kaufmann nodded as if it were of little importance.

Strasser wondered where the SS found people like this. "I want it clearly understood," he said, "that I will not risk my men or my boat if there are hostile naval forces in the area, or if the signal is not given properly."

Kaufmann pouted. "It is essential to the war effort that I return safely to Germany," he said.

The Captain glanced at his watch and stood up. "It is time to transmit the evening radio message," he said. "You will have to excuse me." He paused at the doorway. "By the way, the cook has asked me to tell you that because you missed dinner, he saved you a platter of stew." He smacked his lips. "It's very good."

Kaufmann's eyes bulged, and he buried his face in the bucket.

"I suppose that's a no," Strasser said as he stepped into the passageway.

The moon was obscured by a heavy cover of clouds, and the Irish coast was a vast, shapeless mass of dark against an even darker background. Except for the sound of the waves slapping at her sides, the trawler was silent, engines shut down, lights off, men on deck peering intently into the night. The beam of light flashed once, then, after a long pause, flashed twice in rapid succession.

"That's the signal," said Daly, his voice a hoarse whisper.

The captain of the trawler raised his signal lamp and responded. They waited for the single flash that would confirm their rendezvous.

"That's it," said Daly. "Bring our passengers on deck."

"No need to rush," said the captain. "It will take them at least fifteen minutes to get a boat out to us. Besides, you'll need someone to help you carry the man."

"Now," said Daly. "The sooner we're ashore the better."

When the small motor launch arrived, two crewmen from the trawler lowered Hamilton into the waiting arms of two men on the launch. They carried Hamilton below to a small cabin while a third man helped the two women step aboard.

Daly gave the captain of the trawler a brief handshake, and jumped down to the deck of the launch. "Who's in charge here?" he asked, once he was safely aboard.

"That would be me," said the man who had remained on deck. "Captain Ryan Fitzpatrick, of the Sinn Fein Irregulars."

"Well, Captain," said Daly, "get the women below. Then you can tell me what plans you've made to get us across the border."

"There are more of you than we were told," Fitzpatrick said. "Perhaps you'd better tell me what happened."

Daly pointed to Betty Donaldson, who stood nearby. "We've had an uninvited guest," he said and told Fitzpatrick what had happened. "She might prove to be a problem," he concluded.

Fitzpatrick looked at Betty. "I hope not," he said. "For her sake."

The two crewmen who had carried Hamilton below appeared on deck. "Take the lovely ladies below, and make them comfortable," Fitzpatrick told them. He took the wheel and started the engines. The boat responded with a muffled growl and Fitzpatrick backed her away from the trawler. When he had enough clearance he moved forward in a tight circle, and when the bow was aimed toward land, he slowly increased the throttle so that the steady growl of the engines did not overwhelm the sounds of the waves. "You wanted to know about the arrangements," he said to Daly.

"Yes," said Daly, "How will you get us across the border?"

"We've got a truck waiting ashore that will take you and the others to Downpatrick. It's not safe to be on the roads at this time so you'll spend the night there in a good Catholic house. Before dawn another truck will take you to Crossmaglen. You can cross over at any of a hundred points from there."

"What about army patrols?"

"Patrols?" Fitzpatrick said, and made a rude noise. "You wait until one passes, and then you will have several hours to get across before they return."

"And once across?"

Fitzpatrick gave Daly a small slip of paper. "Memorize that address."

Daly put the paper in his coat pocket.

"Someone there will take you to wherever you want to go."

Everything was coming together, Daly thought. The difficult part was over. The rest seemed relatively simple. There was only one small blemish—the Donaldson woman. He should have killed her in Portpatrick. The thought of his knife against her throat made him smile. The more he thought about it, the more he was certain that under no circumstance could she be allowed to survive.

A harsh wind howled around them as the boat made steady progress against a stubborn tide, and the dark shape ahead, like a photographic print under developing fluid, was becoming more and more distinct. Now he could make out the shapes of the hills and the craggy coastline. Above the howling wind he could hear the surf crashing on the rocky shore.

According to the large map on the wall of the Admiralty tracking room, there were twenty-seven U-boats presently operating in the North Atlantic. Each was marked with a colored counter and its course plotted on an hourly basis. The tracking room's information came from a variety of sources —agents in enemy countries who reported the arrivals and departures of submarines, sightings by ships and aircraft, and reports by vessels under attack. By far, however, the most bountiful, and most useful, source of information was the U-boats themselves.

The U-boats were most often directed to their targets by radio operators in Germany who charted the British convoys by a method similar to that used by the Admiralty to chart the U-boats. Consequently the U-boat captains received frequent messages from their home bases. In order to coordinate their attacks, the captains responded to these messages and sent messages to other submarines in the area.

This constant stream of radio communications from the U-boat captains enabled the British to track each boat. A series of wireless direction-finding stations detected the signals and by a method known as triangulation determined the position of the transmitting U-boat. This method could determine the position of a U-boat only at the moment a signal was sent. Although not infallible, triangulation enabled the Admiralty trackers to ascertain the general operational area of a particular U-boat and to warn merchant ships away from that area.

At a few minutes past midnight on the twenty-second, the wireless direction-finding stations picked up a brief message from a U-boat and immediately transmitted the bearings to the tracking room at the operational intelligence center. This particular submarine had been tracked with more than just the usual interest because its course was out of the ordinary. The U-boat had left the French port of Saint-Nazaire two days earlier and headed for a position in the North Atlantic. But, after taking the usual northwesterly course, the submarine had swung north on a course that would bring her very close to the Irish coast.

The tracker on duty that night, a Sub-Lieutenant Ralston, plotted the new bearings and entered the new position on the map. The U-boat was moving closer to the Irish coast and into an area that was not frequented by British shipping. The latest position placed the boat less than twenty-four miles due west of Dingle Bay and still headed due north.

Ralston sipped his mug of tea. "She's up to something," he

said aloud to himself. He and the other trackers had been alerted to be on the lookout for any unusual submarine activity off the Irish coast. He put his tea mug on his desk and rummaged through a pile of notes until he found the right one. It directed him to call the Special Intelligence Service at Broadway and leave a message for a Lieutenant Bishop. He picked up the telephone and while he waited for the connection, wondered why the SIS was concerned with this particular submarine.

LONDON BOMBED AFTER QUIET DAY; GERMAN
BLITZ ENTERS THIRD WEEK

LONDON, SEPT. 21

◆ *CHAPTER 49* ◆

The single lamp in Josef Benke's sitting room was draped with a cloth so that it emitted only the feeblest light possible. With the blackout curtains drawn and Mozart playing softly on the phonograph, the room was an island of serenity in an ocean of chaos. Benke sat in his favorite chair, a brandy snifter on the nearby table, and with his eyes closed listened to the music. The Mozart helped to drown out the noise of the fire engines as they raced past below his window.

Tonight the Germans had dropped mostly incendiary bombs, and the fire engines and the Air Raid Precaution people had been busy for hours dousing the flames. From the window of his flat in Half Moon Street, Benke could look down the street to Green Park, where a cluster of incendiaries had landed and continued to sputter and flare in alternating flashes of white and green flames.

But, for now at least, the worst seemed to be over.

Tonight's raid, like the blitz itself, seemed to be less ferocious than other nights. In fact, Benke thought, the raids of the last several nights had not displayed the destructive intensity of the raids of the previous week. There had been, of course, great destruction of property and even tremendous loss of life, but nothing close to that incredible first week of bombing. Had the German juggernaut lost its momentum? Was this a permanent shift in the tide of the war or merely a momentary pause so that the Germans might regroup for a renewed onslaught on the British capital?

Benke sipped his brandy and wondered. Even under constant pummeling from the air, the British seemed no closer to capitulation than they had a month ago. In fact, morale was higher now than ever. A quick victory for Germany, a certainty a month ago, was becoming an increasingly remote possibility. His commitment to Germany had been based on the likelihood of an easy victory. If the conquerors were not coming, then perhaps it was time to rethink his commitment.

A sharp knock on his door brought him out of his reverie. He looked at the clock and frowned. It was well past midnight.

"Who is it?" he called.

"Police, sir," said a voice. "We'd like a word with you."

He went to the door. Probably an unexploded bomb in the vicinity, he thought. Or, perhaps, the incendiaries had spread the fire to the end of the street. He opened the door. There were four of them. As soon as he saw the grim faces on his doorstep, he knew that they had not come to save him from the flames. "May I be of some assistance?" he managed.

The man who had knocked stepped back and one of the men in the rear stepped forward. He flashed an identification card at Benke. "My name is Russell," he said, "and I am with the Security Service." He nodded at the man next to him. "This is Lieutenant Bishop of the Intelligence Service. The other gentlemen are with Scotland Yard." He smiled politely. "May we come in?"

Benke stepped back and the four men filed into the small foyer outside his sitting room. "How may I help you?"

Bishop reached into a manila envelope and handed him a photograph.

Benke looked. It was of him and Bernhard Ritter and had been taken in Lisbon, probably during their last meeting.

"The gentleman in the photograph," said Russell, "is believed to be an agent of German Military Intelligence."

"I have no knowledge of that."

"But you do not deny meeting with him."

Benke handed the picture back to Bishop. "Hardly," he said. "Your photographer did an excellent job."

"Who is he?" asked Russell.

"He told me he was a Swiss businessman on vacation."

"His name?" asked Russell.

"I'm afraid I don't recall. Wurtz or Wurst or . . . something."

Bishop reached inside the envelope again and extracted a sheet of paper, which he unfolded and handed to Benke.

Benke recognized it immediately. It was a copy of information that he had given the Germans. "Perhaps you should explain what this is," he said.

"You know damn well what it is, Benke," said Bishop.

Russell gave his colleague a look of disapproval. Such behavior was absolutely uncalled for. "We'd like your assistance, Mr. Benke," he said politely, "in finding Marie Price, whom we believe you know, and Lieutenant Winston Hamilton, who was last seen in her company."

The color drained from Benke's face. "I have no idea what you are talking about," he stammered.

Neither Bishop nor Russell said a word.

"May I remind you, gentlemen," Benke said, "that I am a diplomatic guest in your country."

Bishop turned to the Scotland Yard men, who stood by the door. "Would you chaps wait outside?" He waited until they had gone and then turned back to Benke. "Let's go inside and have a seat, Mr. Benke."

They went into the sitting room, where all three stared at one another in silence until Benke said, "I am sure we all understand the rules of diplomatic immunity, gentlemen."

Bishop chuckled. "Do you understand the extension of Regulation eighteen-b, Mr. Benke?" he said.

Benke shook his head.

"The Treachery Act," Bishop said, "permits the Home Secretary a free hand in the arrest and detention of those deemed likely to endanger the realm."

Benke was well aware that many German and Austrian

immigrants had been rounded up and interned under this act. Ironically, many of those interned had come to Britain to escape Nazi persecution. "But surely," he said, "that legislation does not apply to those in the diplomatic service of other nations?"

"Diplomats in the service of Germany were invited to leave the country last September when war was declared," Bishop said. "Those who chose to remain did so at their own risk."

"But surely," Benke said, "the act would not apply to me." He looked to Russell for help.

"If the Home Secretary deems that you are an agent for Germany, I'm afraid that it will," Russell said.

Bishop chimed in, "You will be arrested, Mr. Benke, and detained at Holloway Prison until you are asked to answer the charge against you."

"And the charge?" Benke asked, his voice quavering.

"Espionage," Bishop said solemnly. "We're going to hang you, Mr. Benke."

"I must call my embassy," Benke said frantically.

"I'm afraid that is not permitted," said Bishop.

Benke looked to Russell for help, but the older man looked away. Benke could see that Russell was sympathetic to his plight but he seemed unable to overrule his aggressive colleague. "Perhaps," Benke began, "I might be permitted a word with you, Mr. Russell . . . alone?"

"If you have anything to say," Bishop said angrily, "you can say it to both of us."

"Let's not be hasty, John," Russell said. "After all, as a representative of the Home Secretary, I am in charge of this investigation."

Bishop stood up. "Highly irregular, Russell," he said. "I'm afraid I will have to report this to our immediate superiors."

"As you wish," Russell said, "but if I might have a moment with Mr. Benke."

Bishop stomped from the room, and Russell waited until he heard the door slam. He shook his head. "Impetuous youth," he said. "Now, what was it you wanted to tell me?"

"First of all," Benke said, "I admit to a certain foolishness in my dealings with Germany, but I intended no harm to your country. I wished only to ingratiate myself to the Germans by providing inconsequential pieces of information."

"I would not describe the documents in our possession as inconsequential, Mr. Benke. I'm afraid the court will see this as an extremely serious matter."

"Is there anything that I can do to extricate myself from this unfortunate predicament?"

Russell shook his head slowly. "I don't really see how."

"I am willing to do anything that is asked of me."

"You would cooperate fully in my investigation?"

"Completely," Benke said. "I will tell everything I know."

"I'm not sure what sort of terms I could offer."

Benke was desperate. "Sir, you have me at a disadvantage."

Russell almost smiled at how thoroughly English this little Hungarian tried to be. "Go on," he said.

"I will accept any sort of terms that saves me from the possibility of execution."

"Do you know what has happened to Lieutenant Hamilton?"

Benke hesitated. "Yes."

"Then, before it is too late, I think you had better start telling me."

"You will give me your word as a gentleman that you will speak in my behalf?"

"Agreed," said Russell. "I will want my colleague to hear this also."

Benke nodded and Russell went through the door and out into the hallway. Bishop gave him a questioning look and Russell nodded. They shook hands, congratulating each other on a job well done.

"He wants to talk," said Russell loudly. "He's not a bad sort, really."

"All right," Bishop said, just as loudly. "I'm willing to listen to what he has to say." As they started to reenter Benke's flat, Bishop whispered, "I still think we should hang the bastard."

Crossmaglen

From their vantage point in the stone cottage by the side of the road they could get a clear view for several hundred yards in either direction. Behind them, a glow in the sky heralded the arrival of the morning, and already the stars, which only moments ago had filled the sky, were fading into a gray background. The field, on the other side of the road, was beginning to emerge from beneath the cover of a damp mist that in concert with the night had obscured the brilliant colors of the land.

The man who crouched beside Daly by the window pointed across the field at the dirt path that intersected the narrow macadam roadway. "Ireland," he said simply.

Daly nodded. Although the name of the country was officially Eire, neither man thought of it as anything but Ireland.

The man's name was Scully. He was close to sixty and wore the weatherbeaten look of the land. He had fought the British most of his life.

The paved road ran parallel to the border and was crossed at right angles by the dirt road less than fifty yards from the cottage.

"Why not now?" asked Daly.

Scully shook his head. "Soon enough," he said, looking at his watch.

They listened for a while and then Scully tapped Daly on the arm. "Listen," he whispered.

Daly aimed his ear to the west, but heard nothing. He looked at Scully, who smiled knowingly. Less than a minute later Daly heard the distant whine of an approaching vehicle that Scully had heard earlier. He patted Scully on the shoulder and said, "I'd better get ready."

Daly crossed the room, pausing to look at Marie, who slept on a cot against the back wall. She was curled into the fetal position and covered with a coarse blanket. He didn't need her now. She was as much a detriment to his mission as the other woman and briefly he contemplated eliminating both of them. His right hand touched the knife in his belt, but the sound of the approaching truck reminded him that he had no time for such matters. It should have been done earlier.

He went out the back door of the cottage. He quickly crossed an open yard and went into a small barn. Inside was an ancient truck, loaded with bales of hay. A man, close to forty, stood guard over the truck and its passengers. His name was Tom and he was Scully's son. He had the slack-jawed look of someone who did not possess all of his mental faculties.

"Everything all right?" asked Daly sharply. He didn't like Tom. He thought the man was too slow for the work that was required, but Tom and his father were a package. Where Scully went, Tom followed.

Tom nodded sleepily. "Ready to move," he said.

The bales of hay on the truck were stacked, like a rectangular igloo, to create a small opening in the center. Daly pulled aside one of the bales at the back of the truck and shone a flashlight down the short tunnel into the opening. Inside, Betty Donaldson and Winston Hamilton, gagged and bound, squirmed like worms under the probing light.

Satisfied that all was in readiness, Daly pushed the bale back into position. He gave the guard a nod and went back to the cottage.

Scully signaled for him to stay low as he entered and he crawled over to the window.

"Here she comes, Sean."

Daly peered from the window, allowing only the top of his head to show. From the west he could see the army truck making its way laboriously toward them. The truck drew closer. He could make out the driver and someone in the cab next to him. Above and behind them, in a makeshift gun turret, was a soldier sitting behind a Lewis machine gun. As the truck approached the cottage, Daly smiled. The man behind the machine gun was fast asleep.

The truck rolled past, allowing Daly a look into the back. Inside were half a dozen other soldiers. Most of them appeared to be asleep, also. If Daly had so desired, he and the two men with him could easily have eliminated the patrol. "Fools," he muttered.

"Just boys," Scully said. "On their way home after a long night."

"How much time till the next patrol?"

"At least an hour, probably more."

"Then let's get on with it."

Daly went to the cot and began to shake Marie roughly. She opened her eyes and sat up. "Time to go," Daly said, and she wobbled sleepily to her feet. Daly took her by the arm and half dragged her to the door.

They went to the barn and flung open the doors. Scully jumped behind the wheel while Tom cranked the handle protruding from the front of the radiator. The old engine turned over twice, coughed, and sprang to life. Tom grinned and patted the side of the truck as if it were a reliable old horse. "Thatta' girl," he said.

Daly pushed Marie in beside Scully and climbed in next to her. Tom climbed up on the hay and banged the flat of his hand on the roof of the truck.

Scully threw the transmission lever into gear and the truck lurched forward. As they cleared the barn he moved the lever again and ground it into second gear with a loud squawk. Daly looked at him but Scully merely grinned.

They pulled onto the roadway and drove the short distance to the dirt road. At the intersection they paused, everyone looking in all directions, and then the truck turned sharply left and, bouncing mightily on the unpaved road, moved south.

At the border there was a barrier of sorts—five oil drums filled with rocks had been placed across the road. Only the two outer drums were actually filled with rocks. Months earlier the locals had removed most of the rocks from the middle three drums so they could cross the border without undue effort. The British patrols, seeing the barrier still in place, never bothered to check. Tom jumped down from the truck and rolled aside the three middle drums. As soon as the truck squeezed through the opening, he rolled the drums back into position and jumped back onto the truck.

"Welcome to Ireland," said Scully.

Daly was already thinking of the next phase of his journey.

When John Bishop arrived for work in the morning he was surprised to find Maxwell Munro sitting in the lower lobby of the building at 54 Broadway. Munro stood as Bishop entered, and Bishop winced when he saw how disheveled the American looked. He must have been up all night. Bishop himself had been up most of the night, but had taken particular care with his toilet this morning so that his appearance did not suffer. My God, he thought, if these Americans ever do get into the war, I hope they don't intend to look like this for the duration.

"Have you heard anything?" Munro asked.

Bishop looked at his watch. "It's barely past seven," he

said sarcastically, "and I haven't been to my desk yet." He relented. "Perhaps you'd like to come up to my office. We can talk and I'll make some tea."

Munro rubbed the stubble on his chin. "I could use a cup of coffee right now."

"I'm not sure I can manage that, but come on up and we'll see what we can do."

They took the elevator to Bishop's office and while Munro waited, Bishop went down the hall and returned with a mug of tea for himself and a mug of hot water. He gave Munro the water and a jar of instant coffee.

Munro made a face as he poured the thick syrupy liquid into his mug and Bishop said, "Sorry, best I could do."

"What have you heard about Betty?" Munro asked.

"Quite frankly," Bishop said, "we've heard virtually nothing. The police report only that she left the Purple Heather last night and did not return."

Munro bit his lip. "What about Price and Hamilton? Have the police found them?"

"There is no trace of any of them."

"They can't have disappeared into thin air."

"We have reason to believe that Hamilton is being taken to Ireland. Price and a man named Daly are attempting to deliver him to the Germans."

"Germans?"

"Hamilton is in possession of information that is vital to either side. If the Germans get their hands on him, I'm afraid it could have rather serious consequences for the war effort."

"Look," Munro said, "I appreciate that you've got a war to fight, and all that, but what do you think has happened to Betty?"

"The most likely scenario is that she was discovered and they killed her." He paused to let his words sink in. "In which case her body is probably floating in the Irish Sea."

"Good God," Munro whispered.

"I'm sorry to be so brutally frank, Captain Munro, but this is a dirty business and you and Miss Donaldson had no right to involve yourselves in it."

Munro sat in the chair, shoulders slumped forward, head in his hands.

Bishop relented slightly. "She may still be alive. There is

always the possibility that they decided to take her with them. When this is over they might simply release her."

"In the meantime," Munro said, "what are you doing to find her?"

"Let me make this clear, Captain. We are trying to find Lieutenant Hamilton. If in the process we also happen to find Miss Donaldson, I will be most pleased."

"But she is not your main priority."

"I'm afraid not," Bishop said. "We have reason to believe that they are taking Hamilton to the western coast of Ireland and that they hope to rendezvous with a German submarine there sometime tomorrow. We are doing all we can at present. We have informants on both sides of the Irish border and hope to get word before they can cross into the south. If not, we hope someone will spot them at some point on their journey and give us their location."

"What if they cross the border before you spot them?"

"Once across the border, they are beyond our jurisdiction."

Munro did not believe him for a minute. He was certain that Bishop was the kind of man who would do whatever he felt was necessary. He would not let Irish neutrality stand in his way. Munro also realized that, as far as Bishop was concerned, Betty Donaldson's safety was only an afterthought. "Well," he said, getting up, "I think I've taken enough of your time."

Bishop made no attempt to dispute him on that point. The woman was dead, he was sure. There would probably be a big flap from the American Embassy and from the American newspapers, but he was too busy to be concerned with that now. He had other, more important matters on his mind.

"I would appreciate it," Munro said, "if you'd keep me informed. The embassy will be anxious for any word."

"If I hear anything at all about Miss Donaldson, you can be sure that I will be in touch."

REFUGEE SHIP TORPEDOED ON WAY TO CANA-
DA; 93 BRITISH CHILDREN, 210 OTHERS
DROWN; JAPANESE INVADE INDO-CHINA;
PRES. ALARMED

WASHINGTON, SEPT. 22

◆ *CHAPTER 50* ◆

He was only eleven and he had followed the sheep up the hillside, unable to get in front of them and turn them back toward the grazing land closer to his home. It made no difference anyway. His mother had sent him off this morning and made it clear that she didn't want him back at the house until much later. He might as well let the sheep roam and follow them wherever they went. It was better than sitting in the valley and watching them graze.

Near the top of the hill the climb was steep and the terrain turned rocky. The sheep stopped climbing, but the boy went on. He pretended that he was in the army and that the Germans were on the other side. When he got to the top he would use the field glasses that his Uncle Willie had loaned him today and he would see how many soldiers the Germans had landed. He would report back to army headquarters and the Irish Army would rush out to save Ireland from invasion. He would be a great hero.

But, at the top of the hill there was, as usual, nothing out of the ordinary. He lay down in the grass and listened to the cries of the gulls and the whistle of the wind. From here he could see the Atlantic. The afternoon was bright, the sky a brilliant blue, and the wind had churned the water into a swirl of whitecaps.

Off to his right he could make out the Slyne Head

Lighthouse, and he raised the field glasses to bring it into closer view. To his left he could see Bertraghboy Bay, the deep inlet cut into the wild coastline. If the Germans came, his boy's intuition told him that it was there they would land.

He let the glasses wander across the landscape, but, in truth, there was little to see. Between his position on the hilltop and the bay there was only a series of fieldstone walls that crisscrossed the meadow, dividing the land into smaller plots, and the old, abandoned cottage that had once belonged to an old shepherd known only as O'Halloran. The shepherd had been dead for two years now and the cottage had been left just as it had been. O'Halloran had a son in Dublin, but the son had never come to claim or even to inspect his inheritance.

He moved the field glasses across the cottage and over the stone wall that ran across the field to near the edge of the cliff that looked down into the bay. Another fieldstone wall cut across the first and circled behind the cottage so that the cottage was surrounded on all four sides by stone walls. Some movement made the boy swing the glasses back toward the cottage. At first he was unable to see what had caught his eye, but then he saw a thin, wispy white line of smoke snaking its way skyward from the chimney in the old cottage. Someone was in there and had set a fire in the fireplace.

The boy watched through the glasses for a long time, but no one ever came to the door and the thin line of chimney smoke never increased. It was almost as if someone was deliberately holding back the fire. The boy thought about it for a while. It must be O'Halloran's son come from Dublin. Finally, after two years, he had come to claim his property.

His first impulse was to run for home and let his mother know. She always wanted to be the first to hear local gossip and this would be the best story since old Mr. Kelley had set his beard on fire with a cigarette. But he knew she wouldn't want him home just yet—not with Uncle Willie visiting again. He wasn't sure if Uncle Willie was his mother's brother or his dead father's, but whenever Uncle Willie paid a visit his mother seemed happy and sent him off somewhere for the better part of the day. Uncle Willie was from across the border in the Six Counties where the heathens lived, and visited the boy and his mother every few months. Sometimes, after supper, he told great stories of men in battle. The stories gave the boy nightmares, but he enjoyed them anyway. The boy wasn't sure but he thought that Uncle Willie might have been a soldier sometime. He walked with a limp and the boy imagined that he had been wounded in one of the great battles that he talked about.

He continued to watch the cottage, wishing that he could run home and tell his mother the news. He wasn't sure why he had to stay away, but knew that the rule was inviolable. Once he had come home early and his mother had cuffed him behind the ear.

He was just about ready to pick himself up and go back down the hillside when a figure appeared in the doorway of the cottage. He trained his field glasses on the figure, and although it was too far for him to recognize the face, he thought that it might be Michael McHugh from Ballyconneely. His mother had told him to give McHugh and his like a clear path. "IRA," she had whispered, as if that were enough to frighten him away.

The man who might have been McHugh was shading his eyes against the late afternoon sun and looking in the direction of the narrow, dirt road that came from the paved road at Roundstone. The boy ran the glasses along the road and sure enough there was a truck coming. He waited and watched and soon the truck pulled up alongside O'Halloran's cottage. Two men and a woman got out, and a third man climbed down from atop the hay that the truck was carrying. The boy wondered why they would bring hay here.

The three men from the truck shook hands with the man who had been inside the cottage, and while they talked, the woman went directly inside. One of the men went to the back of the truck and dropped one of the bales of hay on the ground. He reached inside and began to pull on something and suddenly a man emerged who had been hiding in the hay. The man almost fell and the others had to hold him up, and the boy realized with a start that the man's hands and feet were bound. There was also cloth across the man's mouth as if he were gagged.

The boy watched in amazement as they reached inside the

hay again and pulled out another figure. This time it was a woman, and she too was tied up in the same manner as the man. The man who might have been McHugh, bent forward and lifted the woman across his right shoulder. One of the others did the same with the man, and followed by the other two, they carried them into the cottage and closed the door.

The boy waited until he was sure that there would be no more surprises before he stood up and made his way back down the hillside. When he reached the bottom, he broke into a run. He knew that his mother would want to hear about this. Even if Uncle Willie was visiting, he couldn't wait to tell the story of the people who were tied up and taken to O'Halloran's cottage.

"Two women?" Bishop said. "I never would have believed it."

"Yes, sir," said the aide who had brought the news from the communications room. "That's what the report said. I thought I should bring it to your attention right away."

"And one of the women was tied up? The report definitely said that?"

"And one of the men, also."

"It's them, all right," Bishop said to himself. Perhaps it was not too late. Maybe they could get to them before the Germans. He could feel the excitement of the hunt. "Full transcription of this message on my desk in five minutes," he said. "Copies to 'C' and Sir Duncan."

Less than ten minutes later Bishop was pacing on the Oriental carpet in front of Sir Duncan Sommers's desk. Sir Duncan looked up from the report that Bishop had brought along with the radio transcription. "Please do sit down," he said.

Bishop sat and Sommers went back to the report. The Deputy Chief of the Secret Service wore a look of constant disapproval and it was difficult to determine his reaction to the report from his expression. Bishop reached for the Players pack in his jacket pocket. Sommers, without looking in Bishop's direction, raised an eyebrow, and Bishop certain that he was being given a signal returned the cigarettes to his pocket.

Sommers finished reading. "Quite remarkable that this fellow Riordan was able to spot these buggers so quickly."

"Every contact we have in the North and South has been put on alert. Riordan is on home leave. He was severely wounded in France—shrapnel, I think."

Sommers studied the papers. "Interesting," he said.

Bishop's heart sank. "Interesting" was the death knell for ideas in this office. "I think it could be done," he said.

"Perhaps," said Sommers. "I wonder how the Irish government would react to your mini-invasion. They hardly need an excuse to be even less cooperative than they have been."

Bishop wanted to say, "To hell with the Irish government." Instead, knowing Sir Duncan's dislike of intemperate remarks, he said, "If the operation goes as planned, we would be in and out before the Irish government, or anyone else, knew we were there."

"If," said Sir Duncan, letting the word hang in the air like the barrage balloons that were visible from his office window. Sommers removed his glasses and polished the lenses with his handkerchief. As he did he watched Bishop carefully. The man was a veritable dynamo, he thought. Most of the energy was misdirected, but one could feel the electricity emanating from Bishop's forceful personality. Not the sort of chap that he would have selected for his organization before the war, but things had changed. Headstrong people like Bishop were taking over. Perhaps, when this mess was over, the old guard would get back in control, but for now it was necessary that people like Bishop be given their head.

"I'm not sure that we have very many options available to us, Sir Duncan," Bishop said.

"You are probably quite right," said Sommers, "but this looks like an operation for the SOE."

"I don't think so," Bishop said adamantly. The Special Operations Executive had been created in July by combining the SIS's section D, specializing in sabotage, and a military research section at the War Office. "They're not ready for this kind of operation yet."

"And you are?"

"Yes," he said simply.

"When would you leave?"

Bishop felt his pulse quicken. Sommers was going to agree

to it. "As soon as I could get the men together. Tonight, if possible—tomorrow morning at the latest."

"And you feel that six men will be enough?"

"More might prove to be a burden. I want it quick and clean. In and out."

Sommers chewed on his glasses. If he could have thought of an alternative, he would have suggested it. A full-scale assault force was out of the question. Besides, by the time such an operation had been approved, and put together, the Germans would have come and gone. Bishop's force was small, but that was the beauty of it. If it were discovered, or if things went wrong, the Irish could hardly claim that six men constituted an unlawful invasion of their territory. The operation could be explained away as a miscommunication between a border patrol unit and its headquarters. Although how he would explain that a border patrol unit had gone a hundred miles across the border he did not know. "What if the Germans arrive with a larger force than anticipated?" he asked.

"I doubt very much that they will. They realize, as much as we do, that the Irish are paranoid about belligerents using their territory. I expect a token force. After all, they have no reason to suspect we are on to them. Even if their force is larger than ours, we will have the advantage of surprise."

Sommers was nodding reluctantly. "Gather your men," he said. "I will recommend to 'C' that we go ahead with your operation."

"When may I expect to be notified?" asked Bishop.

Sir Duncan glanced at his watch. Menzies should be arriving at his office shortly. "Within the hour, I would imagine."

"Then," said Bishop, smiling, "I'd best get cracking."

"Perhaps," Sommers said soberly, "I should remind you of the remark that was made about Jellicoe in the last war."

Bishop knew that Admiral Jellicoe had been the Commander-in-Chief of the Grand Fleet at the Battle of Jutland. "Sir?"

"Very few of us," Sommers said, "have the opportunity to lose the war in an afternoon."

"I'll keep that in mind, Sir Duncan."

"I certainly think you should, my boy."

* * *

In the early afternoon Max Munro and Colonel Robert Jackson drove out to Sunningdale in response to a summons from the Ambassador to visit him at his country estate. The drive was pleasant, and both men felt it was a relief to get away from London for a while. There was a false sense of gaiety in the city, a feeling that one must live life now, for who knew what tomorrow might bring. For many, life was lived at a fever pitch that bordered on hysteria.

Jackson did not know why they had been summoned. Munro expected the worst. The Ambassador had made no attempt to contact him since their last, less than amicable, meeting.

"I imagine," said Jackson, "that he must be quite upset about this business with Sutton, and now that Betty Donaldson is missing, he is going to be just delightful. He wants to get home as quickly as he can. These loose ends make it more difficult for him to do so."

As usual, the Ambassador surprised them both. He greeted them cheerfully at the front door, shaking hands warmly, and inviting them inside. Kennedy was dressed casually—white slacks and a gray cardigan over a white shirt. "I've had the cook make up some sandwiches," he said. "I thought we'd have some coffee and a bite to eat while we talked."

The Ambassador led them through the house and onto a rear veranda, where a table had been set. They sat and looked over the grounds of the estate. To the left, some fifty yards from the house, was a tennis court surrounded by high hedges. Directly in front, on the other side of a large expanse of lawn, was a large pond with several swans gracefully dotting the surface. On the right a greenhouse sat in the midst of a flower garden.

"Nice place, huh, kid?" Kennedy said to Munro. "Some English lord, or something, owns it." He laughed sarcastically. "He's probably safely in New York at present."

"A 'dermatologist'?" said Jackson.

"A what?" Kennedy asked.

"Dermatologist," Jackson said. "That's what one of the columnists in the *Daily Mirror*—Cassandra, I believe—calls those who save their skins by escaping to America."

"I don't read the papers much," Kennedy said.

A servant appeared with a pyramid of sandwiches and a pot of coffee. "Real ground coffee," the Ambassador said. "Not that miserable liquid the English call coffee." The servant poured each of them a cup and then discreetly retired.

Kennedy chomped on a sandwich. "First things first," he said, his mouth full. "Let me be the first to congratulate you, General," he said to Jackson.

Taken by surprise, Jackson said, "I beg your pardon, Mr. Ambassador."

"News came with the afternoon dispatches. You've been promoted." Kennedy offered his hand. "Congratulations. It's well deserved."

As Munro offered his congratulations to Jackson, the Ambassador said, "I'll get to you in a minute, young man." He took a bite of a sandwich. "I have it on pretty good authority that the Germans are preparing to invade tomorrow morning," he said. "Our ambassador in Berlin reports that he's been overhearing some pretty scary talk from the Germans. Looks like they're ready to get on with it."

"If our ambassador in Berlin has overheard anything," Jackson said, "you can rest assured that the Germans intended him to. He would be the last person in Berlin to hear anything if the invasion talk was anything more than just talk. The Germans know he will report whatever he hears to Washington, and Washington will immediately report the news to London."

"It's going to come sooner or later," Kennedy said.

"I think the Germans have missed the boat," said Jackson. "They've waited too long. Maybe next spring, but I'm not sure they can pull it off even then."

Kennedy removed his glasses and wiped the lenses with a linen napkin. He was a man who did not like to be contradicted and struggled to maintain his composure. He was determined not to let the meeting deteriorate into a squabble of conflicting opinions. He put his glasses back on and smiled. "And as for you young man," he said, taking on the tone of the headmaster talking to a troublesome but likable student. "How much trouble do you expect to get into while you're over here?"

"Trouble, sir?"

"I got a call at seven o'clock this morning from the Foreign Office, telling me that Betty Donaldson has been reported missing. They tell me that you and she were involved in some kind of scheme to follow a couple of suspected spies."

"Not exactly, Mr. Ambassador. She—"

"You're supposed to be making sure she doesn't get into trouble," Kennedy said, "not encouraging her to go running off on some wild goose chase."

Munro started to mumble a response.

"If I know Betty," Kennedy said, laughing, "she's probably shacking up with someone for the weekend."

Munro stiffened. "I doubt that very much, Mr. Ambassador. I'm quite concerned about her."

"You wait," Joe Kennedy said. "Tomorrow morning she'll show up with some story about being off on assignment."

Munro watched the swans on the pond and wondered how long it would be before he could return to London.

Again Kennedy abruptly changed topics. "I wanted you both to know what has happened with this Sutton business. I'm afraid that he's going to be charged in a British court."

Jackson frowned. "My understanding was that the British were going to kick him out of the country. I was told the Home Office had already issued a deportation order and they wanted him out of the country as soon as possible."

The Ambassador smiled knowingly. "That was before the intervention of Mr. Roosevelt."

"Roosevelt," Jackson said. "I don't understand."

"The last thing Roosevelt wants is to have Sutton come home just before the election. If the American newspapers get wind of this story it will be on every front page from now till election day. This morning the State Department agreed to drop Sutton from the embassy staff, thereby stripping him of his diplomatic immunity. The British can now hold him indefinitely, and under the Official Secrets Act, the press can be denied access to any part of the story. As far as anyone is concerned, it might just as well have never happened.

"Don't you see," Kennedy said. "The British are doing Roosevelt a favor. They'll lock up Sutton until Roosevelt thinks it's safe to let him go." He looked at Jackson. "I think we should convince Munro to go on home before the British try to stop him. He knows as much about this scandal as anyone."

"And when I get home," Max said, "I could talk to my father and to the press."

"Now I didn't say that, Maxwell," Kennedy said defensively. "That would be entirely in your hands. You could, however, be quite a hero back home. Another Lindbergh."

"And join the ranks of the uninformed," said Munro.

"How's that?" the Ambassador said.

"The uninformed," Munro said. "People like Charles Lindbergh, and my father"—he paused and looked the Ambassador squarely in the eye—"and others, who don't really understand what is going on over here." He heard General Jackson's discreet warning cough and saw the Ambassador's eyes flare with anger, but he was on a roll now. "When I first arrived here I was as confused as the others, but not anymore. You said I know as much about what is going on over here as anyone. I don't know if that's true or not, but I do know that the President is right and the others are wrong. If we don't help the British stop the Nazis, maybe nobody can stop them."

Kennedy's face was crimson. He stood up quickly and looked at his watch. "Well, boys," he said, "I'm glad you could come out. I've got some business to attend to now, so if you wouldn't mind seeing yourselves out." With that he turned and left them at the table.

On the way out to the car, Jackson patted Munro on the back. "Good show, Max," he said.

"You know something?" Munro said. "I was more angry about what he said about Betty than the fact that he tried to get me to go home and do his dirty work."

They started back down the drive, the whine of the engine and the crunch of the wheels against the gravel the only sounds. The General allowed Munro his thoughts.

They were on a narrow roadway, the limbs of the trees on either side forming a canopy over their heads. As they drove through this tunnel of flickering light, Munro said, "I want to see Bishop again. To see if there's any news."

"She's going to be all right, Max," Jackson said. He spoke with more confidence than he felt.

"But where the hell is she?"

◆ CHAPTER 51 ◆

From the barricaded window of the stone cottage Betty Donaldson could look out across the green meadow to the edge of the cliff where the land fell away into a cold gray sea. The sun, trapped between cloud and sea, had colored the sky crimson, and Betty remembered the old saying from her childhood—"Red sky at night, sailors' delight." She wondered about the morning.

Winston Hamilton also wondered about the morning, and Betty wished there was something she could say to comfort him. Marie Price had tried to sit with him but he had recoiled from her touch and rejected her attempts at explanation. "I loved you," he said over and over, "I only told you because I loved you."

The three of them were in what had been the bedroom of the cottage. The others were in the larger outer room that had served as living, dining, and cooking quarters. The rooms were musty and damp and the furniture was coated with a heavy layer of dust. The windows were broken and barricaded with wood. Betty stood by the lone window in the small bedroom while Hamilton paced the room. She rubbed her wrists to relieve the pain of where the ropes had been.

Marie stood in the doorway between the two rooms. In this, as in everything, she could find no comfortable ground. "Look," she said, "tell the Germans what they want to know and they'll let you go."

Daly appeared in the doorway. He and the others had been drinking. "Or don't tell them," he said, laughing, "and they'll cut your balls off."

Hamilton sat on the edge of the bed. He stared at the floor. "I don't know anything," he said.

Daly laughed again. "Stick to that story and we're going to have a good time. I understand that the Germans are very good at this sort of thing." He put an arm across Marie's shoulder, letting his hand cup her breast. She pulled away, but he pulled her roughly back toward him.

"When do your friends arrive?" Betty asked Daly.

"Soon enough," he said. He gave Marie Price a pat on the bottom and went back to the other room.

"Pig," Marie Price muttered.

"You might have thought of that sooner," said Betty.

"I didn't realize this would happen," Marie said.

To Betty's surprise, Hamilton spoke. "It's my fault," he said. "I should never have said anything. It was foolish. Damn foolish."

"Do I ever get to find out what the hell is going on here?" Betty asked.

Marie whispered, "Winston knew when and where the London bombing was going to be a day before it happened. The Germans want to know how he knew."

Betty looked at Hamilton's stricken face and knew it was true. The implications of such knowledge were instantly clear. Just as clear was how badly the Germans would want the answer. She covered her mouth with her hand. "Sweet Jesus," she said. She touched Hamilton on the shoulder. "I wish I could help you."

He smiled and Betty thought that there was great dignity in him. "I'm not a very strong person," he said, "I don't know how much pain I can stand."

"None of us knows that," Betty said.

"True," Hamilton said, "but I know that I can make them stop anytime I want."

Bishop was astounded when he was told that Munro was downstairs waiting to see him. He had spent what remained of the afternoon and early evening looking through personnel files and evaluating the men he would take with him. There were a dozen names on his desk and he had to select six. He had already designated his second in command, who was now busily arranging transportation to Ireland. Bishop had decided against a parachute assault as being too likely to attract attention of the target and the Irish government. They would fly into Northern Ireland, using the Coastal Command Station near Belleeck, in Fermanagh. The station was less than a half hour from the border. They would make the rest of the journey in an Army truck, painted to look like a commercial vehicle. If they could make good time they would arrive near the target area sometime in the early morning. Riordan was under orders to keep an eye on the target and inform Broadway if the situation changed in any way. So far there had been no further reports. That could only mean that the Germans had not yet arrived. Thank God for that, Bishop thought.

But what to do about this American who was beginning to be a pain in the neck. If he and his girl friend had not gotten involved, Bishop's job might have been simpler. His orders were that, as a last resort, everyone was expendable, but that he had to make an effort to rescue the American reporter. Things would have been a lot easier if he could simply drop in and eliminate everybody—Hamilton included. People who thought that selective targeting was practical in an operation of this nature had never been in combat.

Bishop was sure of one thing—he wasn't going to risk his own life, or the lives of his men, to rescue a meddlesome woman reporter or a talkative fool like Hamilton. If it came down to it, he would eliminate all of them.

He looked at his watch. Time was already short. He hoped to leave for Ireland within three hours, but now he had this American here again. He would have been happy to ignore him, but the Americans were like a rich uncle who had to be treated carefully in hopes that one would be mentioned in the will. He picked up the phone and dialed. "Have someone bring Captain Munro upstairs to my office," he said.

When Munro arrived, Bishop greeted him with a zest that he did not feel. "Well, well," said Bishop. "I think we have some good news about your Miss Donaldson."

Something about Bishop's attitude did not ring true. Munro was wary. "Yes?" he said.

"If you'll remember, I mentioned a possibility—however unlikely—that she might have been taken to Ireland. Well, it seems that is exactly what has happened. We've had a report from one of our people." He smiled. "They've been seen."

Munro was relieved that Betty was alive but he was still somehow suspicious of Bishop. The Englishman had not invited him to sit down, had not in fact sat down himself. His office, which earlier had been meticulously neat, was a shambles. There were files and notes all over the desk. Bishop seemed a bit too cheerful and a bit too anxious to be rid of Munro. "What now?" Munro asked.

"We're making every effort to arrange for her safe return."

"With whom?"

The smile slipped a bit from Bishop's face. "Beg pardon?" he said.

"With whom are you making every effort? The Irish government?"

The smile was completely gone now. "Not exactly. We feel that it's best if this were handled from our end for the time being." Bishop was wearing his official face now. "I'm really not at liberty to say very much more at this time."

"You're going in after them, aren't you?"

"Not at all." The American had surprised him. He was really much more astute than Bishop had imagined.

Munro sat down. He gestured to Bishop, "Have a seat."

"I'm really quite busy," Bishop began, but sat down anyway.

"It's Hamilton you're going in after, isn't it?"

Bishop was stubbornly silent.

"If whatever he knows is important enough to have him kidnapped and taken to Ireland, it's important enough for you to want him back in a hurry. Now you and I both know that there are two ways to stop him from talking. You could mount a major assault and maybe, if you're lucky, bring him back alive. Or you could quickly put together a small force, go in after them, and not worry about who came back alive as long as nobody did any talking." He paused to give Bishop a chance to deny his scenario, but the Englishman maintained his silence. "You look like a 'let's not take any chances' kind of guy to me."

"I will do everything in my power to see that Miss Donaldson is brought safely back to England."

"I want to go with you."

Bishop laughed. "If such a mission were contemplated, your participation would be out of the question."

"I can handle a rifle, a pistol, automatic weapons, or a mortar. I have made over thirty parachute jumps."

"Very impressive," said Bishop. "I'm sure your cardboard targets were firing back at you."

"Let me put it another way: if I don't go, you don't go."

"I really think you are overestimating your influence, Captain."

"You seem to forget that I'm the guy you arrested yesterday because you thought I was feeding information to the Germans."

"Fortunately you were not."

"I can just as easily give that information to the American press. I couldn't be as easily silenced as Sutton. My father is a rather influential figure in Washington. Your government wouldn't dare lock me up."

"That would be your choice, Munro. Whatever you decide will have no bearing on this mission."

"If the Ambassador finds out about this mission he'll scream like a stuck pig, and his screams can be heard for a long way."

"Even a brief delay would jeopardize the mission's success, not to mention the lives of the people involved," Bishop said.

Munro knew he had struck a nerve. "This must be quite important to you."

Bishop nodded. "If someone possessed a secret that could save your country from occupation by the most heinous band of cutthroats this world has ever seen, would you sacrifice Miss Donaldson, or others, to preserve that secret?"

Munro wouldn't give Bishop the satisfaction of an answer.

Bishop smiled. "You understand the dilemma."

Munro was even more determined not to place Betty's fate in Bishop's hands. "I want to go with you."

"If you were killed," Bishop said, smiling as if that prospect were not unpleasant to him, "how would we explain your demise?"

"Don't. No one needs to know I was with you. It could be our secret. Dump my body in the Irish Sea on the way back."

"I like that part," Bishop said. "But perhaps on the way over?" He smiled an assassin's smile. The truth was that Munro could not stop the mission, but even a temporary delay would make it all meaningless. If the Americans complained, and the politicians demurred for even a few hours, the whole plan might fall apart. He could have Munro arrested and held without charge for twenty-four hours, then released with profuse apologies. That would enable the mission to get underway, but might create more problems than it was worth.

"Why do you want to go, anyway?" Bishop asked.

"Your concern is Hamilton. Someone has to worry about Betty Donaldson."

Bishop made his decision. "You will remain in this building until it is time to leave. You will contact your embassy, on this phone, in my presence, and you will tell them that you are traveling to Scotland this evening in search of Miss Donaldson. You will volunteer no other information. Is that clear?"

Munro nodded.

"You will carry nothing with you that could possibly identify you in case you are captured or killed. You have no rank in this organization, Captain, and you will follow my orders without question. Is that also clear?"

"Yes."

"Then I would suggest that you make your telephone call, and prepare yourself in whatever way you can for a difficult task." He looked at his watch. "We leave in three hours."

The U-boat surfaced three miles from shore under a sliver of moon and a star-filled sky. The Captain and his executive officer scrambled up the ladder from the conning tower to the small bridge, stepping out into the cool, fresh night air. One of life's great pleasures for a submariner was that first full breath of fresh air upon surfacing the boat. They were followed by the lookouts, who manned their posts even though these waters were relatively safe and the submarine virtually invisible on the surface at night.

Short breakers rolled across the deck and a fine spray showered the men on the bridge. The captain listened to the night. Other than the sound of the waves slapping against the superstructure, and the constant rumble of the ocean, there was nothing. "Start engines," he said, and almost immediately a vibration ran the length of the boat as the electric motors shut down and the diesels kicked in. A momentary puff of black smoke escaped the exhausts and then the water turned foamy white as the twin screws churned the waves. "Both engines, half ahead together."

With some difficulty, Obersturmbannführer Otto Kaufmann climbed up beside the Captain and the executive officer. The Captain pointed to the dark shape, three miles off starboard. They could hear the surf pound on the distant rocks.

"Can we get any closer?" Kaufmann asked.

The Captain's look of disdain was masked in darkness. "When we see the signal, we will move in to within a thousand yards of the shore. The signaler will then direct you, through the rocks, into a small cove." He turned his back on Kaufmann and scanned the horizon. "There should be little danger for you or your men," he said over his shoulder.

Kaufmann was uncertain whether the Captain's attitude was disrespectful or merely a function of the relaxed role of command aboard the U-boat. Either way he did not appreciate Strasser's casual disregard for the priorities of rank. After all, he did outrank a mere Korvettenkapitan. "Captain," he snapped, "my men and I will require a relatively short time to accomplish our mission here—perhaps no more than a few hours. I want you to make sure that you are ready to pick us up at dawn. I want to spend as little time as possible on this godforsaken place."

Strasser slowly turned to face Kaufmann, towering over the smaller man in the cramped confines of the bridge. Instinctively, Kaufmann took a step back, bumping into the railing that ringed the bridge. Strasser's voice was menacing. "My boat and I are at your disposal, Herr Obersturmbannführer. We will lie on the bottom until dawn and then surface to await your signal."

Kaufmann, his back pressed against the railing, struggled to keep his voice steady. "Very good," he said. "I will signal by radio or flare pistol when we are ready to be picked up."

They had gone over this several times. "The flare will alert anyone within twenty miles of us," Strasser said. "If anything goes wrong with the radio, a visual signal from the cliffs will suffice."

"I meant, of course, only in an emergency."

A cry from one of the lookouts made Strasser train his field glasses on the coast. Above the cliffs he could make out a light swinging in a wide arc. He lowered the glasses. "Your signal," he said softly. "Reply," he called out to his signal-man, who immediately aimed his hand-held lamp toward land

and flicked it on and off three times in rapid succession. The signal light on shore stopped swinging briefly, then resumed.

"Signal returned," said the signalman.

"Very well," said the Captain. He turned to Kaufmann. "We will move closer to shore. Prepare your men to board the rubber raft."

Kaufmann swallowed a deep draught of air. He nodded but, afraid his voice would betray his nervousness, he did not speak.

On the cliff the swinging arc of light beckoned.

On the rocky hillside above the cliffs, William Riordan lay watching. The boy had brought him here earlier and after sending the message to London, Riordan had returned to watch and wait for reinforcements. He knew only that what was in the cottage was important enough for the British to order him to stand guard and report anything that happened.

His bad leg had throbbed painfully during the second climb and even after lying here for more than four hours the pain had not subsided. He knew that tomorrow he would have to pick out the tiny fragments of shrapnel that constantly erupted from the skin of his left leg.

The night had turned cold and he would rather have been in Jeannie's warm bed. He knew that she would be waiting for him and that the boy would be fast asleep. When the reinforcements arrived she would direct them to his position on the hill.

Nothing had happened until just a few moments ago. Until then no one else had joined the group in the cottage and no one from inside had ventured out. Then, five minutes ago, the door to the cottage had opened and one of the men inside had come out carrying a hurricane lamp. The man had walked across the meadow to the edge of the cliff and after waiting a few minutes began to swing the lamp in a wide arc.

Riordan stood up. He knew what he was looking for. Sure enough, the reply was almost immediate, a brief flashing response from out of the inky darkness told him that there was a ship, perhaps a submarine out there waiting. That, he knew, could mean only one thing—Germans. They had come to claim whatever was in the cottage. He looked back down the hill, hoping to see Bishop and his group on the way up, but there was only the wind and the yelping of a dog somewhere in the distance.

Riordan knew that time was growing short. If they did not arrive soon, it might be too late.

◆ CHAPTER 52 ◆

The pilot of the twin-engined aircraft struggled to keep his plane on course against a heavy crosswind. Every ten minutes or so he asked his co-pilot/navigator for a course correction and, sure enough, found that he was drifting south.

"Be a miracle," he said quietly to no one in particular, "if we can keep this bastard on course long enough to get us where we're going."

The "bastard" he referred to was the Lockheed Hudson, an American design that had been in service with the RAF and the Coastal Command as a training aircraft since before the war. Pressed into emergency service as a jack-of-all-trades, the plane had performed admirably in a multitude of roles, and tonight was no exception. The Hudson normally carried a crew of four, but tonight there was only the pilot and his co-pilot, and, in the aft section where the turret gunner normally plied his trade, the seven passengers bound for Ireland.

The passengers sat grim-faced and silent on the makeshift seats that had been hurriedly installed. They sat, facing each other, three along one side, four along the other, but no one looked at the man across from him. All were lost in whatever thoughts came to men when the possibility of death was near. The men, with the exception of Bishop and Munro, were Royal Marine Commandos, trained in behind-the-lines combat, sabotage, and other "irregular" methods of warfare.

They were dressed in civilian clothing—well-worn tweed jackets, heavy work trousers, flannel shirts, and ankle-high boots. Except for the fact that each man carried a Webley service revolver and a Sten submachine gun, they might have been a group of day laborers or farmers returning from market. On the floor between them were several canvas satchels holding ammunition, grenades and mortar shells. The mortars, two of them, were in the tail section, secured by ropes.

Maxwell Munro looked at Bishop, who sat across from him. Their eyes met and Bishop glared. He had not yet resigned himself to the fact that Munro was a part of this. He would relegate the American to whatever background job was available—anything to keep him out of trouble and out of the way.

Bishop looked at his watch. "Won't be long now," he announced.

The men shifted uncomfortably in their seats, but no one spoke.

Led by McHugh, Kaufmann and his men entered the cottage. There were eight of them: Kaufmann, his interrogator, Sturmbannführer Erich Milch, and the six Waffen SS soldiers of the Deutschland Division who had been assigned to protect them. The Germans wore civilian clothing: sweaters, corduroy trousers, and heavy outer jackets. The two officers wore side-arms and the soldiers carried Schmeisser submachine guns.

Daly, Scully, and Tom stood as the Germans entered and the two groups eyed each other suspiciously. For a moment, each silently appraised the other, the Irish paying particular attention to the men with the submachine guns.

Kaufmann looked around the room, wrinkling his nose as if the odors of the cottage were offensive. He pointed at the table in the center of the room and said something in German. One of the SS guards stepped forward and placed the radio on the table, another lowered a large canvas bag to the floor. "Which of you is Daly?" Kaufmann asked.

Daly stepped forward and extended his hand.

"Obersturmbannführer Kaufmann," said the German, shaking hands with obvious distaste. "This," he said, indicating his interrogator, "is Sturmbannführer Milch."

Milch nodded and clicked his heels. He was in his late twenties, tall and gaunt, his blond hair cropped short. Dark circles beneath his sunken eyes, prominent cheekbones, and protruding teeth gave him the look of a cadaver. His face seemed frozen in a sneer. It was an effort for Milch to mask his feelings about these people. He lumped the Irish with the Jews, Poles, Czechs, and other inferior races. It was his sworn duty to enslave or eradicate all of them, and he found it distasteful to work with them in any capacity.

McHugh looked at Scully and made a face. These were the vaunted Germans? The supermen of Europe? Kaufmann looked as if he'd have trouble seeing over the top of the bar. McHugh almost sniggered. The other one, Milch, looked like he was two weeks past his own wake. Only the six Waffen SS guards at the door, young, tall, grimly determined, were anything like what he had expected.

"I see that your men have got their feet wet," Daly said. "Perhaps they'd like to warm themselves by the fire?"

"That will not be necessary," Kaufmann said sharply. He snapped his fingers and pointed at the door. Without a word the guard detachment filed outside.

Again, McHugh looked at Scully. This time they were more impressed.

"Where is the Englishman?" Kaufmann asked. "I think it is time we were introduced."

Daly snapped his fingers and pointed at the bedroom door. "Bring him in," he said to McHugh.

McHugh hesitated, then sauntered past Daly, muttering under his breath, "Don't be snapping your fingers at me, my boy."

Kaufmann shook his head. No discipline, he thought, no discipline at all.

McHugh opened the bedroom door and stepped inside. Betty Donaldson sat on the bed next to Hamilton. Obviously, she had been trying to comfort him. Marie sat near the door. Hamilton looked at him, his eyes wide with fright, and McHugh, picturing Milch's leering, cadaverous face, felt a pang of regret for Hamilton's coming ordeal. "You've got company, Hamilton," he said brusquely, then added in a near whisper, "Tell them what they want to know, man, and let's all go home."

Hamilton struggled to his feet, and took several deep

breaths. He made his way to the door and then spoke to Betty, who struggled to hold back her tears. "When you get back to England," he said, "tell them I am sorry I made such a mess of things." He paused. "I hope you'll be able to tell them that I did my best to make it right." Followed by McHugh, Hamilton walked into the outer room.

"Ah, Lieutenant Hamilton," Kaufmann said pleasantly, "this is indeed a pleasure. I am Obersturmbannführer Kaufmann." He went on as if he were the host at a cocktail party. "I must introduce you to Sturmbannführer Milch. He and I have some questions for you."

"I regard myself as a prisoner of war," Hamilton said. "As such I am obligated to tell you nothing beyond my name, rank, and serial number."

Kaufmann smiled. "I am aware of your obligations, Lieutenant. I hope you are aware of mine." He went to the door, spoke sharply in German, and two of the guards, Schmeissers slung over their shoulders, came inside. "Perhaps," Kaufmann said to Hamilton, "you will be kind enough to take a seat."

He directed Hamilton to a sturdy wooden chair by the fire and nodded to Milch, who lifted a large bag and placed it on the table in the center of the room. Milch opened the bag, spread a towel on the table, and like a doctor preparing for surgery, carefully deposited each instrument of his profession.

Winston Hamilton could not take his eyes from the array of instruments arranged on the table. There were pokers, knives, straps, hammers, pliers, and various other implements.

Milch spoke for the first time. "I will explain the use of each instrument," he said, the kindly doctor explaining the operation to his nervous patient. He picked up the thick, leather straps. "These are merely used as devices of restraint." His death's head smile attested to his love for his work. "These pliers," he said, snapping the jaws open and closed, "are used to remove toe nails. These larger pliers are used on the teeth. The small hammer is used to break small joints—on the fingers and the toes. The larger hammer"—he grinned—"I'm sure you can imagine." He took several pokers and walked to the fire. He inserted each poker into the coals so that at least six inches of each was buried in the red glowing embers. "I

347

usually don't need these," he said. "My patients tell me what I want to know long before these become necessary." He looked at Hamilton with some scorn. "Something tells me that you will not need to feel the kiss of the metal." He returned to the table and picked up something that looked like a spoon. "Have you ever heard the sound an eye makes when it leaves the socket?" He inserted a finger in his mouth and made a popping sound. "Quite terrible," he said, flashing his teeth in his horrible facsimile of a grin.

A curious calm had come over Winston Hamilton. He knew that he could not for long withstand the kind of pain that Milch reveled in. It was only a matter of time before he told them everything they wanted to know. He watched Milch with morbid fascination, as if the German were displaying some medical technique that would be performed on some other poor, unfortunate creature. None of this had anything to do with him.

Milch picked up one of the knives, but Kaufmann interrupted him. "I think Lieutenant Hamilton understands the point," he said. "Perhaps none of this is necessary. If the Lieutenant is willing to answer one simple question, we will not have to resort to such barbarity."

Milch fondled the pliers lovingly.

"Will you cooperate with us?" Kaufmann asked.

Hamilton did not hesitate. "Yes."

Kaufmann smiled. Daly snickered softly. McHugh, Scully, and Tom sighed with relief. Only Milch seemed disappointed.

"How did you come to know that the Luftwaffe would bomb London on the afternoon of September seventh?" asked Kaufmann.

Hamilton took a deep breath. "As you probably know," he began, struggling to keep control of his voice, "I am employed as a translator with British Intelligence at Broadway in London. It's not a very important job really—sort of a clerk/typist—but sometimes I happen to overhear things. On the day before the raid—the sixth, I suppose—I overheard someone talking in the hallway about a big build-up of aircraft in France. He said that he wouldn't be surprised if London was the target."

Kaufmann's face was expressionless. "You merely overheard this information and do not have any idea how this person knew about the raid?" Kaufmann sighed. "And to think we have come all this way for nothing." He clapped his hands and went to the fireplace. At his signal, the two guards clamped their hands on Hamilton and pinned him to the chair. Kaufmann removed one of the pokers from the fire. The tip glowed red. "So you are telling me that you know nothing?"

Hamilton, mesmerized by the glowing poker, could only nod.

"Most unfortunate," said Kaufmann and thrust the poker against Hamilton's leg.

The smell of burning fabric mingled with the smell of burning flesh and Winston Hamilton gave an ear-shattering shriek. Kaufmann held the poker against the leg and the shriek continued as Hamilton struggled against the men who held him down.

Finally Kaufmann pulled the poker away. He placed it back in the coals. "Now," he said, "how did you know about the bombing?"

Hamilton was whimpering, the pain was worse than anything he had ever felt before. He managed to shake his head.

Kaufmann seemed genuinely disappointed. "You are being very foolish," he said, and turned to the expectant Milch. "He is all yours, Herr Stermbannführer."

Milch flushed with excitement and even Kaufmann shivered with distaste. "Strap him securely to the chair," Milch ordered the guards. His eyes glowed with the fever of anticipation. "And then remove his shoes and socks."

McHugh jumped up and the guards immediately had their Schmeissers at the ready. "I don't want to watch this," he said and walked across the room to the bedroom.

Scully stood up. "Me neither." He looked at Tom, who was white-faced and on the verge of throwing up. "C'mon, Tom," he said. They followed McHugh into the other room.

Kaufmann looked at Daly. "And you?"

Daly's face was immobile. "Get on with it," he said.

Kaufmann was pleased. At least one Irishman had the stomach for what had to be done.

The old dairy truck bounced along the unpaved road at dangerous speeds. The men in the back bounced around, backsides sore, bones aching, teeth throbbing from the constant jostling. The inside of the truck smelled vaguely like spoiled milk, and that, coupled with the bumpy ride and the fact that they were sitting on milk crates, made for incredible discomfort.

Munro sat in the back with four of the others, while Bishop and his second in command were up front. The truck had been hurriedly requisitioned from a local dairy, and was waiting for them when they landed at the Coastal Command Station. Without a moment's delay they had transferred their equipment to the truck and were on their way in a matter of minutes. At the border crossing, the guards had been alerted to their arrival and they did not have to slow down.

Munro had removed his jacket and made a cushion for the milk crate and even though it was cold in the back of the truck the others soon followed suit. By now he knew their names. The other four already knew each other. All were from the same commando unit and considered themselves a match for any comparable unit in the world.

At first Munro's American accent had puzzled them. "What are you doin' along on this?" asked a young man named Simpson.

"I'm here to help with the rescue of an American reporter —a woman."

"No one said anything about a rescue," said MacNair, who seemed to be the oldest. He held a whetstone in his left hand and had been constantly sharpening a wicked looking dagger since the truck ride began.

"That's why I'm here," said Munro. "I want to make sure the woman makes it back. Bishop doesn't impress me as the kind of man who worries about such things."

MacNair tested his blade against his thumb. "There's a war on," he said matter-of-factly. "Or hadn't you heard?"

Munro made the rest of the trip in silence.

The stars cast indistinct shadows across the hillside, playing tricks with Riordan's eyes. Several times he thought he had seen movement at the base of the hill and heard the sound of men on the way up but it had only been the shadows and the wind. Riordan huddled against the cold, hoping that it would not be much longer. He had heard the screams.

He had eaten some bread and cheese that Jeannie had given him and sipped at the flask of whiskey, but only enough to keep warm. From up here the first scream had sounded like the baying of a wolf or the cry of a wounded animal. The wind had dissipated the sound, diminished its urgency, and at first Riordan had not been certain what it was or where it came from. After the next, and the next, there was no doubt that the cry was human and that it came from the cottage.

Sometimes the wind shrieked and Riordan shivered before he realized that it was only the wind. Sometimes there were long silences and Riordan would begin to hope that perhaps it was over—whatever it was. But then running up the hillside, borne on the back of the wind, would come a hideous guttural screech, unlike anything he had ever heard or imagined he would ever hear.

He looked down the other side of the hill, hoping, but there were only the dancing shadows and the whispering wind.

ROBERT MOSES BLASTS NEW DEAL, JOINS DEM-
OCRATS FOR WILLKIE; ROSTER OF DEFIANT
DEMS GROWS

WASHINGTON, SEPT. 23

◆ CHAPTER 53 ◆

The secret, Milch knew, was a maximum of pain with a minimum of damage to the body. If the subject thought his shattered body could not be repaired he might allow himself to be tortured to death. That would never do. The object was to make the subject believe that if he talked he could somehow resume a normal life.

The Englishman had surprised Milch. Hamilton looked like

the kind of man who would capitulate easily to the pain, but he had not. Milch had seen some of the strongest men reduced to blubbering infants, anxious to do or say anything to please him, but so far Hamilton had been able somehow to resist him.

Kaufmann had wisely ordered a rest period. Hamilton was in danger of slipping over the edge where he would be too far gone to do anyone any good. The guards had carried him into the other room and placed him on the bed.

Betty had hovered over him, afraid to touch him anywhere lest the pain prove too much for him. Marie had taken one look at him and begun to sob quietly into a handkerchief. McHugh and Scully came to look, winced, and retreated into the corner they had appropriated for themselves. Young Tom did not want to look.

Hamilton observed them all through the slits of his swollen eyes. He could feel their concern, but actually the pain had been more bearable than he had anticipated. At first it had been worse than he had imagined, but after a while it was as if his brain had begun to reject the signals that his body was sending. He still felt the pain, but it was somehow different, as if it were happening to someone else. Rather than the sharp, wracking, intense agony that he had felt in the beginning, he now felt a long, slow, all-encompassing pain that was indistinct and somehow endurable.

He lay in a semi-stupor and wondered why he was doing this, why he resisted. He knew that in the end he would tell them whatever they wanted to know and, therefore, the pain he had endured was for nothing. He had hoped they might kill him before he told them anything, but had realized early on that Milch was much too skillful for that. They wouldn't kill him until it was over. There was some consolation in that, in knowing that he would not live to see the havoc that his foolishness had wrought. There was also consolation in knowing that he would endure the unendurable before he finally bent to their will.

"Bastards," Betty whispered, and when McHugh looked in her direction she glared at him. "Yes, you, too, you bastard."

"Don't look at me," McHugh said defensively. "This is none of my doing."

"No? This is just as much your doing as theirs."

"This is Daly's show," McHugh said, looking at Scully,

who nodded vigorously. "We're just helping out. Doin' our bit for Ireland."

Betty laughed sarcastically. "For Ireland? When the Germans take over Europe, what do you think will happen to Ireland?"

"We have no quarrel with them."

"Neither did the Danes, or the Dutch, or the Norwegians. Why should the Irish be any different?"

McHugh stood up, and for a moment Betty thought he might strike her. Instead he turned to Scully. "We don't have to listen to this nonsense," he said. "Let's get out of here."

The two German officers and Daly sat warming themselves by the fire. When McHugh and the others entered Kaufmann looked up. "Here are our squeamish revolutionaries," he said. "I thought you would know that nothing is accomplished without bloodshed."

"Don't tell me about bloodshed," McHugh snarled. "I've spilled my share. It's that damn American woman in there. The sooner we're rid of her the better."

Kaufmann smiled and then offered his pistol to McHugh. "Take her outside and get rid of her now," he said softly, matter-of-factly.

"I thought that we were going to let her go."

Kaufmann shrugged. "She knows too much," he said casually. "Both women know too much." He held out the pistol.

"You can do your own dirty work, Kaufmann," McHugh said. "I'm going out for some fresh air. It's starting to stink in here."

He left and Scully and Tom followed. When the door closed behind them, Kaufmann put his pistol back in his shoulder holster. "I think we might have a problem with them," he said. "I don't trust them."

"Vermin," said Milch and then looked at Daly to see if he had gone too far. Daly's face, as usual, was without expression.

"I think," said Kaufmann, "we should let Daly decide what to do about them. After all, they are his men."

Daly flicked his cigarette into the fire. "They are nothing to me. Do as you please."

"And the Price woman?"

Daly shrugged.

353

"Then it's settled," Kaufmann said. "At dawn, before we leave. All of them."

"Such beautiful women," Milch said, "It seems like such a waste."

"You still have until morning, Sturmbannführer," Kaufmann said. "Clear up this little mess quickly and you can have your pick. It will be my gift to you."

Milch beamed, his skin stretched like a reptilian membrane across his face. "Perhaps, then, we should begin again."

Outside, McHugh sat on the stone wall about fifty yards from the front of the cottage. Scully sat next to him. Tom stood with his back to them both. Four of the six SS guards were posted at the corners of the house. Two were on guard at the front door. It was cold and the stars cast a pale, chilling light across the meadow.

"What do you think?" McHugh asked Scully.

"About what?"

"All this," McHugh said, pointing a finger at the cottage.

"Dirty business, to be sure."

"I don't like it at all," Tom chimed in. He had not spoken for hours. "I don't like them one bit. I don't trust them."

"Out of the mouths of babes," McHugh said.

A sudden piercing scream split the night and all three shuddered.

"It starts again," McHugh said quietly.

"What happens when they've finished with that poor bastard?" Scully asked.

"They kill him . . . and the women," said McHugh.

"And us," said Tom.

"Shut up, you dumb bastard," Scully said angrily. "Why would they do that?"

"Just because," Tom said quietly.

"Scully," McHugh said, "your boy may not be as slow as everybody thinks he is." Another shriek made him wince. "That man can't last much longer. They'll be ready to leave as soon as he talks. Have you got any firearms, Scully?"

"A pistol under the seat of the truck."

"My pistol is in the cottage, with my bag. I suggest we get our hands on the weapons in case the Germans try any funny business."

Scully nodded. Another scream sent a shiver down his spine.

Hamilton was finished. He could hold out no longer. He told them everything.

Kaufmann listened in shocked disbelief. It was worse than anyone could ever have imagined. The plans of the entire German war machine had been available to the British on a daily basis. "How many messages a day?" he asked.

"Hundreds," croaked Hamilton.

"How long to decipher?"

"Minutes."

It was incredible. Practically every message of importance sent by the German armed forces—even messages from the Führer himself—had been intercepted and deciphered by the British. For the first time it was clear how the British had managed to resist the might of German arms. They had known every move in advance, had been able to arrange their meager defenses to their best advantage, and the Luftwaffe had flown blindly into their traps every time. No more. That devious game was over. Now the odds would swing firmly in favor of Germany.

Kaufmann turned to Daly, who listened to Hamilton's revelations with a satisfied smile. "I think you should wait outside with the others."

Daly slowly rose from his chair. "I told you we had the right man," he said softly.

Kaufmann waited until Daly had gone, then motioned for Milch to continue the questioning. While Milch scribbled frantically, trying to transcribe the torrent of words from Hamilton, Kaufmann stared into the fire and pictured the honors that awaited him in Berlin.

As long as the British were unaware that their secret had been discovered, it would be possible for Germany to mount a massive deception that could result in the successful invasion of Britain. A sudden increase in Enigma traffic, revealing German invasion plans to the north—somewhere in Scotland, perhaps—would force the British to split their already meager forces. A massive assault directed at England would overwhelm the remaining defenders, enabling the German forces to gain a quick and easy victory.

And he, Otto Kaufmann, would be responsible. His dream was interrupted by a cough from Milch. He looked up.

"I think we have finished," Milch said expectantly. He licked his lips, which had suddenly gone dry.

Kaufmann remembered his promise. "Go on," he said, nodding toward the bedroom door, "but be quick about it. We must contact the U-boat . . . and get rid of the loose ends."

Milch ran a palm across his hair as he went to the bedroom door. He straightened his jacket and raised his fist as if to knock, but thought better of it. He opened the door and stepped inside. The American woman sat on the bed, her legs curled beneath her. The other sat on the chair.

Betty knew why he had come as soon as he walked in the door. What she did not know was whom he would pick. She now knew for certain that the Germans were going to kill them.

"You," Milch said, pointing to Betty. Her heart pounded in her chest and she started to squirm away from him. His voice was sharp, "Outside." He turned his twisted smile on Marie, who slumped forward in an attitude of submission. "Remove your clothing, please," Milch said pleasantly.

Betty moved quickly into the other room, careful to stay as far as possible from Milch. He hardly noticed her. His eyes were fixed on his prey. He closed the door.

At first Betty did not recognize Hamilton, and then it slowly dawned on her that this lump of battered flesh, still strapped to the chair, was him. "Dear God," she whispered, covering her mouth with her hand.

Kaufmann smiled and stood up. "He was very brave," he said. "Very foolish, but very brave. This was so unnecessary."

"I'm sure you would have preferred some other way," Betty said.

The American woman was fiery and Kaufmann liked that. He had been too busy to pay very much attention to her, but he noticed now that she was very attractive. She was tall —taller than he—with excellent bones and the body, hidden under the baggy clothes, was full of promise. Give her a bath, he thought, comb her hair, put her in some beautiful clothes and she would be quite striking. He wondered if she were

Jewish. That would make it even more exciting. His eyes went to the bedroom door, where, even through the thick door, he could hear Milch's animal-like grunts.

"Don't even think about it," Betty said. "It's too much for you to handle."

Kaufmann's face darkened. He was uncertain of the precise meaning of the American expression, but the impression was clear. He looked at his watch. It would be dawn soon. There really wasn't enough time anyway. "I will leave you alone, Fraülein, with your friend." He did an abrupt about face and went outside.

Betty knelt in front of Hamilton. His body was shattered in a hundred places and blood oozed from every orifice. She did not know what she could do for him. She wanted to touch him, to let him know that someone who cared was there, but she was afraid that her touch would pain him even more. His every breath was a groan of pain. "It's going to be all right," she whispered. It was all that she could think of.

Hamilton struggled to open his eyes and then peered at her through the swollen slits. His words came agonizingly slowly through puffed lips and shattered teeth. "Tell them I tried my best."

"I will," she whispered.

The door opened behind her and Betty turned to see McHugh enter. "Is he still alive?" he asked.

"Barely. But do you really think the Germans are going to let us go? Any of us? Above the animal-like sounds from the bedroom they could hear Marie sobbing. Betty aimed her thumb in that direction. "That's what they have in mind for me, I suppose. I just talked shorty out of it, but I imagine he'll be back."

McHugh went to the canvas bag that he had left near the fireplace and reached beneath the extra clothing. He removed a revolver and tucked it into the back of his belt beneath his coat. "I won't let them hurt you," he said.

"My hero," Betty said. "You're a little late, aren't you? Or hadn't you noticed the soldiers with the machine guns out there?"

"Scully has a pistol, too. He's outside waiting for my orders."

"If you were smart you'd both run like hell."

McHugh grinned. "No one ever accused the Irish of being smart."

"What now?" Betty asked.

"We wait."

When Kaufmann and Daly returned, the German went to stand by the fire. "It is very cold outside," he said.

No one responded.

"One must always beware of silence." Kaufmann said.

"What happens now?" McHugh asked.

"We leave within the hour." Kaufmann said.

"What about these people? What happens to them?"

"Are you concerned for their welfare, Mr. McHugh?"

"I just want to know what is going to happen to them."

The flames cast dancing shadows around Kaufmann's face. His puffy cheeks glowed eerily red, and when he turned to face them Betty was reminded of a jack-o'-lantern. "We can't very well leave them behind," he said. "And we can't very well take them with us. It is most unfortunate, of course, but we cannot take the chance that our enemies will discover what has happened here." He smiled. "Does that prospect disturb you, Mr. McHugh?"

McHugh leaned forward in his seat, reached back inside his jacket, and pulled out the pistol. "Just a little," he said softly, aiming the gun at Kaufmann's midsection. "It wasn't in the original plan."

Daly flicked his cigarette into the fire. He leaned forward, muscles tensed, ready to move at a moments notice.

McHugh saw him out of the corner of his eye. "Don't do it, Daly," he said. "I wouldn't say that it would pain me to shoot you. But I'd just as soon not."

Daly relaxed, but his eyes watched for any opening. "It's a foolish thing you're doing, McHugh."

"This doesn't concern you any more, Daly. It's between me and your little German friend here."

Kaufmann bristled at the appelation. "I have six armed men outside," he said. "One word from me and you're a dead man."

"I'll take you to hell with me, Kaufmann. I can promise you that."

"What is it you propose to do?" the German asked.

"Nothing. I'll just sit here with these people and you and your men can be on your way."

"Very well," Kaufmann said. "I'll bid you farewell, then."

Betty couldn't believe it would be this easy. A moment ago she had been sure that her life was almost over, and now she began to hope that she might survive.

Kaufmann moved toward the door, but McHugh froze him with a voice that chilled the marrow, and Betty knew that this was the voice of a man who had killed before and would not hesitate to do so again.

"Don't do that," he said.

"But you said you wanted us to go?" Kaufmann said.

"I have no desire to be trapped inside this place by you and your soldiers. I want you to tell your men to leave their weapons on the table."

Kaufmann grinned. "You are a very wise man, McHugh. Perhaps we can do business again sometime."

"Wise enough to know that I've seen my fill of the likes of you." He waved the pistol menacingly. "Get your men in here," he said in German.

"You are indeed a man of many surprises."

"Do it!" McHugh moved so that he would be behind the door when it opened. "And remember that I have this pistol aimed at the back of your head. One false move and I'll blow your head off."

"I believe you would," Kaufmann said calmly. He opened the door and called to the men outside. They came into the cottage one at a time and, at Kaufmann's command, placed the Schmeissers on the table, and stepped back. "Is that all right?" Kaufmann asked.

"That's just fine," McHugh said, but there was something about the German's attitude that disturbed Betty. There was an air of expectancy in the room, a tremendous tension on the verge of explosion. She hoped that McHugh could sense it, too. She prepared to make a dash for the door when it happened.

"Scully, get in here," McHugh called.

Scully walked into the room, waving an ancient pistol, grinning hugely. Tom followed, his grin as wide. They had just bested the might of the German Army. "Here I am, Chief," Scully said.

"Take one of those machine guns on the table," McHugh said, "and keep this lot covered."

Scully stuck his pistol in his belt and picked up one of the Schmeissers. "Beautiful workmanship," he said admiringly.

"German workmanship, of course," said Kaufmann, opening his jacket to reveal his shoulder holster and pistol. "Perhaps you want my weapon also?" he asked. Without waiting for a reply, he removed his pistol, a Walther P-38, and offered it to Scully.

Scully stepped forward eagerly and Kaufmann shot him once in the chest.

The noise in the close quarters was deafening. Scully's eyes opened wide in surprise. He clutched at his chest and flopped backward over the table, knocking the machine guns and the radio to the floor.

There was a momentary pause, a skipped heartbeat, as if the sound of the shot had paralyzed everyone, and then all reacted at once. The SS guards dived to the floor for their Schmeissers; McHugh raised his pistol to within an inch of Kaufmann's skull and squeezed the trigger; Kaufmann whirled to face him. Again, McHugh squeezed the trigger. Again, nothing happened. His look of amazement matched the dead Scully's.

Kaufmann, with the absolute confidence of a man who knows he has nothing to fear, spoke calmly. He pointed his Walther at McHugh's chest. "Never leave your weapon where others can find it, Mr. McHugh."

The bedroom door opened and Milch appeared, his clothing in disarray, a pistol in his hand. "What happened?"

Kaufmann dismissed him with a snarl. "Get dressed, you fool." Milch disappeared and Kaufmann waved the pistol at the stunned Tom, who stood unmoving beside his dead father. "Get over with the others."

Tom, unable to take his eyes off the body, shuffled over to where McHugh and Betty stood. He was whimpering quietly. Betty took his arm and rested her cheek on his shoulder.

"Quite touching," Kaufmann said. He waved the pistol. "Into the other room, all of you."

They passed Milch on his way out of the room. The Sturmbannführer approached Kaufmann. "Why not shoot them now? Be done with it."

"We leave at dawn. The U-boat will be here then. There is no need to risk attracting attention."

"In this place?" Milch said incredulously. "There is no one for miles."

"Are you questioning me, Milch?"

Milch drew himself to attention. In the excitement he had forgotten himself. "Of course not, Herr Obersturmbannführer."

Kaufmann looked at his watch. "They have until dawn. Perhaps twenty minutes."

✦ CHAPTER 54 ✦

The single shot echoed across the meadow and ran up the hillside. Riordan, who had been listening to sounds from the other side of the hill, snapped his head back to stare at the cottage. Once again, there was only silence.

Low-lying clouds had blocked the glimmer from the stars, leaving the meadow in almost total darkness. Only the glow from the lamps inside the cottage, streaking through the slatted barricades of the windows, gave any light. He listened carefully, his hand cupped around his ear. Nothing. Not from the cottage side, but once again, he was sure he had heard something from the other side. He gave a low whistle and waited.

From somewhere out of the dark below him, his whistle was returned. They were here.

The men struggled up the hill behind Bishop, carrying the heavy equipment. Bishop was gasping for breath, cursing the inactivity of his desk job, while the man beside him, Staff Sergeant Hawkins, who carried one of the munitions satchels, was barely winded. Munro and MacNair carried one of the mortars, Simpson and Smith carried the other. Gordon brought up the rear carrying the Bren gun, a heavy machine gun, and its ammunition.

Maxwell Munro was exhausted. They had left the truck at

the woman's cottage and come at a dead run, carrying their equipment, for several miles. The only thing that kept him going was Bishop's suggestion that he drop out and wait for their return. He dug deep into a reserve of energy he'd been unaware existed. His legs were like lead and the straps of his equipment dug into his shoulders. He willed himself to keep pace with the others.

Several times MacNair whispered. "C'mon, mate. Keep up. Keep up."

The hill itself was torture, but the promise of rest at the summit kept him going. Once when he stumbled, MacNair grabbed him by the collar and dragged him for several yards until he found his footing. Halfway up, they heard what sounded like a gunshot in the distance and Bishop drove them harder.

Riordan came part way down to greet them, then led the way to the crest of the hill.

Bishop paused for a moment to catch his breath. "Was that a shot we heard?"

"Yes," Riordan said. "I have no idea what is going on, but I think we'd better do something in a hurry."

"Perhaps," said Bishop, stealing a look at Munro, who was sprawled nearby catching his breath, but watching and listening intently to everything that went on. "First, tell me what's been happening since you got here." While Riordan told him, he watched the cottage, picking out every detail.

"What about the windows?"

"All boarded."

"Doors?"

"Only one."

"Where does the stone wall at the base of the hill go?"

"Runs toward the house. Stops about fifty yards short. The house actually sits within a square of stone walls."

There wasn't much for Riordan to tell. He told Bishop when the Germans had arrived, how many were inside the cottage, and about the gut-wrenching noises he had heard.

"That would be Hamilton," Bishop said matter-of-factly. "More than likely he's told them what they want to know."

"He held out for a long time," Riordan said.

"Good for him," said Bishop, but there was no hint of exoneration in his voice.

Munro pulled himself to his feet. "When do we go in?"

The commandos looked at him in amazement. To them he was just another soldier. Soldiers did not ask such questions of their commanding officer. Bishop ignored him and asked Riordan, "How long till dawn?" Already a faint glow was evident beyond the first row of hills.

"Fifteen—twenty minutes, perhaps."

"All right," Bishop said, and the men gathered in a semicircle around him. "We have probably less than fifteen minutes of darkness left. That means we have to get into position now. MacNair and I will work our way down this hillside to the stone wall on the left. From there we can work our way along, pretty much unnoticed, to a position perhaps fifty yards from the front of the house." He looked at MacNair, who nodded and went back to sharpening his blade. "Sergeant Hawkins will take Gordon and the Bren gun, work his way along this side of the hill on the right, cut down to the wall which runs behind the house, and set up as close to the house as possible.

Munro cleared his throat, but Bishop ignored him.

"Simpson, you will set up the first mortar here. Smith, find a position at least fifty yards to the right for the second." Finally he looked at Munro. "Munro, you will go with Smith and feed him rounds for the mortar." Munro opened his mouth to protest but Bishop went right on. "Riordan, stay here with Simpson. If you see my signal"—he raised his fist over his head—"put four mortar rounds as close to the house as possible without hitting it. If you see a second signal—he avoided Munro's eyes—"hit the house with everything you've got." Now he looked at Munro. "If we can save the woman and Hamilton, we will do so, but our first priority is to stop anyone from escaping." He did not ask if there were any questions. "Now, let's move," he said quietly.

The men moved quickly to their groups and prepared to leave. Munro went to Bishop. "There are at least eleven men down there. You're taking four of us and you're leaving four behind. If you get in trouble you might need me."

"I won't."

"Look," Munro said, "the house lies between us and the ocean. Obviously their escape route is in that direction —away from us. You've only got two men back there. I could work my way around to help cut off the possibility of escape."

"Don't worry, there won't be any escape."

"Then you won't mind if I go around to the far side of the house?"

Bishop snapped, "Do it, but if anyone sees you before we are ready to move in, I'll kill you myself."

Munro slung his Sten gun over his shoulder, grabbed his extra ammunition clips, and was gone.

Her ordeal with Milch over, Marie sat on the edge of the bed, her eyes closed, her head down. She could think of nothing but what the dawn would bring. She held her torn clothing around her, covering the bites and bruises that Milch had inflicted. If hate were a weapon she would have crushed him with it, but she reserved her greatest hatred for Sean Daly. He had brought her to this. She hoped that someone, someday would make him pay for what he had done to her.

Betty sat near her. She was amazed that her life would come to an end in this lonely place, her death unheralded and, for all she knew, unreported. She had had more excitement crammed into her short life than most, and yet she always wanted more. Always wanted to move on to the next place, the next war, the next disaster. She had always thought that someday she would have her fill of that life and settle down somewhere. She thought of Munro. What had happened to him? Why hadn't he been at the station? Where was he when she needed him?

Tom Scully crouched in the corner, his face a blank. With his father, who had been his constant companion, gone, he wondered what he would do with the rest of his life.

Only McHugh was in motion. He paced the small room like a caged animal, muttering obscenities and pledging oaths of revenge. He would not die easily, he vowed. If there was any avenue of escape, however slight, he would take it. If there was no possibility of escape, then he would struggle till the end. The bastards would see how hard it was to kill an Irishman.

Winston Hamilton, semicomatose and battered beyond recognition, lay on the bed where the two women perched.

Suddenly the door was kicked in, thumping against the wall with a loud crash. Everyone, McHugh included, jumped. They had not expected it to come so soon.

Two guards stood in the doorway, machine guns trained on

the occupants of the room. The guards motioned with the Schmeissers, inviting their victims to follow.

From behind them Kaufmann called, "It is time now."

"Please, no," Marie wailed, in a low voice that rapidly became a shriek. "Daly!" she screamed. "Help me!"

The others began to file out into the larger room. McHugh, looking for any opening, hoped that the woman's screeching would distract the guards for at least a moment. If so, he was ready to pounce. He noted that only Daly, Kaufmann, and the two guards were in the room. That left Milch and the other four outside.

Kaufmann stepped forward. "Stay with her for a moment," he said to Betty. "We will take the men first." Betty retreated into the bedroom.

Kaufmann turned to McHugh and Tom and pointed his pistol at the door. "Outside, please, gentlemen," he said politely.

Outside, in the half-light of early dawn, the other four guards waited with Milch. They had already formed a line and their machine guns were at the ready. McHugh knew that his chances of escape were rapidly diminishing. If he didn't act soon, there would be nothing.

"Over there," Milch ordered, pointing to a spot beyond the cottage, and McHugh realized that they didn't want bullets ricocheting from the stone walls of the cottage. That, he thought, was why they hadn't killed them inside.

McHugh and Tom Scully walked slowly to the spot. McHugh half-expected to hear the blast of the machine guns at any moment. His eyes darted back and forth, and his body was prepared to fly at the first signal.

When the two men reached the designated spot, Milch called, "Now stop and turn around." The firing squad shifted a little, adjusting the line. Tom stood at attention. He had heard that this was how it was done. From the doorway, Kaufmann nodded and Milch grinned. So that his victims would understand what was happening, he gave his instructions to the firing squad in English. "Ready . . ."

From inside the cottage came a woman's hysterical scream.

Bishop and MacNair crouched behind the wall which ran past the front of the house. They watched as the two men came out of the house. "That's eight," Bishop whispered. "Counting the man in the doorway." That meant that as many as four men were still inside with the two women.

Bishop looked down the length of the wall. He could see Hawkins and Simpson, who had not yet made it to the back of the house. He stayed low and held out his right palm, signaling them to wait. He wanted everyone outside before the shooting started.

"Look at this, sir," MacNair said, and Bishop turned his attention back to the house. "Looks like a firing squad."

Bishop watched four of the men line up facing the two who had come outside together. "Good God," he said. "It is a firing squad." For the first time Bishop felt the pangs of indecision. His instinct was to let the Germans shoot whomever they chose to. That would mean fewer problems for him and his men when they started firing, but he had come here thinking that everyone was the enemy. Why were the Germans preparing to shoot these two? Where were the American woman and his fellow Englishman?

"What do we do, Lieutenant?" MacNair whispered.

The woman's scream decided for him.

Bishop raised his hand in a pumping motion to the men who manned the mortars on the hillside and stood up. MacNair stood beside him and both opened fire with the Sten guns.

". . . Aim," Milch said, and then suddenly there was the chattering of machine-gun fire from somewhere close by. Instinctively his men turned to look in that direction. One gave a sharp cry of pain and fell to the turf. The others dived for cover. Milch heard cracking sounds, like a switch whipped in rapid succession, and then the first of several bullets slammed into him and lifted him off the ground. He fell back, eyes wide open, staring at the onrushing dawn.

The first two mortar rounds slammed home, both landing considerably short of the cottage. The earth was so soft that the shells buried themselves before exploding with a muted thump that shook the ground. Huge clumps of sod and dirt were hurled into the sky, but the shells did little damage.

McHugh didn't know if he had started running before the gunfire or after. He was already on the move when he heard

the two explosions behind him, but the sound barely registered. He was alive, his heart pounding, his blood pumping.
He ran from the sound of the gunfire toward the cliffs. If he
could make it to the stone wall that surrounded the cottage he
knew that he would be safe. Once over the wall, he would be
beyond their reach.

Twenty steps from the wall his brain began to calculate how
he would go over. Ten steps to go and he had dismissed the
idea of leaping over the wall; five steps to go and he decided
against diving. The wall rushed toward him at an incredible
pace. He almost laughed. He hadn't run like this since he was
a boy.

One of the German soldiers who had dived for cover at the
first sound of gunfire rolled over onto his stomach. As he did
he saw McHugh running toward the wall. He raised his
machine gun and fired a burst at the fleeing figure.

One step from the wall, McHugh took flight. He leaped up,
right foot stepping firmly on the top of the wall, and threw
himself into the air. Arms waving wildly, legs thrashing
powerfully, he put distance between himself and the chaos
behind him. As he reached the apogee of his flight, the
machine gun burst caught him from behind. One moment he
was soaring, the next he jerked convulsively and plummeted,
dead before he hit the ground.

The third and fourth mortar rounds overshot their mark,
landing beyond the cottage, on the far side of the wall.
Almost immediately two more rounds followed, this time
landing between the wall and the cottage. Again, great
clumps of dirt headed skyward, but little damage was done.
Tom Scully, who had stood motionless the whole time was
thrown to the ground by the latest explosions. He lay there,
face down in the grass, wondering if the world were coming to
an end.

Kaufmann had been standing in the doorway of the cottage
when the first shots slammed into the firing squad. His first
instinct was to step back inside, but as he did, he realized the
cottage was a trap.

All the shooting seemed to be coming from one side, which
meant that he was not yet surrounded. Two men vaulted the
wall at the front of the cottage and came running, firing at the
soldiers who scrambled to return their fire, and he could hear

the crashing sound of a heavy machine gun off to his left. In front of him the wounded SS guard was trying to crawl to the safety of the cottage door. Just short of his goal, geysers of dirt erupted around the wounded man and red splotches stitched their way across his body. He twitched twice and lay still.

Kaufmann grabbed the dead man's machine gun, then threw himself out of the doorway and made a dash to the far end of the cottage. Bullets ricocheted from the stone walls, whining viciously around his head, but he was untouched. He rounded the corner, gasping with the exertion of his short run.

Kaufmann quickly surveyed the scene. Milch was dead and two of his men were trapped inside the cottage with Daly and the women. The remnants of his firing squad were pinned down by machine-gun fire. If he could make it to the stone wall he would have enough cover to get to the beach, his rubber raft, and the flare pistol for signaling the submarine. It could be done, he thought, but he would need help. His soldiers, pinned down by machine-gun fire, had taken cover behind a small outcropping of rocks less than twenty yards in front of him. He screamed at them. "This way! This way!"

They looked in his direction but made no move to join him.

Kaufmann yelled, "I will cover you!"

One of the men seemed to understand. He waved.

"Be ready!" Kaufmann screamed at the top of his lungs and stepped out firing wildly in the direction from which the shots were coming. His men jumped up and made a dash for safety. The first two made it; the third was hit by a fusillade of bullets that knocked his legs out from under him when he was ten yards short of the cottage. The man screamed and held out his hand for assistance. The other two looked at Kaufmann for direction. "Forget him," he said. "He's finished."

The men gathered around him, behind the safety of the cottage wall. "We're getting out of here," Kaufmann said confidently. The men nodded, glad to have someone in command. They were little more than boys. Without the uniforms and regalia of the SS, they seemed less than fearsome.

"Full clips," Kaufmann said, and as the men re-armed, he went over what he expected of them. "You," he said to the man who had first responded to his signal, "will follow me. You," he said to the other, "will stay here to give us covering fire until we reach the wall. When we get to the wall, we will cover for you, and you will follow. Understand?" he barked.

Both men nodded, and Kaufmann said, "Then let's go."

Using the side of the cottage for as much protection as possible, and the machine-gun fire of the other soldier as cover, Kaufmann and the soldier made a run for the wall. The soldier was younger and much fitter than Kaufmann and made the wall a good ten yards ahead of him. He was already over and returning fire when Kaufmann tumbled over onto the turf. When he rolled onto his knees and looked back over the wall, the other soldier was already on his way to meet them. Mini-explosions sprang up around his feet as the bullets dug into the turf around him, but the man led a charmed life and dived over the wall untouched.

Bishop cursed as the German disappeared over the wall. "They're getting away."

Now it was Bishop and his men who were in the open and the Germans who had cover behind the stone wall. Hawkins and Simpson had finally worked their way around behind the cottage, but gunfire from the other side of the wall blocked further advance.

Bishop was in torment. If the Germans escaped it would be no one's fault but his. How could he have made such a fundamental tactical error? Any fool should know not to leave an avenue of escape. He had been so sure that surprise would suffice he had not taken the fundamental precautions that a commanding officer should. Even that damned American had known enough to cover an escape route.

Had Munro made it all the way around? Had he got himself into position between the house and the beach as he said he would? If so there was still a chance the Germans could be stopped. Perhaps the American could slow them enough for the commandos to catch up.

Munro had made as wide a circle as he possibly could around the stone cottage. He descended to the beach, down a

369

well-worn path, and came back toward the house, his boots clattering as he ran across the rocks. To his right the cliffs loomed above him in the burgeoning dawn; to his left the surf crashed against the rocky shoreline. He kept running. His breath was now a gasping wheeze, but the sky was getting lighter and he had to keep going.

At a point where the cliff seemed less steep there was another path to the top. Nearby, someone had left a rubber raft, nestled in the rocks close to the wall of the cliff and partially covered. He didn't have time to investigate. He struggled up the path, his feet slipping in the loose sand that was the wall of the cliff. Once he slipped and slid halfway back down the path. When he reached the top he could see the roof of the stone house. He was less than two hundred yards away.

The sound of gunfire erupted. When he heard the mortar explosions, Munro raced toward the cottage, thinking only of Betty, and what those explosions and shots meant. He was less than a hundred yards from the stone wall on the beach side of the cottage, and still running, when a man leaped into the air from the other side, made a grotesque pirouette, and crashed to the ground.

Munro kept going. There were more explosions. Two geysers of dirt erupted directly in front of him and Munro threw himself to the ground. He was showered in dirt and grass. There was a tremendous exchange of gunfire and Munro knew that Bishop's surprise attack had not been successful. Munro picked himself up and turned back toward the cliffs. The soldier in him knew that he had to hold that position. He tried not to think about Betty. There was little he could do now.

He found a place near the edge of the cliff, behind a grouping of huge boulders. He climbed onto one of the large rocks and found that he could see the wall and the roof of the cottage. Just behind him were the cliffs, and several paths snaking down towards the rocky shoreline. If they came, they would come this way. He settled down to wait.

He did not have to wait long. He saw the first man dive over the wall and come up, his submachine gun firing at the house. Seconds later another man, shorter and less fit than the first, came tumbling over. Moments later a third man followed.

What the hell was Bishop doing? His plan had failed. No one was supposed to escape. Now there were three Germans crouched behind the wall, and at any moment they would head right at him.

◆ CHAPTER 55 ◆

Inside the cottage the sounds of gunfire and explosions were magnified tenfold. Bullets thumped against the heavy front door like giant fists, and several times came through the barricaded windows and ricocheted around the room with a vicious whine.

Betty and Marie huddled in a corner of the back room, hoping that their rescuers, whoever they were, would prevail. With each lull, the women would look at each other, hopeful and fearful that it was over, but then the chatter of the machine guns would start anew. Betty was certain that somehow Max had found her.

The door crashed open and both women looked up fearfully. It was Daly. He pointed a pistol and Betty thought, Dear God, don't let him shoot me now. "You son of a bitch!" she screamed. "Why don't you leave us alone?" If she had had a weapon, she would have killed him.

Daly was taken aback by her outburst. He was used to the easy compliance of women like Marie Price. "Because," he said, "you're going to help me escape." He turned to Marie. "We'll get out of this yet," he said.

Her red-rimmed eyes brightened at his words. She stood up and went to his side.

"The two soldiers in there can't hold out forever," Daly said. "When it's over, we'll go outside and show them our American here. The British don't want to see any Americans

371

get hurt. They're afraid Uncle Franklin will cut off their supplies."

"D'you think they'll just let you walk out of here?" Betty said. "You're crazier than I thought."

"You'd better hope they let us walk out of here. I won't let them take me—or you—alive," Daly said. "We're going to ride Scully's truck out of here."

"You'll never make it," Betty said.

Daly's move was so sudden that he caught her by surprise. He slapped her viciously with his open hand, sending her reeling to the floor. He grabbed her by the hair and pulled her face close to his. "What you do in the next few minutes will decide whether you live or die."

Betty knew that, no matter what, Daly would kill her.

"We will fall back in stages," Kaufmann told his men. "I will go first. You will provide covering fire. When I reach my position there," he pointed to a group of rocks halfway to the cliff, "you will follow one at a time—one covering for the other. When we make it to the rocks, we will repeat the procedure and work our way to the beach." He looked at the two young, frightened faces. "Do you understand?" They nodded. They were German soldiers and would not fail him.

It was the classic fall-back maneuver. Retreat came in ordered stages rather than in panicked flight. In this, as in all things, the German military was supreme. Even though the Wermacht prided itself on being the most powerful offensive military machine in the world, the orderly retreat was a standard military maneuver, practiced over and over again.

Staying low to the ground, Kaufmann headed for the rocks as his soldiers kept up a constant barrage from behind the wall. He was actually beginning to enjoy himself. He was back in control. With only two soldiers, he had managed to outwit at least—he wasn't sure how many British soldiers, but by the time he got back to Berlin it would be at least a hundred. Already he could feel the weight of the Iron Cross that the Führer was sure to pin on his uniform.

At the halfway point he turned and waved to his men. One, running almost doubled over, started immediately. The other continued firing over the wall. Kaufmann hoped that his ammunition would hold out.

The first soldier, puffing from the exertion, arrived next to Kaufmann. He whirled, aiming his submachine gun back in the direction from which he had come. "Ready, Herr Obersturmbannführer," he shouted. "Give the signal."

"Let's go," Kaufmann said. "We must get to the beach."

Kaufmann saw the question in the soldier's eyes and said, "If we are to have any chance of reaching the beach and the submarine, someone must hold them behind that wall."

The soldier took one last look at his friend and turned to Kaufmann, who arranged his face in an expression of sympathy. The soldier nodded sadly. He knew that lives must be sacrificed in war, and that those sacrificed were rarely officers like Kaufmann, but usually men such as himself and his friend.

Together they ran toward the cliffs.

Munro watched them approach his position.

Bishop knew what was happening. He watched the Germans retreat in stages and smashed his fist into the ground in frustration. "Damn them!" he yelled. He hadn't heard Hawkins or the Bren gun for at least several minutes. "Where the hell is Hawkins?"

MacNair, who lay beside him in the turf, could only shrug. They were pinned behind the same clump of rocks where only minutes ago the three Germans had been pinned. The gunfire from inside the cottage was sporadic and posed little threat. Every few minutes someone would fire through one of the barricaded windows, but they obviously were firing wildly. Whoever was inside had not opened the front door since MacNair had riddled it with bullets. It was the man on the other side of the wall who had them pinned down. He had a clear field of fire and a well-protected position.

"There's only one man left behind the wall," Bishop said. "We've got to take him out."

MacNair prayed that Bishop would not opt for a frontal assault. That, he knew, would be suicide. The German was well protected and he could hold them off for as long as his ammo held out. "Hawkins and Gordon must be working their way around from the back side," he offered, hoping that Bishop would wait.

"Cover me," Bishop said. "I'll try to make it to the wall."

"He'll cut you to ribbons," said MacNair, surprising himself with the vehemence in his voice. "Don't be a bloody fool."

"Cover me," Bishop snapped and was up and running.

MacNair jumped up and began firing short bursts in the direction of the lone, remaining German.

Bishop ran, his legs pumping furiously, at an angle to the German's position behind the wall. He counted the machine-gun bursts from MacNair. The Sten gun carried a thirty-two-round magazine, but was normally loaded with no more than twenty-seven or twenty-eight rounds to avoid jamming. That gave MacNair five—at the most six—short bursts before he would have to reload and leave Bishop vulnerable. How many rounds were left in the magazine before Bishop started his charge was the question that he wrestled with as he made his dash to the wall.

The German's head popped up, but MacNair drove him back down with several well-aimed rounds. Bishop was still on his feet, running. Again the German popped up. This time he looked right at Bishop, but again MacNair forced him to take cover. Next time, thought Bishop, he'll take a few shots before taking cover.

Sure enough, the German got off a poorly aimed burst. But this time there was no response from MacNair. He was either reloading or his gun had jammed.

Bishop was still ten strides from the wall when the German stood up and took aim. Bishop was close enough to see how young the German was and how he squeezed one eye shut when he aimed even though he was not sighting down the barrel.

Everything was happening in slow motion now. A fraction of a second seemed like minutes. Bishop was running in a nightmare where his feet were mired in mud. The wall seemed no closer now than it had minutes ago. He could feel the drumbeat of his heart, see the German's finger tighten on the trigger, hear the metallic click of a shell in the chamber. Bishop tried to aim his Sten gun, knowing that it was too late. He swung the gun around, in a slow, ponderous arc.

He heard the obscene chatter of the machine gun and braced himself against the shock of the impact. Even when he saw the German spin in a half circle, his submachine gun wrenched from his hand, he still expected the crushing blow.

The young soldier flopped across the wall, his arms dangling to almost touch the grass. Bishop stopped short and stood gasping for breath. Hawkins appeared from the other side of the wall, Bren gun held high, big grin on his face. He had worked his way around and shot the German when he stood up to take aim at Bishop.

There was no time for celebration. The gunfire had almost ceased after a little more than ten minutes of bedlam, but the job was not finished. Hawkins and Gordon joined Bishop at the wall. "Four men and the two women are unaccounted for," Hawkins said. "They must still be inside the house."

"There is only one way out," Bishop said. "Gordon, you go back and help MacNair keep them bottled inside. Signal Simpson and Smith to come and join you. Hawkins and I will go after the other two. "At all costs, they must not get away."

Munro watched them coming toward him. Both had machine guns. The shorter of the two held his pointing down, running with short, labored steps. The other ran with the long, measured strides of an athlete, the gun held across his chest, one hand on the trigger, the other supporting the barrel. He was the one Munro would have to watch out for.

Munro squeezed himself into a gap between the boulders. He had to decide quickly what had to be done. There were two easy ways to do this. From his hiding place, he could easily shoot both Germans before they could react. Or, he could stay where he was and let them pass unmolested. After all, this was not his fight. His concern was with Betty's safety and this had nothing to do with that. He rejected both alternatives. He could not let them escape, nor could he kill them. He wanted them alive. Munro wanted to see the expression on Bishop's face when he realized that Munro had done what he and his men could not.

They were closer now. He could hear them talking, the short man gasping guttural commands in German.

Ten yards in front of Munro they stopped and looked back. The shooting had stopped. Munro could have shot both without effort. Instead, he pressed his back against the rock.

The silence from the cottage seemed to infuriate the shorter man. He was gasping for breath and held one hand across his fat belly as if to ease some sharp abdominal pain.

He shouted at his companion, then both moved forward again.

Although they passed within ten feet of where Munro hid, neither gave the boulders a second glance. They proceeded to the edge of the cliffs where the shorter one shaded his eyes and looked out to sea. Both had their backs to Munro.

Munro stepped out from behind the rocks, his Sten gun at the ready. Neither of the men noticed his presence until he said, "Don't move."

They turned and saw him, and Munro had the immense satisfaction of seeing the surprise register on their faces. He watched the young one carefully. He was closer to Munro, and his machine gun was still in a dangerous position. Munro's trigger finger itched in anticipation. "Drop your weapons," he said.

The young soldier was too surprised to react, but the other, who had seemed less dangerous, did not hesitate. He took a half-step to the left, placing himself behind his companion, and in the same motion raised the machine gun, pistol fashion, and started firing.

The first three of the German's shots kicked up dirt some two feet in front of Munro. Munro fired his weapon but his shots were wide to the left.

The fourth bullet hit Munro just below the right knee, the fifth caught him in the thigh, the sixth ripped into his abdomen, the seventh shattered his collar bone.

The force of the impact threw Munro back. His submachine gun went flying out of his hands and he toppled backward over the edge of the cliff. He fell silently, spiraling in a slow arc, and landing halfway down on a well-worn sandy path. He bounced twice and tumbled, head over heels, to the bottom, where he lay sprawled amidst the rocks.

Kaufmann raced to the edge, looked and saw that the man was not moving. One leg was bent at an incredible angle and an arm seemed curiously misplaced. There was no movement. "Dead," Kaufmann announced triumphantly. He motioned to the SS guard to follow him and went to the rocks where Munro had hidden. They looked back at the cottage and saw two men vault the wall and start running in their direction. "You will set up here," Kaufmann said, "and hold them off until you get my signal that we are ready to go. I will get to the raft, and signal the submarine. Once I drag the raft to the water's edge, I will cover your retreat down the path.

The soldier was remembering his friend back at the wall. He too had been awaiting Kaufmann's signal. He swallowed once. "Yes, Herr Obersturmbannführer."

It was Hawkins who was aware of the possibility of ambush. He grabbed Bishop by the arm to slow him down and pointed at the boulders. "Perfect spot to wait for us," he said.

"Let's split up," Bishop said. "You go around to the right; I'll take the left. We'll meet on the other side of the boulders."

The German cursed when he saw them separate. A few minutes more and he would have had both of them. Now his task was infinitely more difficult. He watched as one of the men went off at an angle. That one would try to work his way around behind the boulders. In a short time the man was beyond the German's line of sight. The other kept coming. He would take him first.

Bishop slowed his pace. Hawkins and the reminder of what had almost happened back at the wall had made him cautious. He scanned the scene in front of him. Hawkins had been right about the boulders. If there was danger, it was sure to come from there. He waved to Hawkins, over on his right, making a circular motion with his hand. Hawkins waved back, knowing that Bishop would wait for him to get behind the boulders.

The German saw the signal, and he too understood. He could wait no longer. He fired a burst at Bishop, but the range was too long and the bullets dug harmlessly into the meadow. Bishop took cover. The German scurried across the rocks to the other side so that he could force the second man to take cover also, but when he got there, no one was in sight.

On the beach below, Kaufmann heard the shots and worked furiously to free the line that had held the raft anchored to the rocks at the base of the cliff. Finally it was free and he hurled the debris which had been used as camouflage out of the raft. He grabbed at the waterproof case that held the flare pistol and tucked it under one arm. He dropped his submachine gun onto the floor of the raft, threw the line over his shoulder and pulled. At first the bulky rubber boat resisted, but gradually it broke loose and he was able to pull it easily across the smooth rocks of the beach.

Maxwell Munro heard the shots and thought that they were a continuation of the shots that had sent him plummeting over the edge of the cliff. He moved and the intense pain brought him back to full consciousness. He rolled his head to the right, looking down the long stretch of beach. A blurry figure moved across his line of vision dragging a huge, black object.

Munro's left arm dangled uselessly at his side, and a searing pain pounded at his left leg. The pain was nonspecific—it seemed to come from every part of the leg. He rolled over, fighting the jackhammers that slammed into him with every movement, and found that the Sten gun lay nearby. He wondered who had placed it there. He dragged himself to the gun and rested his cheek on the cool metal. He felt better being close to the weapon. Weary from the effort, he felt himself drift into a state of semiawareness.

With one hand, Kaufmann fumbled with the clasp of the flare gun case. He was able to get it open, remove the flare pistol, and drop the case. There were two extra flares in the case, but he hoped that he would not need them. Still dragging the raft, he raised the pistol to the sky and pulled the trigger.

Bishop saw the explosion of light and knew immediately that someone was signaling to a submarine offshore. The flare hung in the sky, glowing white-hot, then burned itself out and dropped into the ocean. There was no time. He jumped up and began running and firing at the same time.

To Munro it was as if the sun was falling from the sky. He watched the flare light, then die, then drop into the sea, like a day in stop-motion photography. He heard the rattle of faroff machine-gun fire and remembered how he got here. He struggled to focus on the scene around him. A shadowy figure was at the water's edge with a raft not more than sixty yards from where he lay. Munro began to drag himself and the Sten gun along the rocky beach.

Kaufmann pushed the raft into the water. He could still hear firing, which meant that the SS guard was still holding them off. He would see that the young boy got some sort of medal, that they all got medals. In knee-deep water he climbed into the raft. He was free of this place.

Beyond the protected cove he could see the flashing signal of the submarine and he laughed. All he had to do was paddle a few hundred yards and they would pick him up. He dug the paddle into the water and stroked with all the strength that he could muster. The raft skimmed across the wavetops. He dug in again and the raft shot forward, only this time he noted that his stroke had sent it more on a diagonal. He compensated by switching the paddle to the other side and the raft swung the other way. Now he alternated each stroke and the raft zigzagged forward. Kaufmann looked over his shoulder. The shoreline was receding but not as fast as he would have liked. He should have been fifty yards from shore. Instead he was only thirty—perhaps not even that.

The raft was made for eight and it was a lot for one man to handle. He was fighting the tide and a wind that pushed against the raft as if it were a giant balloon adrift on the waves. The wind and the tide had pushed him as far along the shoreline as he had managed to paddle out to sea.

Munro looked up. He didn't know how he had done it, but he was getting closer to the man in the raft. He redoubled his efforts, dragging the gun and his useless leg and leaving a wide swatch of blood across the rocks.

Kaufmann couldn't believe his eyes. The man he had shot was crawling after him down the beach. He dropped the paddle into the bottom of the raft and picked up the Schmeisser. The boat bobbed on the waves and it was difficult to take steady aim, but he fired several bursts in the man's direction. Not even close. The man kept coming.

The ricochets kicked up dirt, and sand, and chips of rock all around him, but Munro pressed on. He knew that he was going to get the bastard now. He wasn't exactly sure any more why he had to stop this man, but it was something about secrets and something about Betty and perhaps something about himself. He was almost at the water's edge now and less than fifty yards away from the raft. And getting closer.

Kaufmann saw what was happening. The wind kept pushing the raft, drifting him closer to this madman. He began to paddle furiously and the raft sprang forward, but when he looked back he seemed no more distant than he had been before. Switching from side to side made his task more difficult. By the time he made the switch, he had lost half of his gain. If he kept drifting like this, very soon he would be within easy range of the madman.

Again he grabbed the Schmeisser and emptied a full clip at the man at the water's edge. The bullets churned the water into froth but none struck home. At the top of the cliff he saw two figures pause and then begin a mad dash down the path. They were a considerable distance away, and he knew that he could still make it to safety. He screamed in frustration and went back to the paddle.

Munro propped the Sten gun across a rock and took aim. This, he giggled, was sort of like shooting at clay figures in a shooting gallery. The target went up and down and in and out of focus. He squeezed one eye shut and aimed down the short barrel. The gun danced as he pulled the trigger and the shots went wide of the mark. He needed something to hold the barrel steady. He rested his cheek on the barrel, feeling the cold metal press against his face. He aimed again.

The raft seemed to be moving farther away now and picking up speed.

The wind had changed! Kaufmann was exultant. His powerful strokes now drove the boat forward at a rapid rate, and he could feel the movement beneath him. He looked back at the beach and saw that the shoreline was indeed more distant. The two figures raced to catch up, but it was too late.

Kaufmann raised the paddle in a gesture of defiance just as Munro squeezed the trigger. Years later, Bishop would describe it as the "luckiest damn shot he had ever seen. A man—half dead—with only one arm and lying face down in the rocks, manages to shoot a man from seventy-five yards, with a weapon that has an effective range of about forty yards." Munro kept his finger on the trigger, firing, perhaps, as many as twenty bullets. Most of them flew harmlessly over Kaufmann's head, but one of them hit him in the shoulder, one hit him in the arm, and one took off the back of his head. He pitched forward into the raft, face down, blood and brains mixing with the frigid waters of the Atlantic.

Anticipating Bishop's order, Hawkins threw his weapon to the ground and plunged into the water. He swam after the raft with long, powerful strokes. Bishop watched him for a moment and then, confident that Hawkins would indeed catch up to the raft, went to Munro. He looked at the American and winced when he saw the extent of his wounds.

He had obviously lost a lot of blood and his chances for survival did not look good. Bishop took off his coat and squatted next to him. He removed his shirt and started to tear it into strips for tourniquets and bandages. This would have to suffice until they got back to their equipment on the hilltop. "I'll say one thing, Munro," he said as he applied the first tourniquet above the knee of Munro's shattered leg. "They certainly teach you bastards to shoot in the American Army."

♦ CHAPTER 56 ♦

Bishop left Hawkins with Munro and returned alone to the cottage. He found that Simpson, Smith, and Riordan had joined the others in surrounding the house and that MacNair was questioning Tom Scully, who seemed to be in a state of shock. Bishop sent Smith back to help Hawkins carry Munro.

"What have we here, MacNair?" Bishop asked.

"This lad was with them, sir." He made a circular motion around his temple with his index finger. "From what I can get out of him, there are two soldiers, an Irishman named Daly, two women, Lieutenant Hamilton, and this lad's dead father inside."

"The women are alive?"

"Apparently."

Bishop thought of Munro and said, "Thank God for that." He nodded at the cottage. "What's the situation here?"

"As you said, Lieutenant. No one is going anywhere. Gordon has the Bren gun lined up on the front door. Anytime someone opens the door, he opens up with a few rounds to keep 'em quiet. I've deployed Simpson and Riordan round back in case someone tries to come out the window. Chaps inside don't seem too anxious to continue, but I thought we'd wait for you to get back before we discussed surrender."

Bishop checked his watch. He wanted to be away from here before any of the Irish authorities arrived. Even a country constable could make things awkward at this point. "It's time to end this," he said, stepping forward. "Inside the house," he called, and repeated his words in German. "Throw down your weapons and come out with your hands up."

There was a brief wait and then the front door opened and two submachine guns were tossed outside.

Bishop breathed a sigh of relief. At least this part would be easy. "Put your hands on top of your head and step outside."

The two SS guards had seen prisoners shot in Poland —both in fact had been a part of such atrocities—and were now afraid that it might be their turn. Their options, however, were limited. They raised their hands and stepped outside into the morning sun.

Bishop aimed the Sten gun, his finger tightening on the trigger. He sighed and relaxed. "This way," he said. "Quickly.

"Ladies," Daly said, "it is time to go."

He ushered them from the bedroom into the outer room. The room was more of a shambles than it had been earlier. The front door was chewed with bullet holes, and the boards that had barricaded the windows were shot to pieces. Scully lay where he had fallen, on his back, eyes staring at the ceiling. They stepped over his body to get to the door, Betty first, followed by Daly, and then Marie.

Daly said to Marie, "Search him for his keys. I'm sure they're in the truck, but let's be certain."

Marie knelt next to Scully's body. She could not look at his dead face—it took all of her courage to touch him. Gingerly she went through his coat pockets, then pulled back his coat and saw the pistol stuck inside his belt. She looked at Daly but his attention was directed outside. She patted Scully's trouser pockets, but the old man had only a large pocket knife and some loose change. She closed the coat, covering the pistol, and, for a moment, wondered why Daly wanted her along on his escape. She stood up. "No keys," she said.

Daly nodded. "The keys are in the truck." He waited half a beat and said, "Why don't you hand me the old boy's pistol?"

Marie's face flushed as though she had been caught in a lie. It was as if Daly knew her every thought. She retrieved the pistol from his belt. She held it for a moment, feeling the weight of it, the power of it, but she knew that she did not have the courage to use it.

Prisoners secured, Bishop turned his attention back to the house. As he was about to call to the remaining occupants, Daly opened the cottage door and stepped out. He had his arm around Betty Donaldson's throat and held his pistol against her temple. "Everybody stay where you are," he said. "I'll kill this woman if anyone tries anything."

Bishop groaned. "That must be Munro's woman." He muttered to Gordon, who had the Bren gun aimed at the front door. "No matter what happens, he does not get away."

"She's an American . . . a woman," Gordon said.

Bishop checked the clip on his Sten gun. "Yes, I'm afraid she is."

Bishop walked slowly toward the cottage. Daly stayed in the doorway, protecting himself from any surprise attack from the rear or the sides.

Bishop stopped in front of the doorway and said, "Who are you?"

"Name's Daly, and you're going to let me get to that truck over there."

Bishop raised the Sten gun. "I'm afraid not, Mr. Daly."

Daly moved back a step, pulling Betty closer to him. "I'll kill her," he said.

"You have two choices, Mr. Daly," said Bishop. "You can surrender and be taken back to England, or you can die here and now. There are no other options."

"And what about the woman?" he said scornfully. "She's an American . . . a reporter."

"I'm well aware who she is," Bishop said.

"He'll kill me," Betty said. "He means it."

Bishop shrugged. "I'm sure he does. But I have no choice in this matter. No one leaves."

Daly's finger tightened on the trigger and Betty could hear the touch of metal against metal. The sound was deafening. She heard a voice behind her. It was Marie. "Let her go, Sean," she said. "It's over. They're not going to let you go."

"Shut up," Daly spat. "This bitch is the reason they followed us. It's all her fault."

Marie realized Daly would never let Betty Donaldson go. She opened the pocket knife she had taken from Scully's pocket and walked up behind Daly. "Sean," she said sharply. "Let her go."

Daly half-turned to look over his shoulder, and Marie saw

that the barrel of the pistol was no longer aimed at Betty's head. Marie raised both hands over her head and plunged the knife into the base of Daly's neck.

At first Daly thought she had punched him in the back, but then he felt the blade twisting as he turned to look at her. As he reached back to grab the protruding handle, he released his grip around Betty's neck. He turned and fired two quick shots into Marie Price's chest. She fell dead across Scully. Daly could feel the blood in his throat, choking him, as he tried to pull the knife free.

Bishop screamed, "Get down," and Betty dropped to the ground. Bishop opened up with the Sten gun and blew Daly back inside the cottage. He ran to the doorway, stepping over Betty, and saw that Daly was struggling to get to his feet. Bishop fired again and put him down for good.

Bishop inspected the cottage. In the back room he found Hamilton, who stared sightlessly at the ceiling. Bishop checked his pulse. Nothing. Lucky man, he thought. Survival would only have meant court-martial, disgrace, and probably prison.

The commandos carried Hamilton outside just as Hawkins and Smith arrived carrying Munro between them in a stretcher they had improvised from their coats. At first Betty was unaware that this battered man was anyone she knew, but there was something in the sidelong glances the others gave her that made her realize something was wrong. She looked again. "Max?" she whispered, disbelievingly, her voice cracking. "Is that you?"

They lowered Munro to the ground and stood back. Betty ran to him, and knelt beside him. Her teeth dug into her lower lip as she touched his face gently. She whispered, "Please, Max. Hang on."

His breathing was labored and shallow. He opened his eyes at the sound of her voice and tried to speak but the effort was too great. He saw only blurred shapes blocking the light.

Betty cradled his head in her lap, stroking his hair. "We've got to get him to a doctor," she said. "Now!"

Bishop admired her optimism. He had seen men far less gravely wounded than Munro who had not survived. He turned to Hawkins. "Get Munro into that truck and across the border as quickly as you can. I'll finish up the loose ends here by burning this place and everyone in it."

"I'm going with Max," Betty said.

"As you wish," Bishop said.

As they carried Munro to the truck, Bishop said loudly, "He did a damn fine job back there." He marched over to his men, who sat, backs against the wall, in exhaustion. "All right," he barked. "No time to rest. I want all the bodies put inside the house. Let's not forget the one at the cliff and the one on the beach. Hop to it."

The men clambered to their feet, muttering the things that soldiers mutter. Their well-earned rest would have to wait.

"We're going to burn everything," Bishop said. "Not a trace left behind." He watched them start toward the bodies that lay around the cottage.

Sergeant Hawkins stood beside him. "A most successful operation, Lieutenant."

"Yes, Sergeant. I would certainly say so. Broadway should be pleased."

Their eyes met but could not hold. No one would ever know how close to disaster they had come.

NAZIS IN FOURTH WEEK OF LONDON BLITZ;
FLAMES GUIDE RAIDERS TO NIGHT TARGETS;
GOERING   CLAIMS   BRITISH   MORTALLY
WOUNDED

BERLIN, SEPT. 28

◆ CHAPTER 57 ◆

TIERGARTEN PARK, BERLIN, September 28—The early morning sky above Berlin was a weak watercolor blue that was too thin to hide the brightest stars. It was the first week of autumn and already the mornings had turned cold. The bright, verdant green of summer had subtly changed. The trees were preparing themselves for a hard winter.

It won't be long now, Admiral Canaris thought.

Canaris seemed a figure in miniature on the tall stallion. He wore several sweaters and his old Navy greatcoat against the morning's chill. The Admiral's horse blew clouds of vapor from his nostrils as the Admiral led him along the horse trails of Tiergarten Park. Canaris rode every morning before reporting to the office. He was enjoying this morning's ride more than usual, because for the first time in a long time he was riding alone.

Usually Reinhard Heydrich rode with the Admiral on these mornings. Heydrich talked incessantly, his words often a minefield of misdirection, keeping Canaris constantly on the alert for his many deceptions, and robbing the Admiral of the relaxation that he craved.

Canaris thought, even when he is not here with me, I think about his deceits and his cunning.

Their relationship was a strange one. Heydrich professed to idolize the older man, who had once been his superior, but, in actuality, there was a deep burning animosity that Canaris was at a loss to comprehend.

Although twenty years younger than the Admiral, Heydrich had assumed his position of power only a year later than Canaris. In 1936, when Heydrich took command of the security police, Canaris had been chief of the Abwehr for only one year. Heydrich and his wife, Lena, purchased a home on the Dullestrasse in the same block as Canaris and his wife, Erika, in Zehlendorf in southwest Berlin. Although much younger, the Heydrichs courted the same friends as Canaris and his wife, inviting the same people to dinner, accompanying the same people to the theater and concerts. The Admiral soon realized Heydrich wanted everything Canaris had, and was willing to do anything to get it.

In a perverse way it was flattering, Canaris thought. Heydrich was like a son who loved and despised his father at the same time. No father, he thought, would ever wish for such a son.

At a crossing in one of the trails, the stallion picked up his head suddenly, startled by the approach of something from behind. The Admiral steadied his mount expertly, and saw Heydrich and his black mount approaching at the gallop.

Heydrich reined his horse alongside Canaris. As usual, he was in full uniform, collars starched and buttons gleaming, in striking contrast to the Admiral. The stallions greeted each other with snorts that sent clouds of vapor billowing. The Admiral bent forward to calm his mount with a pat.

"Well, Reinhard," he said calmly. "I thought you would not be here this morning."

When Heydrich did not answer, the Admiral straightened and looked at him. Heydrich's face was beet red, his lips trembling with either grief or anger.

"What on earth is it, Reinhard?"

"I have just received word about the mission to Ireland."

"Bad news, I'm afraid," Canaris said sympathetically.

"All dead . . . or captured."

Canaris was a model of commiseration. "We suspected as much when there was no radio message from your men."

"I've just received the U-boat Captain's report. They arrived in Kiel yesterday. The Captain reports that at dawn on the twenty-third he surfaced and waited for Kaufmann's radio signal. When it did not come he moved to within one thousand yards of the shore. From there he observed through his field glasses a gun battle on the beach. One man signaled by flare pistol and tried to make his escape to the U-boat by rubber raft, but he was overtaken and killed. The Captain has no idea what happened to the others. He waited offshore for more than six hours, but there was no other signal."

Canaris tut-tutted consolingly and even managed to pat Heydrich on the shoulder. "Most unfortunate," he said.

Heydrich wrenched at his reins viciously and his horse whinnied and shook its head in protest.

Canaris, who despised any kind of cruelty to animals, leaned over and patted Heydrich's horse gently. "There, there, boy."

"I will not take this lightly," Heydrich said. His eyes were angry pinpoints.

"What will you do, Reinhard? Send a note of protest to Mr. Churchill?"

"I think the problem lies much closer to home than that," he said. "The British must have been informed about this operation. How else could they have intercepted a small group of German soldiers in an isolated area, well out of the war zone?"

"What are you suggesting?" Canaris asked.

"Only a very few knew of this operation. Reichsmarschall

Goering, Reichsführer Himmler, Obersturmbannführer Kaufmann, Captain Ritter, and you and I."

"Well," said Canaris, "Captain Ritter and I knew of the existence of a plan, but we knew none of the details."

"I think we can eliminate the Reichsmarschall and the Reichsführer as suspects in this matter. I can eliminate myself and you."

"Thank you for your confidence, Reinhard," Canaris said sarcastically. "This was a Reich Security operation. The Abwehr, if you will remember, was opposed to it from the start."

"Kaufmann is dead, I fear. That leaves only Ritter."

"Don't be absurd. Ritter knew only what I knew. He could not have known enough to jeopardize this operation."

"The Captain knew more than he was willing to tell you."

"What do you mean?"

"Ritter enticed Kaufmann into revealing many of the details of this undertaking by pretending he was interested in a position with the Reich Security Office and by offering him tidbits of information about the Abwehr and its operations. Kaufmann, of course, told me what had transpired, but I was unconcerned. I assumed that Ritter was just another ambitious man, trying to move up the ladder."

Canaris knew who had done the enticing. Ritter's ambition had been his only weakness, and now it would be his undoing. It was unfortunate really, but it was obvious that someone had to pay for this mess. "And you think that Ritter is working with the British?"

"It makes sense. Who was it who tried to convince us that it was the Enigma system and not a traitor who had revealed German plans against the British?"

Canaris had to play his part perfectly. "Yes, but I don't see how—"

"And who," Heydrich interrupted, "did not want us to release the information about the Roosevelt-Churchill correspondence?"

"Ritter, of course, but that doesn't mean—"

"It is obvious," Heydrich said, his voice shrill. "Everything he has done has benefited our enemies. I want him arrested immediately."

"But there is always the possibility that Ritter is right."

"Impossible," Heydrich scoffed. "Enigma is unbreakable."

"What if Kennedy does denounce Roosevelt? Would that be proof that Ritter has not worked with the enemy?"

Heydrich reached inside his tunic. "There is more proof." He removed a piece of paper that had been folded several times and handed it to the Admiral. "This was taken from the diplomatic pouch in Lisbon. It is a message from Josef Benke. The envelope was intended for Ritter."

Canaris opened the paper. "It's in code," he said.

"Apparently the two had worked out a simple code. It took only a few hours for my people at Department Six to break it." Heydrich smiled smugly.

"Am I to be informed of the contents?" the Admiral asked.

"A copy will be on your desk before nine A.M. this morning, but I will paraphrase its contents now. Benke says, as instructed, he has informed the authorities of the upcoming operation. He mentions that a German U-boat is involved, and that the British expect to intercept and disrupt the mission. He closes with, 'Sommers sends his thanks.' Sir Duncan Sommers, as you know, is the Deputy Chief of the SIS."

"Benke has been turned," Canaris said. "There is no other explanation for this. They have caught him and forced him to send this message implicating Ritter. Nothing else makes sense."

"We considered the possibility that the message was a deception, but it seems unlikely. However, in deference to you, Admiral, I will place Ritter under house arrest, rather than bring him to Prinz Albrecht Strasse. If you have no objections, I will have Reichsführer Himmler sign the order this morning."

"I have no objections," Canaris said, "but I want it clear that Ritter is to be accorded all the respect of his rank until this matter can be cleared up."

"My aim is to hold him until the intentions of the American Ambassador to England are clear. If Kennedy costs Roosevelt the election, as Ritter claims, then perhaps I am mistaken about him." His face was a death mask. "I am rarely mistaken."

As always, the Admiral's face revealed nothing. He gave his stallion a mild jab with his heels and the horse cantered forward. "Rarely, if ever, Reinhard," he called as he directed his horse to the trail on the left.

What seemed likely to Canaris was that the British were taking great pains to protect their real source of information. Perhaps, he thought, their methods were a little crude, but misdirection and confusion were always powerful weapons in the intelligence game. In Heydrich, who saw treason everywhere, they had found the perfect fish to take their baited hook.

The day seemed warmer than it had, and Canaris looked up at the sky. The blue was more vibrant. Perhaps the winter would wait a little longer.

AMBASSADOR TO RETURN HOME; PLEDGES TRUTH ABOUT AGREEMENTS; PREDICTS "HUGE" ELECTION IMPACT

WASHINGTON, OCT. 22

100,000 CHEER WILLKIE SPEECH, AS CANDIDATE PROMISES TO GIVE AMERICA BACK TO PEOPLE

YONKERS, N.Y., OCT. 22

◆ CHAPTER 58 ◆

LONDON, October 22—Ambassador Kennedy was preparing to leave for home. His departure was sudden, although not unexpected. Less than a week earlier word had arrived in Washington that the Ambassador had been making public pronouncements that he would soon endorse Wendell Willkie and deny Roosevelt the third term. The President had heard enough. He summoned Kennedy home.

At 12:45 P.M. the embassy staff assembled in the reception

hall for the Ambassador's farewell speech. As always, Kennedy kept it short and sweet. He thanked everyone for a job well done, and hoped that he would see them all again soon. Many of the staff were in tears. His feisty personality had been a popular change from some of his stuffy predecessors. "When I get home," he said, "I'm going to badger the State Department to allow each and every one of you a holiday back home. It's the least that I can do for your wonderful service to me and to your country."

General Jackson smiled grimly when the Ambassador said, "I wish I could stay with you throughout the coming ordeal, but I have important duties to attend to in Washington, and I know you can carry on without me." Although the Ambassador had not been replaced, it was obvious he had no intention of returning to London.

There was a round of handshakes and the staff were dismissed. Many of the staff members remained for some private words with the Ambassador, but most of the military people dispersed as soon as the brief ceremony was over. Jackson was on his way up to his office when the Ambassador called to him.

"How's that boy Munro doing?"

"Recovering quite nicely, it seems," Jackson said.

"Any word of the driver who hit him?"

"Hit and run. Probably never find out."

"Terrible thing," Kennedy said. "What's it been? Four weeks now? I meant to get down to—where's that hospital they have him?"

"Bristol."

"Yes, of course, Bristol. But I've been so damn busy lately."

"I'm sure he understands, Mr. Ambassador. He'll be out in another few weeks."

"Tell him I was asking for him, and that I'll give his father the word that he's doing well."

"I'm sure he'll appreciate that."

"You'll be reading a lot about me when I get home. The shit will hit the fan when I have my say. Be lots of changes made."

"You've always been a man who says what he means, Mr. Ambassador."

"Damn right. Roosevelt is going to be sorry that he turned me into a seventy-five-dollar-a-week errand boy."

David Carson approached, holding a yellow sheet of paper. "A message for you, Mr. Ambassador. From the White House."

Kennedy looked smugly at Jackson and took the paper. "Probably wants to make up at the last minute," he mumbled. He read out loud. "Dear Joe, Looking forward to seeing you at the White House as soon as you return home. Please refrain from any statements to the press until we have a chance to chat. Sincerely, FDR." Kennedy crumpled the message in his hand and gave it to Carson. "I'll bet he's looking forward to seeing me."

Kennedy stuck out his hand. "Well, boys, I'm off. Wish me luck."

"Good luck, Mr. Ambassador," Carson said politely.

"Goodbye," said Jackson. He had never understood this man. From the beginning, Kennedy had been what he always was—bold, bright, opinionated, and irrepressible. He had been like a fresh wind blowing around the dusty corners of London, and he had made people think, made them reconsider the preconceived notions of earlier generations. For one brief, shining moment he had seemed in tune with the forces that were to shape the world, and then, as quickly as his moment had come, it was gone. He was whistling the tune when the band had already marched, thought Jackson, and there was no one to tell him that the music had been changed. Jackson was sure of one thing: he would never see Kennedy's like again. And that, he thought, was just as well.

The Ambassador's first stop was at Poole in southern England. He left there the next day on an Imperial Airways Clipper for Lisbon, where he was met by a representative of the American Embassy who handed him another message from the President. It was similar in content to the one he had received in London. After the stopover in Lisbon, he left on the Pan Am Clipper for Bermuda. There, he was met by another representative who again gave him a message from Roosevelt. From Bermuda, he went to New York.

All along the way, speculation raged that the Ambassador was on his way home to denounce the President's policies in

Europe and to break with the Democratic Party. Willkie and his supporters anxiously awaited word from the man they felt could tilt the election in their favor, but Kennedy, whether obeying the President's request, or merely building the drama for his own gratification, kept a strict silence about his intentions.

The Ambassador arrived at New York's La Guardia Airfield on Sunday, the twenty-seventh of October, four days after leaving England. He was greeted by his wife, Rose, and his four daughters and a flock of reporters who were eager to question him about the rash of rumors that he would soon endorse Willkie. Before he could talk with the reporters he was given yet another message by a representative of the State Department. He was invited to the White House that evening and, again, instructed to say nothing to anyone.

"Don't worry, boys," Kennedy told the reporters. "I'll have plenty to say in a day or two. Everyone will know that Joe Kennedy is back."

The President was in his office with the Texas congressmen, Sam Rayburn and Lyndon Baines Johnson, when Joe Kennedy called from his New York hotel suite to announce that he was, indeed, back home. "Joe, old friend," the President said jovially, "it's so good to hear your voice." He winked at the two Texans and made a slitting gesture with his finger across his throat. The Texans muffled their laughter and Roosevelt went on. "I want you to come down to the White House tonight for a little family dinner. I'm dying to talk to you."

On the way down to Washington, Joe Kennedy, as if he were bolstering his courage for the task ahead, continued his diatribe against Franklin Roosevelt. Rose Kennedy, who admired the President and enjoyed the White House invitations immensely, tried to dissuade him from what she felt would be an imprudent course. As usual, her counsel had little effect.

"I'm going to make the bastard pay, Rose," he said.

"Calm down, Joe," she said. "Whatever you think of him, he's still the President of the United States."

"Not for long," Joe Kennedy said.

* * *

Dinner was served in the Roosevelt family dining quarters. The others at the table were Senator and Mrs. James Byrnes, the President's wife, Eleanor, and his personal secretary, Missy LeHand. At dinner Kennedy alternately sulked and complained bitterly about the treatment he had been accorded in London. The others tried to maintain a cheerful, amicable atmosphere, but Kennedy ranted on and on.

Roosevelt's tactic was to agree. "You are one hundred percent correct, Joe," the President said. "Those State Department people had no right to treat you like that. Why, yours was one of the most difficult jobs in this administration."

The President turned for support to Senator Byrnes. "Jimmy," he said, "how many times have you heard me tell people what a valuable service Ambassador Kennedy has done for me and for the country?"

"Many times, Mr. President," said Byrnes obediently. Byrnes, who was sometimes known as FDR's "assistant president," was present that evening for several reasons. He was a jaunty little Irishman from South Carolina who had been one of the President's earliest and staunchest supporters. Being Irish, he had some rapport with Kennedy, and his job that evening was to convince Kennedy to make a major national address supporting the President's re-election.

Nothing anyone said, however, could placate Joe Kennedy. Throughout dinner his foul mood continued, and Senator Byrnes began to fear that the appropriate moment to broach the subject of the speech would never come. The Ambassador had come to have his say and he was going to say it. So far, however, he had not gone so far as to tell the President that he would support Willkie.

The President let him have his say, smiling agreeably, promising that heads would roll at State, assuring him that he was still on the team. Arguing with Franklin Roosevelt was a no-win proposition. He blunted every angry word with a smile, seemed to agree to everything and yet promised nothing. Finally when Kennedy seemed to have talked himself out, the President gave a nod to Senator Byrnes, who coughed into his napkin and began his rehearsed spiel.

"Joe," he said pleasantly, "the Democratic National Committee is hoping, now that you're back, that you'll play a big part in the President's re-election campaign. I've been asked to speak to you about an endorsement speech for the President, Joe. Perhaps a nationwide radio address." Kennedy looked up and Byrnes went on quickly. "The speech is all written, Joe. All you have to do is read it on the air."

Byrnes watched Kennedy expectantly while the President lit a cigarette and pretended that he was not really paying attention. Missy LeHand, amazed that anyone could even think of opposing Franklin Roosevelt, impatiently drummed her fingers on the table.

"I'll tell you what," Joe Kennedy began. "I'll make a nationwide radio address, all right, but I won't parrot some speech written by a bunch of hacks at the Democratic National Committee. I'll write my own speech."

"Of course, if you'd prefer to—" Byrnes began.

"And I'll pay for my own radio time."

"We'd like to have some idea what you're going to say, Joe," Byrnes said.

Joe Kennedy flashed Byrnes a devilish grin. "Tune in, Jimmy. Find out with the rest of the country."

The diners were shocked into an embarrassed silence. Only Missy LeHand was angry enough to speak. She turned to the President. "F.D.," she said sharply, but Roosevelt, still smiling, silenced her with a quick motion of his hand.

"Joe," the President said, "I think it's time that you and I had a chat in my study."

Joe Kennedy stood up. "If you like, Mr. President."

"You will excuse us for just a few minutes, won't you?" Roosevelt said. "Why don't you order some drinks? We'll be right back."

Missy LeHand brought the President's wheelchair from the corner of the room and placed it next to him. Roosevelt swung himself into the chair, spun it around and wheeled himself out. Joe Kennedy followed. The room was still.

The President rolled behind his desk and motioned Kennedy to a seat in front of him. The two eyeballed each other but Joe Kennedy found it impossible to stare down the President of the United States.

"There's been some talk, Joe," Roosevelt said, "about you endorsing the Republican."

"People will talk."

"Important people, Joe. Henry Luce, Charles Lindbergh, and others. They say you're unhappy with my policies in Europe. That you think I'm leading this country into war. I don't believe that for a minute, Joe. You know as well as anyone that I want to keep this country out of war. I've tried to help the British because I think it's the best way for us to stay out of this war. Some people might misinterpret the help I've given, but it has always been with the best interests of the United States in mind."

Joe Kennedy was silent.

"I want your support, Joe. I think I can win without it, but I'd like to have it anyway."

"I can provide twenty-five million votes."

Roosevelt smiled. "Maybe you can, and maybe you can't. Let me tell you what I can do." The President removed his pince-nez glasses and began to clean them with a cloth he kept in his pocket. "I can make anyone with the Kennedy name an outcast in the Democratic Party." He put the glasses back on, carefully spreading the lenses apart before placing them on his nose. He adjusted the glasses by pushing them into position with his index finger. "I can fix it so that your tenth cousin couldn't get elected dogcatcher in the North End of Boston." The President was still smiling. "That boy of yours . . . Joe Jr. He voted for Farley at the convention, didn't he?"

Joe Kennedy nodded.

"I didn't like that very much, but I'm willing to write it off as youthful exuberance. He might have a future in the Democratic Party. He seems like a bright boy. Might even have an outside shot in the governor's race in Massachussets in two years."

Kennedy's eyes widened ever so slightly.

"Not with a Republican in this office, of course. But with a friend in the White House—someone grateful for his family's support—he just might pull it off. You never can tell."

Joe Kennedy thought of all his grievances with Roosevelt over the past year. His concern that this man would drag America into a terrible war. His anger at Roosevelt's secret dealings with Churchill. His misgivings about Roosevelt's liberal advisers. His worries about the Communists and Jews who had the President's ear. His fear that the country was going to hell.

Then he thought about young Joe as Governor of Massachussets. His Joe.

He made his decision in less than five seconds. "Is there anything special that you'd like me to say in my radio address, Mr. President?"

Franklin Roosevelt put his head back and laughed. No laugh was ever more infectious than Franklin D. Roosevelt's. In a moment Joe Kennedy joined in. The others in the dining room heard the laughter through the closed doors, looked nervously at each other, and then gave a collective sigh of relief. Soon they too began to laugh.

KENNEDY IN RADIO ADDRESS SUPPORTS ROOSEVELT; REFUTES ANY SECRET COMMITMENT TO BRITISH; DECLARES, PRESIDENT IS "BEST MAN FOR THE JOB"

NEW YORK, OCT. 29

◆ CHAPTER 59 ◆

SOMERSET, October 30—The embassy sent the largest car they had, a Bentley sedan, to bring Munro home from the hospital in Bristol. Munro's left leg was in a hip to ankle cast and he sat with the leg spread across the back seat, while Betty sat on a small jump seat that pulled down from the back of the front seat. They were separated from the driver by a glass partition.

The day was gray and gloomy and a steady drumbeat of rain pounded against the windshield. The idyllic weather of the summer that had kept the sky filled with aircraft was apparently over. The Bentley hummed softly as it sped over wet roads.

Betty studied the roomy interior. "This must be the car Joe Kennedy used when he went to see the King."

Munro shifted his position slightly; the effort was painful. His left arm was tightly wrapped and secured against his chest.

Betty bit her lip. "Can I help?"

"Yes," he said seriously. "Don't ever run off on your own again."

"Big news from home today," Betty said.

"Is that right?" He was only mildly interested.

"The press dispatches this morning say that Joe Kennedy made a boffo speech on radio last night for President Roosevelt."

"You're kidding." He was interested now.

"He said Roosevelt was the only man for the job. And get this—he said there was nothing to the rumors of secret commitments to the British."

"I wonder what changed his mind. I was sure he was going to destroy Roosevelt."

"Supposedly he had a long talk with the President before the speech. Roosevelt must have done something to twist his arm."

"Just when you think you know someone," Munro said, "they go and do something that seems completely out of character."

Betty leaned forward and kissed him on the lips. "You're right about that," she said, and adjusted his hair. She realized that she had been doing that a lot lately. The first thing she did when she visited him in the hospital was to fuss with his hair. "I don't know where else to touch."

He grinned. "Wait till we get back to my place."

"That should be interesting," she said. "Sort of like making love to the Mummy in that Boris Karloff movie."

He extended his free arm, mimicking the movie monster, but she took his hand and held it against her cheek. Her eyes were damp and he thought she was going to start crying again.

Betty kissed his hand. "I just keep thinking about how you looked that day."

He put his good arm around her and pulled her close. They sat like that for a long time, not saying anything, listening to the rain on the windshield and the hum of the tires on the road. He moved a little to ease the stiffness in his leg, and Betty moved back to her seat in front of him. Before she did she tousled his hair. He smiled and marveled at how she looked and at his good fortune in finding her.

Ritter saw the SS staff car pull up in front of his apartment and knew they had come for him. He quickly went to the bedroom and began to change into his uniform. As soon as he'd heard the news about Kennedy's speech, he had laid out his Navy uniform on the bed, planning to wear it if they were going to take him to Gestapo headquarters. He was just pulling on the tunic when there was a loud thumping at the door.

For those who only imagined what happened there, the basement of the cold, gray building on Prinz Albrecht Strasse was a terrifying place. For those who knew, it was worse. It was dark and damp and smelled vaguely of excrement. The ceilings were low, tomblike; the corridors narrow, claustrophobic.

Ritter was placed in a small, damp cell without windows or light and only a cot to sit or lie on. The single sheet smelled of mildew and the pillow reeked of vomit. He had asked to see Admiral Canaris but had no way of knowing if the Admiral had been informed of his request, or, if he had, if he would come.

He expected to be shot at any time. Every footstep was the footstep of his executioner. For two days he suffered, in total isolation. No charges had been made, but he knew that his days were numbered. He was being made to pay for the failures of others—he knew that. He also knew that his biggest mistake had been to play one agency against the other. Now, when he needed protection, he had nothing to fall back on. If he had stayed loyal to the Abwehr, the Admiral would have saved him from this.

The door opened and the sudden light stabbed his eyes. He shaded them and shrank back from the figure in the doorway. Slowly, painfully, his eyes adjusted and he saw that the figure framed in the doorway was diminutive, almost childlike. His hopes soared. "My Admiral," he said, jumping to his feet. "You've come."

Canaris came into the tiny room. He left the door open so

that there would be light. "Yes, Bernhard. I was told that you wanted to see me."

Ritter offered the Admiral a seat on the bed, but Canaris sniffed once and declined. "What did you wish to tell me, my boy?"

"I had hoped you might speak on my behalf. I have served you well, Admiral. I am being made to pay for the guilt of others."

Canaris stared at the damp walls. "We are all guilty of something, Bernhard," he said softly. "Some of treason" —he looked at Ritter—"some of disloyalty."

Ritter's heart sank. "A foolish mistake, Admiral. A man should not die because of a foolish mistake."

"Perhaps not." Canaris moved to the door and Ritter in desperation blocked his path. The Admiral was surprised that Ritter was on the verge of losing his composure. He raised an eyebrow and Ritter, ashamed of his weakness, stepped aside.

Ritter said, "I am convinced now, more than ever, that the leak is in the Enigma system."

Canaris, who needed no convincing of that, was saddened by the fact that this young man had to die. He could have interceded on Ritter's behalf, but to what end? If Ritter survived and persisted in his claims, sooner or later someone would attempt to verify the accuracy of his charges. Then what? His claims would be verified and men like Heydrich and Himmler would rule Europe for generations. That must not happen. "Someday, I am sure, we will know the truth."

Ritter slumped onto the bed. "I will take that consolation with me to my grave."

The door was closed and the darkness enveloped him.

Reinhard Heydrich was cruel and callous and petty, but he was no fool. As he listened to the taped recording of Admiral Canaris's conversation with Captain Ritter, he was struck by one obvious fact. Ritter was sincere in proclaiming his innocence. He had listened to the pleas of many condemned men. Most, when they realized the end was near, threw themselves on the mercy of their executioners. Ritter had not begged. He had continued to proclaim his innocence.

Heydrich opened the file on his desk and leafed through it. Listed were all the messages sent by the Abwehr in the last four weeks. He had similar files for most of the other agencies in Berlin. These files were provided to him by the Reich Postal Service which was charged with the transmission and collection of all radio, telegraphic, and postal messages in Germany. He observed an interesting fact when he studied the Abwehr file. Since September 19, at just about the time the Irish operation was getting underway, the frequency of Enigma transmissions by the Abwehr had dropped by more than fifty percent. What did Canaris know that he, Heydrich, didn't know? And, why hadn't Canaris, whose men called him the "old man" and doted on him like awestruck children, made any effort to save the life of one of his men?

Was it possible that Ritter was right? Heydrich knew it should have been mathematically impossible to decipher the Enigma machine, but he had seen some of the latest marvels of German science, and was well aware of the successes of the British radio detection system. Was it possible that the British had been able to create something to decipher the Enigma?

He pressed the buzzer on his desk and his adjutant appeared in the doorway almost immediately. "Call Reichsführer Himmler's adjutant and arrange a meeting as soon as possible. Ask if he would contact Reichsmarschall Goering. I'd like him to be there also."

Goering was surprised that Heydrich had changed his mind about a test of the Enigma system, but when his part of the plan was revealed he was only too glad to give his approval. Heydrich was asking the Reischsmarschall to take part in a terror bombing of an English city. Goering had visions of another Rotterdam and quickly gave his approval of Luftwaffe participation.

"What I propose," Heydrich said, "is a massive bombing raid on an English city that has as yet been untouched."

Himmler, as usual, asked all the questions. He sat behind his desk, his lips pursed in that curiously feminine manner, his chin resting in one hand. "Why a city that has been untouched?"

"Because," said Heydrich. "If the message is not intercepted and decoded—and I am quite certain that it will not be—then the raid will take the British completely by surprise."

Goering's eyes narrowed stupidly. The percodan had dulled his senses more than usual this morning. "You mean you are going to inform them that I will bomb one of their cities?"

Heydrich sighed. He wished that the Reichsmarschall would pay more attention to details. "We will use the Enigma coding device," he said. "If they have broken the code, they will be forced to fortify their defenses. If they do, we will know. What we need is a good-sized city, that has not been bombed, and has been left defenseless."

"That's no problem," Goering said. "Most of the cities in the English midlands are undefended."

"Do you have one in mind?" Himmler asked.

Goering rubbed at his red-rimmed eyes. He had not been sleeping well lately. "Coventry is as good as any," he said. "Medium-sized, concentrated city center, no airfields nearby, no antiaircraft weapons in the vicinity." He slapped his sizable thighs. "As the Americans would say, 'she is a sitting duck.'"

Heydrich looked at Himmler, who gave him a nod of approval. Heydrich stood up and clapped his hands together. "Very well then. Coventry it is."

ELECTION RESULT IN DOUBT, SURVEY SHOWS;
CLOSE POPULAR VOTE PROJECTED AS 50 MIL-
LION EXPECTED AT POLLS; BOTH CANDIDATES
CONFIDENT

WASHINGTON, NOV. 4

ROOSEVELT RE-ELECTED PRESIDENT FOR
RECORD-SETTING 3RD TERM; DEMS RETAIN
HOUSE CONTROL

WASHINGTON, NOV. 5

LONDON RAIDS RESUME AFTER WEEK'S RESPIT;
BOMBS FALL AS 1918 ARMISTICE IS OBSERVED
LONDON, NOV. 11

RAF RAIDS BERLIN DURING NAZI-SOVIET
TALKS; MOLOTOFF, HITLER DISCUSS POST-WAR
COOPERATION

BERLIN, NOV. 14

◆ *CHAPTER 60* ◆

November 12, 1940—The machine looked like a typewriter
encased in a teakwood box. At the top, above the keyboard,
were three revolving drums that moved slowly, each revealing a letter of the alphabet through an aperture in the casing.
This particular machine, one of several in use at that moment, was labeled X-3, and was a British copy of the machine
used by the German military to encode and decode messages.

Machine X-3 sat on a table in a large wooden structure
called Hut Number Six at Bletchley Park in Buckinghamshire. The operator, Staff Sergeant Arthur Lewis of the Royal
Air Force sat in front of the machine transcribing the
messages as they were slowly decoded by the revolving
drums. Although there was an air of urgency about the place
and the certainty that what transpired here was of the utmost

importance, the work quite frankly was boring. In the heady days of the Battle of Britain—July, August, September—there had been the feeling that every message might save the nation from the impending invasion. It had seemed then that every other message contained information about projected German bombing raids, and the intercepts had proved invaluable to the overworked pilots of the Royal Air Force.

Now, although the Germans still bombed British cities on a nightly basis, the sense of urgency was gone. The threat of invasion, so real just a short time ago, had passed, and of the hundreds of messages received and decoded each day, only a handful were deemed important enough to go into the priority basket, where messages of obvious value were placed for immediate attention. The rest went into an immense file where they were systematically cataloged by teams of experts on German military procedures. It was suspected that once cataloged the messages were never seen again.

At 11 A.M. on Wednesday, the twelfth of November, the machine had been silent for almost four minutes. Four minutes was an unusually long time. With German troops all over occupied Europe the messages usually came in without pause. Then the machine began to click and the drums to revolve. Staff Sergeant Lewis translated the message as it appeared. Immediately he noticed something different.

"What's this?" he said aloud, and several other operators hunched over identical machines looked in his direction.

Almost immediately the duty officer, Captain Ted Winters, was standing behind him looking over his shoulder. "Got something interesting, Arthur?" he asked.

Lewis handed his translation of the message to Winters. "It's a raid organization. Looks like a big one."

Winters read the message. "Big one indeed." He read aloud. "Four hundred bombers, three hundred fighters . . . Luftflotte Two . . . night of November fourteenth . . . target Coventry." He gave a low whistle. "Better get this one off to the old man."

"Ted," Lewis said. There was little military formality in Hut Number Three.

"Yes?" said Winters.

"Something bothers me about this one."

"What?"

"The name of the target was broadcast in the clear."

Winter's eyes narrowed. "In the clear?"

"Yes. No code name." Usually all targets were referred to in code and the operators had to determine the target's true name. "It came right through on the machine . . . Coventry."

"What do you think? Careless error perhaps?"

"Not likely."

"What, then?"

Arthur Lewis said slowly. "I'm not sure, but it almost looks as if they wanted to make sure that we knew the target."

Both men were silent for a moment. "I hope you're wrong, Arthur," said Winters. "I really hope you're wrong."

"I hope so, too," Lewis said. "Let's hope that it is just as you suggest—a careless error."

"I'd better get this one off to Broadway right away. Let me know if anything else comes in on this. I'll be over at the Registration Room. Let's see what the analysts can make of it."

Lewis nodded and turned his attention to the machine in front of him. The drums were whirring again and the next message was coming in. Automatically he began his translation, but his mind was far away. He realized with crushing certainty that if what he suspected was true, the invasion of Great Britain, that he had come to think was inconceivable, was once again a distinct possibility.

He touched the X-3 machine, letting his fingers run lightly across the keyboard. He believed, as fervently as did anyone at Bletchley Park, that this machine and others like it had saved his country from almost certain defeat. Without the knowledge of the Enigma intercepts, the superior numbers of the German Air Force would probably have overwhelmed the defensive capabilities of the RAF. The intercepts had been the difference between defeat and survival. Now that advantage might be gone forever.

Winston Churchill was in his first-floor study at 10 Downing Street reading the daily dispatches from his military commanders in the field. After replacing Neville Chamberlain as Prime Minister in May of 1940, Churchill had named himself Minister of Defence and since that time had operated as the supreme commander of all British forces in the field. A politician by trade, Churchill considered himself a soldier-statesman and bombarded his military commanders with daily instructions on the conduct of the war.

There was a knock on the door and Churchill's principal secretary, John Martin, entered. "Excuse me, Prime Minister," said Martin, "but I've just taken a call from Colonel Menzies. He and General Ismay request an appointment within the hour."

Churchill looked at his pile of correspondence and considered rejecting the request, but Menzies and Ismay were not the kind of men to bother him with petty details. It must be a matter which needed immediate attention. "Very well. I'll see them as soon as they can get here."

When Menzies and Ismay arrived they were immediately taken to the Prime Minister's study.

"Sorry to bother you with this, Prime Minister," said Ismay, who was Churchill's chief of staff and whose job it was to run the machinery on the military side of the government by acting as liaison between Churchill and the chiefs of staff of the military services. He was one of Churchill's closest aides and a friend and confidant.

They waited as Churchill lit a cigar. "Go on, then," he said, pouring brandy into three crystal glasses on his desk. He slid two of the glasses in their direction and sipped from the third.

"Late this afternoon at Bletchley Park," Menzies said, "we intercepted and decoded a message that apparently originated with Luftwaffe headquarters in Berlin. It was intended for Field Marshal Kesselring of Luftflotte Two headquartered at Antwerp. It's about bombing targets for the next few days—the fourteenth to be exact."

Ismay leaped in. "For the first time an impending target has been named 'in the clear.'"

"The signal clearly stated that Coventry was to be the target of a massive raid on the fourteenth," Menzies said.

Churchill sipped his brandy and waited for Menzies to go on.

"We can't be sure, but it could be some sort of test."

Churchill, puzzled, looked to Ismay.

"Prime Minister," said Ismay, "the Bletchley people think that the Germans may be getting on to the fact that we've been intercepting their secret messages for the past six months."

"If that is true," Churchill said, "it would be a catastrophe of major proportions."

Menzies added, "Not only do the Germans identify the target, they give us two days warning. That's never happened before. Coventry is a major city that has not been targeted before."

"But we have, in the past, used exactly this kind of information to defend our cities from their bombers," said Churchill. "Why is this different?"

"Coventry is virtually undefended. The closest fighter base is more than fifty miles away at Stamford in Lincolnshire. The Germans have every reason to believe that any raid on Coventry, or on a dozen other cities like it, should take us completely by surprise. If we are well prepared—and they've given us ample time to prepare ourselves—they would know that we have broken their Enigma codes."

After a long silence Churchill asked, "What do you propose I do?"

"Prime Minister," Menzies said, "we'd like you to do nothing."

"Colonel Menzies," Churchill said, "what good is this secret of yours—this Ultra secret as you call it—if we are unable to benefit from it?"

General Ismay came to the rescue. "This Ultra secret provides tremendous benefits everyday, Prime Minister."

"But," said Menzies, "the moment that the Germans discover that we possess this secret, our advantage is gone . . . forever."

Ismay was there again. "And, as you well know, Prime Minister, it is one of the very few advantages that we have."

Churchill said, "You wish me to sacrifice the city and citizens of Coventry to preserve this advantage? And you ask me to make this terrible decision without conclusive proof that what you say is true. How can we be sure this drastic step is necessary?"

"We can't," Menzies said. "But, due to the recent problem with one of my men whom the Germans attempted to kidnap, and the unfortunate situation at the American Embassy, I don't think we can discount the possibility that the Germans have some idea of what's going on at Bletchley."

"This," Churchill said, "is more than a military question. It is also a political, moral, even a historical question. What are the political consequences of allowing the destruction of Coventry? What do I say to the mother who asks me why I did nothing to save her child? I'd be booted out of office the moment the facts were known."

Menzies frowned. It had not occurred to him that the Prime Minister would allow considerations of re-election to cloud the deliberations. "No one could know about your decision, Prime Minister. At least not until after the war."

"And how then shall history regard me? As the Prime Minister who stood by and watched the destruction of one of his cities? Shall I be the Nero of British history?"

"This decision," said Ismay, "need never be revealed beyond this room."

Churchill seemed unmoved by these arguments.

Menzies tried to keep the irritation from his voice. "If we lose this advantage, Prime Minister, we may very well lose this war. When Hitler and his hordes march down Whitehall, what will there be to discuss of politics, morals, or of history."

Churchill hid a small smile behind his cigar. He had led his advisers to where he wanted them. It was not enough to make decisions; others must be forced to see the consequences of those decisions. "You are quite right, Colonel," he said. "But I would like you both to leave me while I struggle with this decision."

The Prime Minister had made up his mind before the door closed behind them. Indeed, in some inner recess of his mind, he knew he had made up his mind long before he had forced them to persuade him. There really is no choice, he thought. And then, as if to convince himself, he spoke out loud, "No choice at all."

The air-raid sirens went off just after dusk, but the people of Coventry had heard them before and most went on about their business. When the raid came it was massive.

The first wave of bombers were Pathfinders of Luftflotte 3. Following the Nickebeam directional signals from France and Holland they bore in on Coventery in the early evening and dropped over two hundred tons of incendiary bombs on the center of the city. For the second wave the task was infinitely easier. This larger group followed the bright glow on the horizon which was visible for almost two hundred miles at twenty-thousand feet. Like vultures the bombers droned toward the carnage below. The second wave simply dumped their tons of fragmentation bombs into the midst of the brightly burning city.

It went on for almost ten hours as wave after wave of German bombers followed the dull red glow in the night sky. A new German word was born that night—*Coventrieren,* to Coventrate. The meaning was quite simple—to devastate.

During the raid Prime Minister Winston Churchill was meeting with his chiefs of staff in the underground war room at Storey's Gate. He seemed unusually distracted, his eyes drifting to the red box on the sideboard. The box contained the actual Ultra intercept of the German message.

At slightly past nine o'clock there was a soft knock on the door and Churchill's secretary slipped into the room. He stood quietly until the Chief of Naval Staff concluded his report and then he gave the Prime Minister a brief nod. The raid was on. Churchill emitted an audible groan, but he said nothing and the meeting went on. From time to time Churchill looked at General Ismay who sat to his right. Ismay spent most of the evening avoiding his Prime Minister's eyes.

It was a brief meeting, the shortest anyone could remember. Most were grateful for its brevity. The Prime Minister had not, as he usually did, complained of their lack of effectiveness or aggressiveness, or dismiss them with a long list of recommendations for them to report back to their own staffs. He simply thanked them for their attention and dedication to duty, and dismissed them just before midnight.

After the chiefs of staff had gone Churchill returned to his official residence in Downing Street where he sat in his study in front of the fireplace. He sipped brandy and read reports, but his thoughts seemed lost amidst the dancing flames.

At 1:20 A.M. his principal secretary came into the room. Churchill looked up. "Any news?" he asked.

"The raid is still in progress," John Martin said. "Preliminary reports indicate extensive damage to the city center."

Churchill's eyes closed and his shoulders sagged. "I'll want casualty reports and damage estimates at the earliest opportunity."

"Yes, sir," said Martin and quietly left the room.

Churchill picked up the red box which was now on the small table beside him. He opened it and removed the message. He read the words for at least the tenth time that evening but the meaning did not change. He crumpled the message into a ball and tossed it into the fire. He watched the flames consume the paper and then he buried his face in his hands.

COVENTRY BLASTED IN WAR'S WORST RAID;
1000'S FEARED DEAD IN SURPRISE ATTACK;
MIDLANDS CITY SUFFERS EXTENSIVE DAMAGE

LONDON, NOV. 15

◆ CHAPTER 61 ◆

November 15—Ritter paced his cell nervously, his hands behind his back. Three steps forward brought him into contact with the door; he turned, took three steps and touched the back wall. He was careful not to knock over the bucket that served as his toilet. The wretched smell of the place was almost too much for him. For the last several days he had not been able to eat the foul food they brought twice a day. His only consolation had been in knowing that this would not last for long.

Heydrich himself had visited him more than a week ago and told him there would be one final test of his charge that the Enigma system had been breached. The Obergruppen-führer had told him that he wanted to be as fair as possible, but Ritter knew that Heydrich's only concern was for himself. Heydrich had to protect himself against the possibility that someone would later discover that Ritter had been right.

He had explained the plan to Ritter. It was what Ritter had proposed in the first place. If they had done it then, he

410

thought, instead of the stupid Irish venture, none of this would have happened. Then he might be sitting in one of the upstairs offices, with his feet up on the desk, instead of rotting in this wretched cell.

The door opened and he shielded his eyes from the sudden blast of light.

"Outside," a voice said, and he stumbled to the door.

The air in the corridor was only slightly less offensive than the cell's, but he took several deep lung-filling breaths before squinting at his jailer.

"Follow me."

He followed the black uniform down a narrow corridor, wondering how many unfortunate souls were behind the doors that lined the walls. What impressed him most was the silence. No one made a sound. No one wished to call attention to himself.

They turned left into another corridor and at the end of it he was led into a room that seemed huge in comparison to his quarters. Heydrich sat behind a table. There was a chair on the opposite side of the table. He waited obediently until Heydrich signaled that it was permissible for him to sit.

"Did I tell you that Roosevelt won the election quite easily?" Heydrich said.

Ritter shook his head. He was afraid that if he tried to speak he might be reduced to tears.

"So we have the crippled Jew-lover to contend with for four more years. No matter. His time will come." Heydrich shuffled some papers on the table and Ritter could see there were photographic enlargements on the table.

"You probably want to know how our little operation against Coventry went last night."

Ritter managed a nod.

"Here are the photographs—taken this morning. Look for yourself." He tossed the photographs in front of Ritter, who took them with trembling hands. It was difficult to make out any substantial detail. His eyes were not what they had been only a few short weeks ago.

"That one there," said Heydrich pointing with a pencil, "is the center of the city."

Ritter looked closely.

"Completely demolished," Heydrich said. "Here's another. Total destruction." Heydrich smiled. "You have been part of the most successful air raid of the war."

"Opposition?" Ritter asked hopefully.

"None. Four hundred and fifty aircraft took part. Several turned back because of mechanical difficulties, but none were lost over the target. The enemy was caught completely by surprise."

"There must be some explanation."

"Of course there is, Ritter. You are the explanation."

"They knew," Ritter wailed. "Somehow they knew."

"And let thousands of civilians perish to save your miserable life?" Heydrich laughed. "It's really rather funny when you think of it." He snapped his fingers and two SS soldiers appeared. Ritter had not been aware of their presence in the room.

"Take him," Heydrich said, "back to his cell."

They started down the corridor, but when Ritter reached the turn and started to go right the guards pushed him roughly to the left. Confused, he walked down a corridor that seemed identical to any of the others, but at the next turn he saw the sandbags against the wall.

Almost uncomprehendingly he allowed himself to be pushed against the sandbagged wall. He turned slowly and saw that both guards had already aimed their pistols. He knew he would not be going back to the cell.

That, at least, was some comfort.

♦ *CHAPTER 62* ♦

HYDE PARK, November 23—Two weeks after the presidential elections, Joe Kennedy, and other contributors to the campaign, were invited to the Roosevelt estate in Hyde Park, New York. There was much to celebrate. Although the margin of victory was considerably smaller than in his previous elections, the President had, once again, rolled to an impressive triumph. There were, however, some sobering statistics. Wendell Willkie had been able to wage a much more successful campaign in 1940 than Landon had in 1936. Roosevelt had surrendered only eight electoral votes in 1936. Willkie won eighty-two in 1940. Roosevelt, who had won by almost ten million votes in 1936, defeated Willkie by less than five million. His margin of victory was, in fact, the smallest by any Presidential winner since 1916.

Joe Kennedy lost little time in reminding the President of his vaunted twenty-five million votes, and once again could be heard boasting that he "was the man who put Franklin D. Roosevelt in the White House."

Joe Kennedy had spent his time since his return from England trying to convince one and all that America should stay out of the European war. In an interview with the *Boston Globe* he claimed that democracy was finished in Britain and that if the United States involved itself in the war, democracy would be finished here also. The interview was sprinkled with the kind of anti-Semitic remarks that Kennedy was famous

413

for, but that were rarely published in newspapers. The publication of Kennedy's interview caused a furor in the United States and in Britain. Only the German newspapers reacted favorably to his remarks.

He traveled to Hollywood and tried to convince his moviemaking friends that Jewish money had too great an influence in their productions. Word leaked out that he had implored the studio heads to curb the rash of anti-German films produced in Hollywood. He told the moguls that Hitler, whom he had once characterized as the greatest genius of the century, was offended by their work.

Blithely unaware that his injudicious remarks had offended millions, and unconcerned that the President was among the outraged, Kennedy traveled to Hyde Park, confident that he would be rewarded by Franklin Roosevelt for playing, what he saw as the critical role in the President's re-election. Once again, as he had so many times over the years, Joe Kennedy had misjudged Franklin Roosevelt.

He had also misjudged his influence with the President. Now that the election was over, he was considered a liability. His remarks to the press were a constant embarrassment to the Roosevelt Administration, and the President was not the kind of man who took such things lightly.

At Hyde Park Kennedy insisted on a private audience with the President. He wanted to cement Roosevelt's commitment to Joe Jr.'s gubernatorial campaign in 1942 while the memory of his campaign contributions were still strong.

Reluctantly the President agreed, and, followed by Joe Kennedy, he wheeled himself into his private study. The meeting was short and marked by raised voices. Less than ten minutes later Joe Kennedy emerged to inform Eleanor Roosevelt that her husband wished to speak with her.

Eleanor went into her husband's study and found him flushed with anger. The President had his back to the door and was staring out the window, but she knew his moods and could sense his fury.

"Franklin," she said. "What is it?"

"I want that bastard out of my house," Roosevelt said.

"But, Franklin, he is our invited guest. He's been asked to stay for dinner."

The President was actually trembling with rage. "Give him a sandwich and get him the hell out of here."

Mrs. Roosevelt tried to calm the President down. Even though she had been the target of several of Kennedy's reported comments, she refused to take Joe Kennedy seriously. Hers was the greatest kind of scorn. She refused to be disturbed by anything he said or did. "Can't you just ignore him for a little while?"

The President would not be appeased. "I never want to see the son of a bitch as long as I live," he said. "Put him in a car and get him out of here."

Thus was Joe Kennedy dismissed by Franklin Roosevelt, from politics and from the great drama that was yet to unfold. When war came, he offered his services to the President, but was quietly rebuffed. He spent the wartime years doing what he did best—making money.

In retrospect, it seems clear that Joe Kennedy was wrong about many things, but he was right about how terrible the war would be. It was worse, perhaps, than even he had imagined. Two Kennedys, Joe and Jack, served valiantly and well, but the war did exactly what Joe Kennedy had most feared it would do. It took his eldest son, Joe Jr., from him, and almost took the next in line as well.

There would be no gubernatorial campaigns for young Joe, no opportunities for Franklin Roosevelt to renege once again on a promise to Joe Kennedy. But there were other Kennedys, and other campaigns, and other promises yet to come.

LONDON POUNDED IN ALL-NIGHT RAIDS;
NAZIS RENEW LAGGING ATTACK

LONDON, NOV. 28

♦ *EPILOGUE* ♦

LONDON, Thanksgiving Day, November 28—Maxwell Munro and Betty Donaldson had just come from the Thanksgiving Day dinner at the American Embassy. Max was on crutches and Betty walked beside him as he laboriously made his way down the hallway to his rooms at the Coleridge Hotel. He paused several times, sweat running down his face, before they made it to the door.

Using his key, Betty opened the door and they stepped inside. Munro heaved a sigh of relief and flopped onto the couch in front of the fireplace in the sitting room.

Betty eyed him as she went to light the coal in the fireplace. "You OK?"

"A little tired," he said, rubbing his shoulder. "Shoulder hurts like hell." He saw the worried look on her face. "I feel fine, though. Really. It was good to get out."

She smiled. "Everyone made quite a fuss over you. Do they know what happened? In Ireland, I mean."

"Jackson knows. I'm sure he told some of the others." He laughed. "Studwell gave me the conquering hero's welcome."

"You seemed to be enjoying it."

"It is an improvement over the welcome I had been getting."

"It was enjoyable," she said, then added, "but somehow sad. I'm not sure why."

"I thought you'd know. They think this will be our last Thanksgiving before we get into the war. They know now that the British can hang on until we're ready to come in. It's

417

going to be a long war, and it's only a matter of time before we're in."

Betty stared out the window as if she could see the future there. She shook her head to clear away the picture she had conjured. "At least you'll be going home soon," she said.

"But I'll be back. I know that now."

"I thought you'd had enough of the army."

"Not till this is over." He grinned self-consciously. "I'm a soldier . . . at least for the duration."

Betty sat on the arm of the sofa. She didn't look at him. "What about your injuries? I thought we were going back to Washington together, and I was going to take care of you?"

"They tell me I'll be almost as good as new in a few months," he said.

She tried to keep her voice light and cheerful. "I guess you won't need me when you're back to normal."

"I'll probably need you for a while," he said casually. "At least until I'm better." He was grinning mischievously and she could have punched him for his insensitivity.

"Say it, you son of bitch," she said.

"Say what?"

"Something—anything—romantic. Tell me that with war coming, we'll need each other more than ever. Tell me that you couldn't go on without me." She hated this. She had never left herself this vulnerable to anyone. She tried to look bright and cheerful as if this were all a joke that they could forget later, but her heart was in her throat. "Tell me —something."

He scratched his head. "I'm thinking."

"If you don't say it, I swear I'll break your other leg."

"Why don't we get married?" he said suddenly, as if the idea had just occurred to him.

Betty's eyes widened in surprise. "I hadn't thought that far ahead."

"It's something people do—when they love each other —they get married."

"Since you put it that way—OK," she said, sitting next to him and putting her arms around him, being careful not to squeeze anything that was hurt or broken. She kissed him softly but with passion. "But I'm not naming any of our kids Maxwell."

"Fair enough," he said, putting his good arm around her.

They sat quietly, holding each other for a long time. Both were thinking that life had been good to them, to bring them together at this time and in this place. In the fireplace the flames danced and the coals glowed a dull red.

Outside, the barrage balloons, grim reminders of what might have been and what was yet to come, still swung gently in a chilling breeze.